P9-BZY-083

Count the Ways

Also by Joyce Maynard

FICTION

Under the Influence

After Her

The Good Daughters

Labor Day

The Usual Rules

The Cloud Chamber

Where Love Goes

To Die For

Baby Love

NONFICTION

The Best of Us

Internal Combustion

At Home in the World

Domestic Affairs

Looking Back

Count the Ways

A Novel

Joyce Maynard

wm
WILLIAM MORROW
An Imprint of HarperCollins*Publishers*

FIRST EDITION

Designed by Leah Carlson-Stanisic

Illustrations by MoreVector/Adobe Stock; Alexander Bakanov/Adobe Stock; Alexander Pokusay/ Adobe Stock, Kseniakr/Adobe Stock

---

Library of Congress Cataloging-in-Publication Data

Names: Maynard, Joyce, 1953-author.
Title: Count the Ways: a novel / Joyce Maynard.
Identifiers: LCCN 2020033202 (print) | LCCN 2020033203 (ebook) | ISBN 9780062398277 (hardcover) | ISBN 9780062398284 (trade paperback) | ISBN 9780062398291 (ebook)
Subjects: LCSH: Domestic fiction. | GSAFD: Love stories.
Classification: LCC PS3563.A9638 W57 2021 (print) | LCC PS3563.A9638 (ebook) | DDC 813/.54—dc23
LC record available at https://lccn.loc.gov/2020033202
LC ebook record available at https://lccn.loc.gov/2020033203

ISBN 978-0-06-239827-7 (hardcover)
ISBN 978-0-06-311316-9 (international edition)

21 22 23 24 25 LSC 10 9 8 7 6 5 4 3 2 1

For A., C., and W., who continue to instruct me well in the occasional heartbreak and lifelong joy of being a mother. And for C. and S. The next generation.

I'm sorry.
I love you.
Thank you.
Please forgive me.

—Hoʻoponopono prayer, phrases spoken in any order, for reconciliation and forgiveness

And how can you not forgive?
You make a feast in honor of what
was lost, and take from its place the finest
garment, which you saved for an occasion
you could not imagine, and you weep night and day
to know that you were not abandoned,
that happiness saved its most extreme form
for you alone.

—Jane Kenyon, "Happiness"

How do I love thee? Let me count the ways.

—Elizabeth Barrett Browning, Sonnet 43

Contents

• • • • •

Part 1

Part 2

Author's Note

When a writer chooses, as the basis of her novel, elements that resemble experiences in her own life, it's not surprising for readers to imagine that the book in their hands may not be a work of fiction so much as a fictionalized account of real-life experiences. The better a writer may do her job, the more a reader is apt to suppose that the events unfolding on the pages of a book may have actually occurred.

The characters whose story I chose to tell here are people who emerged from a place I love: my imagination. What is real are the themes I've returned to many times over the course of my long career: home, the making of a family, the costly experience—for children, and for their parents—of divorce and its aftermath.

A writer is apt to tell many stories over the years, but it may well be that her themes change very little, if at all. Long ago, in a novel I wrote called *Where Love Goes*, I explored a marriage and a divorce, as I have done once again in these pages. In a few instances, actual scenes that take place in that early novel appear, in somewhat different form, in this new piece of work.

I didn't know I was revisiting those scenes until a reader of a draft of this novel pointed out a certain resemblance to that earlier one. I was surprised, myself, when I learned that I'd returned to such apparently similar territory. What differs most profoundly between that work—written when I was just past age forty—and this one, written more than a quarter century later, are not simply the characters and events, but the author who created them. Same person. Altered perspective.

My central character this time around, like the author who chose to bring her to life on the page, is a woman who finally—

not without struggle—comes to understand the meaning of letting go of old grievances and bitterness. At the end of the day, this is a novel about the importance of asking forgiveness, and offering it. It's a lesson that comes with age, perhaps—an invaluable lesson no matter when it is acquired.

Count the Ways

Prologue

Toby was just a baby—Alison four years old, Ursula not yet three—the first time they launched the cork people. After that it became their annual tradition.

Eleanor had always loved how, when the snow melted every spring, the water in the brook down the road would race so fast you could hear it from their house, crashing over the rocks at the waterfall. A person could stand there for an hour—and in the old days before children, when she would come to this place alone, she had done that—staring into the water, studying the patterns it made as the brook narrowed and widened again, the way it washed over the smaller stones and splashed against the large ones. If you felt like it, you might trace the course of a single stick or leaf, some remnant of last summer, as it made its way downstream, tossed along by the current.

One time she and the children had spotted a child's sneaker caught up in the racing water. Another time Alison had tossed a pine cone in the brook and the four of them—Eleanor, Alison, Ursula, and baby Toby—had watched it bob along, disappearing into a culvert but showing up again, miraculously, on the other side. They had followed that pine cone along the edges of the brook until it disappeared around a bend.

"If only we had a boat," Alison said, looking out at the racing water, "we could float down the stream." She was thinking about the song Eleanor used to sing to them in the car.

"Merrily, merrily, merrily, merrily," she sang now, in her sweet, high voice.

Life is but a dream.

When they got home, she was still talking about it, so Eleanor suggested that they make a miniature boat and launch it just below the falls. With little passengers along for the ride.

"We could make them out of Popsicle sticks," she said. "Or corks."

Cork, because it floated. Cork people.

Every year after that, usually on the first warm weekend in March, Eleanor laid out the craft supplies on the kitchen table—pipe cleaners, glue gun, string, pushpins, Magic Markers, and corks saved from a year's worth of wine, which wasn't all that much in those days.

They constructed their boats out of balsa wood, with sails attached made from scraps of outgrown pajama bottoms and dresses. For Alison, the future engineer, it was the boats that occupied her attention more than the passengers. But Ursula took the greatest care drawing faces on the corks, gluing on hair and hats. Even Toby, young as he was, participated. Every cork person got a name.

One was Crystal—Ursula's suggestion. She had wanted a sister with the name but, failing that, gave it to a cork person. One was Rufus—not a cork person, in fact, but a cork dog. They named one Walt, after their neighbor, and another was named after the daughter of a man on their father's softball team, who got cancer and died just before they went back to school.

When they were done making their cork people and the vessels to carry them, the children and Eleanor carried them down to a spot they'd staked out, flat enough for all four of them to stand, and one by one, they would lower their boats and the passengers they carried, attached with rubber bands, into the fast-moving waters.

Goodbye, Crystal. Bye, Rufus. See you later, Walt.

They were on their own now, and there was nothing anyone could do to assist them in the perilous journey ahead.

It was like parenthood, Eleanor thought, watching the little line of bobbing vessels taking off through the fast-moving waters. You made these precious people. You hovered over them closely, your only goal impossible: to keep them out of harm's way. But sooner or later you had to let the cork people set off without you, and once you did there would be nothing for it but to stand on the shore or run along the edge yelling encouragement, praying they'd make it.

The boats took off bobbing and dancing. Eleanor and the children ran along the mossy bank, following their progress. They ran hard to keep up, Eleanor holding tight to Toby's hand. Toby, the one who could get away and into trouble faster than anyone.

The journey wasn't easy for the cork people. Some of the boats in which the children had placed them got stuck along the way in the tall grass along the side of the brook. Some disappeared without a trace. If a boat capsized, bearing one of her precious cork people, Ursula (the dramatic one) was likely to let out a piercing cry.

"Oh, Jimmy!" she called out. "Oh, Crystal!" "Evelyn, where are you?" "Be careful, Walt!"

Some cork people never made it through the culvert. Some fell off the vessel that was carrying them on a wild stretch of rapids farther along. Once an entire boatload of cork people capsized right before the stretch of slow, gentle water where, typically, the children retrieved them.

One time, as they stood on the shore watching for their boats to come dancing down the brook, they had spotted a cork person from the year before—bobbing along, hatless, boatless, naked, but somehow still afloat.

Toby, four years old at the time, had leaned into the shallows (holding Eleanor's hand, though reluctantly) to retrieve the remains of a bedraggled cork person, and studied its face.

"It's Bob," he said. Named for one of Cam's teammates on his softball team, the Yellow Jackets.

Ursula pronounced this a miracle, though to Toby there seemed nothing particularly surprising about the unexpected return of an old familiar character.

Cork people went away. Cork people came back. Or didn't.

"People die sometimes," Toby pointed out to Ursula (older than him by a year and a half, but less inclined to confront the darker side). Not only people whose songs you listened to on the radio and people you heard about on the news, and a princess whose wedding you watched on TV, and a whole space shuttle filled with astronauts, and a mop-topped rock and roll singer whose songs you danced to in the kitchen, but people you knew, too. A neighbor from down the road who showed you a gypsy moth cocoon, and a guy who came to your parents' Labor Day party and did an imitation of a rooster, and a best friend who took you to a water park one time. And dogs would die, and grandparents, a child to whom you once offered your last mozzarella stick at your father's softball game, even. And even when those things didn't happen, other terrible things did. You had to get used to it.

But here was one story you could count on, one that never changed. Spring, summer, fall, winter, the water flowed on. These rocks would be here forever—rocks, among the things in the world Toby loved best, and as much as Toby had considered the losses around him, the thought that he and the people he loved best would ever cease to exist was beyond his imagining.

In Toby's mind, their family would always stay together, always loving each other, and what else really mattered more than that? This was the world as they knew it. This was how it seemed to them then, and maybe even Eleanor believed as much, once.

Part 1

1.

a familiar road

The sound reached them all the way down to the field where the chairs were set up—so loud that if Eleanor hadn't been holding Louise as tightly as she had, she might have dropped her. A few people screamed, and someone yelled, "Oh, shit!" Eleanor could hear the voice of one of the assembled guests begin to pray, in Spanish. Louise, observing the scene, burst into tears and called for her mother.

The noise was like nothing she'd ever heard. A crash, followed by a low, awful groaning. Then silence.

"Oh, God," someone cried out. *"Dios mío."* Someone else.

"We'll find your mama," Eleanor told Louise, scanning the assembled guests for her daughter, Louise's mother, Ursula. Eleanor herself took in the event—whatever it was—with a certain unexpected calm. Worse things had happened than whatever was going on now, she knew that much. And though the piece of land on which she now stood had once represented, for her, the spot where she'd live forever and the one where she would die, this place was no longer her home, and hadn't been for fifteen years.

It was impossible to know, at first, where the sound came from, or what had caused it. Earthquake? Plane crash? Terrorist attack? Her mind went—crazily—to a movie she'd seen about a tsunami, a woman whose entire family had been wiped out by one vast, awful wave.

But Eleanor's family was safe. Now she could see them all around her—dazed, confused, but unhurt. All she really needed to do at a moment like this was to make sure that Louise was all right. Her precious only granddaughter, three years old.

At the moment they heard the crash, Louise had been studying Eleanor's necklace, a very small golden bird on a chain. "You're okay," Eleanor whispered into her ear, when they heard the big boom. All around them, the guests in wedding attire were running with no particular sense of a destination, calling out words nobody could hear.

"Everybody's fine," Eleanor said. "Let's go see your mother."

Cam's farm—she was accustomed now to calling it that—lay a little over an hour's drive north of her condo in Brookline. She had made the trip to bear witness to the marriage of her firstborn child, Ursula's older sibling, at the home where she once lived.

After all these years, she still knew this place so well that she could have made her way down the long driveway in the dark without benefit of headlights. She knew every knot in the floorboards of the house, the windowsill where Toby used to line up his favorite specimens from his rock collection, the places glitter got stuck deep in the cracks from their valentine-making projects, the uneven counter where she rolled out cookie dough and packed lunches for school, or (on snow days) fixed popcorn and cocoa for the three of them when they came in from sledding. She knew what the walls looked like inside the closet where she'd retreat, holding the phone she'd outfitted with an extra-long cord, in a time long before cell phones, when she'd needed to conduct a business conversation without the sounds of her children's voices distracting her.

And more: The bathroom where her son once played his miniature violin. The pantry, shelves lined with the jam and spaghetti sauce she canned every summer. The record player spinning while the five of them danced to the Beatles, or Chuck Berry, or *Free to Be . . . You and Me*. The mantel where they'd hung their stockings and the patch of rug, in front of the fireplace, where she spread ashes to suggest the footprints of a visitor who'd come down the chimney in the night.

Eleanor knew where the wild blueberries grew, and the lady's slippers, and where the rock was, down the road, where they'd launched their cork people every March when the snow thawed and the brook ran fast under the stone bridge. The pear tree she and Cam had planted, after the birth of their first child. The place in the field where cornflowers came up in late June. Just now starting to bloom. A shade of blue like no other.

And here she was, attending the wedding of that same child. In another lifetime, they'd named that baby Alison. They called him Al now.

There stood Eleanor's old studio, and Cam's woodshop, where she would sometimes pay him late-afternoon visits and they would make love on a mattress by the woodstove. The crack in the plaster over the bed she'd chosen to focus on while pushing their babies out into the world.

How many hundreds of nights—a few thousand—had she stretched out on the bed, her children in their mismatched pajamas with a stack of library books, the three of them jostling for prime position on the bed (three children, but there were only two sides next to their mother)? Downstairs, she could hear Cam in the kitchen, washing the dishes and whistling, or listening to a Red Sox game. Outside the window, the sound of water running at the falls. Moonlight streaming in. Her children's hot breath on her neck, craning to see the illustrations in the book. *Just one more. We'll be good.*

Sometimes, by this point in the day, she'd be so tired the words on the page she was reading would no longer make sense, and she'd start speaking gibberish, at which point one of them—Alison, generally—would tap her arm, or Toby might pat her cheeks.

"Wake up, Mama. We need to know how it turns out."

They were all grown up now.

Older people (the age she was now herself, midway through her fifties) making small talk at the grocery store, back in the days her cart overflowed with breakfast cereal and orange juice—when there was always a baby in the front and someone else scrunched up among the groceries—used to tell her how fast your children grew up, how quickly it all passed. At Stop & Shop one time, Toby got so wild—sticking carrots in his ears and pretending he was a space alien—that she'd abandoned her cart full of groceries, there in the middle of the aisle, whisking the children out to the car until her son calmed down enough that she could resume their shopping. Bent over the wheel of her late-model station wagon while her three children cowered in the back, she imagined hightailing it to someplace far away. The Canadian border, maybe. Mexico. Or half a mile down their dirt road, to spend one entire morning with her sketch pad and pencils, just drawing. Only there were the children to think about. There were always the children, until there weren't.

All those small injuries, sorrows, wounds, regrets—the hurtful words, the pain people inflicted on each other, intentionally or not, that seemed so important once. You might not even remember anymore what they were about, those things that once made you so angry, bitter, hurt. Or maybe you remembered, but did any of it matter, really? (Who said what? Who did what, when? Who hurt whom? Well, everybody had hurt everyone.)

Now here you were at the end of it all, opening your eyes as if from a long sleep—a little dazed, blinking from the brightness of the sun, just grateful you were there to wake up at all. This was Eleanor, returned to the home of her youth on the wedding day of her firstborn child. Concentrating on the one thing that mattered, which was her family, together again. Beat up and battered, like a bunch of Civil War soldiers returning from Appomattox (whatever side they'd belonged to, it made no difference) but still alive on the earth.

Earlier today, when Ursula introduced her mother to her daughter, her voice had been polite, but wary—the tone a parent might utilize when overseeing her child's first meeting with a new teacher, or with the pediatrician in preparation for receiving her shots.

"This is your granny, Lulu," Ursula explained to Louise, who had shrunk back in the way a three-year-old does with a stranger. Then to Eleanor, "How was your drive?"

"I missed you," she said, getting down low, studying her face. Memorizing it. She could see her daughter in that face, but mostly what she saw was a whole new person. "I was hoping I'd get to see you."

This was when Louise had noticed her necklace. Amazingly, her granddaughter had climbed into her arms to study the small golden bird more closely.

Eleanor could see, on Ursula's face, a look of caution and concern. She studied her daughter's face now—her middle child, now almost thirty-one years old—for some familiar reminder of the girl she used to be, the one who liked to start every morning singing "Here Comes the Sun," the one who arranged her vegetables on her plate in the shape of a face, always the smiling kind, the one who'd sucked her thumb till she went off to first grade. At which point she herself had begged Eleanor to paint her thumb with the terrible-tasting medicine, to make her stop. (Eleanor hated doing this. It was Ursula who had insisted. Ursula, so deeply invested in fitting in.)

Ursula was the one who, when Eleanor tucked her into bed every night, liked to say, "I love you more than the universe. More than infinity." If you left the room before she got a chance to say the words, she'd make you come back.

It was three years since Eleanor had seen Ursula. Easy to keep track, because it had been three days after the birth of Louise. They were in the kitchen of Ursula and Jake's house; Ursula had just finished nursing the baby. Eleanor was holding her when her daughter had stood up from the table. She took the baby from Eleanor's arms.

"Don't come back. Don't plan on seeing your granddaughter ever again." Those were Ursula's words to Eleanor as she sent her away that day. Then three years of silence.

"I love our family," Ursula used to say.

Our family. She spoke as if the five of them, together, constituted some whole entity, like a country or a planet.

This would have been in the mid-eighties, when the children were all in single-digit ages. She had been so busy with the children, most of all Toby, that she hadn't noticed her marriage to their father unraveling. But her younger daughter did. Sometimes back then, observing Eleanor's worried expression, Ursula had placed her fingers—one from each hand—in the corners of Eleanor's mouth to form her lips into a smile.

At the time, Eleanor was always playing the same one song on her Patti LaBelle album, "On My Own." She was always worried about money, worried about work. Mad at Cam. That most of all.

Ursula was just eight at the time, but already she had designated herself the family cheerleader, the one who, through her own tireless efforts, would make everyone happy again. Ursula, the one of Eleanor's three children who had, for a while, refused to read *Charlotte's Web* because she'd heard what happened in the end and didn't want to go there, though in the end she did. Ursula, the perpetual peacemaker, the optimist, the girl committed above all else to the well-being of everyone she loved (possibly ignoring her own feelings along the way). Sensing trouble between her parents, she was always thinking up things they might do to bring them all together.

"I call family hug!" she'd announce, in that determinedly cheerful tone of hers.

Who wants to play Twister? Let's build an igloo and go inside and sing campfire songs! Tell us the story again, Dad, about how you met Mom.

Now their endlessly hopeful younger daughter had a second child of her own on the way, evidently. Her first—whose birth had been followed, three days later, by Eleanor's disastrous visit—nestled into her grandmother's arms as if she'd known her all her life.

Ursula had known the comfort of those arms herself. But she'd forgotten, to the point where the simple fact of Eleanor's ability to hold a three-year-old in her arms without eliciting screams had seemed to surprise her.

"It's okay, Lulu," Ursula said to Louise, when Eleanor bent to pick her up. "She won't hurt you."

Why would anyone ever suppose otherwise? Least of all her own child.

2.
intimate strangers

In no other way that she could think of would Eleanor be called a superstitious person, but there had been a time when she could not round the final bend in the long, dead-end dirt road that led up to this place without saying the words out loud, "I'm home." Maybe some part of her actually believed that if she ever failed to speak the words, something terrible might happen to one of them. How would she ever survive if it did?

Only, she had.

The first thing she'd always see, approaching the house, was the ash tree. Nobody remembered who started this, but they had called the tree Old Ashworthy. The oldest in town—a rare survivor of the hurricane of 1938 that had wiped out so many of the biggest trees, their neighbor Walt told her. The tallest, anyway.

The trunk had been massive, its girth so vast that one time, when Cam and Eleanor were still together, and the children were little, the five of them had all held hands and circled it, or tried to.

It had been Ursula's idea. "I have a plan, guys," she'd announced. At her instruction they'd formed a circle around the base of the tree in their front yard—their backs against the scratchy bark, faces looking out, fingers touching, Alison with that dark, worried expression that seldom left her by this point—rolling her eyes, no doubt, and wanting nothing more than to be left alone—and sweet, vague Toby not fully grasping the concept of what they were trying to do here but ready as always to oblige.

Eleanor had tried to touch Cam's fingers that day, but Old Ashworthy's circumference exceeded their reach. In the end, even with Cam's long arms, they couldn't reach all the way around the trunk, or even close.

Even this—the failure of the five of them to execute her plan of a unifying hug around the tree, and the ominous sense of failure they might have taken from this—Ursula had managed to transform into a signal of something good.

"You know what our family needs to make this work?" she said. "Another baby!"

Looking back on that day now, Eleanor realized that her husband must have already given up on their marriage by then, though it said something about how distracted Eleanor was at the time that she had failed to notice.

All three of their babies had been born on this farm. The worst pain Eleanor had ever known—the worst physical pain anyway, the sense that her body was ripping in two, sounds coming out of her she would not have believed herself capable of making. Then the part where this whole new person showed up, and you looked into her face, wrapped your arms around her wet pink body.

"It's a girl."

She'd driven Al to Logan airport, the day she saw her firstborn off to college. It was back before Homeland Security prohibited you from walking up to the gate with someone you loved, or being there to watch as she came off the plane when she came home.

Only Al might not be coming home much, she told Eleanor. She had turned to face Eleanor, just before boarding the plane, to deliver the news.

"You might not be seeing me for a while," she said. "I need to be on my own to figure everything out."

Figure out what? Can't I help you? I always used to be able to do that.

Al walked down the ramp then, into the tunnel that led to the plane. Standing at the gate, watching her go, Eleanor felt a stabbing in her chest, as real as a knife.

Sometimes a person has to leave home to become who they need to be.

That was a long time ago now. Her child had accomplished what he'd set out to do. If you hadn't known him before, there would have seemed nothing out of the ordinary about the appearance of the man who stood there beneath a homemade arbor of grapevines, hair slicked back, wearing a suit and tie and a pair of lace-up oxfords, a sprig of lilac pinned to his pocket. Kissing the bride.

If you had told Eleanor this would be part of her family's story—the child she had thought of as her daughter, who had sent her a letter to say that he was actually her son—she might have imagined this as their family's central challenge. But Al getting to become the person he always wanted to be turned out to be one of the best things that could have happened.

Eleanor had thought it would be strange, seeing Al for the first time—Al, a man. But it wasn't. When she pulled up that morning, he was standing on the porch in his wedding suit, with the bride's two brothers along with Toby and Elijah—Cam's son from his second marriage. The five of them were fixing each other's boutonnieres.

As much as Al had changed since she'd said goodbye to him that day at the airport, she recognized him instantly—his eyes, his hands, that dark hair with the familiar cowlick, now tamed with hair product.

But he was different, too, in ways that had nothing to do with the assignment of gender. The child who used to be Alison was never quick to smile. The young man Eleanor encountered on the porch now—her son Al—looked happier than she could ever remember. There was a lightness to him. He was actually laughing at something one of the future brothers-in-law had said.

"It's good to see you," Eleanor told him. The blandest words. Had they ever meant more than they did now?

Eleanor put her arms around him. He did not resist her embrace, as he might have done once. For a few years there he had been angry at everyone, himself included, no doubt. Angry at the world.

She should have recognized sooner that Alison had never felt she was born in the right body. She told no one when she got her period, though when Eleanor saw Alison's underpants, hand-washed, hung to dry in her closet, she had put her arms around her daughter and asked, "Why didn't you let me know?" When Ali's breasts developed, she told Eleanor she wanted to chop them off.

Back in those days hardly anyone ever talked about things like that. You didn't consider the possibility that there might be another way for a person like Ali to make her way through life, and if you did elect to do something about it (the hormones, the surgery), that would have seemed like the worst thing you could imagine your child going through.

Now here he was, Eleanor's son Al, on his wedding day. Strong, handsome, happy.

"I want you to meet Teresa's brothers," he said, his hand on her shoulder.

"Mateo, Oscar. This is my mom."

From where she stood, holding Louise near the back of the assembled guests, Eleanor had met the eyes of Teresa's mother, Claudia—born in Mexico, raised in Texas, a woman who, years before, would have gone shopping with her daughter for a quinceañera dress. Forty years married, Claudia had told her earlier. Hers, a church wedding. Catholic.

"All that matters is love," she had said to Eleanor, when the two of them met before the service. "Our daughter is happy. *¿Qué más necesitamos?* What more do we need?" For her, the only issue about the match between her daughter and Eleanor's son had been their refusal of a church wedding, but once they'd gotten a priest to give his blessing she'd gotten over it.

It was possible that Miguel and Claudia remained unaware of Al's early history. What mattered to them was who these two adult children were now, not who they had been. When a person has been born in Michoacán, and lives now in a Dallas suburb, she knows all about letting go of the past. Making her peace with it, at least.

Eleanor studied the faces of the other guests, as many as she could see from where she stood. There was the Seattle crowd, Al's programmer friends from his start-up, all unknown to her. The Mexican American contingent. But there were others she recognized—from school potlucks long ago, nights at the softball field, playground fundraisers, drop-offs and pickups at each other's houses, times the children got together to play. They all just looked a lot older, but then so did Eleanor.

None of them had escaped large sorrows. A child in and out of rehab over the last ten years. A child dead by suicide. A son who lost a leg in Iraq. Scanning the assembled guests, Eleanor's thoughts went to the friend who, if she were still alive, would have taken her for pre-wedding pedicures, and to her old neighbor Walt, who'd quietly loved her all those years—dead now for a dozen years. So many of those her age were no longer married to the wives and the husbands of their youth. Eleanor and the man with whom she'd raised three children among them.

It was never difficult to locate Cam in any crowd, given his height and his hair, which had retained its color, though now there were strands of gray among the red. If this event had taken place a couple of years earlier, the woman who'd replaced Eleanor as his wife would be seated next to him, but she was gone.

Maybe because he'd been busy setting things up, they had not spoken to each other yet, but now Cam turned his head, which allowed Eleanor to see his face for the first time in many years. It was deeply lined, but still handsome, though he was thinner than she'd ever known him to be. Gaunt, even. Cam had always been a lean person, but as a young man he had a certain heft to his body. Now his face was so drawn you could almost see the actual bones of his skull under the skin. When she caught sight of him he was staring off in the distance, his expression impenetrable.

It was a familiar image to Eleanor: Cam, with his attention someplace else. If the occasion inspired in him some memory of a day, long ago, when it had been himself and Eleanor standing in this field looking into each other's eyes, swearing their love for all time (neither one of them able to imagine the day their hearts would not beat faster in the presence of the other), nothing on his face betrayed it.

Cam had never been a man inclined to consider the past. When a person left, she was gone. When an event was over, it might as well never have happened.

They'd met at a craft fair in Vermont when Cam was just getting started with his woodworking.

"Cam," he said, when she'd stopped to inspect a bowl, running her finger over the smooth interior. It took Eleanor a moment to understand he was speaking to her.

"I thought you'd never stop at my table."

He looked like an illustration out of an old book of Greek mythology she'd owned as a child, with that flowing red mane. His lanky presence was something she often registered (this was later) even before he walked into the room, ducking his head slightly as he passed through the doorway—a habit acquired from long experience of the many times he had hit his head on some low-hung New England lintel. He exuded utter self-assurance and a quality whose implications for her own life she would only understand later—a kind of coolness she never came close to possessing. Worries that consumed Eleanor rolled off his back, or seemed to. He didn't hold on to things the way she did. He had an easier time than most letting go of things, and people, though she didn't know that part yet.

She probably fell in love with Cam the moment she met him—with his shirt open and a black-eyed Susan tucked behind his ear, reaching out his hand in her direction. A cleft in his chin. Perfect teeth. That smile. "Cameron, actually," he told her. "But nobody calls me that except my mother."

Eleanor had never known a person with redder hair. Not strawberry blond, but true red, curling down to his shoulders—like a man with his head on fire, she used to say. She could still remember the feeling of her hands raking through that hair, and of how, when he lowered his body over hers, those curls fell over her face. She had loved his body, loved his seemingly endless capacity for any new experience, mystery, joy. She could not get over the fact that a person like him would have noticed her and sought her out. There had been nothing remotely self-assured about Eleanor, but maybe that was what had drawn him to her.

He spoke of babies the night they met.

He moved in with her—here, on this farm—the week after they met. They were married that summer. Watched their first child born on their bed the winter that followed, and within less than four years, two more.

How does it happen that a person with whom you have shared your most intimate moments—greatest love, greatest pain, joy, also grief—can become a stranger?

3.

some tree

Earlier that afternoon, shortly after her uneasy arrival at the farm, but before she'd located Al or Ursula—or known whether Ursula would even be speaking to her, or if she'd have a chance to meet Louise—Eleanor had spotted a very old woman sitting off to herself under the tent. It took her a moment to realize that this was her former neighbor Edith, from down the road. She did not approach her.

Edith had never liked Eleanor, probably because her husband, Walt, had liked her too much.

Walt had died years ago. All those years living down the road from Eleanor—before her marriage to Cam and after—Walt had been as good a friend to her as anyone. Especially in the days when she'd lived here on her own, Walt used to stop by just to check up on Eleanor and see if she needed his assistance with anything. He'd delivered cordwood for the stove and split it for her, and he helped her get rid of a family of skunks who'd moved into the shed. After she got together with Cam, he'd been less quick to come over, but he still left zucchini and tomatoes from his garden on their doorstep.

"You know the old man's got a thing for you, right?" Cam had told Eleanor, after one of Walt's visits.

"He's just my friend," Eleanor said. "He likes to look after me." Not a whole lot of other people had.

It had been Walt into whose arms she had collapsed that day Cam told her he didn't want to be married to her anymore, that he'd fallen in love with someone else.

"Your husband's a fool," Walt said, stroking her hair, the one and only time he'd done so. They had stood there like that for no more than thirty seconds, probably—the longest he'd ever dared embrace her, the only time. Then he'd climbed back onto his tractor.

It had been Walt who carried her boxes of possessions out to the U-Haul the day she moved out. Walt who drove the truck.

"I still don't get it," he said. "Why it's you that has to go."

Eleanor didn't explain this to Walt, but she knew the answer. Sometimes you leave a place because you don't like being there. Sometimes you have to leave because you love it too much.

The brothers were rounding everyone up now, with instructions to gather in the lower field behind the house, the spot where a guitarist was playing and someone had constructed an arbor. The ceremony was due to begin, and they were anxious to get on with it, in part no doubt because everyone had been studying the sky, whose darkening clouds suggested a coming thunderstorm.

As the best man in the day's ceremony, Eleanor's son Toby—the youngest of their three—stood next to the groom, with that familiar shock of unfathomably red hair, that wistful look, like a visitor from some other planet, still trying after all these years to figure out how life was conducted on this one. Unsure how long he'd be sticking around.

This was Toby—twenty-eight years old now, but with the face of his five-year-old self barely changed, his expression perpetually dreamy. Toby, the sweetest boy alive—hard to think of him as a man, who trusted everyone and bore no grudges and wept at the death of a baby lamb or a bird who crashed into the window. On a day when her daughter had met her with wary formality and her older son, distraction, Eleanor felt gratitude that the face of her youngest child had lit up when he spotted her. He still called her Mama.

Just the act of taking the ring from his pocket to hand to his older brother had seemed to take place in slow motion. *His brother,* a concept to which Toby had adapted more swiftly and with greater ease than any of the rest of them. What did it matter if this person called himself a man or a woman? He was someone Toby had loved all his life. It was that simple.

Sitting there with Louise still fingering her bird necklace, Eleanor studied the groom—the son who used to be her daughter, staring at his bride—his gaze full of love, his face familiar and unknown, both at once. Here they all were, on the same piece of land where they'd started out, the same cast of characters, more or less, all these years later, though with the happy and unexpected addition of Teresa's large Mexican American family come to celebrate, along with Elijah. And Louise.

"I now pronounce you husband and wife." The familiar, old-fashioned words, spoken in Spanish by a Jesuit priest, a cousin of Teresa's, assisted by a friend of the couple from Seattle, ordained for the day by the Universal Life Church, who added, "You may now kiss the bride."

Al and Teresa finally released each other from their long embrace and turned to face the assembled guests. A trio of mariachi musicians who'd flown in from Texas began to play. Now everyone was milling around—taking pictures, admiring the floral arrangements, checking themselves for ticks. Having worried all afternoon about the possibility of a thunderstorm, a sigh of relief seemed to overtake them all as the final words of the service were spoken. The sky was overcast, nothing more. Disaster averted.

Eleanor had gotten up from her seat, Louise in her arms, and headed for a spot a little ways over on the hill. "Grammy!" Louise pointed to a plastic bottle she'd left on the ground by the chair. "My bubbles." Feeling like an outsider, Eleanor felt glad to have a job to do, retrieving it.

That was when they heard it. The crash.

First had come the lightning, a crack like the sky splitting in two. A person might have mistaken it for gunfire. One shot, followed within a fraction of a second by a volley of others, like nothing she'd ever heard.

Then came a different, deeper sound, louder than the first, and not from the sky this time, as a flash of light shot down, like a message from God in some old painting. From where they'd gathered for the service, at the foot of the hill, nobody had seen it yet, but this was the moment Old Ashworthy came crashing to the ground.

Ursula's old lab, Matador, reached the spot first. He was barking loudly. The rest of the group made it up the hill a few moments later.

Huddled together in the pounding rain, they could see it all plainly then: the giant tree lay lengthwise, from the grape arbor all the way to the pond, its branches splayed in all directions, as if the whole world had just gone sideways. Three centuries' worth of growth—spring, summer, fall, winter, a few hundred years of the cycle repeating itself, the tree growing taller and thicker, branches reaching out in a leafy green canopy for as long as any of them remembered and long before.

Lightning had split its trunk down the middle. Limbs and splinters lay spilled in all directions like a bunch of pickup sticks, leaving leaves and branches scattered across the grass over the perennial bed and down onto the field.

Long ago—the year their marriage was falling apart, though Eleanor had been too occupied with everything else to recognize it—Ali had built a fort in this tree, a getaway from what was going on in the house at the time, probably. Now Eleanor could make out, through the tangle of fallen branches, the remnants of the rungs Ali had hammered into the trunk. If she and Cam hadn't been so distracted that year—Eleanor consumed by anger and grief, Cam drunk on new love for a girl who could still view him as a hero, not a disappointment—they would have inspected that ladder and recognized how unsafe it was, how easily those rungs might have given way.

And now look. It was not the sketchy ladder that presented the greatest risk, or the long fall. The rungs had held fast. It had not been the wooden slats that gave way but the tree itself.

There stood Eleanor's children—adults now, all three of them older than she and Cam had been at the moments of their births—standing in a semicircle around the wreckage, their hands to their faces. Only Toby spoke—Toby, for whom life appeared less complicated than it did for the rest of them. Toby, whose vocabulary contained so many fewer words, yet those he spoke sometimes identified the truth with greatest clarity.

"Some tree," he said, shaking his head.

4.

fixer-upper

In the spring of the year Eleanor turned twenty, she bought a secondhand Toyota Corolla and set out on the road to buy a house. It was late May the first time she laid eyes on the farm.

She'd driven a couple of hundred miles that day—that day, and a dozen before it. There was something comforting about all that driving. Put a person in a car with a full tank of gas, give her a road map, and never mind if she can't think of one hopeful thing to look forward to. She can listen to the radio and keep driving.

The Watergate hearings were in full swing, though Eleanor had only the vaguest idea of what any of that was about. A year had gone by since the defeat of the Equal Rights Amendment. The first issue of *Ms. Magazine*. Title IX. All around her, women were making it clear, for good reason no doubt, that they no longer wanted to be defined by life in the home. But for Eleanor, it was home that mattered more than any of the rest. She'd gone looking for hers.

Eleanor put a thousand miles on the Toyota in those days she spent on the road, driving around Maine, Vermont, New Hampshire. She didn't listen to the news much. She kept a mixtape playing, of songs she loved, most of them sad. George Jones fit the bill, as did old Irish ballads about love gone wrong, and, equally, certain old R&B singers, but only the ballads. Otis Redding singing "These Arms of Mine" got to her every time, as did Edith Piaf. The heartfelt lyrics of James Taylor songs never really spoke to her, but Joni Mitchell's did—her yearning for love, her endless disappointments, and the realization she seemed to have acquired, young as she was, that for all her handsome rock star boyfriends, she might be alone forever. Alone on a two-lane highway, Eleanor sang along with Dolly Parton. *In my Tennessee mountain home / Life is as peaceful as a baby's sigh.* And with Joni. She played *Blue* on repeat all the way from upstate New York to the New Hampshire border.

There had been nothing particularly distinctive about Akersville when she stopped there. No cute coffee shops. No traffic light even. Most cars that passed this way drove on through.

It had been a random choice on Eleanor's part, pulling into this town. For close to two weeks she'd been staying at a different motel every night, living on handfuls of raw almonds and bags of carrots and Dannon boysenberry yogurt, picking up real estate flyers at rest stops with one idea in her head: to find a safe landing place.

Eleanor had pulled up in front of Abercrombie's Realty, with its row of straggly pansies and the faded wooden sign "Where Dreams Come Home." The agent on duty was a man in his late sixties, from the looks of it, nursing a Styrofoam cup of coffee. "Ed Abercrombie," he told her, extending a hand.

Not many people Eleanor's age went real estate shopping. Even if they had the means, they wouldn't have possessed the inclination. But if Ed Abercrombie felt surprise or curiosity about any of this, he concealed it well.

More often than not, when Eleanor had stopped at some Realtor's office on her odd, solitary road trip, they didn't take her seriously. Maybe they detected a certain sense of melancholy desperation tucked under the surface of her greeting as she entered their offices—her tight smile, her unnaturally vigorous handshake. She probably appeared too eager (she usually did), her needs too urgent. A person might sense, meeting Eleanor that spring, that her desire to buy a piece of property suggested a hunger deeper than that of the ordinary client.

Ed's only question concerned her employment. Not a whole lot of jobs in this area, he told her. That might be a problem.

Only it wasn't.

"I make books for children," she said. (Did he notice her fingernails, bitten down below the quick? The very slight trembling of her hand as she brushed her hair out of her eyes?)

"You make a living doing that?" he said. "Don't like to pry, but the bank's going to ask you. Taxes aren't cheap around here."

"It won't be a problem," she told him. To the surprise of no one more than Eleanor herself, her first book, published the previous year, had sold almost a hundred thousand copies. She'd be getting to work on the fourth one soon.

"I write about a little girl without any parents who travels around the world having adventures."

"A writer," he said. "What do you know? My wife used to write poetry."

Actually, Eleanor explained to him, she was more of an artist. She made pictures with stories attached. She could have gone on to explain to Ed that since she was five years old—younger maybe, an only child left to her own devices for long stretches—she'd seldom found herself without a pencil in her hand. She'd spent her childhood making up characters to keep her company and stories about the things that happened in their lives, things that never in a million years would have happened in Eleanor's. Some of these stories featured a girl named Bodie whose parents had died in a car wreck, who headed out to explore the world in search of a mysterious great-aunt she'd always heard about but never met, who was an archaeologist. Eleanor's English teacher at boarding school had suggested she send one of her Bodie stories to a publisher, along with the illustrations she'd made.

She had not yet graduated when the editors at Applewood Press had invited her to their offices to meet them. One week later, not yet in possession of a car, she had ridden the bus to New York City to meet with them. Now, in addition to *Bodie Under the Sea,* there was *Bodie Goes to the Potato Chip Factory* and, soon, *Bodie in Zanzibar.* Just before setting out on her epic journey in search of real estate, Eleanor had signed a contract to deliver *Bodie, Queen of the Desert.* She hadn't collected the check yet, but when it came, it would be a large one.

She had tried for a while there to do the things other young people did. Go to college. Fall in love. More than publishing children's books, what Eleanor had hungered for was a normal life, or something resembling that.

Only Eleanor never did well at normal life. She had lasted at college exactly one month shy of finishing her sophomore year. That was when she moved out of her dorm, packed up her mixtapes and albums, bought the Toyota, set out on the road.

She had thirty-seven thousand dollars in her checking account—the advance from her publisher for *Bodie in Zanzibar,* along with royalties from her first two Bodie books. Plenty of money, no place to live. This was when she decided to buy a house. Maybe, if she had a house, all the other parts that came with that—the things that happened in people's houses, in people's lives, so absent in her own—might also be within reach.

There was nobody to tell her this wasn't a good idea. This was the problem, in fact. Apart from her editor, who just reminded her when her next manuscript was due, and her agent, who read over the contracts, there was nobody to tell Eleanor anything.

Now here she was in Akersville, New Hampshire, listening to Ed Abercrombie talking about a log home he'd just listed, with vinyl siding and a mother-in-law unit out back.

Eleanor didn't know much, but one part was clear: the place Eleanor was looking for didn't have to be very large, but it would have land around it, and be far enough from town that you could see the stars. She needed good light, she told Ed, for making artwork. She'd never had a garden before, but she wanted to grow tomatoes and maybe peas, lettuce for salad. Zinnias.

Close to water would be nice, Eleanor told Ed. If not on the property itself, nearby.

Well, there was this one place, he said. Right down the road from a swimming hole and a waterfall. The owners hadn't actually put it on the market yet, but he could show her.

"This one's a real fixer-upper," he told her.

The old Murchison homestead had been unoccupied for five years at this point—and even before that, the family only came up summers. Nobody had spent a winter in the house since before the war, and Ed wasn't talking about Vietnam or even Korea. There was an ancient furnace but no insulation. The town no longer plowed the road, though if Eleanor lived there in the winter—he studied her face here, assessing the likelihood of this—she'd have a right to request it.

Ten minutes later, she was in the passenger seat of Ed's Oldsmobile headed north out of town.

On their way, Ed handed her the sheet with the listing information, but Eleanor chose to look out the window instead. Though she took in a number of fine old colonials and capes—the kind with stone walls around them and apple trees out back—this wasn't one of those prettied-up New England towns featured on postcards and calendars. There were two-hundred-year-old houses like the one Ed was taking her to, but there were also double-wide trailers and ranch houses with cars in the yard that didn't appear drivable. A pizza place, a Laundromat, a gas station, a church next to which were cemeteries with gravestones that went back to the seventeen hundreds, Ed told her.

They passed a row of mailboxes. A farm stand, not yet open for the season. A sign that said "Deaf Child."

Not a whole lot else.

The house sat on a rise at the end of a long dirt road—the kind in which a strip of grass marks the space straddled by a car's tires. It looked out over a hillside: a few acres of open land, and beyond those, another thirty of woods, Ed told her. No streetlights, of course—they'd passed the last of those a couple of miles back. This was a place where a person could look out at the night sky with no light competing with the constellations but that of the moon, no sound but the cry of owls and, in the fall (though she would only learn this later), the gunshots of hunters. The nearest neighbors lived a good half mile away.

It was lilac season when she first laid eyes on the property, and the trees were leafing out. One in particular dominated the view: an ash that had somehow survived the famous hurricane that people in these parts still spoke of, Ed told her. The tree sat just far enough from the house so as not to block the sun, but its branches seemed to fill the sky and span the horizon.

"How's that for a tree?" Ed said, as he pulled the car up alongside the door to the porch. "I'm guessing this one got started right around the time my great-great-great-grandfather hung out the first sign for his dry goods store. That would be more than two hundred years back. Maybe longer. I'm going to wager you're looking at the oldest tree in town."

A person could hang a hammock here. If she ever had the time to put her feet up, that is. With all the work a property like this required, not to mention coming up with the tax money, there might not be much time for snoozing.

Never mind that. Eleanor wasn't looking for something easy.

She stood there out front for a while, taking it in, before stepping onto the granite slab by the front door. She made no comment, asked no questions. She could feel the beating of her heart.

5.

where the happy people lived

The house was small, but she liked that. Her childhood home had been large and lonely. When she had children, she'd keep them close.

She stepped onto the porch first—a screen porch, with a trestle table. From all the stuff stored there, it looked to Eleanor as if whoever used to live here knew how to have good times together. Hung up along the back wall with the kind of care that suggested the sun shone regularly here were a croquet set and an assortment of badminton racquets, shuttlecocks, Ping-Pong paddles, baseball bats, fishing poles, horseshoes, skates and sleds in a variety of sizes. There was a hammock and a dartboard, an old pedal car.

There was a miniature cannon. Every Fourth of July, Ed explained, the family had fired off three shots. You could hear it all the way over to the Pouliots' place.

Everywhere Eleanor looked lay evidence of a life full of good things. Gardening tools. A toboggan. There were board games and a Victrola with a stack of old 78s. (Benny Goodman. The Andrews Sisters. Bing Crosby.) The wall by the door featured pencil marks indicating the heights of various children. *(Mickey, 4th of July weekend 1952 four foot six. Susan, July 1957. Bobby, five foot eight! Peter, five foot eleven. Look what happens when a boy eats his vegetables!)*

It looked like a house where people who loved each other had lived.

In the kitchen, a fireplace occupied most of one wall; in another century the woman of the house might have set a loaf of bread in the baking oven. The floors were wood, counters Formica. At one end of the room was an old Coldspot refrigerator. "You'd want to replace this," Ed told Eleanor, but she knew she wouldn't.

Off to one side of the kitchen lay a small pantry whose shelves had been covered with red-and-green flowered contact paper, most likely laid down in the fifties. Running her hand along one of these shelves, Eleanor pictured mason jars filled with vegetables canned in the pressure cooker, sitting on a top shelf alongside cake toppers and packages of birthday candles and little yellow plastic corncob holders, with plates to match shaped like corn husks.

Out the pantry window she could see blackberry bushes. If this house were hers, she'd make jam and write the dates on the labels, line them up along the shelves. She'd grow tomatoes for a winter's worth of sauce.

The other end of the kitchen opened to a tiny space—barely large enough for a single bed—that Ed referred to as the borning room. In the old days, this was where the woman of the house gave birth to her babies, Ed told her. Another bedroom, larger than this one, faced out to the front of the house, with another, smaller fireplace and windows opening south and east. Morning sun.

There was a small front hall, and a living room with a third fireplace and old nails on the mantel suggesting that some December long ago, children had hung stockings here. Wide pine beams spanned the ceiling of the room, as they did in the kitchen.

There was a surprising brightness to the space, thanks to the windows, looking out to a field no longer tilled, stone walls, a few old apple trees, and beyond them, woods. And that enormous tree, of course. The ash.

"The Murchisons never did much in the way of upgrading," Ed told her. He said this as if it might be a problem, but Eleanor loved that about the house. The walls still bore decades-old wallpaper (roses in the bedroom, farmers and milkmaids chasing cows across the living room, a row of their buckets spilling milk, a row of dancing children below them). The floorboards were wide and rutted, and not even close to level, though not enough to suggest major issues with the foundation, Ed assured her, as if she might be worried about that, which she wasn't.

Upstairs (steep risers, bowed in the middle from 150 years of use) there was a single room, divided in the middle by the massive chimney from the fireplaces below, with a window seat where a person might place herself and take in the scent of lilacs. Children should sleep here.

At this point in the tour Ed suggested that Eleanor might like to see the basement, but she was more interested in studying the dishes in the pantry (a complete set of Fiesta ware, and a Blue Willow teapot, and cast-iron frying pans and muffin pans and an old popcorn popper). In the living room cupboard were at least two dozen boxes of jigsaw puzzles, which, when completed (give or take a piece or two), might reveal the image of a covered bridge in fall, or a New England churchyard surrounded by snow, along with an ancient Monopoly game with the original pieces in lead.

He took her out into the field, to the spot where the green of young grass met the trees, so she could look up the hill toward the house. Already she thought of it as her house. When she looked down, she saw moss and a patch of lady's slippers.

There was more: the tool shed, an old plow, a wooden wheelbarrow. "You probably wondered about the well and the septic system," Ed said to her.

She hadn't.

He was saying something then about what it would cost to insulate the place, and to install a new furnace (essential) and double-pane windows. The roof was old, but they built them right in those days. She'd need to install a new water heater.

She barely heard him. He had already explained that the owners were selling the place with everything in it: dishes, furniture, sheets and towels. An old hand-crank ice cream maker. The Bing Crosby 78s.

They were standing under the giant ash tree, with the front door behind them. The door was blue, but needed paint.

"Hear that?" he said. It was the sound of water. "There's a stone arch bridge just down the road, over Hopewell Falls. This time of year, with all the rain we've had and the runoff from the snow, the water's running high. If you favor trout fishing, the swimming hole below the falls is the spot for you. Nice place to cool off on a hot day."

She had no idea how to catch a trout, and less what she'd do with one if she succeeded. But the part about the waterfall got to her.

"I'll be buying this house," she told him.

6.

who should we call?

Eleanor was sixteen, the winter of the crash. Her parents, Martin and Vivian, had been driving home to Boston from a ski trip in Vermont. Nighttime black ice on a two-lane highway, tires locked, a skid into the path of an oncoming Pepsi delivery truck. Impact sufficiently violent that one of her mother's boots had turned up fifty feet from the side of the highway. Her father would have been smoking, which explained why the windows were open, though how it was that the boot made it out of the car was one of about a hundred questions Eleanor preferred not to consider, same as she chose not to think about how—if things had been different between them—she would have been there in the back seat when they hit the truck. Some teenagers would have been with their parents on that ski trip, but Martin and Vivian were happiest when it was just the two of them.

She was halfway through her junior year at her Connecticut private school when she got the news. Sometime a little after ten that night—a Sunday—came the knock on her dorm room door.

Later she would remember the sound of showers running in the bathroom they all shared, down the hall. Simon and Garfunkel on somebody's record player. *I am a rock, I am an island.* The smell of marijuana from the joint her roommate, Patty, had lit earlier, and Patty opening the window next to her bed at the sound of the knocking, the voice on the other side of the door announcing the presence of a faculty member.

"Eleanor? It's Mr. Guttenberg. We need to talk."

"Oh, shit," Patty said, just before Eleanor opened the door. For a moment they had actually believed this would be the big catastrophe of the night: Patty getting put on probation or kicked out of school, even. But as it turned out, a drug violation had been the last thing on Mr. Guttenberg's mind.

At the time Eleanor had been painting her toenails. For weeks the evidence remained. One foot with all blue nail polish. The other, three toes only.

After he told her the news—"Head-on collision," "died instantly," "at least they didn't suffer"—Mr. Guttenberg patted Eleanor on the shoulder, almost as if he were petting a dog. (Somewhere in the background, Patty was wailing. *Oh my God, oh my God*. Eleanor made no sound.)

"Who should we call for you?" he asked her. The emergency numbers on the forms she'd filled out back in September listed her parents' number. No point calling that one now.

"My mother had a second cousin in Illinois," she said. Or maybe Wisconsin.

She actually slept that first night—an odd, dead kind of sleep, more like a blackout. The next morning there had been a moment when she woke up and, for a few seconds, forgot what had happened. She heard the sound of the girls along the hall and the clanging of radiator pipes. Then it came to her.

"Who can we call for you?" the headmaster's wife asked her when she stopped by that morning with a plate of blueberry muffins. There was nobody. Her family had consisted of three people. Two of whom were now dead.

Eleanor had never asked her mother the reason why she was an only child. She had the feeling that after they had her it must have occurred to them that they really hadn't wanted to have children after all, and the best they could do was not have any more.

She was probably no more than three years old when she made up her imaginary brother, Anthony. He was older, and very handsome. He played dress-up and later Candy Land with her—a game her mother said was boring—and when she walked to school he held her hand. Somewhere along the line he turned into a teenager who carried her on his shoulders and drove her places. By this point, she no longer talked to him in her head the way she had when she was little, but even in her Holcomb Academy days, she sometimes let herself picture what it would be like if Anthony were there. Calling her up, or driving to see her on Family Weekend and taking her bowling. She knew what kind of car he'd drive. A VW Bug.

Or maybe she would have had a little sister. "I'll always take care of you," she would have told her sister that she never had. She pictured herself wrapping her arms around a little girl who resembled herself, but smaller, pressing her tight against her chest and not letting go—the same exact thing she would have liked to have someone do for her.

As things were—in real life—there was nobody to talk to about what happened. The people she used to have, with whom she might have discussed losing her parents, were the parents she'd lost. But the larger truth was that she couldn't have talked to them about it anyway. Martin and Vivian had died that night, but they had been largely absent forever.

It was just Eleanor then. One other distant relative somewhere in the Midwest that she'd met a couple of times when she was little. No grandparents.

She'd made the trip home to Newton by herself; her father's law partner, Don, picked her up. She'd met him a few times over the years, at her parents' annual cocktail party, where her job was passing the hors d'oeuvres, but didn't recognize him when he came up to her at the train station and, a little awkwardly, offered what passed for a hug. From there they went straight to the funeral home.

Later that weekend she'd made her way through the rooms of their house figuring out what to do with all their stuff. Only she couldn't figure it out. How was a not-quite-sixteen-year-old supposed to begin taking apart a house full of furniture and clothes, books, records, papers, photographs, ski equipment, tax returns? All the odd things that nobody talked about: Her father's underwear and a collection of *Playboy* magazines from the sixties. Her mother's diaphragm. The liquor cabinet containing six different bottles of whiskey, ten of vodka; the clock over the television in the family room: *No drinking until 5 P.M.* Every number on its face a five.

Eleanor knew people whose parents viewed their children as the center of their universe, but that was never how it was in her own small family. She had friends whose parents barely spoke to each other and never touched, might even have slept in different bedrooms, but never missed their children's games or band concerts. In Eleanor's world, it was nothing like that. Her parents had already been together almost twenty years when she was born, and it had always appeared to Eleanor that they never fully got over viewing her as something of an interloper in their private world.

She could remember, from earliest childhood, the cries coming from their bedroom, late at night, a strange and confusing combination of what sounded like wild joy and injury. Her father's eyes anytime her mother walked in the room. Her mother's eyes meeting his. Herself, off in the corner with her colored pencils, close to invisible.

Thursday nights, watching Dean Martin—the two of them with their martinis. Friday afternoons, happy hour at a bar they liked at Coolidge Corner. Sunday mornings, she understood not to disturb them in bed till after ten o'clock, and used to watch the clock, waiting. "Adult time," they called it. This took place not only Sunday mornings, but at dinner, too, when her mother put on one of her silky lounging outfits and the two of them shared their bottle of wine, and if Eleanor was quiet, she got to listen in to their conversation. Sometimes alone in the living room, they put on Mantovani records and danced. Eleanor could have set the drapes on fire when they were dancing that way. They wouldn't have noticed.

Other times she heard her father's voice, loud and angry. They were crazy about each other, but sometimes, they were just plain crazy.

Somebody would throw something. Somebody threw something else. Then came the sound of breaking glass. Their voices, saying terrible things. Then—not right away—the laughter. Then their voices were quiet again. Then the sounds from the bedroom.

This was the part to the story nobody mentioned at the funeral. Nobody spoke about Martin's drinking, or how Vivian had matched him, drink for drink. Cocktails after work every night. Bloody Marys on Sunday mornings, and other mornings, too, often. Wednesdays. Mondays. You name it.

None of the people who'd come that day—men who knew her father from Rotary, or golf, or the law firm where he practiced, women who'd done volunteer work with her mother—would have recognized this other side of the two of them that Eleanor had known. The angry dad who tore through the house one time, cursing, because he couldn't find the *TV Guide*. The one who, when the liquor store was closed one night, drove to five different convenience stores to find a particular brand of whiskey. The one who, when she asked him if he could not have so many drinks when her friend Marcy came over, sent her to her room. After, she could hear him tearing around the kitchen, ranting to her mother. *Can you believe? Our daughter thinks I'm some kind of alcoholic bum.* At some point in the evening he had torn into her room and grabbed her colored pencil set, which she was always careful to keep organized by color family. He threw the open box against the wall, pencils flying in all directions.

Eleanor had a word for times like those, when one of her parents—sometimes Martin, sometimes Vivian—spun out over the edge. She called it Crazyland. They didn't live in that place all the time, but you never knew when they might go there. It was always just around the corner.

Eleanor never told anyone about Crazyland, but the fact that she had been there—witnessed it, anyway—was why she didn't invite Marcy or Charlene for a sleepover, ever. Knowing Crazyland was always nearby made her try to be very good all the time, to keep her parents from going there.

Looking back on the house where she grew up, it came to Eleanor—later—that she had seldom seen her parents completely sober. Her father's drink of choice, Jack Daniel's on the rocks. Her mother's, a Manhattan.

The accident that killed them had been a head-on collision, and all anyone said at the time was that there must have been ice on the road. Maybe the tread on their snow tires was not the best.

But Eleanor could guess why it was that their car had crossed over into the other lane that night. They would have stopped at their favorite bar on their way home. One of their many favorite bars.

They must have loved her. That's what parents did. But it had been their idea, not Eleanor's, that she go to boarding school, and although they seemed sad when they dropped her off that first time, Eleanor couldn't help but notice a sense of relief underlying their farewells. "We'll see you at Parents' Weekend," they said, but they didn't make it.

After he picked her up and brought her home, the law partner, Don, told her she could leave everything till the summer, when school got out. But when school got out, and Eleanor returned to Newton, it was no easier to figure out what she was supposed to do with a houseful of the possessions of two dead people who in many ways she barely knew. In the end, somebody called in a company that ran estate sales, who promised to empty the house by July, so it could go on the market.

Eleanor spent an afternoon alone there. "Pick out what you want, honey," Don told her. She started making a pile, but at the end of an hour the things she'd set out filled most of what had been their dining room. Where was she supposed to put all of this stuff, anyway?

In the end, Eleanor walked away with her father's clarinet, her old cereal bowl decorated with Beatrix Potter animals, a dress of her mother's from the fifties, and a pair of velvet pants that weren't even her size. She took the photograph albums, of course, though it would be a few years before she opened any of them, and when she did, she was struck by how many photographs there were of Martin and Vivian, how few of herself. Judging by the slightly off-kilter way in which the images had been captured, she guessed she had served as her parents' photographer. Anyone else, leafing through the album, would have no way of knowing that Eleanor had been along on those trips at all.

She was eleven years old when they'd traveled to New York City to take in the World's Fair—riding an escalator past the *Pietà,* flown in from Italy; taking in water-skiers and a parrot at the Florida pavilion and the World's Biggest Cheese at the Wisconsin pavilion. Later that afternoon, her parents drank so many mai tais at the Hawaii pavilion (seven, based on Eleanor's count of the paper umbrellas) that they had trouble making their way back to the parking lot.

The next day, after a breakfast involving a large pitcher of Bloody Marys, as they were walking along Fifth Avenue—Eleanor a few steps behind the two of them, as usual—she had decided to simply stop walking. Just stand still on the sidewalk and see how long it took before they noticed.

Her parents had gone more than a block before they looked back, and even when they did, they did so with an unnerving measure of calm.

Oh, there you are, her mother said. Her speech was only very slightly slurred. Nobody would have noticed but Eleanor.

The last time she'd seen her parents, Eleanor had told her mother she didn't plan on going skiing with the two of them over break.

Did it ever occur to you to ask my opinion about what I'd like to do instead of making all these plans and then letting me know? Did it ever occur to you that I might have my own ideas about what I'd want to do, besides tagging along after the two of you, watching you order cocktails and stare into each other's eyes? Cleaning up the broken glass in the morning?

That Christmas they'd given her a pair of warm gloves and a parka, a watch, an art kit of the sort best suited for a child around eight years old who may or may not have expressed an interest in painting, and a gift certificate for Filene's. Eleanor was in her room, packing her suitcase, her face still hot from the argument with her parents. Her mother appeared in the doorway, without a drink.

"Are you sure you don't want to come skiing with us?" her mother asked, again. She put her hand on Eleanor's shoulder. She seemed relieved when Eleanor said no thanks, she was going to visit her school roommate, Patty, over winter vacation.

At the funeral, someone who'd seen Martin and Vivian at the mountain the day of the accident had told her how great the conditions had been. How happy the two of them had looked, sitting in the lodge after their last run, sipping their Irish coffees.

"In a way, it's sort of perfect that they died together," a friend of her father's had suggested. Imagine either one of those two without the other.

They'd ended their lives side by side in the front seat of their Oldsmobile, with their only child at school a few hundred miles away.

Once again, Eleanor had been left out, and though this time it was a good thing, it seemed to her that really, she'd been on her own forever anyway.

Who else did Eleanor know who—as she discovered, cleaning out their kitchen, after—had one whole cupboard devoted to swizzle sticks? And another containing two dozen jars of maraschino cherries?

7.

one small step for man

Patty's parents, the Hallinans, invited Eleanor to spend her summer vacation with their family in Rhode Island. Patty was going to be away working as a camp counselor for most of the summer, but Alice Hallinan said that only made them all even more eager to have another teenage girl around, so they wouldn't miss Patty so much.

Jim Hallinan found Eleanor a job doing daytime kitchen prep at a restaurant owned by a golfing buddy of his. And the best part was, their son, Matt, would be home from college, retaking a class he'd flunked the year before and studying for the law boards, so he could drive her to work and look out for her.

An older brother. Eleanor had envied Patty for having one. It was her Anthony dream in real life.

She moved into Patty's room, with its twin canopy beds and the poster of Donovan on the wall, along with Patty's swim team medals and a collage of pictures from family trips to the Cape. Alice—who'd told Eleanor to call her Mom, not that she did—had cleared out half of the drawers for her clothes, though she didn't have that many. Their dog, Buddy, licked her shin. She'd always wanted a dog, but that wasn't her parents' style.

"We all want you to consider yourself one of the family," Alice said.

On the ride over to her first day of work at DiNuccio's, Patty's brother, Matt, turned on the radio. Eleanor recognized the warbly strains of "Crimson and Clover."

"My sister goes for all this sugar crap," he told her. "But I'm thinking you might appreciate Led Zeppelin." He changed the station.

He was back at the restaurant at four to bring her home, and every day after that, he drove her. Both ways.

"This must mess up your plans," Eleanor said. "Having to go back and forth to DiNuccio's all the time."

"I have no plans," he told Eleanor. "My dad's got me on a short leash on account of my grades. He basically laid down the law: if I don't pass this stupid Spanish class I need to graduate and get a decent score on the LSATs, he's taking back the car. The good thing about driving you is I get an excuse to bust out of the coop twice a day."

Eleanor liked sitting in the front seat with Matt, listening to the radio. Sometimes they rode without speaking—Matt pounding on the steering wheel when a good song came on, Eleanor looking out the window—but more and more, he talked with her. She felt special and grown-up, that a boy as old as Matt would pay attention to her this way. It was almost like having a real brother.

One day he handed her a joint. "You smoke?"

She never had, but she didn't want to seem like a goody-goody. "Sometimes."

She inhaled, more than a person should. She started coughing.

"Not much I guess, huh?" he said. His laughter sounded like some kind of animal. A hyena, or the way hyenas sounded in cartoons anyway.

"What do you figure the story was with this guy Billie Joe McAllister?" he asked her. "Ode to Billie Joe" had come on. "Like, why *did* the guy jump off the Tallahatchie Bridge?"

Eleanor didn't know what to say, so she kept quiet. Something about "Ode to Billie Joe" always made her uncomfortable. Nobody ever explained what they threw off the Tallahatchie Bridge.

"You have a boyfriend?" he asked her.

"No."

"You ever have a boyfriend?"

For a minute, she thought she'd lie, but she figured he wouldn't believe her anyway. "Not really."

"Any guy ever kiss you?"

She shook her head.

They were at the point in the road where, if he went left, they'd be back at the Hallinans' in around two minutes. There was another road, off to the right. Smaller. No sign of houses. She'd never been down that one.

That's where he took her. Not saying anything, he pulled the car over.

He leaned over to her side of the wide bench seat and put his hands on her shoulders. He pressed his face against hers. At first the kiss was the normal kind, as much as Eleanor had imagined. Then his tongue was in her mouth.

After that, he always turned down the other road when he picked her up after work. They didn't talk about it. This was just something he did, and Eleanor let him. It usually lasted only a few minutes. Then they went back to the house.

After a couple of times Matt started putting his hand down the front of her shirt. Inside her bra, pinching her nipple. She wondered if that was supposed to feel good. If someone had told him it did. If he cared about things like that.

Then he had his hand in her underpants. The next time—middle of July, probably—he pulled her skirt all the way up. He unzipped his pants. Except in museums, on statues, and one time when she'd walked in on her parents, Eleanor had never seen a man's penis. Now he was pressing his against her. Then he was thrusting it inside. At first it wouldn't go, but then it did.

Eleanor lay there on the seat, letting him move up and down on top of her. She closed her eyes.

It got to be a regular thing. Driving to work, listening to the radio. Eleanor tried hard to focus on that, rather than what would happen in the car with Matt.

They always seemed to be playing Creedence Clearwater that summer. "Bad Moon Rising." Though sometimes Matt put on the news.

There was a riot in New York City in reaction to some policemen beating up homosexual people. As far as she knew, Eleanor had never met a homosexual, but she couldn't understand why anyone would want to beat them up.

"That's one way to get out of the draft," Matt said, listening to the broadcast about the Stonewall riots. "Just tell them you're a fag."

Eleanor hardly ever said anything in the car with Matt, but this didn't seem to matter. He was mostly just talking to himself, probably.

"Me, I'd rather take my chances in the army," he said.

That summer there was a lot of talk about the moon, of course. The Apollo 11 astronauts were going there soon. Not just orbiting, but landing this time, actually walking around. Mrs. Hallinan had already made plans to host a neighborhood moon walk party.

"It's a night you're going to remember your whole life," she told Eleanor. "We're living in the middle of a historic moment."

One time, on the drive home from work, when he pulled her underpants off, he'd seen the string of her tampon hanging out. He put his penis in her mouth that day. "No offense," he said, "but I get sick at the sight of blood."

That week, the cover of *Life* magazine had featured a photograph of the lunar landscape—those vast, empty craters with nothing around them but blackness and stars.

Remember the moon. Forget the rest.

"You ever wonder what the astronauts do about going to the bathroom in space?" Matt asked her.

"No."

"They have a special bag in their suit," he said. "Then they release it into outer space. Gross, huh?"

He made the right turn. He always did. She had learned now, when he got on top of her, to put some other picture in her head and focus on that one.

Sometimes she pictured the dog, Buddy. Sometimes the moon.

Matt's biggest concern that summer was Vietnam. He wasn't that political, and the Hallinans wouldn't have approved of their children attending protest marches, but he knew that among the consequences of his failing to get the credits he needed and a good enough score on the law boards to get into some law school, the worst was the strong possibility of getting drafted. Whenever President Nixon's voice came over the radio, Matt got particularly agitated.

"No way am I going into some jungle with a goddamn M15," he said. He had a backup plan for the law boards. A guy he knew would take the test for you, with a fake ID in your name. It wasn't cheap, but if you paid him the money, he guaranteed you a score over 700.

In other circumstances, Eleanor might have said something. As it was, she just sat there letting it happen again: The turn in the road. The engine going, so he could keep the radio on. Her underpants around her ankles that she'd pull up, after. The vinyl seat upholstery sticking to her skin and later, back at the house, Mrs. Hallinan in the kitchen offering a snack. *No, thank you.*

She could smell it on herself. Matt Hallinan's semen dripping down her leg.

"You're wasting away," Alice told her. "You aren't going anorexic on us or anything, are you?"

Up on the bed in Patty's room, after, Eleanor would put on *Clouds*. Sad as she sounded, Joni Mitchell always made Eleanor feel better, or maybe simply less alone. First she took a shower, always. Then set her colored pencils out to draw. She knew that if she said anything to the Hallinans about what happened with Matt, they wouldn't believe her. The whole thing—her job at DiNuccio's, her Rhode Island summer, Mrs. Hallinan offering to take her back-to-school shopping, her friendship with Patty—would be over. Not that any of those things were so great. But where else was she supposed to go?

This was the summer Eleanor started working on the Bodie stories—the adventures of a ten-year-old girl orphan who met all sorts of kind, wonderful people in places like Maine and Antarctica and Paris. With no parents around, but also nobody like Matt Hallinan. Bodie was a girl who got to do whatever she wanted, and nobody told her what it should be. There were no boys in the story, no kissing, or any of the rest of it.

The day of the moon landing, Mrs. Hallinan prepared pigs in a blanket and deviled eggs and they all gathered around the TV set—not just the Hallinans and Eleanor, but a dozen neighbors from up and down the street—to watch Neil Armstrong walk on the moon. Privately, Eleanor wished he hadn't stuck that flag there. She liked how the craters looked with nothing on them. When she thought about the moon, which she did, in the car, it looked the way it did in *Life* magazine. Empty craters. No flag.

The next time Matt drove her home from work, he pulled over same as he always did. She closed her eyes, as usual.

As he entered her body—a sensation that had felt like a poker going into her the first time but no longer did—he put his face against her ear.

"One small step for man," he whispered.

Patty returned home from her job at the camp the second week of August, and the five of them—Mr. and Mrs. Hallinan, Patty, Matt, and Eleanor—spent five days together in Maine. There was a music festival going on somewhere in upstate New York that week. "Bunch of hippies," Mr. Hallinan said. "Probably pals of that nutcase that murdered the movie star."

Alice told Matt he should take Eleanor out on the speedboat, show her how to water-ski, but she said no thank you and mostly stayed in her room that week. She didn't even get a tan.

One night near the end of their time at the lake, she had heard Patty and her mother in the kitchen, discussing the situation. "I wish we hadn't even brought her," Patty said. "She turned out to be such a drag."

"You have to remember what Eleanor's been through," Alice told her. "It hasn't even been a year. I'm not saying it's easy having her around all the time, but let's try to be understanding."

A couple of days after they returned to Rhode Island it was time for the two of them to go back to school. As she was struggling to get her bag down the steps, Jim Hallinan called out to his son.

"Matthew! Get your butt down here. I expect you to carry out Eleanor's bag. And while you're at it, give our girl a nice big hug."

She stood a little ways off as he placed her bag in the trunk, next to Patty's.

"Good luck on your test," she told him.

"See you next summer," he said. "Sooner than that, actually. You'll be back at the ranch for Thanksgiving, right?"

"Like I keep telling Eleanor," Alice chimed in. "We're your family now."

"Family. Everybody's gotta have one, right?" Matt grinned. "Even Charlie Manson knew that."

8.

like someone just ran you over with a truck

She was back at school—rooming with Patty again, not that either of them felt particular affection for the other at this point.

Her period was due the week classes started, but it didn't come. By November she knew why.

She had thought she'd never have to speak to Matt Hallinan again, but now she found his number in Patty's address book, the frat house where he lived. Someone else picked up, a boy nicknamed Ratso, who'd changed his name from Bill after he saw some movie called *Midnight Cowboy,* Patty explained to her. Loud music in the background. A party going on. A minute later, Matt was on the phone.

It had taken him a minute to place her, but then he did. When she told him she was pregnant, he didn't deny it. He just kept saying, "oh shit oh shit oh shit."

He picked her up at school that weekend. Not on campus, obviously. Nobody could find out about this.

He'd gotten the name of a doctor from one of his fraternity brothers who'd recently had to deal with a similar problem. The doctor, who was up near Poughkeepsie, could take care of it, no questions asked. Eleanor had no way to get that kind of money without asking her father's old law partner, Don, but Matt worked out that part, not that it wasn't a pain.

Five hundred dollars. *Fuck.*

They didn't talk in the car. Five hours. He kept the radio on. Neil Diamond. The Fifth Dimension. They must have heard "Light My Fire" six times, on the drive north, but the Doors song that got to her most was "The End." She couldn't get Jim Morrison's dark, haunted voice out of her head.

The address Matt had been given turned out to be an apartment on the outskirts of town. A woman answered the door. She brought Eleanor to a room in the back where a man was waiting. He didn't have a beard, exactly, but he needed a shave. He told her to climb up on the table.

The doctor must have had one of those operations where they take out your vocal cords. The voice that spoke to her came out of a machine.

When it was over, the woman came into the room. She gave Eleanor a very thick sanitary napkin for right away and another one for later.

Matt must have paid while she was having the procedure. They left as soon as she could stand up. He dropped her off a couple of blocks from her dormitory a little before nine thirty.

Patty was in the room, changing her nail polish.

"No offense, but you look like someone just ran you over with a truck," she said.

Eleanor had to carry the blood-soaked pad out to the dumpster behind the dorm—that one, and the others she used over the course of the next six days—so Patty wouldn't see and wonder. Normally, she used tampons.

At Thanksgiving—never the greatest day, even when her parents were alive—Eleanor opted to stay in the dorm, and to Alice and Jim's frustration—though Patty's relief, probably—she did the same at Christmas. The following summer, Eleanor was accepted into an art program in San Francisco, where she finished the drawings for the book that became *Bodie Under the Sea*. When her English teacher back at school saw the book, she suggested that they send the book to her editor friend at Applewood Press, and by Thanksgiving she had a contract.

Eleanor never went back to Rhode Island. When everyone else at school was visiting colleges with their parents and filling out applications, she was correcting her book galleys. Alice Hallinan offered to bring Eleanor along on a college tour with Patty, but Eleanor said no thanks. She had other plans. A girl she knew from history class had told her about a school she'd visited in upstate New York that seemed pretty and easy to get into, where they didn't have any math or science requirements. Eleanor sent in an application and a few weeks later got the letter of acceptance.

The summer before college, with the money from the advance on her book, she rented a room in Boston. She took a class at the Museum of Fine Arts and finished another Bodie story.

That fall she went off to college, but mostly what she did there was make pictures in her notebooks and think up more stories. Near the end of sophomore year, with her grade point average hovering around 2.8 and embarrassingly large royalty checks arriving in her campus mailbox every six months, she decided she'd had enough of school. She bought the red Toyota and set out on the road to buy a house. Thirteen days later, she landed in Akersville.

9.

a blue-eyed boy and a good dog

Eleanor made a full-price offer on the farm at the end of the dead-end road with the giant ash tree in the front yard. Ed himself even suggested she try a lower number first, see how the sellers—the various Murchisons, living far away, the children and grandchildren of the people whose names and annual heights were recorded on the pantry wall—might respond. But Eleanor saw no reason to dicker. The house was worth the price they were asking, so why not just pay it?

The day she moved in, her neighbors Walt and Edith showed up to introduce themselves. Edith looked dubious when she saw how young Eleanor was. Not Walt. "Anytime you need a little help around the place, give me a holler," he told her.

She painted her name on the mailbox and with Walt's help she hung a swing from one of the lower branches of the giant ash tree out front.

There was more substantial work to be done, of course, and plenty of it. Nobody had lived in the house year-round for more than fifty years, so she hired a crew to blow in insulation and install a new oil burner and water heater, new windows, new floorboards to replace the ones that were giving way. An electrician upgraded the wiring and an outdated fuse box. It turned out the septic system was failing. Until she'd bought the farm, Eleanor hadn't known what a septic system was.

What she loved most was furnishing the place, adding to what was already there: quilts and pillows, tablecloths from the fifties, an old electric mixer, a picnic basket outfitted with tin plates and silverware with Bakelite handles—all the stuff to make a life, except the characters to populate it.

All summer, Eleanor went alone to auctions in search of treasures: an old sleigh bed for upstairs, a set of wicker furniture for the porch. At a yard sale she found an old worktable that she set up in the barn. She laid out her colored pencils and India inks then, and her drawing paper, to get to work on the new Bodie book.

Every afternoon around four o'clock she walked down to the swimming hole below the waterfall and jumped in. Sometimes there'd be a couple of teenagers sharing a beer or making out on the rocks.

(*Making out.* These kids were only a few years younger than she was. Still, for Eleanor now, the idea of kissing someone, feeling a pair of arms around her, hands on her body, felt as remote as the memory of her childhood home. In her mind's eye she saw herself and Matt, that Rhode Island summer—his big sweaty hand on her breast, his other hand on her stomach and moving down. She could remember how it was, her work uniform pulled up around her waist, her thighs sticking to the vinyl seat under her, his fingers digging into her flesh.)

One time down at the waterfall she brought her sketchbook. She was drawing a group of boys fishing for trout. One of them had come over. He hung back, but he seemed to want to see what she was doing. He stood a little ways off, watching. "You can take a look if you want," she told him.

From the looks of him, she figured he was probably twelve or thirteen years old. But the voice in which he spoke to her was deep, and there was something strangely mature, almost manly, about him.

"You must be an artist, huh?" he said.

"I just like to make pictures. You can do it, too, if you want." She pointed to her extra sketchbook, lying next to her on the rocks.

"I'm no good at art," he said. "I just like looking at it."

His name was Timmy. His family used to run Pouliot's Garage out by the dump, only they closed it last year on account of his dad died. She'd probably seen the place.

She didn't ask, but he volunteered the next part. "He shot himself," Timmy said. "I was the one that found him."

His teacher had a poster up on the wall in his classroom, by this artist named Vincent van Gogh. Some people said he must have been a weirdo because he cut off his ear, but Timmy had memorized that picture. He thought it was the best artwork he ever saw. Then he found out this artist, van Gogh, had killed himself, just like his dad.

"My dad died, too," she told him. "I know it's hard."

Though in Eleanor's case, anyway, it hadn't been that great when he was alive. Not in Timmy's, either, most likely.

"Why don't you give it a try?" Eleanor said. She held out a piece of charcoal.

He shook his head. "If I was an artist I'd make a picture of you."

A voice called out. His older brother, probably. "Hey, Romeo. We're leaving."

"I have to go," he told her. "See you around."

Timmy was a few yards away when he turned around one more time. She'd never known a person to have bluer eyes. "Do you have a boyfriend or anything?" he said.

She laughed.

"I think I'm a little old for you," she told him. Seeing his face when she said that, she wished she hadn't. He had meant what he told her and she had acted like it was the most ridiculous thing ever and flicked him off like a deerfly.

She was going to say something else, like "Come back again and I'll let you try my watercolors." But he was gone.

That July she'd gone to the ASPCA and adopted a dog—a mutt she named Charlie who loved chasing squirrels and chewed up a box of oil pastels one time when she'd left the barn door open and her work out.

"You better watch that pup of yours come hunting season," Walt told her. "You don't want him to go chasing deer."

What Charlie seemed to love best were squirrels and butterflies. He had no chance of ever catching any, of course, but that didn't stop him. Sometimes, at the end of the day, she'd sit out under the tree and watch him. One minute he'd be stretched out with his head in her lap, but suddenly he'd sit up and a look of total concentration would come over him. Then he was off like a shot on his joyful, futile pursuit. There was a dog's life for you: no memory of losses, no expectation of future reward. No heartbreak when the squirrel disappeared up the tree. All Charlie appeared to care about was the feeling of the sun on his belly and the racing of his heart, no doubt, when some small animal or fluttering creature came into view. The endless, uncrushable hope that one day he would actually catch that squirrel.

His devotion to Eleanor was absolute. Wherever he was in the house, whatever he was doing—including sleeping—she had only to walk past him and he'd slap his tail against the floor. When she came home to that empty house—and it was always empty when she came home, empty of human companionship, anyway—he'd be there at the door, waiting for her.

No family. No man, only a dog. No man, though Walt stopped by in his truck to check up on her and put on the storm windows when the cold weather came. A man of few words, though it occurred to her at some point that if he didn't stop by, as he did nearly every afternoon, she'd miss him.

In the warm weather, he brought her vegetables from his garden. (Zucchinis above all else. More zucchinis than a person could eat in a year.) In the fall, he came with a basket of apples. After a snowstorm, she could count on Walt to show up with his plow, and after he finished with the plow he climbed down from the cab of his vehicle and cut her a path to the driveway with his shovel.

She knew from Edith that she and Walt had been married thirty-two years by this point, and when Edith was around, she did all the talking. But when he came by on his own he'd linger longer than was necessary and never said no to the coffee she offered. Once he showed up when she was still in her nightgown, and she could feel the heat of his gaze. She guessed that Edith, though she saw none of this, disliked her.

"Don't you get lonely, out here by yourself?" he said to her once.

"I was an only child," she said. "I'm used to it." The loneliest she'd ever been, probably, was in the front seat of Matt Hallinan's car, though nights with her parents back at their house, in Crazyland, came close. There was more than one way of feeling lonely.

Fall came. Her tomato plants were hit with frost. The ash tree's leaves turned red and for a week every time she stepped out the door of the house she just stood there, taking in the color and the way the light illuminated them, the brilliance of that red against the sky. The leaves fell, and the branches were bare against the sky—brown leaves swirling in the wind. By three thirty she had to turn the lights on over her desk. There was an album of very sad Irish ballads she loved, and one by Leonard Cohen, with "Suzanne" on it, that she played so much it was all scratched up. She lit candles and sketched images of the new Bodie adventure, as distant from anything going on in her own life as Neil Armstrong's walk on the moon. Sometimes she made popcorn for dinner. More often than not she was in bed by nine.

Driving into town at the end of the day—Charlie in the seat beside her, with the window cracked even though it was cold, so he could take in all the smells—she could see into the houses of the families along the road, fixing dinner and watching TV. Maybe things weren't really all that great in those houses, but through the windows, it looked pretty nice.

The first time Eleanor built a fire in the woodstove the house filled up so swiftly with smoke that she opened all the windows. The next day she called Walt, who told her she'd left the dampers shut. After he cleaned the chimney he told her she was lucky to have avoided a fire. "That thing was so full of creosote, it's a wonder any smoke got out at all," he said.

"You can always call me. Not easy, a girl like you living by herself way out here like this without a family. Without a man."

She heard from Patty now and then. Her old roommate was finishing college a year early, engaged to a Yale guy she'd met at a mixer, pre-med. "My mom always asks about you," she said. "You should come for Christmas this year. My brother asks about you, too."

Patty wrote again six months later. Engagement off. Her ex-fiancé had wanted to settle down and start having babies right away and she wanted a career. She had moved into an apartment in New York City, the Upper East Side. Just a studio, but it had a balcony where she could set up a fondue pot. She'd gone out with her brother and his girlfriend to some club where she saw Liza Minnelli. At least she thought it was Liza Minnelli. It could have been some guy dressed up like her.

Eleanor did not pay a visit to the Hallinans that Christmas, preferring to spend the holiday alone with Charlie.

That winter, the snow was so deep it covered most of the downstairs windows, and even with the furnace going—also the woodstove—it was so cold she slept with a hot water bottle. Days went by, sometimes, when she wouldn't make it down the driveway to pick up her mail, though when she did she could usually count on at least one letter, forwarded from her publisher, from a child who'd read one of her books.

"I love how brave Bodie is," one girl wrote to her. "I wish I was brave like that. I get scared just asking for a hall pass at school."

"I never told anyone this before," another child wrote. "But my dad hits me a lot. Sometimes I like to pretend I could be Bodie, and just go away someplace by myself and have adventures like she does, with nobody yelling at me or saying I'm stupid or taking out their belt."

When Eleanor got letters from children about her books, she always wrote back.

Months passed, marked by days at her desk, late-afternoon walks with Charlie to Hopewell Falls. She saw Timmy Pouliot now and then, fishing with his brother at the falls or riding his dirt bike through town. If he recognized her, he showed no sign.

10.

wish I had a river

Eleanor had been living on the farm for two years now. Days went by sometimes in which she barely spoke, except to her agent or her editor or her dog, and occasionally Walt and Edith, on her daily walk to the waterfall.

There was a woman Eleanor observed sometimes at the swimming hole. She had a little girl, and the two of them would sit on a flat stone by the edge of the swimming hole and dangle their feet in the water to cool off. The woman didn't swim and the little girl didn't go in the water, either. She'd stay for about as long as it took to smoke a cigarette, then pick up her daughter, gather her toys in a bag, and head back to her car, an old Chevy so rusted Eleanor wondered how it ever passed inspection. Something about this woman—sitting on the rock, staring out at the water—made Eleanor want to be her friend.

One time, the woman looked so upset that Eleanor had spoken to her. "Are you okay? Anything I can do to help?"

"No big deal," the woman said. "It's just my husband. I should leave the jerk. But it's not like I've got anyplace to go."

Her name was Darla. Her daughter was called Kimmie. "Why don't you come over for tea?" Eleanor said.

Darla showed up with a six-pack.

"No offense," she told Eleanor, "but I never understood this whole tea thing. Sitting around drinking hot water with a bag of crumbled-up leaves."

They sat in the living room with their Budweisers. Darla took it all in: the vases of cut flowers, the Matisse reproduction tacked to the wall, the plate of Brie, the record albums. She spotted a box of books on the table, newly arrived from Eleanor's publisher. With Eleanor's name on the front.

"Hey, that's you," she said, studying the picture on the back.

"You should take one for your little girl," Eleanor told her.

"You're not from around here, are you?" Darla said. "Wild guess."

Darla wasn't, either, it turned out. She came from northern Maine. Potato country.

"We were a mill family," she said. "You know what that means? Payday's Friday. You can count on your dad being drunk through Sunday night, hungover Monday."

Darla's father had a habit of slapping her mother around when he was drinking. "I guess with five kids and no job of her own, she figured there wasn't much she could do about that."

To look at her, you might have thought Darla was closing in on forty, but she was twenty-eight. She had met her husband, Bobby, at a motorcycle rally in Loudon. Not too many women came to the track at Loudon on their own bike—as opposed to riding on the back of some man's—but Darla did. A Suzuki 350.

Eleanor didn't know anything about motorcycles.

"For your information," Darla said. "A three fifty isn't the kind of bike a person takes to Loudon. But I was just happy having any bike. Bought with my own damn money."

"I never won anything in my life," Darla told her. "But I used to buy a lottery ticket every Friday, and one week they pulled my number. Two thousand dollars. That's how I ended up with the Suzuki."

She went to motorcycle school and everything. "I wasn't going to be like my mother, with a houseful of kids and a drunk husband by the time she was thirty, sweeping the floor at a beauty parlor for three dollars an hour," Darla said. "I had this plan to ride my bike to California, camping along the way. Not that I knew what I'd do when I got there but it was 1967, you know? Summer of Love."

Then came Bobby. For a good ten minutes she thought the love might be right there, at the Loudon track. "He was sweet to me that time," she said. "He had this shirt on that said, 'If you're gonna do it, do it on a Harley.'

"First thing he said, when he came up to me at the rally, was 'You actually ride this thing? Or is it, like, an accessory?'

"That's Bobby for you. Master of the putdown," Darla said. But at the time it hadn't bothered her. That's how her dad always was, until he ran off with his second cousin. And Bobby was funny. Used to be, anyway.

He told her she didn't need a bike of her own. She could have a seat on the back of his. He'd take her to California.

"Big talk," Darla said. "Bobby's whole family comes from Akersville. Grandparents, stepdad, half sisters, you name it. The guy's never been farther than Salisbury Beach. He just said those things to get in my pants."

The biggest mistake of her life was selling the Suzuki, she said. They used the money for a down payment on their trailer. Three months later, what do you know, there's a baby on the way.

Robert Junior was born with a hole in his heart. ("Took after his father," Darla said. "Bad joke.") He lived seven months.

"I could've still got out at that point. Nothing keeping me besides the damn mobile home. But you know what happened? After I lost Robert Junior, all I wanted was another baby. That was Kimmie."

She was four years old now. "Light of my life, I'm telling you," Darla said. "One thing's for sure, no way she's ending up in a double-wide with a guy that stays up all night watching TV."

They didn't even ride together anymore, Darla told Eleanor. She could, but there was Kimmie to consider. "If it was just me out on the road, going ninety up Route 89, I'd take my chances. But I'm not going to leave my kid without a mom, you know?

"You've got the right idea," she said to Eleanor, looking out the porch screen at the field below the house, where Eleanor and Walt had planted her vegetable garden. "No man telling you what to do. Nothing holding you down except the dog, and all he's going to do is lick your hand and wag his tail. Right, Charlie?"

He thumped his tail on the floor.

After that it got to be a regular thing. The two of them would sit in Eleanor's kitchen while Kimmie played with the Monopoly pieces or colored with Eleanor's pencils and Darla told Eleanor stories from her life or offered her observations of the world beyond Akersville that she'd never gotten to explore.

"Can you believe that Patty Hearst?" Darla said. She might be the daughter of a millionaire, growing up in San Francisco and all (*San Francisco!* The place Darla was heading when she met Bobby), but in a funny way, Darla identified with her.

"She had it all," Darla said. "Then she meets this guy and he takes her away and they start robbing banks. Next thing you know, she's calling herself Tania and she's on the front page wearing some damned camo gear, holding an M16."

According to Darla, this was what love did to a person. You got brainwashed.

She stayed home with her daughter now. She would've liked to work, but Bobby wouldn't let her. He had lots of opinions about how she was supposed to be.

"It could be worse," she said. "He could be on drugs. He knocks me around sometimes but nothing serious."

She cleaned houses for summer people. Bobby didn't know anything about the housecleaning jobs. He wouldn't like it if he did. The only house Darla was supposed to clean was their own. His house, actually. That's how he put it.

When she had enough set aside, she was going to use it for a down payment on an apartment for her and Kimmie. Not in this town. Someplace far away. Manchester, maybe, or even Boston.

"I always wanted to go to college," she said. She knew this probably sounded weird, but she wanted to get certified to be an undertaker.

"Some people might find that kind of work creepy," she told Eleanor, "but dead people don't bother me. Plus, you deal with the families. You work with people at the saddest time in their life. If you do a good job, you can make a difference."

"If I told any of this to Bobby, he'd belt me," she told Eleanor. "But it's OK. I'm getting out soon."

Darla did most of the talking, those afternoons on the porch. She had a lot to say, and Eleanor was probably the only one she could say it to. But one afternoon, Eleanor told her what had happened with Matt Hallinan.

"Let's make an oath," Darla said. "One of these days, you're going to stick it to that guy. Same as one of these days I'm leaving Bobby in my dust. We just have to wait for our moment."

One time when they were out on the porch, a little later than usual, Bobby came by looking for Darla. Charlie hardly ever barked, but when he heard Bobby's Harley coming down the long driveway, he did, and when Bobby stood in the doorway, he hid under the table.

"I had a feeling I'd find my wife here," he said to Eleanor. Then he turned in Darla's direction. "I know how you love chitchatting with your girlfriend," he said, "but it's time to go."

Darla's voice sounded different when she spoke to him. "You go on ahead, hon," she said. "I'll be home soon."

He turned toward Eleanor again. "Your friend here has her responsibilities."

"I'll just pack up Kimmie's pictures," she told him.

"I said now." He picked up a drawing his daughter had made. A stick figure meant to be a portrait of Charlie.

"I wasn't finished with my picture," Kimmie said.

"This woman here," Bobby said, placing his hand on Darla's neck, tight enough that Eleanor could see her flinch. "She's something in the sack."

"Stop it, Bobby," Darla said.

"You ashamed of what I do to you, baby?" he told her. "How I drive you crazy? You tell your friend how you're always begging for more?"

"I'm sorry," Darla said. "This is what happens when he drinks."

"This is what happens when a man comes home and his wife isn't there to make him dinner," he said.

He roared off on his bike. Darla, in her car, with Kimmie in the back, followed behind.

It was late November, heading into Eleanor's third winter alone in the house. The ash tree out front had been bare for weeks, and now she'd turned back the clocks, which left her needing to turn on the lights by three thirty and stoke the woodstove all through the day. There had been a telephone conference with her editor about *Bodie Goes to Space*, and by the time she hung up the phone she realized the room was dark and it was nearly dinnertime.

It was the third week of deer season, that time when hunters who hadn't bagged one yet started feeling desperate. Driving into town the day before to pick up groceries, Eleanor had passed two houses in front of whose garages hung the upside-down carcasses of recent kill. Men in orange vests were everywhere. All day, shots had rung out from the woods.

As she usually did, she ended her workday with a walk to the waterfall, wearing an orange hat on account of the hunters. Normally, Charlie would have accompanied her, but when he didn't come, after she called him, she figured he was probably off chasing squirrels.

Rounding the last bend in the road, where the old ash tree came into view, she expected to see Charlie stretched out on the step, but he wasn't there, and she realized then that it had been hours since she'd seen her dog. She walked to the edge of the woods and called to him in the growing darkness. Nothing.

She was back in the kitchen, vaguely uneasy without having anything to do about it, when she heard the sound of tires. Living at the end of a dead-end road as she did, hearing the sound of a car was a rare event. Just about the only visitors Eleanor got out here were the Federal Express man or Darla or Walt, come to check up on her. (Most recently, there had been a sudden infestation of bats in the big upstairs open space. Walt had spent the afternoon getting rid of them for her, refusing payment. One more thing for Edith to be annoyed about.)

But it wasn't Walt's truck she saw coming down the road. It was a police car. There appeared to be something on top of the vehicle. As the car got closer she could make out the body of an animal, but not a deer. She stepped into the driveway to get a better look.

It was Charlie, held to the roof with a couple of bungee cords, a single stream of blood running down the windshield. His tail, which never failed to wag when she came within range, hung down the side of the car, unmoving.

Eleanor ran to the police car, her hand to her mouth. She might have screamed but no sound came out of her. The officer stepped out of his vehicle.

"This your animal? I spotted him up the road a ways, chasing a deer. Sorry about your pup here, but we've got procedures to follow when an animal does that."

From inside his patrol car Eleanor could hear the voice of the dispatcher, crackling. From the house, the voice of Joni Mitchell. *I wish I had a river I could skate away on.*

"You got two options," he told her. "I can leave the body here for you to take care of, or we can dispose of it back at the station. Animal control."

She stared at the spot on Charlie's body where the bullet had entered his chest. When the officer lifted him up slightly, she took in how much blood there was. She would bury her dog under the ash tree with a pile of stones to mark the spot. Walt would give her a hand.

The death of Charlie changed everything. Until then, even in her loneliest times, Eleanor had viewed her life on the farm as a romantic adventure. Though she had no idea of what might happen to change things—or where the children were going to come from, whose bedroom awaited them—she believed, a little like her character, Bodie, that sooner or later, amazing things would happen to her. She would fix the house up to be something like the illustrations in her book of Carl Larsson drawings. She'd have this great garden, exploding with flowers. She'd create these magical stories, one of which would feature herself as the heroine. One day, in the not-so-distant future, her rescuer would appear, and their life together, *her real life,* would begin.

In the weeks and months after the police car came down the long driveway with her dog lashed to the roof, a new and terrible thought came to her. Maybe how things were now was not simply a temporary state she'd pass through on the way to her real life. Maybe this was her real life—sitting by the fire listening to sad songs with a bowl of popcorn for dinner, drawing pictures of a made-up child.

Darla and Kimmie came by now and then, and Walt, but days went by sometimes in which she spoke to nobody. Before, she could have counted on the sound of Charlie breathing at her feet. Now, except for times she played music, the one sound she heard was that of her own pencils on the paper. The house was that quiet.

II.

a red-headed man

Normally, Eleanor worked all day, writing and illustrating her Bodie stories. Seven days a week she put in her hours, not winding down until around four thirty, when she'd take her walk to the waterfall and, in warm weather, swim.

But she'd seen a poster for a craft fair that weekend, a few towns north, and decided to give herself a break.

It was a gorgeous day. Late April, the leaves on the ash tree out front just starting to unfurl themselves, the first crocus breaking through the soil where a few last patches of snow had not yet melted. In the car on the way to the fair, she put on a Doc Watson tape. "If I Needed You" started playing—a Townes Van Zandt song she loved. She sang along with the tape. *I'd swim the seas for to ease your pain.*

The fair was housed in the parking lot outside the Masonic lodge of the town, though most of the craftspeople displaying their work were hippies rather than Masons. If a person wanted a very solid ceramic casserole or a mandala, or a mug that probably wouldn't break if you threw it on a concrete floor, this was the place to find it. Also macramé plant hangers and hand-stenciled wrapping paper and hooked rugs and homemade soap and braided rugs and patchwork quilts. Breadboards in the shape of the state of New Hampshire.

She had spotted him the minute she walked into the hall. Hard to miss a six-foot-three-inch red-headed man, curls circling his face like a halo, with a goat tied to his display table. A simple hand-lettered banner was stretched across the front: "Cameron. Maker of Beautiful Things." A small cluster of people had gathered—ostensibly to sample the cheese he'd set out, though Eleanor guessed they had been drawn to the red-headed man's table for the same reason she was. The man.

He was talking about the products he made, apparently, and a group had assembled to listen to him. Women, not surprisingly. He may have been the most handsome person Eleanor had ever laid eyes on, but there was more to it than that. Anyone could see this person had an air of assurance about him, with his checkered shirt and his red bandanna and his one pierced ear and his leather boots that looked as if they'd been made by some wonderful old Italian shoemaker, though it was also possible he'd made them himself. He was the kind of person other people probably tried to imitate, but they weren't likely to succeed. Wherever it was he was going, you'd want to come.

In addition to cheese, the red-headed man made hand-turned bowls from tree burls. Some of these were so small all they could hold was a handful of nuts, though there was one burl bowl on display so large it could have held salad for twenty people.

Eleanor visited all the other craft tables before making her way to the red-headed man's display.

She cupped the smallest bowl in her hands, stroking the wood. The goat was chewing on her skirt, but Eleanor kept her gaze on the inside of the bowl. If she looked directly into his eyes, she knew it would be all over.

He spoke his name to her. "I thought you'd never stop at my table," he said.

He extended his hand. Not as rough as you'd think, for a man who worked in wood. Later she would learn that he rubbed oil on his palms and fingertips every night, to soften them.

"You know what I really want to do with this bowl," she said. "I want to put it up to my face so I can feel it against my cheek." After she said this, she wondered what came over her. She didn't usually talk this way, particularly to a person she'd just met. Particularly a man.

"What's stopping you?" he said. "I have a policy that if I feel like doing something, unless it's going to hurt someone, I do it."

Years later Eleanor could still remember how he looked that first night, when he brought her back to the little cabin he'd built, a few miles outside of Brattleboro.

They brought the goat out to the shed first. He'd made a sign on her pen, out of a burl, with her name carved into it. Opal. "I wanted to name her Alison," he said. "But I decided to save that one for when I have a daughter."

Even that first night he spoke of children. She told him about the death of her dog, which seemed at the time to loom larger than the death of her parents.

"Charlie was like my best friend," she told Cam. "Not *like* my best friend. He was."

Back in the house—the air chilly now, though it was April—Cam lit the stove. He took off his shirt in the firelight—his skin freckled and glistening, his face so finely chiseled it was as if she could see the skull beneath his skin. His body was as keenly defined as a figure in the old anatomy book she kept on her desk back home—every rib visible.

"I'd like to draw you," she said. She surprised her own self with her boldness. She was not a person who could talk about sex, or his body, or her own. But from the moment they'd met she had felt strangely at ease, safe even, in his presence. "I never go anyplace without my drawing pencils."

"Draw me? Nobody ever did that before," he said. "Cool."

He stepped out of the rest of his clothes with as little self-consciousness as if he were peeling a piece of fruit, and for the next hour she sat there making a portrait of him on the back of a piece of newsprint laid flat on his kitchen table.

He knew how to keep perfectly still. He didn't try to talk, and neither did Eleanor. She was perfectly concentrated on the act of studying his body and re-creating it on the page. His gaze remained fixed on her.

It was two hours later when she set down the pencil. Still naked, he walked over to the table and studied the image she'd made of him on the page.

"You got me," he told her. "Not a lot of people do."

Up until this, Eleanor had felt a surprising absence of self-consciousness, probably on account of focusing as she did on her drawing, but now she felt the warmth in her face and, more so, deep in her body.

"I don't know about you, but I'm starving," he said.

He pulled on his pants and cooked for her on the tiny gas stove in his one-room cabin overlooking the river—table, chair, apple crate with a few pairs of long underwear and jeans, a couple of T-shirts folded on top, a futon. The dish he made featured olives and sun-dried tomatoes, eggs, goat cheese courtesy of Opal, some herb Eleanor should have recognized but didn't, cumin maybe. Before he set the meal on the floor—the floor, not the table, because he had only one chair—he had laid out an Indian bedspread and a couple of pillows. He lit candles—not one, but five or six—and put on a recording of some Celtic singer. Partway through the meal, he had leaned in and studied her face. "You have sauce on your chin," he said, and licked it off.

This was the moment he kissed her, long and slow, with his hands circling the back of her neck, almost as if he were some weary traveler, finally arrived at a watering hole. They stayed that way, pressed up against each other, neither one of them moving, for a surprisingly long time.

"I know this might sound crazy, but I want to make babies with you. I have this feeling you'd make a wonderful mother" he said. "I want to make a family."

"I've only had sex with one person, ever," she told him. She did not add that it happened in the front seat of the car of her roommate's older brother, with her eyes shut and her fingers gripping the seat, waiting for it to be over.

"That other person you were with, before," he said, "I'm guessing he hurt you. But I won't."

That first night, they slept together. It was nothing like what had happened with Matt that summer in Rhode Island. She didn't want to close her eyes. She wanted to see his face. When they finally fell asleep, Cam's arms stayed wrapped around her. When she woke up, he was still holding her.

He moved into her house ten days later with two apple crates containing his tools, Opal the goat, a sack of goat feed, the harmonica he intended to learn how to play, and his dog, Sally, who sniffed

Charlie's old dog bed briefly, then settled in. Two months after that Eleanor was pregnant.

When they learned she was going to have a baby, they danced in the kitchen. Cam got down on his knees and kissed her belly—still flat, though by fall it had begun to swell, as her breasts did. Neither one of them cared whether it was a boy or a girl. "Just so long as one of our children learns to play the guitar," Eleanor said.

She loved almost everything about being pregnant. She didn't feel sick that much, but when she did, she got under the quilt on their bed with her copy of *Spiritual Midwifery* by a woman named Ina May Gaskin and her husband, Stephen, who had founded a commune in Tennessee called The Farm, where people came from all over to deliver their babies. Eleanor had the birth stories in the book practically memorized. Sometimes now, driving next to Cam in his truck, she'd read out loud to him from its pages.

"Let me get this straight," he said, when she read him the part about the most important things a woman's husband could do when she was in labor. "You're lying there yelling and screaming and I'm supposed to give you this long, passionate kiss?"

"Stephen says it helps a woman's cervix dilate," Eleanor told him. "So the baby can get out easier."

"Fair enough," Cam said. "Kissing you always sounds like a good idea."

They were married that August—a wedding pulled together so fast that the only people in attendance were Patty (still living on the Upper East Side of Manhattan, working for an ad agency), and Darla (accompanied by Bobby, who wouldn't let her attend without him), and Walt and Edith, and a couple of friends of Cam's who raised goats in Vermont. Cam's parents, Roger and Roberta, made the drive from Amelia Island, in Florida, arriving the day before the ceremony and taking off the morning after. His brother, Roger Junior, came from Dallas with his wife, Annette—the first time the brothers had seen each other in years, evidently. Darla's daughter, Kimmie, in her role as flower girl, scattered petals along the path to the makeshift arbor Cam had built, out behind the house, where they said their vows. Cam's mother sprayed bug repellent wherever she went, and stayed close to Roger Junior and Annette.

Eleanor wore a Gunne Sax dress—unfastened in the back because it didn't fit over her belly—and a garland of flowers in her hair. Cam wore a white shirt and suspenders and a pair of tuxedo pants she'd found for him at a thrift shop in Keene. A friend of his—one of the goat farmers—played the guitar and sang an Eric Andersen song, "Close the Door Lightly When You Go." Given that the lyrics were about a couple breaking up, it wasn't what you could call a wedding song, but Cam had explained that it was one of the few songs whose lyrics Jeremy remembered, so never mind the part about "Fare thee well, sweet love of mine." The main thing was that he knew all the chords.

They spoke their vows in the field below the house, a few hundred feet from the giant ash tree at the top of the hill. Eleanor read the vows she'd written the afternoon before, on a rock at the waterfall. "I promise my heart will stay open to every single chapter in our lives together, even the hard ones," she told him. "I know there will be some."

Cam had a piece of paper, too, that he took from his pocket. She had never seen him cry, but that afternoon, reading the sonnet he'd chosen—Elizabeth Barrett Browning—his voice cracked.

"How do I love thee? Let me count the ways."

12.

the money part

They made love a lot that summer, and throughout the following fall. In the field behind the house—a mossy patch, their clothes flung on a nearby rock, and under the ash tree, on a blanket Cam laid down for them, and once, around dusk on the kind of drizzly afternoon when nobody was likely to show up for a swim, at the swimming hole below the waterfall. After years of being skinny, she loved the way her body felt as it filled out—as if she were some very ripe piece of fruit.

They kept a record player in their bedroom and put on music every night, a soundtrack to their life. Van Morrison singing "Tupelo Honey." Cam's favorites—the Grateful Dead—and Eleanor's—Emmylou Harris, Buffalo Springfield, Doc Watson. The old albums of sad songs no longer spoke to her as they once had.

"I used to feel sad, even when my parents were still alive, that I wasn't anybody's favorite person," she told Darla. "But I'm Cam's favorite. I never knew what that felt like before."

All fall they ate meals of vegetables and grains, healthy food, but she also baked pies and cookies, brownies, poppy seed cake. After the years living alone in the house, it felt good having someone to make meals for. More often than not, they ate naked on the rug by candlelight.

Walt surprised them by stopping by one night with a package that had been delivered to him and Edith by mistake—a gift from Cam's parents, a mobile featuring Disney characters that played "It's a Small World."

Eleanor, when she heard Walt's truck pulling up, had grabbed her shirt and started pulling on her maternity pants. Cam just sat there, butter from the corncob trickling down his beautiful, freckled skin. But Eleanor buttoned up her shirt as she went to the door.

After Walt gave her the package and drove away, they burst out laughing.

"Maybe he'll think twice about dropping by unannounced next time," Cam said later. "Come to think of it, with these breasts of yours, he'll be stopping by every night now hoping to get a look." He reached across their shared slice of pie to touch her skin. She felt like the goddess of fertility.

"We should make six babies," he told her. "Ten."

"Let's see how this one goes first," she said as he pulled her down onto the rug.

Until that winter they had worried surprisingly little about money. Sales of Cam's burl bowls didn't bring in much, but he set up his workbench in the barn and turned Eleanor's writing space into a woodshop while Eleanor moved her desk into the house. Every morning, she worked on the next Bodie book. Every few months she could count on a royalty check showing up in the mailbox from the previous ones. They didn't live extravagantly, but if she wanted to buy an expensive crib or a pair of earrings or beautiful handmade slippers for Cam, she didn't think twice about it.

Sometime around Thanksgiving, Eleanor got a call from her agent. "We just got the latest sales figures on the new Bodie book," she told Eleanor. "It's just not selling. There's been a shift. All the kids are into fantasy these days. It's looking like the Bodie thing has run its course. They aren't renewing your contract."

She spent the month of December working on proposals for a new series. Nobody in New York was reading book proposals over Christmas, but in January, when they finally did, all that came in were polite rejections.

In February, property taxes would be due, and the Toyota needed new tires. Then the transmission on Cam's truck died, and the cost of the repair came in greater than the value of the vehicle. The people who wanted burl bowls all seemed to have bought them by now, with few new customers on the horizon.

A call came from the bank. For the first time ever, the check Eleanor had written for the mortgage on the house had bounced. Insufficient funds.

Cam never let this kind of thing worry him. It had been something Eleanor had loved in the past—how relaxed and carefree he always seemed, how totally oblivious to the practical considerations she lay awake thinking about. But now when she sat at her desk, her head throbbed. She looked down at her huge belly. She finally had the family she'd dreamed about. But all she wanted to do was bake bread or climb into bed and read recipes and seed catalogs. Or maybe do nothing. Her chest constricted.

She started her day making lists of avenues to pursue. Cam started his day running to the waterfall and back. Eleanor was getting frown lines in her forehead. Not Cam.

Often, now, lying in bed at night, Eleanor thought about money. She calculated the cost of installing a washing machine compared to visits to the laundromat and the hourly rate of day care they'd need once their baby was born and she was ready to get back to her writing and drawing—assuming someone would actually pay her again for the work she did there.

"I guess I got spoiled," she told Cam. "For all these years, my work was in big demand. I never worried about earning a living." What had seemed unattainable then had been the family part. And look, now she had that.

"You'll figure things out," Cam told her. His choice of pronoun did not go unnoticed. The summer he moved in they'd gotten a bank loan to build him a woodshop out behind the house and he was finishing the roof now, but they both knew—though did not discuss—that his income from the sale of his woodworking projects in no way offset the cost of its construction.

Still, much of what they had was good. Eleanor loved the hum of her husband's tools out in the shop, and the sound of his whistle when he came back in the house at the end of the long day to wrap his arms around her where she sat in the rocking chair by the woodstove, reading her well-worn copy of *Spiritual Midwifery*. But she could feel a very small knot forming in her, too—questions she didn't like to ask herself, but sometimes did. Who contributed what, and how much? Thoughts entered her mind now of a kind that had never arisen before. Why was it always Eleanor who had to figure out where the money came from?

Eleanor's relationship with Cam was nothing like Darla and Bobby's, of course. When she talked to Darla—who was still setting aside money to leave Bobby—she felt nothing but lucky that the man she had married was not just handsome and talented but supportive and loving. Nights in their bed, when her husband reached for her—or she for him—her skin still came alive. Just the sight of him stepping in the door at the end of the day, shaking the snow off his boots, still made her draw in her breath. What was a steady paycheck compared to the feeling she got when he put on Donna Summer and he took her in his arms—she with her eight-months-pregnant belly—and twirled her around the kitchen.

"With the baby coming, and me not having another book contract yet," she said to him one night, in bed, "we might need you to get a real job."

His expression, when he met her gaze, was not anything she'd seen before.

"I have a real job," he told her. "I make bowls."

Usually they made love every night, but that night they didn't.

She knew he was trying to bring in more money. Saturdays, he set off for craft fairs to sell his work—driving greater distances than before, gone longer hours—and sometimes, though not always, he came home with some cash in his pocket.

Occasionally, Eleanor would go along. A woman in her early twenties, who was wearing earrings made from the feathers of some exotic bird and a pair of handmade sandals, had fallen in love with a burl jewelry box, one of the nicest pieces he'd ever made. When she told Cam she couldn't afford the price—fifty dollars—he'd placed the box in the young woman's hands. Her name was Fiona, she told him. She was an astrologer.

"Take it," Cam said. He put up his hand and stroked the feather dangling from her right ear. "I'll enjoy thinking about my box holding those beautiful earrings."

"Let me guess," Fiona said. "You're a Scorpio."

Even Eleanor, who didn't believe in astrology, knew what that meant.

She watched Fiona float off, feeling the heaviness of her own body—her swollen ankles, her puffy face. Their baby kicked all day long now, and her back ached. As an economy measure, she had stopped buying the expensive cream she used to ask Cam to rub over her belly. When the ritual had ended, somewhere around her fifth month, he seemed not to have noticed. The skin of her belly was covered with striations now. Fiona had worn a midriff top, with a peasant skirt that hung low on her hips.

Another beautiful young woman approached Cam's table. Didn't anybody but gorgeous, penniless twenty-two-year-olds love burl bowls?

Eleanor told herself not to worry. The money part would work out. She was part of a family now.

13.

here's your daughter

They didn't have health insurance. Even if they'd had the money for a hospital, she and Cam had decided after studying *Spiritual Midwifery* that their baby would be born at home. Eleanor had located a midwife who lived outside of Concord, a thirty-mile drive from Akersville. Valerie was in her early forties—a single mother of three girls, who sometimes came along with her to attend births. Once a month, Eleanor traveled to Concord for her checkup. In the fall, when she'd failed to get a new publishing contract, she had asked Valerie if they might pay the last installments for attending the birth with a large burl bowl. When Valerie agreed, Eleanor realized that saving the money accounted for only part of her happiness in the arrangement. It felt good to know that Cam was contributing to supporting their baby's care. "If only we could pay the property taxes in bowls," she said, the day they delivered Valerie's.

Two weeks before her February due date, with Cam off in Vermont at another fair, she made the thirty-mile drive to the midwife by herself. It was already snowing lightly when she took off that morning, but by the time she set out for home—with the news that she was three centimeters dilated—the road was slick and the windshield kept icing up. A couple of miles from home, Eleanor hit a patch of ice and crashed into a tree. When she looked up the car had spun a full 180 degrees.

The instant before impact, her hand left the wheel to rest on her belly—the baby not yet born but already her instinct to protect it overtaking everything else, as it would continue to do a few thousand times in the years to come. Later, Eleanor would see the bruise from where her forehead hit the windshield and feel the throbbing in her neck. But at the time, all she felt was the quick, firm kick of the baby—the now-familiar foot, or maybe it was a hand, pressing out just under her rib cage.

"You're okay," she said out loud. Nobody else in the car but her not-born baby.

The engine had stalled on impact, so she turned the key. Nothing. For a few minutes all Eleanor could do was sit in the driver's seat of their undrivable car, her parka no longer zipping up over her belly, staring out through the shattered windshield at a tree branch resting across the glass. Sitting in the front seat, the little pine-scented cardboard tree still spinning—and outside, snow falling around her—Eleanor tried not to think about what came next. When she stepped out of the car, she took in the crumpled front end of the Toyota—the same vehicle their handful of friends had decorated with tin cans and brown-eyed Susans on their wedding day the summer before and painted with the words "Call Us Crazy, We Did It."

Now that day felt like a hundred years ago.

Walt and Edith's house was not that far. She knew once she got there, Walt would drive her home.

Later, when Cam got back, they had the car towed, but it was beyond salvaging. Nothing for it then but to wait for the insurance money to come through, and hard to say, when it did, what kind of vehicle they could find with the eight-hundred-dollar settlement. But Eleanor wasn't hurt, and the baby was fine—all that really mattered.

"You shouldn't have been driving by yourself like that," Walt had said to her, as he stoked the woodstove after driving her home. "Where is your husband?"

Over the days that followed, as the snow kept falling and she crossed the days off the calendar, they made do with what they had in the freezer and a delivery of quiche brought in by their neighbors Simon and Tilda down the road, on snowshoes.

Darla had a low opinion of the home birth plan, observing that her own three days at the hospital following the birth of her daughter, Kimmie, six years earlier had been the only time she could remember when someone actually took care of her, as her husband, Bobby, definitely did not.

"Take advantage of the vacation," she'd told Eleanor.

The snow kept falling. Even in the midst of her worry, there was no denying the beauty of what they saw out the window, and most of all its aftermath—the snowdrifts, like sheets draped over the furniture at some old English country estate, covering up the mess (rusting propane tanks, the busted washing machine discarded back in the spring) so all you could make out was a single expanse of white, vast and unbroken. On the last night of the storm, the snow had turned briefly to freezing rain, so when they woke up every branch and twig—also the electric wires to the house, and the clothesline, and the two mismatched socks still dangling from it—were encased in ice. The sun came out then, and for a few hours the sight of it all was so brilliant that when he went outside to shovel, Cam had to put on his sunglasses. He looked, that morning, like a movie star.

The world never looked more peaceful than it did right after snow fell. The only vehicles on the road were the creeping snowplows scraping the frozen dirt, but it would be hours before one of those reached their little farmhouse. For a few days, Eleanor occupied herself with baking—casseroles from her Tassajara cookbook, granola, whole wheat muffins that she wrapped in foil and stored in the freezer they'd bought with what was left of the advance from the last Bodie book. The pregnancy, and the worries about money, had left her with a fixation on storing food. (She left one muffin out of the batch for Cam, but took none for herself.)

"Take a picture," she said to Cam, placing the stash in the one spot not yet filled with all the other foods she'd prepared, for their future. Better to see it all there, with the labels facing out, and the dates, than to actually consume any of what she'd set aside. The contents of that freezer were the closest they had to money in the bank. It occurred to her, as he took the picture that day, of her in his stretched-out hockey shirt—her amazing breasts, her belly presented to the camera like some prize she'd won at a fair—that this would be the only photograph she had of herself pregnant. Cam was never one for taking pictures. "I keep it all in my head," he told her.

That afternoon—day nine since the snow had begun falling, almost nonstop—standing at the sink filling the teakettle, Eleanor felt a burst of warm water trickle down her leg.

"It's going to happen today," she said to Cam, dialing the midwife. Valerie lived half an hour's drive away, but she had four-wheel drive, and the plow had finally made it down their driveway sometime in the early hours of morning. There was one good thing.

She put on her Doc Watson record. *Shady grove, my little love, shady grove, my darling.* Happy songs, mostly. This was not a Joni Mitchell moment, or one for Bob Dylan, either. She heated soup and set a bowl of bread dough next to the woodstove to rise. "By the time it's baked there might be another person in this house," she told Cam. Someone who didn't enter through the door.

By midafternoon, the contractions were coming strong, the spaces between them shorter in duration. She called Valerie again.

Walt stopped by in his truck. She could hear him talking with Cam in the kitchen. "Back when Edith delivered Walt Junior and Cassie, they made the fathers sit outside in the waiting room," he said. "Times sure have changed."

"Or gone back to how it used to be," Cam pointed out. Theirs was not the first baby born in this house.

"You got a point there," Walt told him. "If it ain't broken, why fix it?"

After Walt left, Cam's friend Jeremy showed up with supplies—a box of Cocoa Puffs and his recycled copy of the *Sports Illustrated* swimsuit issue for Cam, and a tie-dye T-shirt in size zero. From the bedroom, Eleanor could hear the two of them, her husband and his friend, whooping it up about the Celtics game—John Havlicek had just pulled off a miracle shot from mid-court—and the swimsuit model he found particularly hot. Jeremy had a bead on a car for them: a Plymouth Valiant, always a good bet. The car had twelve years on it, all but the last few months of them spent in the state of Georgia.

"This one's a peach, buddy," she heard Jeremy tell Cam. Slant-six engine. Push-button transmission.

Their neighbor Betsy stopped by with her daughter, Coco, in tow. "We thought you might like some banana bread," Betsy said. "Coco made it herself." Eleanor got up briefly to say hello, and because she thought the pain might not be so bad, standing up, but it was. She took in the sight of their neighbor's little girl just for a moment, Cam, kneeling beside her so they were at eye level, explaining how burls formed on trees.

More contractions now. Sharper than before, and so close together that as soon as she caught her breath from one, another overtook her. Eleanor knelt on the floor, her cheek against the wood, remembering the nights she and Cam had made love in this spot.

Now came the strongest contraction yet. Eleanor pictured Valerie at the wheel of her four-wheel drive, making her way along the snowy roads toward the farmhouse. *Come soon.*

A sound came out of her then that she'd never heard before, the sound a person makes when she's doing the hardest thing she ever attempted. From the living room came the roar of the fans, and Bob Cousy announcing some amazing play. She heard whooping from Jeremy in the living room; the Celtics must be winning.

Valerie arrived—door swinging open, door slamming shut, her daughter Asa in her sleeper suit, carrying the Fisher-Price farm set. Eleanor heard Valerie talking to Cam—"You won't even know she's here." Then the sound of the faucet—Valerie washing her hands, laying out towels and a bowl of water, warming a stack of blankets on the woodstove, unpacking her roll of implements. Cam, back at Eleanor's side, telling her she was doing great. Asa, in the corner, making animal noises.

Eleanor, in the brief calm between contractions, lay on the bed, legs apart, knees bent.

Valerie returned to the room and inspected her. "You're almost there," she said. "Eight centimeters." She laid her towel out on the table by the bed and set out swabs, speculum, scissors. A pitcher of water. A bowl of ice cubes.

"It's good to walk," Valerie told Eleanor, but her body had started to tremble, in a way that had nothing to do with the temperature in the room, which was plenty warm enough. That morning Cam had stoked their woodstove to the top and opened the dampers.

Another voice at the door. Darla's. The sound boots make when you slap them against the side of the woodstove to knock the ice off.

It was dark out, a full-moon night. The moonlight came in the bedroom window, slashing across the blue double-wedding-ring quilt. From the kitchen, Asa was asking if they had any chocolate milk. Darla was talking to Cam, who had defrosted a steak when the contractions first started. Now he was setting it in the pan.

"I wasn't sure my car would make it." Darla was in the doorway now. "Thought you might like these."

A bag of Florida oranges tumbled out on the bed and rolled onto the floor. From her spot at the foot of the bed (Eleanor breathing hard now, sweating), Darla dug into the peel of one with her thumbnail, and a spurt of orange sprayed into the air. Between breaths, Eleanor took in the scent like a meal.

From the kitchen, another smell, but this made her feel sick. The odor of meat. Cam's steak, sizzling in the pan.

"Take it outside," Eleanor said, between contractions. "I'm going to throw up." A look came over Valerie's face—impatience, irritation, the expression of a woman accustomed to the failures and disappointments provided by men. This was not the first time in her days as a midwife that a father had proved himself oblivious to the strains of his wife's labor. Not the first time a sporting event provided the soundtrack to a child's birth.

The contractions got stronger. Cam returned, taking his place on the bed next to Eleanor. From the living room, she could hear the sound of the basketball game.

Then no more words. Everything coming fast and faster. Cam was pulling Eleanor up on the pillows, bracing her back, Darla rubbing her shoulders. At the foot of the bed, with the reading lamp in position to illuminate the place where the baby would make its entrance, knelt the midwife.

Cam leaned in to kiss Eleanor, as recommended in *Spiritual Midwifery*. An open-mouth kiss, meant to help Eleanor dilate those last two centimeters. Eleanor could smell steak on his breath.

On the third push, she was overcome by the most searing pain—like hot metal branding flesh, like her whole body ripping in two, a jagged tearing of her softest, most tender part.

Then the baby spiraled out of her, and everything else—steak, Celtics, swimsuit models, Fisher-Price animals, oranges—fell away.

They saw her face first—small and round, and wailing, with large black eyes and a full head of hair. Valerie ran a hand over the creamy white substance covering her skin and placed it on her own cheeks and around her eyes.

"Vernix," she said. "The best moisturizer ever invented. How else did you think I got to be this age without any wrinkles?"

Laughter. More talk of basketball. Jeremy entering from the living room, where the game had ended by now.

"She looks like Bill Walton," he said.

What was he doing here anyway? Eleanor wanted to be alone with Cam.

"Here's your daughter," Valerie said. Then Alison was in her arms, and nothing else mattered.

14.

second fiddle

A week after Alison was born—March now, snow melting, mud season—the insurance check for their wrecked Toyota showed up in the mailbox, and they purchased the 1965 Plymouth Valiant with Georgia plates. There was just enough money left over for a car seat and a Johnny Jump Up, recommended by Darla.

Eleanor's milk came in, her breasts cartoonishly inflated. She wept at the sight of her body—her belly still protruding, everything soft. Nobody had prepared her for this part. Her husband could enter into fatherhood with his body unscathed, his stomach as flat as it ever was, those same abdominal muscles rippling over that perfect chest. But after delivery, Eleanor bore stretch marks and shredded skin in the most intimate place of her body, not to mention thirty extra pounds.

Three weeks after the birth, a woman who saw Eleanor in the grocery store asked, "When is your baby due?"

Afterward, out in the parking lot, she leaned against the steering wheel and wept.

There was one part that thrilled her, though: the power she possessed, within her own body, to nourish their daughter. When Alison cried, all she ever needed was Eleanor's nipple, and the world was right again. Eleanor gloried in the wild, animal connection she had with this child. She had only to hear Alison's voice—and sometimes, had only to walk into the room and see her lying there—for milk to come pouring out of her.

Cam loved Alison, too, of course. But it was different for him. At this point in Alison's life the most important thing in her world was getting fed, and Cam couldn't provide that. Eleanor considered, for a moment, how it must feel for a man at moments like these—

holding his infant daughter, hearing her scream, and knowing there was nothing he could do for her but hand her to her mother. The powerlessness of that.

"I know he's trying," Eleanor said. "But at this point, Cam almost feels"—she felt guilty saying this out loud—"superfluous."

"Tell me about it," Darla said. "All Bobby wanted to do, after Kimmie was born, was hand out cigars and drink shots of tequila and ask if we could have sex yet."

Eleanor did not share Darla's bitterness. But the thought had occurred to her that once the impregnation part was over, there wasn't a whole lot for a father to do besides folding and changing the diapers and standing around, trying to be supportive.

She thought about her parents, and how, for them, she had been a kind of interloper in their love affair. Her birth had been grudgingly accepted—her presence in their lives like the regrettable but necessary visit of a relative from out of town who overstays her welcome.

For Eleanor's child—Eleanor and Cam's—it would be different. Alison's birth marked the beginning of a new kind of love affair—hers with their daughter. If there was an outsider in the story, it was Cam. "I didn't know it was possible to love anybody so much," she said to Walt and Edith, when they came by to see the baby.

Walt had patted Cam on the back with the air of a man welcoming a comrade into a new and unfamiliar club.

"From here on out, you play second fiddle, bud," he said. "Might as well get used to it."

15.

ships in the night

It was hard to understand how one very small infant who slept most of the time could have created so much upheaval in their lives, but Eleanor was exhausted all the time, inhabiting a state that somehow combined euphoria with sorrow.

They had created this precious, miraculous person. Whole hours passed in which all Eleanor wanted to do was hold Alison and study her face. But there was this other part: her body belonged to her child now. She could hardly remember who she had been before. Somehow, in the course of becoming a mother, she had lost a piece of herself.

The sadness came to her, in a rush, every time she placed Alison on her nipple to nurse. Some hormone must have released itself into her bloodstream, she figured, but knowing it was her own body chemistry playing tricks didn't make any less real the feeling that she was plummeting down some bottomless well.

For Cam, none of the same hormones came into play, but he felt the effects of Eleanor's. Her breasts, that had been, for Cam, a source of seemingly endless pleasure—never more so than during her pregnancy—were vessels of milk now, whose sole function was to feed their child. One night, in bed, not so long after the birth of their daughter, he had reached over to touch them, and she recoiled as swiftly as if she'd received an electric shock.

Afterward, she apologized. "It just doesn't feel right anymore, you touching me there," she told him.

They were having sex again by this point—not so often as before, or as energetically. It was disconcerting to Eleanor that more often than not, when they made love—no matter how quietly—Alison would wake from her sleep in the little basket they put her in at the side of their bed, and cry out—as if she knew something was going on that wasn't about her, and she didn't like it. Here came the reminder: she was the center of their universe now.

"You don't have to pick her up right this second," Cam whispered. "She's okay."

But the mood was broken.

Alison was six weeks old when Eleanor returned to her desk. In the absence of a new book contract, she was drawing illustrations for a series of elementary school reading textbooks. The work didn't bring in much money, and it was unexciting, but it provided regular checks, and they needed those.

She figured out a way to hold her daughter—nurse her, even—while she was drawing. She had figured out a way to sit with her legs folded in a kind of modified lotus position, with Alison cradled against her mother's thigh, and propped against her nursing breast.

There had been a time when Eleanor would visit Cam in the barn almost every afternoon when their work was winding down, with a beer for them both, and more often than not they would peel off each other's clothes and lie down on the foam mat he kept out there, for just this purpose.

This happened less frequently now. One day, when she'd come out to the woodshop—she needed his signature on their tax return—Cam mentioned that he couldn't even remember the last time they'd made love.

"Oh, God," she said. "I'm just so tired." These days, if there was ever a half hour when the baby was sleeping and there was no laundry to wash, all she'd want to do with it was to be alone.

They no longer spoke about the old dream of ten children, or six, or even four. They'd catch sight of each other across the room, like two people who had met once, long ago, but couldn't remember where.

One time, out on the road, when she was driving into town—a grocery run, a trip to the dump—Eleanor had passed Cam, driving the opposite direction, at the wheel of his old green truck they'd finally managed to get running again. And for a split second, catching sight of her husband, she actually failed to recognize him. For a moment there, seeing his face, she thought, *What a handsome man.* Then she remembered: she was married to him.

Ships passing in the night. It sometimes felt that way. And yet it was also true that having made this baby together—this person—and sharing in the strange and mysterious adventure of these early days with her had brought them closer.

Days went by that Eleanor didn't get out of her sweatpants. Some nights, all they could manage to throw together for dinner was a bowl of canned soup. But sometime in early September—just when the leaves were starting to turn and the first frost hit their tomato plants—Eleanor decided to make a special dinner for the two of them—spaghetti carbonara, with the last of their garden greens on the side, and homemade brownies for dessert. She picked up a bottle of Chianti at the liquor store. (Candles, they always kept on hand.) She waited until they had Alison in her crib, then changed into the one nice dress she owned that she could still fit into. She put on her Al Green album. Then lipstick.

Cam, when he came in from his run, looked around the darkened room—just three candles and an oil lamp burning—with puzzlement. It had been that long.

"What's the occasion?" he asked her. "Did I miss something?"

"Nothing in particular," she said. "I just thought we should remind ourselves where all this baby stuff came from in the first place. You and me."

They ate by the fire, the way they had in the old days. (Not so old. It hadn't even been two years since they'd met.) At one point during the meal, Cam had reached across the table to take her hand and brought it to his lips. "You're still a beautiful woman," he told her.

"I don't feel that way."

After, they brought the candles into the bedroom. Since Alison's birth, Eleanor had been undressing in the dark, mostly, and sleeping in a nightgown, unbuttoned in the front to make it easier when the baby came into bed with them to nurse.

"Let me see you," he said, holding out the oil lamp.

Six weeks later, her period was late.

"I didn't think you could get pregnant while you were nursing," she said, when she told him. She had worried that Cam might be upset. She wasn't sure herself how she felt about the idea of another baby, so soon after the first. But he threw his arms around her and let out a whoop.

"I have no idea how we'll pay for this," she said.

"There you go again." He grinned. "It's only money."

16.

a first baseman's wife

"I joined a softball team," Cam told her, hopping out of the truck after a Saturday morning run to the town dump. "They're called the Yellow Jackets."

To Eleanor, this seemed like an odd moment for her husband to take on a commitment to play ball three nights a week. It was April, six weeks past Alison's first birthday, with three months to go before the new baby came. He was already headed to the garage to look for his old glove.

"They made me first baseman," he said. "Long-armed lefty. How can I go wrong?"

That Tuesday night, he went alone to his game, but when he came home he told her how all the players' wives liked coming to the games. "It's a great group of guys," Cam said. "I bet you'll like the women, too. Everybody's got little kids and babies on the way. You're always saying you wished you knew more people in town."

After that, Eleanor never missed a game. Cam was right: it was fun sitting on the bleachers at the dusty ball field with Alison in her arms or on a blanket next to her on cool spring evenings (and, later, warm summer nights). Half watching the players, but mostly (always with an eye on the older children, playing in the dirt a little ways from the field) talking with the other wives—an experience she'd never had before—about all the small, seemingly insignificant details of their children's lives that, at the time, consumed them: whether to use a pacifier, when to start solid food, what to do if you observed your four-year-old masturbating. They talked about other things besides the children, too. Recipes, for sure. But also, particularly after a beer—and there was always beer—the conversation came around to sex. Who was having it. Who wasn't. Who still cared about it.

Cam was among the younger players when he joined the team—the others were in their thirties, mostly, though the catcher, Buck Hollingsworth, was probably over forty, judging by his hairline and his gut.

Rich McGann was the Yellow Jackets' main pitcher (his wife, Carol, was a nurse who sometimes arrived late to games, still in scrubs). Sal Perrone played second base, no doubt unaware that back in the bleachers, his wife, Lucinda, was making appreciative comments about every reasonably nice-looking man who came up to bat, drawing unfavorable comparisons to Sal. Sal was the slowest runner on the team, but he could hit. He had more home runs than anyone, though every time he hit one, this look of astonishment came over his face, as if he couldn't quite believe a person like himself had accomplished this.

The weakest player on the team was Harry Botts, who'd opened a coffee bar that sold used records in a long-abandoned storefront on the main street of Akersville. Every year or two, some outsider would move to town and open some interesting little business: a bookstore, a ceramics gallery, a health food co-op. Usually they closed within the year. But Harry's record store had survived a half dozen seasons, mostly because he had a trust fund, people said.

The Yellow Jackets were the first team Harry had ever played on, and they'd put him in the outfield, where he had yet to field a single ball. His at-bats were understood to be guaranteed strikeouts. But the players maintained a certain amused affection for Harry, and it helped that he never showed up without a cooler of good German beer. That, and his Cubs hat. Nobody knew what had brought Harry from Chicago to Akersville—an unlikely move—but they embraced him as a kind of mascot. He might not know anything about the game of softball, but he never failed to show up with the beer.

Eleanor's most frequent companion on the bench was Peggy Olin, whose husband, Bob, played shortstop. Every time he slid into a base, Peggy groaned. "You know how hard it was getting out the grass stains last time?" she said to Eleanor.

Peggy and Bob had a daughter, Gina, a year older than Alison, and an older daughter, Katie, who led games of red light, green light and tag with the younger kids. The summer they met, Peggy had recently read a book by Adelle Davis that inspired her to transform her family's diet. She handed out samples of healthy but barely edible snacks that the children generally disposed of once they were out of sight while, off at the hot dog stand, her husband scarfed down fries.

Peggy believed in breastfeeding on demand—was still nursing three-year-old Gina, and never missed an opportunity to comment when she saw one of the other mothers taking out a bottle of formula. "Don't they know all the health benefits their child is missing out on when they give them that stuff?" Peggy said to Eleanor. Eleanor breastfed, too, though not as determinedly as Peggy did. (Two years later, Peggy would still be giving her daughter her breast on occasion, though by age four Gina could unbutton her mother's shirt and ask for it.) Gina was large for three—a pale-skinned strawberry blonde who mostly sat on the bleachers with her mother and required constant reapplication of sunscreen and bug spray.

Observing this, Bonnie Henderson—wife of the third baseman—rolled her eyes. Bonnie was that other type of mother, whose parenting philosophy, if she had one, mainly involved giving her two sons a large bag of cheese puffs and a Coke at the beginning of every game and shooting a stream of ice-cold water from her boys' squirt guns in their direction any time one of them acted up. Back before kids, she'd worked as a corrections officer at the state prison, and still employed a few of her old techniques.

"If I'm walking a little funny today, girls," Bonnie told them one evening, "it's on account of all the crazy stuff Jerry and I were up to last night." Her stories tended to feature times their children had come into their bedroom at an inopportune moment—which could have been just about any moment, to hear Bonnie tell it—or surprising places where they'd had sex.

"I think she's making it up," Carol said.

"I don't know," Lucinda offered. "Did you see the way Jerry cupped his hand around Bonnie's butt the other night, after he came in from hitting that home run?"

Partly, the women were shocked. More so, envious. Though none of the women seemed deeply unhappy with their lives. They were young. Their children were healthy, and so were they. The banter of those summer nights felt less like complaint than a ritual of bonding, a way for the women to make connections with each other, over the shared travails of children and husbands, judgmental mothers-in-law and losing the baby weight.

Partway through the season, a new player joined the team. Two of them, actually: Ray and Timmy Pouliot. Ray was a relief pitcher whose specialty was a knuckleball. He worked as a carpenter and wore wifebeater shirts that showed off his muscles. It took Eleanor a few minutes to realize that Timmy, drafted for right field, was the same person she'd met years before, that day she'd gone to the falls, when he'd admired her drawing and asked her if she had a boyfriend. Eleanor remembered the story Timmy told her about finding his father in the garage that day. The gun.

She figured he must be eighteen years old, and he had filled out. He had a compact build, and a tattoo of his father's name on his bicep, but Eleanor still recognized a certain angelic softness in those incredibly blue eyes of his—sadness maybe—that set him apart from the other men on the team.

The Pouliot brothers rode motorcycles. The two of them generally arrived just as the game was starting, roaring up to the ball field on their Harleys, no helmets; you could hear them coming all the way from Main Street.

Timmy's girlfriend that summer was Mandy, who worked at the Stop & Shop checkout. At the beginning of the season she'd sat on the bleachers with the other players' wives, but when the conversation turned as it generally did to pregnancies and breastfeeding, day care and playgroups, she drifted over to the edge of the field in her midriff top and short shorts to help Coco with whatever project she'd taken on that evening—French braiding everybody's hair, more often than not—or else she'd just stand there watching the game. When it was over, she hopped on the back of the bike and wrapped her arms around Timmy's waist, and the two of them took off in a cloud of dust.

Eleanor was eight and a half months into her second pregnancy by this point in the season. Her back ached all the time now, and she'd developed an odd rash on her face. That night, lying with Cam in the dark, her head nestled into his chest, she spoke of the Pouliot brothers.

"That was some catch Ray made," Cam offered.

"That girlfriend Timmy brought to the game has an amazing body," Eleanor said. She had not yet lost the weight from having Alison when she'd gotten pregnant again. "Mandy," Eleanor said. "The blonde."

"I hadn't noticed," he told her.

17.

black ice

A few miles down the road from where they lived, there was a lake where they'd skated, that first winter before Alison's birth. Eleanor's center of gravity was off, due to her large and growing belly, but she'd managed to get across the ice, with Cam's arm around her for support. The ice was uneven, though, and Eleanor's back hurt. They only stayed out for a few minutes. But it was a good day.

A year later, newly pregnant with Ursula, with a baby to care for now, it had been harder to get out on her skates. Then came one of those rare and precious days (sometimes whole years went by between them) when the perfect combination of meteorological events took place: A hard freeze. No snow. Rain maybe, followed by frigid temperatures that left a layer of black ice over everything. Perfect skating conditions.

They discovered this on a night they'd been at the movies—a rare evening out, Darla babysitting for Alison. Eleanor and Cam had pulled over by the side of the frozen lake to take in the full moon.

"You know what we need to do," Cam said to Eleanor, as they stood on the embankment, looking out.

They kept their skates in the back seat for moments like this. Now they laced them up and stepped out onto the ice. With no light but what the moon provided, they took off across the lake, just the two of them.

That night the ice was glass—Eleanor's skate blades newly sharpened, her husband's arm around her waist, one of her mittened hands in his. A sensation came over her—she could still summon it—as close to flight as Eleanor would ever know. *Remember this moment,* she thought.

They'd heard a strange groaning sound under their skate blades then, like an ancient sea creature waking from a long sleep to find himself trapped under the ice and pushing to escape. Eleanor had thought the frozen lake was giving way, but Cam told her it was just the ice expanding.

"We're safe," he said. "I won't let you fall through."

The months after the birth of Ursula, that July, stretched out in a kind of milky blur for Eleanor. There was always someone who needed to be fed and held and someone who needed to be changed and a basket of laundry to be washed and a sinkful of dishes to be washed and somewhere in there, someone had to be earning a living. That turned out to be Eleanor, mostly. Cam was an endlessly entertaining father—funny and tender and surprising. You never knew when he might burst into the door with a jar of tadpoles he'd collected in the brook for the children to keep in a bucket and study, or a hand-carved dog he'd made for Alison (he spent all day on that), or, one winter, a snowy owl he found dead on the road, frozen in a storm and perfectly intact. One day he came home with a stack of 45s from the 1960s that he'd picked up at a yard sale on the way back from a craft fair. Alison was only three at the time, and Ursula only just walking, but they put them on, one after another, and had a dance party in the kitchen—with Ursula in Eleanor's arms and Alison on Cam's shoulders.

More than anything, he loved showing them artifacts from the natural world: he'd put his hand in his pocket and, when it emerged, set down a strange, mysterious pellet that turned out to be animal scat—coyote, possibly, or fox, or moose even—that, when you picked it apart, contained small pieces of bones and fur from whatever the animal whose scat it was had eaten for dinner the night before. He knew the names of the constellations and the stories that went with them, and he could carve a doll with his penknife or make a fort out of an old cardboard box covered with an umbrella. He brought home finger paint, and let the girls cover one whole wall of the garage with it.

Still he wasn't the kind of father with whom Eleanor could leave two small children for a stretch of hours while she worked. She'd set up a desk at one end of the kitchen, close enough to keep an eye on the children, but it was hard to concentrate there. "I'm happy to help you out," he'd say—a phrase that would once have sounded benign but now struck Eleanor as carrying with it the implicit belief that primary care of their children rested with her. She started to say something about his easy, offhand assumption but stopped herself.

There had been a time, and it lasted years, when all Eleanor supposed she needed was to love someone deeply, someone who loved her back, and she had this now. And she had her family—the thing she'd wanted above all else. But there was also, now, a place in her where something like a small, hard nut of resentment resided. She could almost feel it there sometimes—watching the cool ease of the way Cam mounted his bicycle and headed out on a ride some Saturday morning, with the dishes from the waffles he'd made—he was a joyous but messy cook—still stacked high in the sink.

"When do I get to take a Saturday morning off to go on an adventure?" she asked, out in the driveway as he pumped up the tires.

"Be honest with yourself, El," he said to her. "Do you actually see yourself getting on a mountain bike on a Saturday morning?"

He had nailed it, of course. So much time had passed in which she had no time that she no longer knew what she'd do with herself if she had any.

18.

people you care about start dying

Ursula was still in diapers, and Alison not so long out of them, when Eleanor realized she was pregnant again. This time, it had not been the result of a romantic interlude with a soundtrack from Al Green, or a dinner by the fire after the kids went to bed, with a bottle of wine. Those didn't happen anymore. She had been flat-out for so long, she just hadn't noticed the small tear in her diaphragm. Maybe she'd even noticed, but she hadn't gotten around to replacing it yet. She'd gotten pregnant once before, while breastfeeding—but even though she only nursed Ursula at bedtimes now, she'd allowed herself to believe it couldn't happen a second time.

That August, the day of the lunar eclipse—their daughters three and a half and two—Cam piled everyone in the truck to get the best view from the top of Hopewell Hill. "Maybe they won't remember," he said. "I just like to show them things."

This was what you did. You took your children out in the darkness to watch the moon disappear. You dissected coyote scat with them. You led your two-year-old down to the garden to press a handful of radish seeds into the soil and handed her the spatula to lick when you made chocolate pudding and turned the pages of *Richard Scarry's What Do People Do All Day?*, pointing out the animal characters and naming their jobs. You gathered autumn leaves, pressed them with an iron in between two sheets of wax paper, and taped them on the window, where you'd set an avocado seed in a glass of water to watch it sprout; and carried your three-year-old outside in your arms at night—her and her sister—to let them catch snowflakes. Who knew what they'd remember, and what they'd make of it, but the hope was there that if nothing else, what they would hold on to from these times was the knowledge of being deeply loved. You showed your children the world. It was up to them to determine what they'd make of it.

One morning that December—Alison nearing her fourth birthday, Ursula two and a half, Eleanor two weeks away from her due date—Walt stopped by with a load of firewood. As he was throwing the split logs off the back of his truck, he asked if they'd heard the news. "Remember those boys they had on *Ed Sullivan* a while back?" he said. "The ones with the hair, that all the girls used to scream about? You know the one with the Japanese wife?"

Nobody but Walt would have chosen to identify John Lennon as one of the singers from *Ed Sullivan*.

"Somebody shot him last night," he said. "Dead on the spot."

Walt was saying something else now, about New York City—how dangerous it was, why would anyone want to live there? Eleanor couldn't focus on the rest of what he was saying.

"I figured you'd want to know," he told her. "Seeing as how you're always playing those records."

Eleanor went back in the house. She thought about that Sunday night so long ago, at her parents' house in Newton, when she'd heard the Beatles for the first time—she and a few million other people. She had been ten years old. Most of the girls liked Paul the best, but for Eleanor it was always John. The picture came to her of Charlie, her dog, lashed to the roof of the police officer's car that day, shot for chasing deer. She stood at the sink, watching Alison, on the couch with a half-eaten bagel, Ursula propped up on pillows beside her with her bottle, the gaze of her two daughters totally focused on the television screen, where Bert was explaining to Ernie why it was a good idea to carry an umbrella.

So much is going to happen to them.

There was nothing she and Cam could do about most of it.

She heard his truck in the driveway. When he came in the door, he put his arms around Eleanor. He'd heard the news in the car, driving home from town.

"I know it's crazy to be this sad about someone I never knew," she said. "When people are dying every day, all over the world. I just never pictured it happening to one of the Beatles."

"The older you get, the more bad things happen," he said. "Good ones, too. People you care about start dying. There's no getting around it."

19.

a web-footed boy

The odds were long, given what she knew about the gene for red hair—recessive—but finally, with their son Toby, they got their red-headed baby. A Christmas Day boy, he burst into the world weighing ten pounds, and howling. A couple of hours after his delivery, holding him against her breast, examining every inch of him, she had discovered a magical trait. The first of many, as it turned out.

"Our son has a webbed foot," she told Cam, not with any dismay. More like wonderment.

"Maybe he'll swim the English Channel," Cam said. "Or to Cuba."

"I get this feeling he's going to be different from the other two," Eleanor said. "Not just because he's a boy, or a redhead. He's like some foundling child who shows up in the cabbage patch. Like some magic person."

"Here's all I know," Cam said. "We're outnumbered now."

Even then Toby had this surprisingly deep voice. He was like a man trapped in a baby's body, she used to say. Impatient to grow up.

Eleanor loved her children equally, but Toby occupied a particular place in her heart. It seemed to Cam and Eleanor as if he'd landed from another galaxy—a strange and miraculous alien baby come to live at their house.

He had the most unusual ears, like shells, but pointed at the tips. Somewhere in those first minutes Eleanor spent inspecting every inch of her new son's body she had discovered a thin, almost transparent piece of skin connecting each of the toes on his left foot—only the left, and very briefly this had worried her, though soon enough her son's webbed left foot would become another of the things she loved about this otherworldly child. When Ursula and Alison's friends came over to play, the girls would remove his shoe and his sock, if he wasn't barefoot already, to display this magical feature of their amazing brother.

He was born in the bathtub, and maybe because of this he seemed drawn to water. Wherever a body of water lay, Toby made his way to it and, whenever possible, jumped in. The special toes on his left foot made him swim fast as an otter, he told them. Or a muskrat. Where had he learned about muskrats? In some other lifetime, maybe.

Alison had not yet reached her fourth birthday when Toby joined the family, but she begged to hold her brother, and Eleanor knew Alison would sooner let her arm fall off than drop that baby. He had entered the world the way he entered every room, from that moment on—like a rodeo bull released from the pen, bucking and kicking. Though there was this other side to Toby. Of the three children, he was the one most hungry for touch, the one for whom rubbing up against the skin of another human being seemed more vital than food.

In that brief stretch of months before he started crawling—something he did younger than the others, or any baby she'd ever observed—Eleanor kept his infant seat on the girls' craft table at a height at which Ursula, when she ran through the room in the middle of some game, could pat his head as she flew by, like Cam's beloved left fielder Carl Yastrzemski tagging third base on the way to completing a game-tying home run. His eyes stayed locked on his sisters as they ran past him, off to play in the snow or dig in the sand. Even then you could tell how crazy it drove Toby that he couldn't run after his sisters, but once he could crawl, then run, he never stopped. Wherever the girls went, he followed.

That March—when Toby was just three months old—they made their cork people for the first time, and the boats to bring them on their journey along the brook. The idea had come to them on a morning right after Ali's birthday. After a solid month of below-freezing temperatures, a freakishly warm couple of days had melted much of the snow, and when they took their daily walk to the falls, they saw how the water had risen from all the runoff. Water crashed over the rocks; the brook was running again.

"If only we had a boat," Alison said. "We could float down the stream."

It wasn't a river, of course. The brook was only a few feet wide in most places. Deep enough for trout, but not for the kind of vessel that might transport a person. But when they got home, Eleanor announced they were making boats to sail down the river.

"We need people," Ursula said. "To ride in the boats."

"No problem," Eleanor said. "We'll make some."

So they crafted a half dozen little boats, and the day after, with the water racing faster than ever, they brought them to the brook—Eleanor holding tight to the girls' hands, one on each side, with Toby in the front pack.

They spent most of the afternoon launching their boats and running along the water's edge, following them. When they got back to the house, Eleanor made hot chocolate.

"Let's always do that," Ursula said. "Every year. Our family tradition."

That was Ursula for you. She never wanted anything to change. Neither did Eleanor, actually. The difference was, she knew, as her children didn't yet, that this was impossible.

20.

this was her artwork

Sitting in the front of Eleanor's shopping cart at the checkout one time, Ursula had spotted an issue of *People* magazine dedicated to the upcoming wedding of Prince Charles and Lady Diana. Maybe it was the word "princess" that captured Ursula's attention—that, along with Diana's beauty. When Eleanor explained what the story was about, Ursula begged her to buy the magazine, which she carried around with her and took to bed, to study the pictures. On the morning of the royal wedding in London—a July day when the temperature hovered around ninety—she had sat on the living room floor, eyes glued to the television set. She wanted to know how a person got to be a princess, and if she could be one, too.

Even very young, Alison had acquired her sharp, witheringly honest way of addressing her sister, and everyone else in the family.

"Nope," she told Ursula. "You'd have to be rich. Your parents have to live in some fancy house. Forget about it."

But Ursula didn't. She wanted to know who the other princes were that hadn't found wives yet. She was particularly interested in Diana's tiara, and the coach she and Prince Charles rode off in after the ceremony was over.

After, she always kept a picture of Princess Diana taped to her wall. As time passed and the story unfolded, she added others, until there was a whole collage that included Prince William and Prince Harry and her favorite, of Princess Diana dancing with John Travolta. When Eleanor explained that Prince William would probably be the king someday, she decided to marry him.

"I already explained to you," Alison told her. "It's hopeless." But Ursula was an incorrigible optimist.

"Party pooper," she told her sister.

Cleaning up Ursula's room one day—vacuuming around her Barbie hospital, the papier-mâché puppet of Madonna—Eleanor found herself studying her daughter's wall of tacked-up Princess Diana photographs. Those beautiful gowns, all those exotic trips with Prince Charles, the pictures of Diana and her sons. Whatever was difficult or possibly crazy about having three children so close together in age, Eleanor always knew this: there was nowhere she'd rather be, nothing she'd rather be doing with her life. On the rare occasions when her hands were free, and there were no more diapers to wash or laundry to fold, Eleanor set her magical red-headed baby on his blanket and took out her sketchbook, trying to capture it all. Not that she ever succeeded. Still, there was a quality to the drawings she made at this time in their lives that had not revealed itself in anything she'd made before, a kind of tenderness.

There was something else, too. She could feel how quickly time was passing, how fast her children were growing, and though every stage that disappeared signaled the arrival of another (crawling, to walking, to jumping, to skipping), she felt the changes with a twinge of loss. Eleanor remembered how she had felt when Toby lost interest in nursing (and she knew by then that he was the last). She had registered the moment as a small death.

No more babies. A chapter had closed. That wonderful stretch of months when all this particular child needed was right there in her own body, and all she had to do was unbutton her blouse to provide it, was over. She could begin to reclaim her body, maybe. Allow herself thoughts and ideas that weren't centered on those three small people who had occupied her every waking moment for the last few years. Maybe ideas for books and pictures would begin to come to her again. Her stalled career might revive, if she was lucky. She and Cam would reclaim their bed for lovemaking, or uninterrupted sleep. But every springtime after that when they stood at the side of the brook, launching their boats, it would occur to her that she was one year closer to the day her son and daughters would no longer live with her and Cam. How would she ever bear that?

Years later, looking back on those days, Eleanor would try to pinpoint when it had started—the slow, relentless leak of passion from her marriage, so gradual you'd barely notice any change, and Cam's regretful resignation as he began to drift away from her, like one of the boats they made for their cork people every March, floating dreamily down the brook. It had taken place so gradually that maybe neither of them noticed until somewhere along the line she'd looked up and he was gone.

"Jesus, what's happened to us?" Cam said one night, as the two of them sat across a table from each other at the pub in town, having a steak dinner. "I'm sitting here with my wife, and it's the first time we've actually been alone together in—what? Four months? Maybe six? And we're talking about whether we need to put tubes in Ursula's ears because of all the damned infections, and if we can afford to buy Alison a bike."

He reached across the table then to take her hand. "When we get home tonight, let's have sex," he said.

She nodded and smiled. Back at the house, Cam paid the babysitter—Coco, in their children's eyes the goddess of the softball field, now thirteen years old—and drove her home. While he was gone, Eleanor lit candles in the bedroom and put on music and inserted her diaphragm —a new one. She checked on the children—all asleep, in their own beds for once—and climbed into the one she shared with Cam. No nightgown for a change.

The next morning, when she got up, he was already shaving.

"What happened to our plan?" she asked him. He laughed, a little ruefully.

"By the time I got back from dropping Coco off you were sound asleep," he told her. "Never mind. You probably needed the rest."

More than many men (Darla's husband, Bobby, for instance, who reportedly had never changed a single one of Kimmie's diapers, or given her a bath), Cam reveled in fatherhood. But it was abundantly clear that he was the fun parent, Eleanor the practical one. Eleanor was the parent who made sure the children got to bed at a reasonable hour and knew that if you decided to make s'mores in the fireplace at eight thirty, this was unlikely to happen. Cam was the one who built crazy snow forts and got them out of bed to see a meteor shower and oversaw the preparations for a Mother's Day with breakfast in bed: waffles and maple syrup they'd made from tapping their trees, and a bunch of dandelions in a jar. "You wouldn't believe how the kitchen looked when I got up," Eleanor told Darla.

Never mind all that. Here at last was the thing she had always wanted above all else. Where Eleanor and Cam had always slept naked, skin touching skin, before the children, now there were small, warm bodies in sleeper suits that occasionally smelled faintly of pee separating the two of them most nights. Never mind that she wasn't making children's books anymore, and that editors no longer called her, or that she had to lose the twenty pounds she was still carrying from the last pregnancy, or possibly the one before.

This was her artwork. This family.

21.

over the coals

Summer came, and softball. In one of the last games of the season, Harry Botts, running in the wrong direction for a ball, slammed into Cam as he stood at first base. The impact broke Cam's ankle. The snap of his bone carried all the way over to the hot dog wagon out beyond right field, where Coco was doing Ursula's nails.

They had to borrow a couple thousand dollars from Cam's parents to pay the medical bills. In one way, it was easier, not having to pack up all the children—preparing the many Tupperware containers of snacks, assembling the sweatshirts and shoes—and head out to games all those nights. But Eleanor missed the games. Not so much the softball, but the society of the women in the bleachers—watching the children in the grass, handing out Goldfish and boxes of Juicy Juice and sandwiches. Studying the figure of her red-headed husband guarding first base, his right arm outstretched, just waiting to get the next batter out.

Halfway through softball season, Eleanor ran into Timmy Pouliot at the liquor store, buying beer.

"I've missed seeing you at games," he told her.

"Come to our Labor Day party," she said. It was that time of year again already. "Bring your girlfriend."

Eleanor and Cam had not yet made plans for their annual end-of-season potluck, but now—though money was in even shorter supply thanks to the broken ankle, not to mention a third baby—it seemed important to maintain the tradition. Cam was still on crutches, but able to man the grill. Eleanor fixed pitchers of mojitos, and Harry Botts came through with the beer. They set their stereo speakers in the yard, blasting Blondie—the first album they'd bought on CD, *Parallel Lines*. Even with his ankle out of commission, Cam danced by the fire, as sparks rose around him in the darkness. Eleanor leaned against the porch door, holding tight to her son. Even then—not yet walking—he was the kind of child a mother couldn't let out of her sight.

Eleanor had started doing the Jane Fonda workout, but she hadn't come close to reclaiming her body. The one she used to have. She'd bought a sundress for the party, shorter than anything she'd put on in a while, with a halter top that exposed more skin than her usual.

It had disappointed Eleanor that Cam hadn't noticed her dress. Handing out the ice cream bars to the kids (Sal and Lucinda Perrone's son Joshie complaining, as usual, that someone had pushed ahead of him in the line), she'd gotten waylaid by one of her least favorites among the team wives—Jeannie Owen, who hadn't been seen out of maternity clothes since 1978. Now she was pregnant with her fifth. Her oldest, Paulette, had an ongoing problem of constipation, she told Eleanor. She wanted to know Eleanor's thoughts on enemas, though really, it appeared, she was more interested in sharing her own.

Darla—always quick to recognize a situation—called out to her. "I need you in the kitchen, El."

They were clearing away dishes when she heard the roar of a motorcycle. It was Timmy Pouliot with that summer's girlfriend on the back of his bike.

"Let's see who Timmy's brought with him this year," Darla said. "The one he brought to your party last year would be hard to top."

The new girlfriend was named Amber. She had on an outfit that reminded Eleanor of the actresses on *The Dukes of Hazzard*, a show her children loved. Feeling suddenly ridiculous in her pink-and-green-striped sundress with its pointless ruffles and too-short skirt, she ducked into the bedroom for a sweatshirt to throw over her outfit.

After Timmy parked his bike and grabbed a beer from the cooler, he joined the other men at the spot in their field where Cam had set up horseshoes. Amber headed in the direction of the mojitos. She was a good ten years younger than any of the other women. She took a long swig of her drink.

She made her way to the horseshoe pit. Every man on the team watched as she crossed the lawn and bent over to toss her horseshoe.

Standing at the sink, Eleanor looked toward the barbecue. It was never difficult to pick her husband out in a crowd—the tallest man, the reddest hair. He had a beer in one hand, and the other on the shoulder of one of his softball buddies. He was the life of the party. If she'd never met him before, she could have fallen in love with him all over again that night.

He didn't see her watching him. He was looking at Timmy Pouliot's girlfriend. Who wouldn't?

Eleanor caught her reflection in the window—the ridiculous outfit she'd chosen for the party, her hair, with the bangs she'd cut herself recently, in a misguided attempt to cover her frown lines.

She took out a Brillo pad to scrub the pan she'd cooked the ribs on.

"Need help?" A man's voice, behind her. "I like that dress, by the way," he said. It was Timmy Pouliot, carrying in glasses.

"Now I know you're lying," she laughed.

"Honest to God," he said. "You looked great even when you were popping out all those babies. That's my opinion, anyway."

"Your girlfriend's really something," Eleanor said. "None of the guys can take their eyes off of her."

"You know how it is," he said. "Show a bunch of guys a girl in a tight getup and they all go nuts. We're all like a bunch of dogs with our tongues hanging out, but it doesn't mean anything."

"It doesn't?"

"Don't you know I've always been in love with you?" His voice sounded different. Huskier. He set down the tray of glasses. One by one, he arranged them on the counter, as if he were setting up chess pieces on a board. As if he wanted to take as much time as possible.

"How much have you had to drink tonight?" she said.

"You think I'm joking?"

She had been scrubbing hard, but now she turned around. Timmy stood there, holding the empty tray—a soft, sad expression on his face. Later, she would remember this—the sound of the children calling out "red light, green light" in the darkness, the smell of the meat on the grill, Debbie Harry singing "Heart of Glass." Timmy Pouliot, just standing there with those blue eyes of his. Not even Cam, in their first days together, had ever looked at Eleanor the way Timmy Pouliot did at that moment.

22.

my body keeps wanting to be bad

Except for her father's periodic visits to Crazyland—the fights when her parents got not simply drunk but plastered, and the cries of their lovemaking in the night—Eleanor's childhood home had been eerily quiet. She spent a lot of time in her room, with her colored pencils. There was conversation at meals, but it seldom involved Eleanor. The house was immaculate, mostly because so little went on there.

The house they lived in now, at the end of the dead-end road, in the shade of Old Ashworthy, was almost never even close to tidy, and except for the nights, never quiet, but to Eleanor that suggested only good things. Life happened here. Children played. Walk in the door from the porch and there'd be art projects on the kitchen table. Bug collections on the windowsill. Neon-colored shoes and action figures and mateless socks and experiments, pictures and magnet alphabet letters on the refrigerator, sprouting avocado seeds, skates, crayons, swords, naked Barbies with their hair chopped off, half-finished Fruit Roll-Ups, Smurfs, rocks. There was a dog underfoot, a chart on the refrigerator awarding stars for peeing in the toilet (for Toby, though once he abandoned diapers, he preferred to pee outdoors, even in winter. Whooping and laughing, he pulled down his pants if he wasn't naked already and squirted yellow designs in the snow).

Where Ursula maintained a virtually perpetual air of steadiness and good spirits, Toby was, from the first, a child of wildly fluctuating emotions, big passions, and large feelings—ecstasy or despair. Unlike Alison's frequent dark moods, which often lingered for days, then disappeared as mysteriously as they'd arrived, Toby's moments of sorrow—from when he was just a few months old—touched down like a tornado, swift, powerful, then gone, all within the space of a few minutes.

He spoke earlier than either of his sisters, and even before he was two, he was offering up all these surprising revelations. "I hear music in my head all the time," he said, in that deep voice of his. He hummed a lot, sometimes even when he was sleeping. He danced, whether or not a record was playing.

It had been Ali, though, with whom Toby made up his own language, which only the two of them understood. Sometimes, sitting at her desk, drawing, Eleanor could hear their strange, unknowable conversations, made of sounds unlike any in the English language. Though when he chose to communicate in words the rest of them understood, what he said was almost equally otherworldly.

"I was talking to God the other day," he'd begin. He was not yet three when he said this.

"Did you know I used to be a buffalo? Before I came to live in our family?"

He was a boy now, he conceded. But a boy like no other. His rock collection was lined up five deep along the wall of the borning room, where they'd set a mattress on the floor for his bed, and he could tell you what patch of ground, what spot in the woods, every one of them had come from. He knew things without anybody explaining them, and regularly offered up observations about life and the world that seemed to indicate he'd been around a few hundred years before the rest of them. All day long, he barely stopped running—or dancing, or leaping—but when bedtime came, and they all curled up together on the couch with the most recent haul of books from the library, it was Toby who pressed up alongside Eleanor the closest, stroking her arm with a look of reverence as he held on to a piece of ribbon he'd had since he was very small—once pink, now gray—that he twirled around one finger and liked to brush against the inside of his ear. "I want us to be like this forever," he said.

The family had only recently celebrated Toby's second birthday when he explained to them all, at dinner, "My brain keeps wanting to be good. But my body keeps wanting to be bad." That was the day when Toby's day care teacher had called Eleanor and Cam to come down to the school (not the first time) because he was in trouble again. He'd taken a pair of craft scissors handed out for a project in which he had no interest and cut off a piece of Amanda Dunfey's hair. He just thought it was so beautiful, he told Eleanor in the car on the way home—his low, husky voice (almost a man's voice, coming out of a two-year-old) rueful, but baffled. She could grow it back! He just wanted to have that tip of her ponytail—well, maybe more than just the tip—to take home and put in his special box, with all his other treasures.

"Amanda has the softest hair, Mama," he told her. "I wanted to brush it on my cheek."

23.

a non-comic strip

Early in her marriage, after the sting of her book publisher's rejection had faded—and with no particular belief that anything would come of it—Eleanor had started drawing a comic strip about their life on the farm. For reasons still unclear to herself—perhaps because it was too fragile, and maybe too precious to bring out into the light—she kept this project a secret. She hadn't even shared it with Cam.

This wasn't the kind of strip that featured jokes, or made you laugh out loud. What she liked to do in her panels was to give an honest, loving, but unsentimental picture of the life of a family. She never saw the strip as providing income or becoming any kind of career. It was the thing she did at her desk—early in the morning, generally, before anyone else woke up—for the pure joy of it. Years earlier, before her marriage, she had often known the feeling of such pleasure in her work. With the strip she found that she was able to reawaken a part of herself that might otherwise have disappeared during those long, tiring, and occasionally mind-numbing days of caring for a young child, and then another one, and another after that.

As the years passed, the cast of characters in Eleanor's strip expanded—a fictional family, but one that bore a strong resemblance to her own. The central character was the mother, Maggie, a librarian who played ukulele in a local rock and roll band—a woman who was always trying without success to get in better shape (she did the Jane Fonda workout, but followed up every session with a brownie). Maggie's hair, like Eleanor's, usually looked untidy (except in the strip about the time Maggie gave herself a disastrous perm). The father, Bo, was a handsome potter who was part of a local men's basketball team and made beautiful mugs that hardly anybody ever bought.

Eleanor's non-comic-strip family featured two older girls—Jessie and Kate—and a younger son named Jasper, who collected rocks and got into trouble a lot. With all the other characters in the strip, Eleanor had taken pains to insert fictional details into the story that distinguished them from the real people who'd inspired them. But when she got to the character of Jasper, she felt a need to model him more closely on her real son.

Most of the themes she explored in what she called her non-comic strip stayed close to her experience. There were all those peaches to puree, all those Legos and Playmobil people to pick up.

She wanted to tell stories, but ones that were about real, hard things in a person's life—about a mother who drove back and forth over the same stretch of road for an hour, looking for a lost Playmobil Pirate sword, or a very young son who stuck his face in a bowl of jello to see what it felt like.

My brain keeps wanting to be good. But my body keeps wanting to be bad. Eleanor had included that observation—made by the Jasper character, of course—in the last panel of an early strip.

Eleanor wanted to present a picture of parenthood that went deeper and truer than the kinds of things she saw in the women's magazines—an ongoing look at family life and parenthood that didn't soften the edges or ignore the hard parts. Her passion for the job of raising children would be at the center of every strip, but she would look squarely, unblinkingly, at the other part of the story: how difficult it was, and frustrating, and lonely; the stress it put on a person's marriage. She wanted to explore how it might be possible to be both a stay-at-home mother with children *and* a feminist of her generation, all within the same twenty-four-hour day. She wanted to portray all those hours spent lying on the rug with a baby reading *The Very Hungry Caterpillar* seven times in a row or playing Candy Land, her most hated game, and the one Ursula loved best. (*More,* she used to cry out. *More. More.*) She wanted to share the humor and boredom and love in those moments—and the lessons they taught her. Also—

and maybe this explained why, for a long time, she showed her strip to no one—she wanted to explore the complexities of making a marriage, and the ongoing struggle between her love for her husband and the many aspects of being married that frustrated her.

A couple of years after she'd started drawing it she sent one of her strips to the local paper, the *Akersville Gazette*. They published it and asked if she had another. (Yes, actually. A hundred, probably. And new ones coming to mind every day.)

Nowadays her strip was a staple of the weekly paper. She called it *Family Tree*, in honor of Old Ashworthy, which was often pictured when a panel featured an outdoor scene. The pay was just twenty-five dollars a week. But it felt good to be working.

The truth was—and it felt almost dangerous saying this, when women her age were trying to rewrite the history of their housewife mothers, creating careers outside their homes—that for Eleanor the raising of their three children remained the primary focus of her life. Eleanor saw her days with her children as a kind of artwork, and as with the practice of making art, much that you attempted didn't work out. Still, the act of doing it felt as demanding and precious as the creation of any book.

In her occasional conversations with Patty—off in New York in her Diane von Furstenberg dresses and heels, complaining that whatever man she was seeing at the time distracted her from her career—Eleanor's life looked hopelessly outdated and out of step with the times. She didn't mind.

She and Cam were old-fashioned parents, who still sang grace before the start of every meal and went for walks to the waterfall rather than to the mall. They had decided that there would never be a Nintendo at their house. She wanted to portray, in her drawings, the picture of a family that had somehow managed to hold on to a simple, uncomplicated way of life in a fast-moving world.

They baked pies and glued doilies onto construction paper for valentines and caught fireflies. They made cork people. But the couple in her strip struggled with their relationship, too. In the course of supporting their children's hopes and dreams, they frequently wondered what had become of their own.

Eleanor liked to think of herself as putting a frame around the events of her day in such a way that they took on a kind of significance they might not otherwise have possessed. Setting down her stories within the five frames of a weekly comic strip allowed Eleanor to take a few steps away from her life. She could make a series of panels about something as small as the despair she had felt when her daughter rubbed a chicken pox scab off her scalp, knowing that she would have a bald spot there forever—or her husband's choice of a new toaster for her birthday present the year she turned thirty, or the day her son's beloved cowboy hat had been lifted from his head by a gust of wind as they stood at the edge of the waterfall and plunged into the water—and her own anguish at his grief. Every time she memorialized these moments, large and small, by drawing the characters and putting the words they spoke in bubbles over their heads, she was able to locate the larger meaning in what she had chosen to do with her life.

One week she drew a series of panels featuring the character of the mother, Maggie, on the couch in a living room whose yard sale furnishings and braided rug looked a lot like the ones in their own living room—reading a book to the younger daughter, Jessie. The book Maggie was holding, in the drawing, happened to be one Eleanor had once read to Ursula—a story called *The Dead Bird*.

The cartoon child, Jessie, who sucked her thumb, just as Ursula did, asked Maggie where her own parents were.

"They died," she said. Like Ursula, when she'd put the same question to Eleanor, Jessie had been quiet, taking this in.

"Are you going to die sometime?" the child asked her mother.

"Not for a long time, honey."

Then the hardest part: "Am I going to die someday?"

In the final panel, the Maggie character just sat there, pondering her child's question. Sometimes there were no good answers.

"We're outnumbered now," Cam had said, laughing, after the birth of their son.

Eleanor had loved this—loved the way their family, unlike the quietly lonely one in which she was raised, was loud and boisterous and always a little chaotic. She knew, from observing the way Cam's parents greeted their son, and even their grandchildren, on their annual Christmas visit, and again, when they pulled down the driveway every August in Roger's Lincoln Town Car—with clubs in the back for Roger's annual game of golf with his son, and matching sweaters for each of the children, and the same observations every year ("Look how you've grown" and "How's school?")—that the home in which her husband was raised must have been similarly lacking in warmth.

This was what Eleanor had wanted for her life: the constant whirl of activity, the small warm bodies tumbling into her lap, the jumble of shoes by the screen door, which swung open and closed all day long, as the children headed in and out, the chorus of their sweet, high voices calling out. (And then Toby's, that had been surprisingly deep almost from the beginning. He never seemed like a baby. More like a very small man.) The three of them piling into the bed after their baths, the smell of baby shampoo, Ursula flinging her arms around Eleanor's neck, Alison (the one who hung back) smoothing her brother's wet curls, Toby twirling his ribbon in his ear, his small foot (the one with the webbed toes) stroking her own. Why did people think having a tidy home, or a quiet one, was such a great thing? To Eleanor, the sound of her family's voices was music. Even when they drowned out her own. Even when they drowned out her husband's.

She saw the two of them—herself and Cam—like two white-water rafters, off on class 5 waters. You didn't have time to debate your choices or question them once they were made. There was no space to think or even worry. You held on tight, paddled hard, and surrendered to the experience, hoping you'd make it to the spot, wherever it was, where you brought your craft into shore. But your heart beat so hard you thought your chest might explode. First you got wet. First the water swirled around you, tipped you over, or came close. You never knew if you'd make it, but you couldn't stop.

Eleanor was too consumed with children and work to consider her goals in life. (It continued to amaze Eleanor the way her friend Darla—even in the middle of a messed-up marriage—never lost sight of hers. She still spoke regularly about leaving Bobby, saving up for a deposit on a place of her own for her and Kimmie, and signing up for undertaker school, where all Eleanor could think of was getting through the day.)

Somebody always needed her. Food, bathroom, shoelaces, lost toys, Barbies, rocks, Band-Aids, unwanted dresses, volcano dioramas, insects, Legos, popcorn, sorrow. Joy again.

Come look. Come play. An event was not wholly real in her children's lives unless they'd told her about it, unless she'd borne witness.

She knew every inch of their bodies, but seldom gave thought to her own. And though she knew this was not how women should live their lives—devoting themselves solely to the care of babies and children, and particularly the women of her generation, who had challenged the old definition of a woman's role—she harbored an almost guilty pleasure concerning her love of caring for her children, to the exclusion—or the vast compromise, anyway—of her own sidelined dream of making art. And to the detriment of her marriage, probably.

These were not stories Eleanor explored in her *Family Tree* strip. She barely explored them in her own mind. Long ago, Eleanor had promised herself she'd never let a son or daughter of hers feel excluded the way she had. Instead, maybe, the one she relegated to last place was her husband. Somewhere along the way, she was losing sight of him. He was losing sight of her, too.

Maybe the problem went deeper than that. Maybe she had lost sight of herself.

24.

the Wieniawski Polonaise

From early on in their time together, Cam had told Eleanor that his brother, Roger Junior, was his parents' favorite. To Eleanor, the idea of feeling greater love for one of your children over the others was unimaginable. But it may also have been true of Toby that he inspired a particular brand of wild love unlike anything she'd known. He was wild himself, so much so that one time, at the end of her rope, she put him in the borning room and stuck a broom through the door handle to keep him from breaking it down.

"I'm having quiet time," she told him, as—through the door—he offered up that he'd be good from now on, for the rest of his life. He was weeping and so was she.

"I've reached my limit," she told him, as—thirty seconds later—she let him out.

"Poor Mama," he said, flinging his arms around her neck, licking the tears off her.

That summer, Eleanor had her best crop of tomatoes ever. In late August, she picked four bushels, with the plan of taking out the pressure cooker the next day to make a winter's worth of spaghetti sauce. The garden had yielded a good crop of basil, too. She set the tomatoes in baskets in the kitchen, planning to work on the sauce that afternoon when the day cooled off.

She left Cam in charge while she drove into town to buy canning jars. Even before she set foot in the house, she could feel—all the way out where she parked, by Cam's woodshop, that something had happened. Maybe it was the uncharacteristic stillness, the quiet.

One step into the kitchen and she saw it all, what looked at first like a crime scene. Her son had gotten into the tomatoes. It had probably started with a single one—a big, juicy Jet Star, maybe, or an

Early Girl, poised on the top of the overflowing basket calling out to him. He had probably only intended to fling that one tomato, but once he'd done this, the thrill of throwing it and the desire to keep going had been too much for him. By the time Eleanor stepped into the room, her four bushel baskets were empty. Tomato juice, tomato seeds, tomato skin covered the cupboard doors and walls. Her son stood there in the center of the room, his face containing, simultaneously, a look of rueful regret and ecstasy.

"I couldn't help it," he told her, shaking his head so his curls bounced wildly, his face like that of an angel.

Cam ambled into the house in the aftermath of the tomato disaster, his mellow demeanor unaltered. "Hey, buddy," he said, swinging Toby high over his head as Eleanor, on the floor, mopped up tomato seeds and skins. "Looks like you had yourself some fun." He stripped off his son's clothes, then his own, and stepped outside to turn on the sprinkler. From her place at the sink, wringing out the mop, she watched them dance. Her two darling redheads.

Toby had only recently turned three when he saw a show on television featuring a child prodigy violinist from China named Mei Mei Ling, playing a piece of music called the Wieniawski Polonaise. The moment Mei Mei set down his small violin, Toby told Eleanor he needed one of those.

The first time Toby mentioned his desire for a violin, she imagined it was probably a fleeting whim, though even then he was not prone to those. His passions were clear and abiding—snails and other crustaceans, rock collecting, long hours spent studying Tintin books, swimming in the brook down the road every chance he got, and chasing their boats of cork people downstream—and it had been Eleanor's experience that once Toby developed an interest, rather than diminishing, it only intensified.

In the case of his rock collecting, he filled his pockets daily with stones found on their property and, when they ventured out on hikes, beyond—so many rocks that the floor of his room was lined with specimens from his collection. The first thing Eleanor did now, before washing his pants, was to empty the pockets of that day's latest finds.

Likewise, he had a terrarium filled with snails, and knew all their names. On the seventeen-hour car trip they made once (once, and never again) to visit Cam's parents on Amelia Island, he had occupied himself for the entire drive with a library book about the species of snails found in South America.

He brought up the topic of the violin again that night when Eleanor put him to bed, and again at breakfast. He volunteered to sell his Troll collection—also, if necessary, his Ninja Turtles and Smurfs—as a way of earning money to buy the instrument. He promised to take on jobs. When they'd set out in the car later that day, to do errands, he asked Eleanor, "Are we going to get my violin now?"

In the end, they bought him a one-quarter-size instrument and signed him up for Suzuki lessons. Because Eleanor had no time to study with him, as she would have done in earlier days, Alison agreed to go to lessons with her brother and learn the violin alongside him. Within a couple of weeks he had surpassed her and she lost interest in the lessons, but it didn't matter. Toby was happy practicing alone.

His location of choice for doing this, on account of the acoustics in the room, evidently, was their bathroom—which was problematic, since they had only the one. Many times, when Toby had installed himself in the bathroom to work on his scales, one or another of them would end up hammering on the door needing to use the toilet.

"Come on in," he said. "I don't mind if you see me play."

He had books with sheet music for simple pieces, but found them insulting. "I want that one we saw on TV," he told Eleanor. Meaning the Wieniawski. Cam had located a recording of the piece (though not, as Toby would have preferred, performed by the child prodigy from China) at a store in Boston. Toby asked them to put the record on for him multiple times every day.

Sometimes now Eleanor would find him standing in front of the record player, listening, tossing his wild red hair like a conductor he'd seen on television one time, a look on his face of the most intense concentration.

Though his Suzuki teacher followed a conventional approach to learning the violin, Toby had developed his own method for mastering the particular piece of music he loved. From listening to the record he had worked out the first eight or ten notes of the Wieniawski. He played them over and over. Every day he tried adding two or three more notes.

Eleanor liked to stand in the bathroom doorway, just taking in the sight of him—her strange, miraculous, web-footed, red-haired son, whose fingers barely reached across the neck of the small violin.

He didn't seem to be aware of her presence. More often than not, at these moments, or when one of his sisters, having given up on privacy, came in to pee, Toby would keep playing his instrument while one of them sat on the toilet. Maybe he noticed. More likely he did not.

"Damn Wieniawski," Cam said one afternoon, coming in from the woodshop to the ever-present sound of Toby's practicing his piece.

"He'll either end up in Carnegie Hall or San Quentin," Eleanor said. One thing they knew, he would have a life like nobody else's.

Eleanor was in the garden, shoveling a load of manure onto her squash hills. Suddenly Cam was beside her.

"I thought you were giving the children a bath," she said.

"I took off their clothes and turned on the sprinkler," he said. "It accomplishes the same effect."

"We'd better get back to them," she said. It never took Toby long to find trouble.

"We'll go back," he said. "I just needed a moment."

She had a shovelful of manure in her hands. Dirt on her face no doubt. She was wearing her old overalls, and she must have smelled of cow manure. "What's the matter?"

"I just wanted you," he said.

He put his arms around her. He pulled off the bandanna she had used to hold her hair back. He pressed his mouth against hers and kissed her hard. A phrase came to her, something Sylvia Plath had written in her journal long ago, about the night she met the man she would marry, Ted Hughes—the father of her future children—describing how, that night, *he kissed me bang smash on the mouth and ripped my hairband off, my lovely red hairband.* That was how Cam kissed Eleanor that afternoon in the garden.

Eleanor knew the rest, of course. Sylvia Plath had babies. Ted Hughes had an affair. Sylvia Plath ended up with her head in the oven.

That wouldn't be Eleanor and Cam's story. Only the kissing part.

25.

sex in the air

Now that the children were getting older, Eleanor was taking on more freelance jobs. She missed spending days at her desk, making up stories and drawing pictures to illustrate them, but it had become clear, after her publisher declined to renew her contract, that she had better come up with a new way of meeting their expenses. Bodie's adventures traveling around the world, an orphan with a pet pig and a red suitcase, had got them a house, paid for Cam's woodshop, allowed her to stay at home, able to work in her pajamas all those years surrounded by her colored pencils. Once Eleanor had supposed she could keep doing that forever.

Now she just wanted to be sure the bills got paid every month. When there was something left over, she could buy Alison the insect book she wanted or take a trip to Santa's Land—a place Ursula had seen in a brochure and was crazy to visit. The truth was, most of their best times took place right here on the farm—putting on plays, making valentines, building snow forts in winter, sailing their boats with their homemade cork people every spring, and when it got warm enough, walking down to the falls every afternoon to jump in the swimming hole. You didn't need a lot of money for any of that.

By the time Alison reached first grade, and Ursula was enrolled in kindergarten, their lives had fallen into something resembling a routine. Toby went to day care four mornings a week (the fifth, Fridays, he stayed home with Eleanor). Friday nights, in winter, they went out for pizza, and on rare occasions—fewer and fewer of these—they left the children with Coco and took in a movie. Three nights a week, in softball season, they headed to the ball field.

Cam still had his woodworking projects, but, with strong encouragement from Eleanor, he had added a sideline: making hand-carved spoons. Four different craft shops carried them now, and though the income from sales never came to much, for the first time in their married life he had become a legitimate financial contributor.

But the primary responsibility for making the mortgage and taxes on their property still fell to Eleanor. She got to work most mornings by eight, as soon as the children left for school and day care, and she stayed focused on that till four, when the children got home. Then it was time to hear about everyone's day and get dinner on the stove while the girls worked on their homework and Toby stretched out on the floor, building tepees or showing her a new rock he'd found for his collection or teaching Sally a trick.

Standing at the stove, listening to the radio and the hum of children's voices around her, Eleanor could let the worries of her day evaporate, and not even the news that their house needed a new roof, or a letter from Toby's day care informing them of his most recent escapade, not even Cam's increasingly long absences at craft fairs as far as Portland, Maine, could shake her feeling about their life. Darla would talk forever about leaving Bobby. Patty, back in New York (her love affair with a sportscaster in Boston finished), was stressed out about not being made a partner in her ad agency, when so many less-qualified men had accomplished that. The women on the bleachers at Cam's softball games fantasized about a getaway to Hawaii or Florida, with or very possibly without their husbands: but for Eleanor, there was no other place she'd rather be than this one.

Before they ate, everyone held hands and sang grace—a Shaker song Eleanor had taught them, "Simple Gifts." But once it was over the meal took on the air of a happy free-for-all—Ursula offering up the news that Gina Olin had thrown up on the bus and some interesting fact she'd learned about her current passion, Iceland, or describing the outfit her glamorous kindergarten teacher, Miss Thibeault, had worn that day. (A purple velvet pantsuit! A monkey-print skirt with a shirt to match! Earrings shaped like unicorns!)

At this point Alison, who never had any patience for Ursula's fashion commentary, might lay out her options for an experiment she wanted to replicate that she'd read about in a book. Invariably one of them would spill their milk, at which point Cam might jump up from the table to suggest that maybe instead of refilling the glass, he should fix everyone a root beer float. Was it possible that Toby had never experienced one of those?

"Not until he finishes his dinner," Eleanor said. And then to Toby, "I don't want to see one single piece of broccoli on your plate, mister." At which point Toby would stick a piece into his ear.

"Broccoli all gone, Mama," he told her. Cam reached for the root beer.

Eleanor looked across the table to Cam. No need to say anything. Here was the one person on the planet who understood what they were doing here, what they had made. If, a minute later, Toby spilled his float, or stuck the straw into his nostril, or blew into it so hard that root beer poured out onto the table, as, very likely, he would, they might shake their heads in a kind of mock despair, but the truth was, they'd wanted this—this six-year-old daughter, bent over her Mandarin vocabulary book, her younger sister, drawing a picture of Miss Thibeault's amazing shoes, in this too-small kitchen with a too-large dog who invariably planted herself directly in the center of traffic where a wild red-headed boy now flung himself on top of her to bury his face in her fur.

Toby worshipped his sisters. Strong-minded as he was, he remained ready to submit to anything they wanted so long as they included him—dressing him up, pulling him in the wagon, assigning him roles in the plays they put on. His performances were wild, exuberant, anarchic. Even when caught in the act of doing something he'd been forbidden to do, as was true at this particular moment, when he upended a bowl of rice over his head, announcing a snowstorm, it was almost impossible for any of them to speak sternly to Toby. You tried to be mad, but ended up laughing.

When it was all over—and the children had had their baths, and the chapter from whatever book they were reading at the moment, or a game of Uno, and they were in bed, finally, the dog snoring by the woodstove—the two of them could stumble off to bed themselves, peel off their clothes, and drop onto the bed. If Cam no longer reached for Eleanor, or Eleanor for Cam—was that what mattered most anymore? They were lucky, Eleanor reminded herself. They loved each other. They lived on a beautiful farm at the end of a long dirt road near a waterfall. They had three healthy children. That most of all.

There was a rhythm to their lives now, marked by the seasons in part, and by everyone's ages—who needed naps, who needed diaper changes. (And then the great moment: nobody did anymore.) In winter, they stoked the woodstove and shoveled the car out, made valentines, stayed in their pajamas all day with a stack of library books. At the first sign of spring they made cork people. Then came softball season.

Eleanor looked forward to those games. Not so much for the games as for all the things that went along with the actual play—the pleasure in watching other people's children and how they'd grown since last year's season, the company of other women, the cold beer on a warm night. Three nights a week Eleanor packed sandwiches and drinks and Tupperware containers of Goldfish and animal crackers and headed out in the station wagon to the ball field. She never got tired of watching her husband standing out there on first base, his red curls spilling out from under his cap, his long arm reaching out for the ball with his lefty glove, the graceful way he ran when he made a hit, as he could usually be counted on to do. There were more powerful hitters on the team, but nobody could run like Cam.

Eleanor had been surprised to see Walt at the ball field that first night. He wasn't a player anymore, but he served as umpire for games. He knew the rules of softball better than the Pledge of Allegiance. He brought folding chairs for himself and Edith, when he could persuade her to get out of the car. Mostly she stayed in the front seat reading a magazine, or knitting.

And there was more going on than what took place on the field. High school girls selling hot dogs, a summer fundraiser for next year's class trip to Washington, D.C., and the boys who came to hang out there, talking about their cars and trying to impress the hot dog girls. Younger boys on lowrider bikes lolling by the fence, spitting in the dirt and passing around the headphones to somebody's Walkman. Older women of the town, selling Avon products or just come to watch the game. Maybe they used to be married to someone who played softball here once, but if so it was long ago.

From where Eleanor sat in the stands with the other players' wives, she could hear the crack of the bat against the ball, the men calling out to each other, sometimes approval, sometimes trash talk. The wives called out to them, too, sometimes: *Way to go, Rich. You've got this one, Timmy. See the ball, Bob.*

Then there was Coco, their neighbors Evan and Betsy's daughter—now their occasional babysitter, a long-legged teenager with golden skin and a ponytail that bobbed when she ran. Warm summer evenings in softball season, she and her girlfriends had taken to riding their bikes to games. Maybe in part because she was an only child of older parents, she liked spending time with Eleanor and Cam's family.

Eleanor had first met Coco on the night of Alison's birth, when she'd stopped by with her mother during the early stages of Eleanor's labor, bearing banana bread. Even back then, young as she was, there had always been something about Coco. When she showed up at the field, all the younger children looked up from playing in the dirt and clustered around her. They knew that she would do something thrilling—organize a play, or teach them cat's cradle or gymnastics moves. When Coco got into position to execute a cartwheel, all eyes on the stands moved from the ball game to the girl on the grass. The children worshipped Coco, of course, and the mothers loved how she kept the children entertained. "That girl's going to drive men crazy someday," Peggy Olin observed, watching her.

"Someday?" Bonnie Henderson said. "Try now."

That was the summer Coco taught Alison and Gina—daughter of Peggy and Bob—how to execute a cartwheel. Neither of them had been able to pull off the move the way Coco did, but they spent all July and August trying.

It seemed to Eleanor that Coco must have the longest legs of any fifteen-year-old ever. There was a glorious effortlessness to the way she tumbled across the field, one turn of her long, lithe body spinning into the next, with Alison and Gina alongside her, executing their own floppy versions of the move, and the younger children following behind like ducklings—leaping and tumbling—the sound of their voices high and joyful out beyond the third-base line.

"Have you ever seen a more amazing pair of legs?" Peggy said.

In the beginning of the season, Coco had only shown up at games now and then, but more and more as it progressed, she had become a nightly presence on the field, her ponytail whipping behind her when she ran.

"I think Coco's got a crush on you," Eleanor told Cam one evening as they pulled up to the ball field to see her standing next to her bike waiting for them. She appeared to be wearing mascara, which was new.

It had not escaped Eleanor's attention that every time Cam came up to bat, Coco stopped what she was doing to watch him.

"You're reading too much into it," Cam said. "She's just a lonely kid. Only child. You know the story."

"Just be aware of it," Eleanor said. "She admires you so much, and she's getting to that age. I'd hate to see her hurt."

There was this feeling, on softball nights—palpable as the crackling of mosquitoes landing on the bug zapper—of sex in the air: Women watching their men. Men performing as heroically as they could for their women. Their own, or somebody else's. Some nights, you could almost feel the heat coming off the field, of the women watching the men, or watching the other women.

Whoever it was who'd been chosen to be Timmy Pouliot's girlfriend that summer would be leaned against the fence, with a beer in her hand, away from the wives. When Timmy hit a home run, or just tagged home even, on a base hit, the girlfriend would plant a kiss on him and sometimes pat him on the butt. One time, when he made a home run, she jumped into his arms, and the kiss she gave him went on for a while.

Eleanor didn't feel this way herself, but a lot of the wives hated Timmy's girlfriends. Eleanor figured they were just jealous of a woman who still had her body, and time to apply polish to her toenails and run around on the back of a Harley.

"Did we ever look that good?" one of them asked, taking a long sip of Budweiser Light.

One night, Bonnie's husband, Jerry, hit a particularly well-timed home run that brought home three runners to win the game. As he rounded the last base and slid into home, Eleanor turned to Bonnie. "That's got to be the best feeling," she said.

Bonnie had tossed her head back and laughed.

"Second-best feeling, maybe," she said. There was pride in her voice, and maybe a certain awareness that among the assembled mothers there might not have been another who could have echoed the sentiment.

The women on the bleachers went strangely silent after that.

"You're too close to the parking lot," Eleanor called out to Toby. That was the thing about her life. She never had time to think about anything very long before somebody needed attention.

That night, driving home from the game, she decided once again that as soon as they got the children to bed, she and her husband would make love, but this time, the person who'd fallen asleep was Cam. And anyway, Toby had climbed in next to her. The hand that ended up on her breast that night was his.

26.

the amazing catch

The Yellow Jackets were playing a team from Franklin, one of the tougher competitors in their league. In the ninth inning, the team led by a single run, with the guys from Franklin getting the final at-bat and one of their best hitters on deck.

Out on the mound, the Yellow Jackets' pitcher, Rich McGann, threw a ball, followed by a strike, two more balls, another strike. The batter—the Franklin second baseman—positioned himself for the next pitch. Strike. Out.

Eleanor looked over at Cam, poised a few feet from the bag on first base, waiting to tag out an advancing runner. They had to keep the Franklin boys from scoring and make another two outs to win. It had been six years since that night in his Vermont cabin when he'd taken off his clothes so she could draw him. He still had a beautiful body.

Franklin's power hitter stepped up to the plate. Swung. They could hear the crack of the bat. Another few inches and he would have had a home run on his hands, but it was a foul. Strike one.

Another pitch. Another strike. Even Eleanor, who—even after all these summers—knew little about the game and mostly spent her time on the bleachers keeping an eye on her children, could tell from watching the batter that this was the kind of guy who, if he got his swing just right, could hit it to the far end of the field.

On the third pitch, he did just that. Even the two-year-olds, gathered around Coco as she handed out Rice Krispies treats, looked up from the dirt at the sound of the wood smacking the ball. Eleanor shaded her eyes from the sun to watch as it sailed over the outfield.

Then came an amazing moment. Harry Botts, the player who had never once in his seven years on the team actually made a catch, ran toward the spot where the ball was arcing down. Harry had a funny, loping run—not particularly fast—and his arm, as he reached out with his glove, seemed like a wet and floppy noodle. The way he held out his arm, he looked not so much like a ballplayer as he did a person going for a jog and checking the sky for rain first, to see if he needed to take his umbrella.

He caught it. More accurately, maybe, the ball landed in Harry's glove.

The Yellow Jackets went crazy. So did the wives and girlfriends on the bleachers. Nobody could believe what had just happened, including Harry Botts.

He stood there, frozen, in the middle of the field, still holding on to the ball and shaking his head.

"I caught the ball," he said. "I can't believe I caught it."

Harry just stood there. He was still gazing at the ball, still looking stunned. His teammates were calling out to him to field the ball to second base for a double play. Harry just stood there.

"Throw to second, Harry," someone called out. Everyone did.

But Harry Botts just stood there. You couldn't even be mad at him. He was just so amazed at what he'd done, it did not occur to him.

The other team scored, but the Yellow Jackets cheered for Harry anyway.

27.

Hawaii Ho

Labor day again. Cam and Eleanor's annual potluck. The Hendersons came, and Sal and Lucinda Perrone with their son, Josh, the Olins with their two girls, Katie and Gina. Harry Botts—always alone. Ray and Timmy Pouliot, on their motorcycles.

Walt and Edith came, of course—Walt bearing his cider press and a bushel of Cortlands for the children to run through the press. Coco's parents, Evan and Betsy, showed up, and their neighbors Simon and Tilda, who lived in the geodesic dome down the road, though like every other Buckminster Fuller follower they knew who'd constructed one, they'd had a "For Sale by Owner" sign out front almost since they'd built it.

"You know how hard it is to put furniture or hang pictures in a house with no right angles and no normal walls?" Tilda said. They were hoping to move to Oregon, but nobody wanted to live in a geodesic dome anymore.

Darla came without Bobby, which was fine with Eleanor. She still couldn't understand why Darla stayed with her husband.

That night she showed up with a black eye, which she told everyone came from walking into a door.

"I'm just waiting for the right moment," Darla told Eleanor. The familiar line. "I just need a little more housecleaning money in the kitty to make my getaway."

Eleanor no longer made any comment when Darla said this.

The Labor Day blowout was a potluck—everyone bringing a casserole or a pan full of grilled potato skins or a pot of chili, buffalo wings, tacos, and in Edith's case, a deadly-looking meat loaf made with Hamburger Helper. After everyone went home, Eleanor set it out for Sally, but she wasn't interested.

That year, Eleanor had taken her party theme inspiration from a feature in *Family Circle,* "Aloha! How to Throw Your Own Backyard Luau." She hung paper lanterns with white lights across the yard and followed the recipes for coconut shrimp and pineapple upside-down cake, and though Cam told her that really, the guys would just as soon have beer, she mixed piña coladas in the blender. Toby had got his hands on the mix and downed a whole blender full—before they'd added the liquor, fortunately.

She had checked a record out of the library—Don Ho, *Hawaii-Ho!* When the sun went down, the garden was illuminated with tiki lights. Still carrying an extra ten pounds of the baby weight from Toby, she chose a loose, muumuu-style dress. Cam went shirtless that night, looking as fit as he had been the night she first went back to his little cabin in Brattleboro. Lucinda Perrone—with her husband, Sal, the only ones among their guests who appeared to have noted the Hawaiian theme—had shown up wearing a grass skirt and a bikini top. Sal wore a shirt he'd bought at a Jimmy Buffett show.

At some point in the evening, Eleanor observed Lucinda, piña colada in hand, laughing with Ray Pouliot by the big ash tree. She was demonstrating her hula moves, tossing her hair, touching his arm. Eleanor found Sal, in his too-bright parrot and hibiscus shirt, sitting by himself at the edge of the field, studying the moon. He'd probably consumed more than a few beers. He sat hunched with another cold one in his hand.

"You tell me," he said when she approached him. "What do women want these days, anyway? I try to be a good husband, but I can never please my wife."

"I'm sorry," she said.

"We hardly ever talk to each other, except about who's going to pick up the kids. All we do is watch TV."

Eleanor didn't know what to say, so she just sat there. Sometimes the only thing you could do was listen.

"I try to make her happy," Sal said. "She had her heart set on Disney, so we took the kids. The middle of July when it was a hundred degrees in Florida, standing in line at some ride so you can sit in a boat watching mechanical pirates. I'll be working overtime all year to pay for it. And every night, back at the hotel, she was telling me all the ways I disappoint her. I'm not exciting enough. I should go to the gym."

Eleanor knew all about the Disney trip. Lucinda had sent her a postcard from Orlando. "Joshie threw up on Big Thunder Mountain Railroad," she wrote. "Greta pitched a fit because we wouldn't buy her a Snow White costume that cost sixty dollars. Goofy gave Jessica a hug and she burst into tears. Sal and I aren't speaking to each other."

"She says I'm not romantic," Sal said. "One of her girlfriends' husbands gave her a diamond pendant for her birthday. Nothing I do ever surprises her."

"It's a different kind of romantic, being dependable," Eleanor said. Her voice was quiet.

"Lu and I hardly ever have sex anymore," he told her. "She's always too tired."

"It's not so easy, after a long day with the kids." The picture came to Eleanor of Cam, reaching for her as he had a couple of nights back. How she had pretended she was sleeping. "I understand where she's coming from."

"You know how I would have liked to spend that vacation?" he said. "In a tent in Maine, cooking over a fire. Sleeping under the stars with my wife next to me."

The two of them sat on the grass, far enough from the pit where Cam was grilling lamb kebabs that the smoke wouldn't get in their eyes. Eleanor and Lucinda Perrone had a superficial kind of friendship, from years of having each other's children over to play, and softball nights, but the truth was that Eleanor had never liked Lucinda. Still, she understood how easy it could be, when you had kids, for two people to lose track of each other. There they'd been, all of them, back in their twenties, going to Grateful Dead shows in Vermont and reading *The Joy of Sex,* or just having a lot of it. There was a time when even Lamaze classes had felt sexy.

Now there were all these children to show for it. And they'd forgotten what got them there in the first place.

Eleanor and Sal sat there for a while, looking out at the old ash tree and the field beyond it, taking in the night peepers, the distant sound of Don Ho singing "Tiny Bubbles" and Coco teaching the dance that was Toby's current obsession, the Moonwalk, to the younger children. (When had her body filled out this way? All those Friday nights, paying her for babysitting, Eleanor hadn't noticed, but suddenly, in addition to those long legs of hers they'd all observed, softball summers, cartwheeling along the perimeter of the ball field, she had these breasts. Now Eleanor found herself staring at them.)

There was a full moon that night. The children who were still awake were roasting marshmallows, Evan had taken out his guitar. To anyone dropping by, this could look like a perfect scene—the kind Eleanor used to imagine other families besides hers engaged in, back when she was growing up, the kind she had wanted to create with Cam. Only there was Sal's wife, whispering something to Ray Pouliot, Ray nodding his head as if she'd made the most amazing observation ever, and here was Sal Perrone confessing to Eleanor (as he never would have if he hadn't drunk all those beers) that sometimes, late at night, he sat out in the garage smoking pot and looking at old issues of *Penthouse*.

"That's my sex life," he said. "Sitting on a camp chair, fantasizing about some Miss November from 1968."

Eleanor felt no attraction to Sal, but she could see how easy it might be, at a moment like this one, to imagine that some person other than the one you were married to might provide the answer to your difficulties. There was Sal, doggedly bringing home the paycheck, as Cam never had. There was Lucinda, hanging on the words of Ray Pouliot. There was Walt, cranking the mill on the cider press and Edith telling him he was doing it wrong—Walt, so often there when Cam was not.

And once again, Eleanor didn't know where Cam was. No place in sight.

Off in the field, where Coco had organized a game of moonlight tag, she heard Toby's voice rising above those of the others. Something about dog poop, followed by the sound of another child—Joshie Perrone, maybe, who was always a crybaby and a tattletale. She figured she had better investigate. Toby could get into trouble faster than any child she'd ever known. She found him on a branch in Old Ashworthy. He said he was pretending he was an owl.

It was late when the last of the guests left—sleeping children in their arms, most of them—leaving a mountain of dishes to wash, the leftovers to wrap up and put away. To Eleanor, the best part always came after, when they got to take off their clothes and climb into bed. Eight years into marriage, they might not have sex so often anymore, but they pressed up next to each other.

"Lucinda Perrone is going to leave Sal," Eleanor said.

"She told you that?"

"I can just tell."

"Let's never let that happen to us," Cam said. He pulled her toward him. "The children would never get over it." He put a hand on her breast.

"Remember what these used to look like?" she said. "This is what nursing three babies does."

"I don't care about that," he told her. She took note of the fact that he didn't contradict her assessment of her breasts. Just said it didn't matter, what had become of them.

"They fed our children," he said. "That's the important thing."

A wave of sadness passed over Eleanor. But something else, too. Acceptance, maybe. This was what happened. What had happened to them, at least. Some things disappeared, but in their absence, there was this strange and deep bond that came in part, probably, from the knowledge of their mutual disappointments. *Here we are,* she thought. Under this roof, at the end of this road, living this life.

The rest of the world fell away then, and it was just the two of them on the bed. Just the two of them, until sometime in the middle of the night when one or another or even all three of their children padded into the room to climb in next to them.

But for this one middle-of-the-night moment, they could be alone together in the dark, nothing but the sound of an owl—a real one this time, perched in the high branches of the giant tree, just beyond the window. Out the window, that long, mournful cry. A moment later, from some other tree, some other owl—his mate, perhaps—called back in response.

28.

the no-cry pledge

Winters were hard at the end of their long dirt road. Cold mornings, car battery dead. Icy roads. Short days. The long process, every time you left the house with the children, of zipping up the snowsuits, finding mittens, hats, scarves, boots. It was a safe bet that by the time they were all dressed, someone would need to go to the bathroom, and all the gear would have to come off again. Then came the task of hanging up the wet clothes, drying out the boots, mopping. "Sometimes it feels like all I do, from November through March, is mop the floor," Eleanor told Darla. Times like these, she allowed herself to dream, briefly, of what it might be like to live in a place like California. Only briefly. She knew she would never leave the farm.

When the weather was on their side—cold temperatures, no snow—Eleanor loaded the children into the car and went looking for a pond, then laced up the children's skates. They put a low wooden chair on the ice for Toby to push, and sometimes Ursula set him in the chair and pushed him around the ice. One time Eleanor brought out a boom box and put on a cassette of old Beatles songs, but the cold must have affected the batteries, so the songs started playing slower and slower, turning Paul McCartney's voice very low, and the guitars weirdly off-key. Cam was a beautiful skater, whipping past them on the ice with his hockey stick, scooping Ursula up in his arms and taking her for a spin. "I'm flying," she cried out, her arms spread wide, as if she were embracing the whole sky. She knew her father would never drop her.

For Eleanor, there was little opportunity for tearing across the ice, if she even managed to get out there. She would no sooner have everyone's hats and mittens assembled and skates laced up than Toby would need to go to the bathroom or Alison would say she was too cold. They'd head back to the house for popcorn and hot chocolate then, and reruns of *The Love Boat* or a movie on their newly acquired VCR—*Herbie Goes to Monte Carlo. Old Yeller.* Disney in your own living room! Imagine.

Even with the stove cranked up, it was hard keeping the house warm, especially upstairs where the children slept. Every night, twenty minutes before she put them to bed, Eleanor filled three hot water bottles to put under the covers so no matter how cold the room was, it would be warm when they climbed into bed. In bed—seldom late; most nights they were worn out by nine thirty—she wrapped her arms around Cam's hard, firm chest, felt his heart beating. Now was the time—the only one, often—when they could talk about their day.

"Do you think we should be worried about how much time Toby spends lining up rocks in his room?" she'd say. "Sometimes when I talk to him while he's playing, he doesn't even hear me. You don't think he could be autistic, do you?"

"I think you're worrying too much," Cam said. "Get some sleep."

"What do you think it means that Alison threw out that dress your mother sent for her birthday?"

"You have to admit, it was a pretty ugly dress," he told her. He was not prone to analyzing every aspect of what went on in their children's world the way Eleanor did.

"How about we focus on you and me for a change?" he said, pulling her close.

"The dress wasn't really that ugly," Eleanor told him.

They worked on craft projects a lot, in winter, and baked—cookies, muffins, bread. When they started to go stir-crazy, Eleanor piled the children in the station wagon and headed for the bowling alley, the one big attraction in town, other than the dump. A couple of games for the four of them—plus shoe rentals—wasn't cheap, but sometimes, particularly when the temperature had been hovering around zero for three days straight, they all just needed to get out of the house.

The one problem with bowling was Toby. As the youngest and

smallest, it was not surprising that he had a harder time than his sisters knocking the pins over. But his pride made it unacceptable for him—even at age four, even at three—to accept the idea of using bumpers to keep his ball from ending up in the gutter every time his turn came up.

Inevitably, he'd end up the low scorer. Then came the heartache. More than once, a happy afternoon at the bowling alley would conclude with Toby flinging his body on the floor in the spot they'd just tallied up their points, like a mourner on a funeral pyre. Inconsolable.

In the end, Eleanor had instituted a tradition in which each of them was required to recite what she called the No-Cry Pledge—a two-sentence promise to stay calm, whatever the outcome of the game, written on the sun visor of her station wagon, which she'd flip down for the occasion before they entered the bowling alley. Of the four of them, only Toby was at risk of falling apart over a losing score (and it was Toby who lost every time). But all of them, including Eleanor, recited the pledge. Toby took his vow seriously. He never had another tantrum at the bowling alley.

There was one good thing about winters, particularly the hardest ones. When the cold finally lifted, and spring came, you'd be left with a greater sense of joy than any resident of California or Florida could understand or appreciate. Then it was time to make cork people. Then the leaves on the ash tree unfurled and the lady's slippers pushed up through the soil and burst out their strange, vaguely sexual, purselike blossoms. The air filled with the smell of lilac, which always reminded Eleanor of the first time she'd driven down this road. Ursula picked a basketful of blossoms and laid them on her pillow, so she could breathe in the smell all night long. Toby dug for earthworms and tried teaching them tricks. They launched their boats. Home again, after, they grieved the losses of the cork people who didn't make it all the way down the brook and set the survivors on a high shelf until next year's launch. A reminder that hard as winter might be, spring always came. Just when you reached your limit.

Then it was time to plant the peas. Then it was softball season again.

29.

sometimes even breast milk isn't enough

That was the year Eleanor and Cam built the pond.

They'd been talking about this for years. Every afternoon in warm weather, the five of them walked to the waterfall (four, if Cam was off on his mountain bike or at softball practice), and sometimes they brought their poles to fish downstream, but it wasn't a place for young children to swim—the water too rough and swirling, the stones too sharp.

A few months before, Eleanor had sold an article to a women's magazine. It was a story about Alison's decision, when she was six, to stop answering to any name but Little Joe. She had fallen in love with the character played by Michael Landon on *Bonanza* reruns on Nickelodeon. For her birthday that year, all she wanted was a pair of cowboy boots.

It was a funny story. "Your daughter has some imagination," one of the softball wives had observed.

Because the money felt like a windfall, Eleanor and Cam used it to hire a backhoe. For ten days straight, Buck Hollingsworth, the Yellow Jackets catcher, had shown up at their place every morning at seven to dig out the pond site.

Alison found the machine too noisy and stayed in her room a lot during this period, working on a scale model of the *Titanic,* but Ursula and Toby were transfixed by the process. They sat on the grass for hours every day watching Buck work, and when he asked if they'd like to come up in the cab with him and help operate the machine, Toby looked as if the doors of heaven had just opened. Ursula, always the caretaker, yielded her time in the cab of the backhoe so her brother could stay there longer, working the controls with Buck.

After the hole was finished and Buck made his way down the driveway that last day, Toby looked as bereft as if he'd lost his best friend.

In the days that followed, the water began to fill the hole, frogs appeared out of nowhere, and the dirt turned to the most wonderful mud, and for the rest of the summer, all any of them wanted to do was play in it. Even Alison—though she was always quieter and more reserved—slathered the rich dark goop over her legs and arms and face and lay in the sun till it dried. Once the water got deep enough, they all jumped in the beginnings of their pond. Self-conscious about her body, even when very young, Alison kept her swimsuit on, but Ursula and Toby spent much of that summer naked in the mud. Just about the only time they put on clothes was when they all piled into the car to attend one of Cam's softball games.

Eleanor and Peggy Olin had one of those friendships formed through children. The fact that Peggy's daughter, Gina, was older than Alison and Ursula, conferred a certain authority. Peggy regularly advised Eleanor on which kindergarten teacher she favored and where to get winter boots at the best price. Other than Bonnie Henderson's bulletins on her sex life, no deep exchanges occurred on the bleachers at Yellow Jackets games. But for a few summers there, Eleanor regarded Peggy as her closest friend, after Darla.

Then one day—late May, black fly season—Peggy was absent from the bleachers, Bob gone from the field, and one of the other wives told them the news: Peggy and Bob's daughter Gina—the child raised on brown rice and tofu—had been diagnosed with a rare form of cancer.

The team took up a collection. Someone suggested a bake sale and someone else passed around a card for all the team members and wives to sign. Peggy and Bob were driving to Boston that weekend to consult with a specialist at Dana-Farber. Then they were going to Johns Hopkins. St. Jude's. Then they were visiting some clinic in Arizona.

By Fourth of July weekend, with no word from Peggy, Eleanor knew she should call. But every time she began dialing their number, the thought of what she might hear about Gina's condition made her stop.

Here was the awful truth about being a parent. From the moment of your children's births, you did all these things to protect them. You made your own baby food; you checked to make sure the fabric of their pajamas wasn't flammable and there was the correct space between the bars of the crib. When, in your second pregnancy, you read about a rare disease contracted from cat feces in a litter box, you got rid of your cat.

You read the books all the experts had written, and you followed their advice. Sometimes, in the middle of the night, when one of your children was sick, you stepped quietly into the room where they slept, to listen to their breathing.

And still, there was no protecting them. You could burn every spinning wheel in the kingdom—the image that haunted Eleanor, when she rented *Sleeping Beauty* from the video store—and still, the fair-haired princess in your care could prick her finger and fall into that deep and terrible sleep.

Look at Gina Olin. Breastfed until age four. Bald now, from the chemotherapy.

All that summer, Bob Olin still presided over the outfield, but his daughter's illness had changed him. He seemed to run after the balls with a kind of manic ferocity absent in previous seasons, as if everything wrong in his life, which was just about everything, might be obliterated if he could just connect his glove with that one line drive coming his way. Men were supposed to protect their families, at all costs. But how was he supposed to protect his child against attack from inside her own body?

Peggy still brought Gina to games sometimes. She was in a wheelchair now, her body thin as a leaf, her eyes glazed. Toby offered her a mozzarella stick one evening, but she just looked at him as if he came from a whole different planet. Or she did. There was a look on her face as if she saw things nobody else did. She was floating high above the ball field. More like a cloud than a person.

Word on the bleachers was that Peggy and Bob had brought their daughter to see a healer in Quebec who was said to cure hopeless cases by touching a person's forehead and placing a drop of a special water on their tongue, but when they got back, Gina was weaker than ever. By August, Peggy must have lost ten pounds. She wore the same clothes every game, and seemed to have given up brushing her hair. They'd discontinued chemotherapy by now, on the advice of the doctors, who'd told the Olins to bring their daughter home and make her as comfortable as possible. Bonnie Henderson told Eleanor that Peggy had approached one of the younger wives on the team, who was due to give birth any minute, about getting a vial of her breast milk for Gina once she delivered, to boost Gina's immune system. To the women on the bleachers, her quest sounded crazy, but what else could she do? How was a mother supposed to give up trying to save her child's life?

The others—the ones with healthy children—sat quiet, watching, vowing to never again complain about rowdy four-year-olds or six-year-olds who wouldn't finish their sandwiches. Eleanor was one of these. Looking at the pale, shrunken form of Gina Olin in her sticker-bedecked wheelchair, with a Cabbage Patch doll propped up in her lap, she made a silent promise to herself that she would ask for nothing, ever again, but that her children stay healthy and safe.

This was the terrible part of being a parent. The more you loved, the more you had to lose. It might as well be your own heart the pitcher was firing off toward the plate, hovering out in midair, ready for some bat to smash into it. Once you had a child you were never safe again.

Gina died that August. When Eleanor told the children, Alison fell silent for a minute, then opened her homework. Ursula flung herself on the couch, weeping. Toby wanted to know where they were going to put her body, and what would happen to her soul.

Later that night, in bed—Toby pressed up against her body on one side, Cam on the other, the sound of their son's breathing a soothing presence in the darkened room—Eleanor lay awake looking out the window at the moonlight, coming through the branches of Old Ashworthy. Somewhere off in the woods she heard the barking of a dog, and farther away, a howling that sounded like a pack of coyotes.

She pressed her face against Cam's chest.

"You awake?"

"I am now," he said.

"Let's always remember today," she said. "How much we have. How lucky we are. Having this family. Living here. Being together."

"Sounds good," Cam told her. He was only half awake.

"I don't need one more thing," she whispered. "Just this."

By September the hole Bud Hollingsworth had dug for them, at the hopeful start of summer, was nearly filled with water. They had a pond. That winter they skated on it, and the next spring, as if by magic, tadpoles appeared. Cam and Eleanor still brought the children to the waterfall most afternoons to take in the sight and sound of that roaring water, but they swam now in their own family pond. They named it Tadpole Lake and planted lupine along the sunny side from seeds they'd gathered on a camping trip to Maine.

That Labor Day, on the day that would have been their annual softball team potluck, Cam and Eleanor attended Gina Olin's memorial service. "If there's anything I can do," Bonnie Henderson offered, that day at the church. They all knew there wasn't.

Home again, standing at the kitchen counter, looking out the window at the pond, the tree, the garden below, Eleanor could almost feel her heart expand in her chest. Two sensations came to her. Wild happiness at the sight of her three children, terror at the thought of what it would be to lose one of them. If it was possible to love someone any more than this, she could not imagine how.

30.

Barbie shoe

Maybe it was knowing all the enormous things outside of her control as a parent that contributed to Eleanor's obsession with the small ones. Cancer was a rogue villain. But there were problems of a scale Eleanor could handle (and therefore, tried to fix): lost toys, birthday party invitations that failed to arrive, sorrow when the bottom of the box of Cracker Jacks fails to yield the particular miniature whistle your child was hoping for. The look of sorrow on Alison's face when the ride she loved—small boats going around in circles at the annual Foliage Festival—came to a halt. Another ticket cost a quarter. Who wouldn't buy it?

Cam, probably. "You worry too much," he told her. "You can't make everything right all the time."

When was the moment her obsession took hold, to spare her children the pain of loss? As if any parent could do that. As if it would be a good thing, if she could.

Eleanor knew the reasons for her own inability to endure her children's small losses. In her life as a mother, she was rewriting her childhood—creating, for the children she and Cam were raising, the one she didn't get to have herself. Somewhere along the line—here came trouble—she ceased to notice her own sorrows, she was so busy attempting to protect her children from theirs.

Opening the presents at her sixth birthday party, Ursula received, from Emily Finster, the gift of Crystal Barbie—the one that came with clear plastic shoes like Cinderella's glass slippers.

"Let's put those shoes up on the shelf till your guests have gone home," Eleanor advised her. But Ursula wanted to carry those shoes around with her all afternoon, until the terrible moment (or what used to qualify as a terrible moment, in the world as they knew it then) when she realized one of the shoes was gone. Somewhere—in a house filled with ripped-up wrapping paper and ribbon, paper plates and half-eaten cake and melted ice cream and candle wax and party favors and three different guests' allergy medicine and little baskets of M&M's and melted M&M's that fell out of the little baskets and Joshie Perrone complaining that Emily got a bigger piece of cake than he did, somewhere a Barbie shoe lay hidden. And here was Ursula, good, patient Ursula, who always wrote thank-you notes and emptied the dishwasher without being asked and looked out for her friends and her siblings before herself and never did anything unkind; here was Ursula, sitting in the middle of her birthday party, weeping inconsolably over the loss of a clear plastic Barbie shoe the size of the nail on her pinky finger.

After the other children went home—the mothers who picked them up lingering less than normal, on account of the birthday girl's unprecedented meltdown—Eleanor had ripped the house apart to locate the shoe. She took cushions off the furniture, crawled under the table, poured the trash onto the kitchen floor, picking through ketchup-smeared French fries and frosting, in search of the lost shoe. Observing the scene, Cam had put a hand on her shoulder, briefly. "Do you really think this is necessary?" he said, before retreating. There was a game on. The Red Sox vs. the Yankees.

At some point in the afternoon—Eleanor having moved to the children's bedroom upstairs in her search for the shoe—the balance between sanity and madness shifted as clearly as if the two main characters in the drama sat on opposite sides of a teeter-totter. Ursula had become the calm, reasonable one; it was Eleanor who'd gone crazy—whipping off bedsheets, upending the laundry basket, all in her quest for the Barbie shoe, while Ursula, her tears gone, watched uneasily, offering up soft, gentle supplications. *It's okay, Mom. I didn't need it after all. I like it when Barbie goes barefoot.*

Too late now. Without a single drop of Jack Daniel's in her, Eleanor had crossed over into that old familiar country of her childhood, Crazyland. She was tearing around the house now, as if the only thing separating her child from heartbreak was whether or not she'd succeed in locating the Barbie shoe.

Door to the liquor cabinet thrown open. Then other cupboard doors. Every one in their kitchen, but she had moved on to the pantry—her father's voice in her brain: Where did you put the damned olives, Vivian? Is it too much to ask when a man comes home from a long day at the office that there'll be the makings of a martini waiting for him?

Still no Barbie shoe. An hour after she'd started her search, every room in their house had been ripped apart—the kitchen, also the bathroom, and the porch.

Sometime after dark, Eleanor found the shoe on the windowsill. "Oh, I put it there so it wouldn't get lost," Ursula told her—her face revealing a level of fear greater than what might be attributed to the loss of a plastic object. This was about her mother appearing, briefly, to lose her mind.

"I forgot."

Eleanor placed the shoe in her daughter's hand and collapsed on the sofa. Off in the doorway, beer in hand, her husband had observed it all unfolding but he kept his eye on the game.

"I'm sorry," she told him. "I don't know what got into me."

He put his arms around her.

"I couldn't stand it. Thinking about Ursula being sad on her birthday. When the real thing that probably made her sad was me."

"You were just trying to make everything perfect," he said. "But it won't ever be that way. Our children have to get used to that."

"If anything really terrible ever happened to one of our children, I couldn't survive," Eleanor told him.

"Hard things will happen," Cam told her. "They always do. It's called life."

Eleanor wondered whether there was such a thing as loving your children too much. Maybe her problem was caring too deeply, knowing that because this was so, her love probably felt suffocating and oppressive to them. They might not have said as much, or even acknowledged this to themselves, but she imagined there were times when Alison, at least, probably hated her mother for how much she did, how hard she tried, and above all, how she suffered their pain—sometimes even before they'd had a chance to experience it themselves.

There was an afternoon that fall, at Alison's T-ball game. Watching her daughter on the bench, waiting her turn at bat, Eleanor had recognized that Alison needed to pee, but wasn't going to risk missing her turn to do something about it.

Eleanor could tell, even as it was happening, the exact moment when, seated on the bench, awaiting her at-bat, Alison wet her pants. Alison's back was to her, but Eleanor could imagine the look of horror on her face.

It was her turn now to step up to the plate. There would be a yellow stain on her uniform. Everyone would know.

Eleanor didn't even need to think about what to do next. She leapt up from her seat on the bleachers, a few feet away, grabbing the Coca-Cola of the mother sitting next to her. She moved toward the bench, crossing directly in front of Alison with the open can—positioned herself, awkwardly, directly in front of her daughter, at which point she appeared to trip, spilling the contents of the can as she went down. She spilled it, with exquisitely precise aim, directly on the crotch of Alison's pants, so the only stain you could see there now was the one made by the Coke.

"Jeez, Mom," Ali had said, looking down—her tone one of utter and complete disdain. "Could you be any more of a klutz?"

How could they understand? Not having grown up as Eleanor had, with parents who cared too little rather than too much, it was easy for her children to feel impatient with their mother, and to favor the effortless no-strings affection their father provided. If Cam was less likely to make sacrifices for his children, this was probably, in their eyes, nothing but a relief. When a person gave less, he required less in return.

31.

a career in dry-cleaning

When she started drawing her strip about their life on the farm, Eleanor never pictured anyone actually reading it. (Well, Walt did. And Darla. But that was about it.) Telling her stories had been like having a conversation with herself, a journal that she happened to publish in the local paper.

As the months passed she started tackling tougher topics—the difficulty of getting through Mother's Day without her mother, the time Cam forgot her birthday. (All day she'd been waiting for something to happen, figuring he must have a surprise in store for her, but it turned out the date had slipped his mind. The drawing she'd made to illustrate that part in the story had shown a lanky man with long curls coming out the sides of his baseball cap, slapping his forehead when he realizes his mistake, with a bubble over his head that read, "Maybe I can get the date tattooed on my forearm before next year.")

After that strip appeared in the paper, his fellow softball team members had given Cam a hard time. "You made us all look pretty bad, man," Jerry Henderson told him. At the hardware store, replacing a drill bit, the guy behind the counter had suggested he bring home a gift for his wife along with the drill bit he'd just bought. A hummingbird feeder, maybe? A pair of flower-print gardening gloves?

"You've got a lot to make up for with that gal," he said. "And if you don't mind the suggestion"—now came a reference to an earlier *Family Tree* installment—"don't bring her any more weed whackers." That had been his birthday present to Eleanor the previous year, later memorialized in her strip.

Until now, it had not occurred to Eleanor that Cam might take issue with her telling stories about their life. The kinds of things she wrote about were the kind that happened to most people. What was the big deal? And anyway, she doubted that Cam read her strip.

She had been drawing her *Family Tree* strip for almost five years when she got a call from a newspaper syndicate in New York. Someone there had become aware of the strip and felt Eleanor's work could reach a broader audience. Would she be interested in having them pitch *Family Tree* to papers around the country?

By the time Toby entered nursery school, Eleanor's stories about Maggie and her family were running each week in over fifty newspapers nationwide—a milestone Eleanor marked by buying herself a real drawing table. Every month now, Eleanor collected a check for a couple of thousand dollars. They weren't rolling in money, but it was more than she'd made since the days of her Bodie books, long out of print.

No similar breakthrough occurred in the world of hand-crafted burl bowls, but now that Eleanor was making such good money, she didn't worry about that so much. The hard part was finding time to work. She still got up before sunrise to write and draw, and if she was lucky, and nobody was home sick, and it wasn't a snow day, she had the hours the children spent at school—just half days for Toby—to work at her drawing table. But she suggested that Cam might pitch in a little more.

"So the idea is, your work is more important than mine now, because they pay you the big bucks?" he said. There was an edge to his voice that she hadn't heard before, a look that reminded her of times during his parents' infrequent visits, sitting in the kitchen with Roger and Roberta, as they recounted the accomplishments of his brother out in Texas. Cam would pour himself a glass of Jack Daniel's then (a rare event) and sit across from them, whittling some piece of wood into no particular shape, saying nothing.

What she heard from him now wasn't anger so much. He wasn't disputing her position. Eleanor would never have imagined that Cam was the sort whose ego would be wounded at the idea of his wife supporting the family, but maybe she was wrong about that.

"I'm not saying my work is more important than yours," Eleanor told him. "I just need a little more help."

She spoke the words in a quiet, even tone of voice, but she could feel an edge of bitterness creeping in that hadn't been there before. Later, scrubbing potatoes for dinner, she reflected on how women spoke about domestic responsibilities, compared to the language their husbands employed. Eleanor couldn't imagine any of the mothers she knew speaking of "helping" their husband with the housework or "babysitting" their own children.

"Did it ever occur to you," she had asked him, as she was packing the snacks for a night at the softball field to watch her husband play, "that I might like to go off and do something fun, too?"

"I never knew you played softball," he said. He stood behind her, his arms on her shoulders. He was stroking her neck. "You'd be an improvement on Harry Botts, anyway. And definitely cuter."

"I wish you wouldn't make this a joke, Cam," she told him. "You know what I mean."

"Listen, Ellie," he said. "Anytime you want to take up some kind of hobby or pastime, I'll be a hundred percent behind you."

"Somebody around here has to earn a living," she told him.

His face, when she said that, reminded her of Toby's, the day she sent him to his room for picking every one of the squash blossoms in her garden, before they turned into squash. All she wanted to do, seeing that expression of sorrow and remorse, was reassure him.

"It's okay," she said. "We're fine. You do other things."

Maybe it was getting to Cam that his father, Roger, off in Florida, still expressed concern about the unlikelihood of his son ever making a decent living selling wooden bowls. Cam's mother, Roberta, had never had a paying job, though in Eleanor's estimation, taking care of Cam's father was a full-time occupation. Roger had recently reminded his son, for the third time, of his willingness to bankroll a business of some kind for Cam to manage in Akersville. A dry-cleaning establishment, possibly. There was good money to be made. Maybe not as much as Roger Junior took in, with his real estate development firm, but enough that he could pull his own weight and sock something away for retirement.

"Thanks, Dad," Cam told his father. "But dry-cleaning isn't my thing. Besides, Eleanor and I like the work we do."

It ended there, but not really.

The only times Eleanor had ever seen, in her husband, evidence of anything like melancholy were these—visits with his parents, and more so, after they left. Sometimes, after one of their rare phone conversations, he'd disappear into the woodshop and be gone for hours. His parents' annual holiday trip north for Christmas could plunge Cam into a daylong silence.

After his parents had driven away the last time—when Roger had raised the dry-cleaning idea—he'd headed out on a hike. Normally, at least one of the children would have accompanied him, but this time they could all sense it: he didn't want company.

It was hours later when he returned. The children were watching a video, Eleanor just about to put the lasagna in the oven. One look at his face, as he walked in the door, and she put her arms around him.

"I'm sorry," he told her. "I sometimes think I've dedicated my whole life to making sure I'm nothing like my dad."

"Well, you've succeeded," she said. This was a good thing.

"I wish I could be a different kind of person for you," he said.

"Then you wouldn't be you," she told him.

He buried his face in her hair.

In the end, they hired Coco to come over after school five days a week. The children loved having her around more, naturally. Her presence on the farm made everyone happy.

"Where would I be without Coco?" Eleanor observed to Darla. Coco was the most easygoing, helpful teenager she'd ever laid eyes on. When she'd gotten her license, Eleanor figured she be off all the time with her girlfriends, or boys, but coming over to the farm and organizing games for the children down at the softball field had remained her priority.

"My daughter would probably pay *you* for the chance to hang out with your family," her mother, Betsy, told Eleanor.

"And my children would probably rather spend the afternoon with Coco than with me," Eleanor said. "She's a lot more entertaining."

On her second day of babysitting, Coco brought over her soccer ball. Afternoons now, when Eleanor sat at her drawing table, she could look out the window and see the four of them—her children and Coco—kicking the ball across the field, Coco with her wonderful long legs and her ponytail flying, graceful as a gazelle, the children following behind her like a flock of ducks. Except for Ali, their skills were pretty comical, but it didn't seem to matter to any of them that sometimes Toby would pick up the ball and run with it or that Ursula tended to forget which goal she was shooting for. One afternoon Cam joined them in their pickup game. Bent over her sketch pad, Eleanor took in the sound of their voices, glad to know her children were having a good time. Having that thing she'd wanted for them more than any other: a happy childhood.

After a few weeks it became a daily event that Cam closed up his woodshop early to play with them. Boys against the girls, they decided. Cam and Toby versus Coco, Alison, and Ursula. The matchup left them close to equally balanced, though one day Eleanor had looked out the window to see all three of her children playing on Coco's team, with Cam on his own as the opposition. When they defeated him—with a questionable shot, from Toby, in which he'd run the ball between the goalposts—Cam had collapsed on the grass in mock agony. The children tackled him then. Their voices—announcing their victory and laughing—carried all the way up the hill.

One time, when she finished her work earlier than usual, Eleanor decided to join them. She had to dig into her closet to come up with sneakers suitable for running through the grass, and a pair of shorts she hadn't put on since before her first pregnancy. When she got down the hill to the spot where the game was going on, she called out to them.

"Can you use another player?"

"Come be on my team, Mama." Toby flung his arms around her. The girls hung back.

"No offense, Mom," Alison said. "But I just don't think you're the soccer type."

Ali was right, of course. Eleanor sat on a rock instead, watching them, cheering equally for everybody. In a few minutes it occurred to Eleanor that she should probably head back up to her desk. This was the hour of day when, often, her editor at the syndicate checked in with questions about her strip before it went out over the wire.

"I guess I'll be going," she said, but nobody appeared to notice. They had moved on from soccer to their other favorite Coco pastime—cartwheels. Even Cam, tall as he was, spun gracefully across a patch of field before collapsing in the grass.

For a moment, seeing them all together that way, Eleanor thought of running back to join them. But she headed to her desk instead.

Eleanor watched from the window after that, looking up from her work now and then when the sound of the voices of her children playing in the field suggested that someone—Coco or Cam—had scored. She could always tell when Coco and the children managed to get the ball past Cam, from the sound of their four high voices crying out, followed by Cam's mock despair. He'd throw himself on the ground and lie there on the grass as if he'd been shot.

"You got me," he moaned. Toby and Ursula jumped on top of him then—in a pile of legs, arms, sneakers, laughter, ponytails. Even Alison joined in.

Not Coco. Since turning sixteen, she had become more self-conscious, particularly around Cam.

Watching her family from where she sat, bent over her drawings for that week's strip, Eleanor felt relief to see them having so much fun together. She was working long days now on *Family Tree.* It felt good, making enough money finally that they didn't have to worry all the time. Not that Cam ever seemed to worry about anything.

There had been a time when she had loved that about him.

32.

bûche de Noël

That was the Christmas—Christmas, also Toby's birthday—when Eleanor made the *bûche de Noël*.

She had gotten the recipe from a cookbook she found at the dump. ("I think I know why someone threw this out," Darla had said, flipping through the pages, when she'd come over later and found the book on Eleanor's table. "Who has time for all this stuff? Or money for the ingredients? What the hell is 'almond paste'?")

Long ago, at one of their annual holiday parties when she was growing up, her mother had served a *bûche de Noël*. Store bought; Vivian wasn't much of a cook. Eleanor had been fascinated by its construction—not so much the layers of frosting and whipped cream, but the way whoever constructed this dessert had managed to create a cake that resembled a real log, with moss and mushrooms and tiny woodland creatures, all made out of marzipan. Eleanor had asked her mother (she was probably thirteen at the time) if they could try making a cake like that themselves, next Christmas, but they never did. Baking projects—projects of any sort—had not been Vivian's thing.

It was a crazy undertaking that called for making a sheet cake first, spreading it with mocha frosting, and rolling it up to form a log-shaped cylinder that you covered with more frosting. Then you got to work on the decorations—forming marzipan mushrooms and leaves, marzipan holly berries, marzipan moss.

Nobody needed a cake like this. The girls—sprawled out in the living room, inspecting their loot, with Alvin and the Chipmunks playing, Toby in his golden birthday crown with a number four on top, and Sally at work on her holiday bone—would have been just as happy (more so, as things turned out) if she'd served vanilla ice cream, or Jell-O. This was Eleanor wanting to give her children what she herself had missed, of course. Eleanor, trying to make everything perfect.

When she finished decorating the cake, she set it on the counter. She still had to truss the turkey and bake the sweet potatoes, along with the dozen other jobs before Cam's parents arrived from the airport for their annual twenty-four-hour holiday visit.

Now here was her husband, standing at the door, winding the Christmas scarf that Alison had made for him on her Knitting Nancy. He had chosen that of all moments to head out cross-country skiing. "What a day, huh?" he said, as he laced up his boots. "Perfect snow conditions."

She looked at him—this handsome man she loved and sometimes hated. Wrapping paper and packaging from toys were scattered everywhere. Sally had gotten hold of Toby's new stuffed meerkat and had chewed off the ear. In another minute, when he discovered this, he'd be crying. Cam, heading toward the door, reached for his winter hat.

"You've got to be kidding," Eleanor said. "You're leaving now?"

"Can't a guy have a little fun on Christmas?" he said.

The *bûche de Noël* sat on the counter, freshly decorated. From the record player, the voices of Alvin, Simon, and Theodore: "Silver Bells."

What happened next seemed to take place in slow motion—slow but deadly, irrevocable. She picked up the cake. With no visible trace of anger—yet—she walked to the trash bin. Threw it in. Smashed it down hard, past all recognition.

But she was only getting started. She whirled through the house then, stuffing pieces of used wrapping paper into a trash bag.

"Merry Christmas," she said, tearing through the living room, wading in the mountain of presents she'd spent all of December picking out, wrapping. A He-Man figure, a Lite-Brite, a microscope. A baby doll.

"Happy New Year."

Ursula and Toby just stood there watching. Alison retreated upstairs.

Eleanor had gathered up a pile of wrapping paper now. She was heading toward the fireplace.

"I was going to save that piece of ribbon for my dolls," Ursula said quietly. Nobody else seemed able to speak.

"Count to ten, Mom," Ursula said. Toby sat mute, studying a rock he'd picked up on their walk to the waterfall a few days before and humming the Rudolph song. Cam, pulling the hat over his ears, walked out into the snow.

33.

he got hold of the Reddi-wip

She heard from Patty—working in advertising in New York City and living with her latest boyfriend, the bass guitar player with a band called Manic Depression. They were driving to Vermont to spend New Year's skiing and wondered if they could stay over for a night on their way north.

Eleanor spent the whole morning, the day of the visit, cleaning the house. She bought scallops for a special dinner—coquilles St.-Jacques. Cam, watching her preparing the meal, a Julia Child cookbook propped on the counter, ingredients lined up—had surveyed the scene on his way to his woodshop, looking amused.

"Who are these guests of ours, anyway—Charles and Diana?"

"They live in New York City," Eleanor said. "They're not the macaroni and cheese type."

"It could be an exotic experience," he said. "Let them find out how the natives live, in the backwoods."

But she made the Julia Child dish. Also chocolate mousse and French-cut beans amandine. Before their arrival, she sent Cam to town to buy a bottle of wine.

"What kind?" he asked her. Neither of them knew anything about wine, beyond "white" or "red."

Expensive, she told him. The safest bet.

Patty had told Eleanor they'd get to the house around five thirty, but it was past seven when they arrived. Eleanor had gone ahead and fed the children. Toby and Ursula were having their bath, Alison upstairs with a book on some kind of computer programming language. More and more these days, that's where Alison stayed these days: off with a book.

Patty and Philippe pulled up in a bright red Porsche. The last time

Eleanor had seen Patty, she was a brunette, but her hair was platinum now. She was very thin and dressed in the kind of outfit that would have identified her, immediately, as having come from someplace other than Akersville. Eleanor wished she'd put on something besides the thrift shop Laura Ashley dress she'd chosen for the occasion.

"Come meet our guests." Eleanor stood at the foot of the stairs, calling up to her children. She might not be thin or fashionable, or have a sports car, but she had the best thing of all: them. This was what she'd been doing with her life while her boarding school friend got to be partner at her advertising agency: making a family.

Patty and Philippe had brought a gift from the city: an orange tin full of a kind of Italian cookie that came wrapped in very thin special paper that, when you lit it on fire, floated up into the air in wispy clouds of smoke and ash. The children didn't like the taste of the cookies so much, but Toby and Ursula kept reaching for more just so they could watch Philippe set the papers on fire. Alison—present, but still holding on to her book about MATLAB programming—kept herself apart from the group, watching.

"You didn't tell us your name," Philippe said to her. When she answered, he started singing the Elvis Costello song. She knew it, of course. At one point, when Philippe forgot the lyrics, she sang them herself. This was rare, for Ali. But she loved that song. It was a big thing for her, that there was a song with her name in it.

"So did Elvis Costello have the hots for you or something?" Philippe asked her. "Did you two, like, hook up at some point?"

Of their three children, Alison was the most literal, the one least capable of recognizing a joke. Philippe's question seemed to worry Alison, as if she was afraid she might disappoint him with her answer. "I never met any famous musicians," she said. "I'm just seven."

"Well, keep up with the singing, babe," Philippe told her. "At some point, you might want to learn how to stay on key."

"If you want to know the truth, buddy," Cam said, "my daughter won first prize in the talent show at school, singing that song. Maybe you need to get your hearing checked."

"I was being nice," Philippe said. "Maybe people around here aren't familiar with the concept."

Eleanor had set the table in front of the fireplace. She lit oil lamps and put on a record, trying to imagine which of their limited selection might seem cool enough for a person like Philippe. When she put on Talking Heads, Philippe told them he'd played at CBGB a couple of months earlier. He kept talking about this person named David, which Eleanor finally realized meant David Byrne.

"So, I guess you didn't hear what my big brother's been up to," Patty said. "He got elected to Congress. His Christmas card this year was a picture of him and the family at some big dinner in Washington, with Ron and Nancy."

Eleanor said nothing, but Cam did.

"So what's his platform?" he asked her. "The issues he campaigned on."

"Here's the wild thing," Patty told him. "After all those years of making sure he didn't get drafted and . . . shall we say . . . partaking of the white powder, Matt's turned into this *rah-rah* Republican. He's all about family values and the Pledge of Allegiance and increasing military spending. *Just say no.* You don't want to hear what he has to say about women's rights. It's bizarre."

"That must be difficult for you," Eleanor said.

"Not really," Patty told them. "It's just politics. It's not like my brother really believes any of that stuff. He was just trying to get elected."

Toby came downstairs, wearing one of Cam's T-shirts that he liked to sleep in. He was carrying his violin.

"I was wondering if you'd like to hear the Wieniawski Polonaise," he asked them.

"How cute is that?" Philippe said to Patty, after he'd finished the twelve measures he'd learned so far. "We got to get ourselves one of those."

"The boy or the violin?" Cam asked.

Eleanor waited until their two youngest children were in bed before serving the dinner. Alison had disappeared back into her room. After an appetizer course of avgolemono, Eleanor brought out the coquilles St.-Jacques, served in real scallop shells bought for the occasion.

"Jeez, this looks fabulous," Patty said, studying the shells set before them—four scallops per person. "I guess I forgot to tell you we're vegetarian."

"I'm not totally vegetarian, actually," Philippe said. "I just don't eat shellfish. Allergic."

Because the main dish was off-limits, Eleanor figured she'd leave as much of the French-cut beans as possible for their guests. As Cam spooned a generous portion on his plate, she tapped his leg under the table, but he seemed not to have taken the hint.

Afterward, there was chocolate mousse with whipped cream. Another Julia Child recipe.

"Don't get the idea this is how we normally eat around here," Cam told them. "My wife just wants to impress you. She thinks if you saw our real life you might get the idea we were a bunch of backwoods hicks. Which we probably are."

Patty scraped the whipped cream off her mousse and raised her spoon to her lips. From the kitchen, Eleanor could hear a sudden whoop from Toby. A moment later, Ursula was in the doorway.

"He got hold of the Reddi-wip, Mom," she said, with a look on her face that combined regret and pride. Then Toby appeared, naked. His penis was covered with whipped cream.

"You know, Baby, I'm thinking we should hit the road tonight," Philippe said to Patty, massaging his temples. Maybe the prospect of having a four-year-old of his own had lost some of its appeal.

Eleanor walked out to the car with them. "I wish you could have stayed over," she said. "We were going to make waffles."

"I can't wait to tell Matt everything," Patty said. "He still asks about you."

There it was again. That sick, hollow feeling Eleanor got whenever she remembered that summer in Rhode Island. She stood in the driveway, watching their car disappear down the road, and a while after.

Later, in bed, Eleanor brought up Cam's comments to Philippe.

"You know how embarrassing that was?" she said. "When you

said what you did about me trying to impress them with the fancy food?"

"It was a joke, for Pete's sake," Cam told her. "But you've got to admit I had a point."

"It's true," she said. "I did want to impress them. I guess there's some part of me that still feels I should be doing something important with my life."

"You are," he told her.

"You know the truth?" Eleanor said. "Until tonight I completely forgot. I never actually liked Patty."

34.

you have to make compromises

There had been a time when Eleanor had told people, if they asked, that she was a writer and an artist, but over the years—and even now, with her *Family Tree* strip gaining traction—she had put that part of herself away. Exhausted as she was at the end of each day, Eleanor would not have traded places with Patty—off in New York City, working at her ad agency, and flying to London four times a year. She didn't envy the writers she knew from back in the day when she went on book tours to promote her Bodie books. Some of them were still out there promoting new books and signing big contracts. But if she were doing those things, she figured, she couldn't be home with her children, rolling out cookie dough or planting radish seeds or curled up on the couch with a bowl of popcorn watching a show about penguins.

Eleanor knew she was out of step with women like Patty and her New York friends—determined to let no man, and no child, get in the way of their careers. She had the thing she'd wanted most, a family. Still, the other part—earning a living—was always on her mind.

There was nothing glamorous about Eleanor's work life now. She has her non-comic strip of course but, in her spare time, she created company logos, textbook illustrations, the wedding invitations of a wealthy summer resident who wanted a pen-and-ink drawing of the bride and groom, framed by a heart. She hardly ever turned down work. It didn't matter if the job she was hired to do failed to inspire her. She found her inspiration in her *Family Tree* strip. And in the family that inspired it.

One time, a Harvard graduate student, working on a thesis about the difficulties of women artists raising young children, tracked Eleanor down. The young woman had been a fan of the Bodie books when she was growing up. Nothing else could have explained why Eleanor's name would have made it to her list.

The graduate student, Ashley, had driven up to the farm from Cambridge to interview her. Eleanor was hanging out the laundry when her car pulled up.

"I didn't know anybody still did things like this," Ashley said.

"Here comes the crazy part," Eleanor told her. "I love hanging out the laundry. You know how much better clothes smell when they've been hung out in the fresh air to dry?"

Ashley appeared unconvinced. "But your husband participates, too, right?" she said. No way was this young woman going to use the term "helps out."

Eleanor laughed. "Cam may or may not know what a clothespin is," she said. "But *no* is probably the safer bet."

"Doesn't it make you mad?" Ashley said. "The double standard? All the things women artists put up with that men never would?"

It was funny. Eleanor knew there were all kinds of things she could feel angry about, if she started thinking about them. She chose not to. Or maybe she actually was angry, and she just hadn't admitted it to herself.

The bûche de Noël *smashed in the garbage pail. Cam heading off on his mountain bike. Her words as he headed out the door: "When do I get to take a Saturday morning off to go on an adventure?"*

"I'm not angry," she said. "Where would it get me if I were?"

"I mean, it's got to deplete your creative energy," Ashley went on. "Housework. Childcare." She didn't even know the other part. The part about who earned most of the money.

"You know where my creative energy comes from?" Eleanor told the young woman. "Them." She gestured in the direction of the field where, at that moment, her three children were engaged in a game that seemed to involve an old tennis ball and a flyswatter. "In one way or another, all the best things I've ever done come out of the things I've learned raising my children."

She fixed the two of them a lunch of broccoli quiche and salad that they ate on the porch—the children racing in on occasion, and then back out to play.

"Do you ever, you know, imagine what you could be doing, if you didn't have all these kids?" Ashley had asked her. From the way she said it, Eleanor got the impression that she found it a sad and possibly even tragic turn of events that Eleanor had gone from bestselling children's book author to carpool-driving mother working freelance and cutting the crusts off Toby's bread.

"It's true," she said. "Taking care of my children means I have a lot less time to put anything down on paper. But when I finally get to my desk, I have a lot more to say."

She was speaking about her non-comic strip, of course, though the truth was that until recently the majority of Eleanor's time at her desk was spent drawing logos for plumbers and insurance companies. Not that she'd mention that part to this young woman who had started out their visit by telling her how the Bodie books had changed her life.

Even without knowing that part, Ashley looked dubious. "I get it," she said. "But you have to feel angry sometimes, right? At all the things that are expected of women that men take for granted? Wouldn't you like to have a room of your own to work in? Instead of a kitchen table?"

"I don't think about that much, actually," Eleanor said. "For me, being a feminist means manifesting the strength and confidence and tenacity to pursue whatever it is you most want to do with your life. In my case, the goal was having a family. I'm doing that. If I don't get to make art that much at the moment, I can live with it. Nobody gets everything in life. You have to make compromises."

Ashley left in the middle of the afternoon. After, standing at the sink, washing the dishes, Eleanor thought again of the younger woman's question. Maybe she was angrier than she knew. Maybe she just didn't allow herself to admit it.

And maybe she just didn't have time to think about it. Eleanor woke early to get to her desk—piled high with school papers and grocery store coupons—before the children got up. She had bought an extra-long cord for their phone so if a client called, she could stretch the cord and take the call in the downstairs closet without the sound of children's voices in the background. She was trying to give the impression, to anyone on the other end of the line, that she was a professional person sitting in an office somewhere, instead of a woman in a pair of stretched-out sweatpants with a naked four-year-old banging on the other side of the door, wanting to show her his poop.

She hadn't bought new underwear since her last pregnancy. But she wasn't a martyr, she told herself. She had her family. She had made this choice.

Sometimes, standing at the counter, stirring cheese into the macaroni, Eleanor would listen to the sounds of her children's voices coming from different corners of the house—Ursula's Barbies having conversations with each other about fashion; Alison teaching herself Mandarin from a tape she'd checked out of the library; Toby, in the bathroom, at work on the Wieniawski; even Sally, asleep in front of the woodstove, making noises that suggested she was dreaming of chasing squirrels.

"This is *my* radical act," she had told the young Harvard woman. "Raising three human beings who will go out and change the world."

35.

family values

She was driving to pick Ursula up at gymnastics with the radio on. Usually Eleanor favored music, but for some reason the dial had been set to news. A segment came on about rising stars in politics. A familiar voice came out of the speaker—one she hadn't heard in a long time, but even before she could put a name to it, her stomach clenched.

"We've got all these welfare recipients out there, sitting around watching TV and collecting checks," he said. "It's time to start thinking about hardworking middle-class Americans for a change."

There was more. Something about church, old-fashioned family values. The sacredness of human life, from the moment of conception.

This was Matt Hallinan. Now representing the state of Rhode Island in the United States House of Representatives.

She could still hear his voice whispering in her ear and remember his hands on her shoulders, and then her face, pushing her down.

Eleanor turned off the radio and pulled over by the side of the road. Knowing what was coming, she stepped out of the car. She threw up.

36.

Female Party Guest Number Four

That spring, Alison's teacher had sent a note home to Cam and Eleanor. She wanted them to come in for a conference.

Plans had begun for the annual show, a musical version of *Cinderella,* and all the girls in class—all but those cast in the roles of Cinderella, the stepsisters, and the stepmother—were supposed to play guests at the ball. When the teacher directing the play, Mrs. Ferguson, had shown all the girls the ball gowns they'd be wearing for their roles in the show (a move intended to make them feel better about not having speaking parts), Alison had refused to try hers on. She wanted to play one of the male party guests. That, or the prince.

"This is actually the first time any of us has seen Alison assert herself so forcefully," Mrs. Ferguson told Eleanor and Cam at their conference. "She's always been so quiet. She's always gone with the flow. But I have to say, this whole thing brought out a side of your daughter I wouldn't have expected. It's been very difficult."

"Can't you just let our daughter wear a suit jacket if that's what she'd prefer to do?" Cam said. "The whole point of this show is to let the kids enjoy themselves, right? Clearly, putting on a fancy dress is not Alison's idea of a good time."

"Once we start bending the rules for one student, there's no telling what the others will start asking for," the teacher told them. (This seemed bogus to Eleanor. How many other eight-year-old girls in the class shared her daughter's aversion to putting on a dress?)

In the end, Alison agreed to play Female Party Guest Number Four. But her acquiescence struck Eleanor as closer to defeat than acceptance. The night of the performance she had a stomachache, and the family stayed home.

Later that night, Ursula had come to her parents' bedroom. "I think you should know," she told them, "Ali says she's really a boy. You just made a mistake when she got born."

This was one story from their lives Eleanor would not be including in her *Family Tree* strip.

37.

no more cork people

That spring, when they launched their cork people, Alison stayed home—the first time any of the children had failed to participate in their tradition. "It's just dumb," she told Eleanor. "I don't get the point of dumping a bunch of stupid boats in the water with some stupid corks attached and getting your shoes all muddy chasing after them. Then Ursula starts bawling if one of the people falls off the boat. Like they're actually real."

"They *are* real," Ursula told her. "Real cork people."

Ten more newspapers signed on to run *Family Tree*. Eleanor was getting invitations to appear at events in other cities now. Staying in hotels, like in the old days. But in the old days, there were no children.

It was difficult, leaving home. Cam, unfailingly good at impromptu art projects and backyard sports—igloo building and nature hikes—was not very reliable when it came to school pickups and getting children to soccer practice and music lessons. Whenever she left him in charge, she'd come home to find they'd missed appointments, failed to turn in homework—and had a great time. Once, after a weekend visit to a newspaper convention in Chicago, she returned to find they'd painted a mural on the living room wall. Another time, Ursula had applied a T-shirt decal of Michael Jackson's face directly on Toby's stomach. For weeks after, it remained on his skin, slowly peeling off, until all that was left was a faint outline of one eye and part of a mouth.

When she first started traveling for work, Eleanor had counted on Coco to step in with babysitting, but Coco—almost eighteen now—was a senior, applying to colleges, and had cut back on her hours.

Eleanor put an ad in the paper. When she thought about the best person for the job, it felt as though the most important thing was finding someone energetic enough to run after Toby—and above all else, reliable in ways his own father never was.

In the end, she hired Phyllis, a fifty-two-year-old divorced woman who'd raised a couple of children on her own. Ten years of teaching Jazzercise at the Y had left her in excellent shape. She cooked. And she could knit.

"Give me a few months with your family and you'll all be wearing new sweaters," she told Eleanor. But what really sold Eleanor was how Phyllis responded to Toby.

Some people who met their son, observing his explosions of wild energy, didn't know what to do with him, but Phyllis seemed unfazed. The first time they met, she had spoken to him in a calm voice, not baby talk, and when she saw that he had a couple of rocks in his hand, she asked if he would show them to her. He laid them in her hands and she studied them closely before speaking again.

"I like rocks, too," Phyllis said.

"You want to see my collection?" Toby asked her. He took her hand and led her into his room. A minute later she heard music. He was playing his violin for her—the twelve measures of the Wieniawski Polonaise he'd mastered.

"One more thing," Eleanor heard her son telling Phyllis. "Did you know I have a webbed foot?"

38.

old wonderful life

"If only we could just stop the world," Ursula said. "If it just could always be the way it is right now forever."

It was a Sunday the week after school got out. For three days they'd been experiencing a heat wave—unusual for that time of year, with the temperature never going below ninety and spiking over a hundred at midday. All that week, Ursula kept making trays of juice Popsicles—the only food besides watermelon that anyone felt like eating.

That week, Cam and Eleanor slept naked, no longer for the touch of each other's skin, but only for the purpose of receiving as much relief as possible against the heat—and when they got up, they took long showers and rubbed ice cubes over their faces, squirted themselves from spray bottles. Jumped in the pond. It occurred to Eleanor that no babies would be born nine months from this. Nobody would be crazy enough to make love in this heat.

That day, Darla and Kimmie had made plans to take Alison and Ursula to a water park up north, Magic Waves—a place Ursula had been dreaming of going to since she spotted a brochure for the place at Friendly's one night. But they had a strict minimum height requirement at the park, and Toby was too short. The morning Darla came to pick the girls up for the water park adventure, he'd sat at the window, watching them pile into the car, and for the next hour he wandered around like a man without a country, asking Eleanor when his sisters would get home.

The girls were back right after lunchtime. There'd been an electrical storm at the park and everyone had to get out of the water.

When his sisters burst in the door, he leapt into Ursula's arms.

"I found you," he called out.

"They gave us passes to come back another day with an extra for a friend," she told him. "I bet by then you'll be big enough to go."

"It wasn't really so great anyway," Alison offered. "I have a feeling people had been peeing in the water."

"You came back," Toby said, stroking their hair—Ursula's first, then Alison's, his favorite people in the world. To Toby that day, it probably seemed as if he had conjured his sisters back home by the sheer force of his yearning for them.

Cam came in from the woodshop and cut up a watermelon for them, and after, they built a fort out of the box from a refrigerator delivered that week—the old Coldspot having finally given up the ghost—with a pulley leading to a second structure Alison called the Kasbah, made by draping a couple of old bedspreads over the rose arbor. All afternoon they sent messages back and forth on pulleys between the fort and the Kasbah, until everyone was too hot and too tired. Ursula ran into the house and came out with a pile of pillows and library books and smell markers and a giant bag of Goldfish.

They spread a blanket under Old Ashworthy and Alison read out loud to them for a while—*Charlotte's Web,* their favorite. Then they made Toby a sword decorated with foil that Ursula had been saving from some chocolates, and Alison read them another chapter, and then Ursula and Toby took off all their clothes and raced into the pond together, holding hands, even though the water was still very cold.

When they came out, they wrapped themselves in towels and Ursula painted Toby's toenails and her own, but not Alison's, naturally.

Toby climbed up onto the picnic table then, naked except for an old straw hat of Cam's, with his purple toes, and performed his current favorite song, "Shipoopi." He'd learned the song from a soundtrack record of *The Music Man* they'd found on one of their recent dump-picking missions. He alternated this performance with his other beloved song, "Thriller." Though the *Thriller* album had come out some time before, he particularly loved the video with Vincent Price and Michael Jackson turning into a werewolf. Toby knew all the moves, and performed them with amazing accuracy and, more than that, style.

They could smell dinner cooking—fried chicken with corn bread—and they knew there would be apple crisp later, too, with vanilla ice cream, and that afterward, the family might snuggle up on the couch with Sally to watch a movie on the VCR, with a fan going on account of the heat. The weekend before, they'd picked out a movie about a scientist who goes up to the Alaskan tundra to study wolf behavior, and because they hadn't returned the tape to the video store yet, there was a good chance they could persuade their parents to let them watch it again, since it was one of those movies their mother believed instilled good values, like kindness, as well as courage.

That was the afternoon when Ursula had made her observation about wishing she could stop the world.

It was true. This may have been the best day ever. (And the funny thing was, they never even got to ride the giant slide at the water park.)

Later, the girls would remember exactly where they were when Ursula said this: lying on the plaid TV blanket in the sideways refrigerator-box fort, munching the last of the watermelon, juice dripping down their chins. "Let's all hold hands and close our eyes," Ursula said. "So we remember."

Alison had been the one who suggested making the time capsule. Some time back, she had dug an old metal safe out of a pile of trash at the dump, and though it wasn't easy getting this thing up the hill to the station wagon, she had persuaded her mother the safe was a treasure worth salvaging.

It had been sitting in the garage for at least a year. That afternoon, they hauled it out. The three of them spent the better part of an hour scrubbing off the dirt.

The plan was for each of them to put something in the safe. "It shouldn't just be some dumb piece of junk or some prize you got with a Happy Meal," Alison said. "It has to be something that really matters to you. It might be something you have a hard time giving up, but that just goes to show it belongs in our box."

Nobody was supposed to tell the others what they were putting in the time capsule. They wrapped their items in toilet paper. Each of the girls composed a letter to their future selves—or whoever it might be who one day discovered the box. These, too, remained secret.

Toby wanted to write a letter also, not that he knew how to write. Alison suggested she'd help him with this but he said no, he'd do it by himself. Reaching for a purple smell marker (grape), he spent a surprisingly long time—five minutes, at least—composing his note.

When they were done, and each of them had placed their time capsule treasures in the box, along with their letters, they located a shovel in the garage. They considered carefully where the best spot might be to bury the time capsule.

It was almost dinnertime; their mother was calling them in. "Five minutes!" they called back to her.

The sun was hitting the leaves on Old Ashworthy just right, so they seemed almost to glow, and the sky was cloudless.

This was the place, of course—under their special tree—but far enough from the biggest roots that the shovel could break through the earth.

"What if we forget where we buried it?" Ursula said.

"I don't think that would happen, but just in case, we'll draw a map on the wall of the woodshed," Alison said.

They would not forget this or anything else about that afternoon. It was the last day of their old wonderful life.

39.

pocket of stones

Monday was the day her *Family Tree* non-comic strip had to be delivered to the syndicate, and the heat wave hadn't let up. Eleanor had gotten up even earlier than usual, hoping to get her work done before the brutal heat settled over them. Most of the time she had a dozen ideas for stories to write, but that morning her brain was empty. She wrote the word "Hot" on the top of the page. Then nothing.

From her drawing table off the kitchen, Eleanor could hear Ursula washing out the ice cube trays, singing the song that had been her favorite all last summer, "We Are the World," in that high, thin, bright voice of hers. Alison was upstairs with a Japanese fan and a stack of old *National Geographic* magazines. Sally just lay in the dirt panting.

Phyllis had taken the day off to go to the doctor, and Coco was off checking out a holistic healing school in Vermont that she was thinking of attending, as an alternative to college. A little grudgingly—because one of the guys from the Yellow Jackets had stopped by suggesting they go take a look at a truck he was thinking of buying—Cam had agreed to watch the children.

Early that morning he had turned the sprinkler on and set up the Slip 'N Slide, but nobody had much energy for running around. At one point Eleanor looked out the window to see Ursula and Cam stretched out on the grass while Toby squirted them with water from a spray bottle. Cam was reading out loud to them from a collection of Shel Silverstein poems. It was almost too hot to waste energy on laughing.

Eleanor turned back to the panel she was drawing, of a woman vaguely resembling herself—this was her continuing character in the strip, Maggie, the mother—sticking her head in the freezer.

After, Alison said she remembered Toby wandering off, but she hadn't been worried because a minute later she heard him playing his violin back in the house. He had recently learned a couple more measures of the Wieniawski.

After, they would find his violin leaned up against the tub, as if he was planning to get back to practicing later. This was Toby for you: He could focus in like a laser beam. Or race off to something totally different with an explosion of energy like Super Mario. Maybe, in the middle of practicing, he'd heard Sally barking. Maybe it occurred to him that he needed to go say something to Alison in that secret language of theirs. Maybe he spotted a bug on the windowsill and decided to take it outside to find its mother. That would be Toby for you.

Maybe their web-footed boy just decided to take a swim.

Ultimately, all they ever knew was that at some point Toby had wandered off into the woods looking for rocks, another of his pastimes. They figured out that part from the rocks in his pockets when they found him.

Back on the grass, Cam had fallen asleep with Alison next to him and the Shel Silverstein book open on his chest. Ursula had gotten up to refill the spray bottle with water from the hose. That's when she'd seen it: her brother's small, sturdy body lying facedown in the pond, his long red curls fanned out around his head like a sea creature, his arms stretched out as though he were making snow angels, one flip-flop still on his foot, the other floating a few feet away among the lily pads.

Toby was not simply on top of the water but underneath it, deep enough that his face appeared to be touching the bottom of the pond. He wasn't moving.

Ursula called out for her parents. They came running—Cam from the lawn, instantly awake, Eleanor from the kitchen. She was the one who reached their son first, wading into the pond and wrapping her arms around him, pulling his limp body from the water, screaming for help.

After, they understood what had dragged him under and kept him there. All those stones he'd been gathering in his pockets.

By the time Eleanor had laid Toby on the grass the rest of them had reached the spot. Alison ran in the house to call 911. Cam knelt over Toby, pumping his chest, trying to recall what he'd learned years ago in lifeguard training.

None of them had any sense of time as it was happening, but Cam probably kept pumping Toby's chest for many minutes. Eleanor knelt on the ground beside their son, rubbing his cheeks, his feet, his hair. Alison, who'd returned to the spot after phoning for the ambulance, stood on the grass with an arm around her sister's shoulders and her gaze locked on her brother's face. Except when he was sleeping, they had never seen him so still.

It wasn't only Toby who wasn't breathing. It felt to Eleanor, at least, as though none of them was. Somewhere far away—though really, this was happening right next to her—she could hear the sound of Ursula weeping.

The shirt Toby was wearing that day featured a picture of a Teenage Mutant Ninja Turtle on the front, Donatello. Cam, pumping on Toby's chest, said something Eleanor could not make out. A prayer, maybe. Eleanor herself, kneeling on the grass, made a silent bargain. There was nothing she owned she wouldn't give to see her son draw a breath of air into his lungs.

He lay unmoving. His face had taken on a bluish color. His hands—fingers callused from all those hours practicing the Wieniawski Polonaise—lay at his sides like two dead fish.

Let Toby wake. This was the prayer Eleanor made. Not out loud, but in her head. This farm could burn to ash, if their magical boy might only be restored to them. She chose, at that moment, to offer, in sacrifice, the thing most precious to her other than her children.

A minute passed. Possibly five. They could hear the siren down the road now—a sound they'd never heard outside of town. For a fraction of a second Eleanor thought, *Toby will love this.* Toby—lover of backhoes and excavators and fire trucks and anything that made a loud noise. A lover of flashing lights and men in uniforms and vehicles driving fast.

The truck was just pulling up under the ash tree when the miracle happened: Toby's body, that had been totally limp, suddenly jerked up off the grass as if an electric current had passed through him. Then he was spitting water—water and mud. He didn't cry, but his whole body was shaking.

By the time the EMTs reached Toby, Cam and Eleanor had him in their arms, and he was making more sputtering sounds—the glorious noises of a living, breathing boy. His skin was returning to pink. He had his arms around Eleanor now, and she was pressing her face in his hair, and he was staring at the sky and at Sally, who had raced over and was licking his feet. Those wonderful webbed toes.

You're okay, they said. Over and over. *You're okay. We were so scared. We got you back. Nothing else matters. Just this.*

But he was different. He was crying, but not in the way the old Toby cried, on the rare occasions when he cried at all—not wailing, or angry, or indignant.

Now his voice, that had always been big as a man's, was barely audible, not a cry so much as a whimper, and there was none of the old ferocity in him. Eleanor remembered a bird that had crashed into the plate-glass window of the kitchen one time. The bird had dropped to the ground and, for a minute there, showed no signs of life. Then it had begun flapping its wings, making odd chirping noises, finally dragging itself to a standing position. After flopping around for a bit, it flapped its wings again, and took off in strangely tentative flight before lifting off and disappearing beyond the tree line.

It would be like that with Toby. It made sense that for a few minutes he would lie there in Eleanor's arms with his family on all sides stroking his face, his hair. First he would have that look on his face, like a character in a comic strip who gets bopped over the head and stars explode around him. Any moment now he would shake his beautiful mop of hair—wet from pond water—and burst out with that big, deep laugh. He'd look around, shake himself again, and take off like the bird.

Only he didn't. He sat there staring at them all, still looking dazed, as if he was thinking, *Who are these people?*

"You okay, buddy?" Cam said. "You sure gave us a scare."

Now Eleanor could put her arms around Ursula, who could not stop shaking. "If it wasn't for you, Ursie, we might not have got to him in time."

What she didn't say, because she hadn't worked through to this part yet, was that if Cam had been doing what she asked of him—if he had been watching their children as he had promised—Toby would never have been in the water in the first place. If he had been doing what he was supposed to, instead of falling asleep, he would have kept their son safe.

One of the EMTs was performing some tests now—shining a flashlight into Toby's eyes, telling him to follow the light. He was taking Toby's blood pressure, listening to his heartbeat.

"You learn the alphabet yet, pal?" the EMT said to Toby. This was Toby, who could recite the alphabet before his second birthday, and had recently been working with his older sister on counting to twenty in Mandarin. Also the times tables and the capital of every state and the name of every dinosaur, even the ones nobody else ever heard of, and the first thirteen measures of the Wieniawski Polonaise, not to mention every mineral in his *Encyclopedia of Rocks and Minerals* book. He looked blankly at the man. "K," he said. "K. L. Z." His head flopped onto his chest.

"He's still a little groggy," Eleanor said. "It's understandable, given what just happened." She could hear, in her own voice, a certain note of terror just below the surface. Who was she trying to convince? Herself, probably.

"I'm not sure I could recite the alphabet myself at the moment," Cam told the EMT.

"Just take it easy, Tobes," he told their son.

Alison stood a little ways off, hands in her pockets, as if she already knew. Not Ursula. Kneeling beside her brother, she brushed his hair out of his face, arranged his curls.

"A, B, C, D," she sang. "How 'bout we sing it together?" She must have thought this was like school, where if you didn't get the answer right, you could get in trouble.

"X," Toby said. He sounded like an astronaut, coming to them from somewhere out in space. "W." His eyes looked glazed, unfocused. His skin was so cold.

"Listen," the EMT said to Eleanor. "I'm sure your son's going to be fine, but we need to bring him in to the ER for a little testing. Just to be on the safe side. They'll probably hook him up to an EEG. We need to be sure his brain is functioning like we want."

They were buckling Toby onto the stretcher. It was unlike him to offer no resistance. One thing about Toby, he was not a boy to pin down.

A terrible sick feeling had started to come over Eleanor. "No, no, no," she told the EMTs. "I want to keep him here." So long as they were on their farm, he'd be all right.

"Can't we do this another day?" she said.

"We have to do this, El," Cam told her. He led Eleanor toward the station wagon.

Jackie Kennedy in Dallas. The pink suit, with the blood.

Eleanor wanted to get in the ambulance with Toby, but the EMTs needed to be there with him. "You follow behind," one of them told her. There wasn't room for more people.

Cam drove. Nobody said anything. There had been a cassette in the tape player when Cam turned the ignition on. The soundtrack from *The Music Man,* right at the spot where they'd left off, when she'd last pulled into the driveway, with the three of them all singing "Seventy-Six Trombones" in the back. Toby loudest of all.

"Turn off the music," Eleanor said.

40.

that moment has passed

The tests, when they got the results back, left them no room for fantasy. Mild to medium brain damage resulting from oxygen deprivation. The doctor started talking about lobes and hemispheres, but they couldn't take in the rest.

"This is just temporary, right?" Eleanor said. "How long before he's back to normal?"

The doctor just looked at her for a moment and took a long, slow breath. "There are people who can help your son retrain himself so other hemispheres take over some of the function of the damaged portions of his brain," he told them. "But injured brain cells do not regenerate."

She could see his lips moving, but the words made no sense. She must have heard this wrong.

"Your son can still live a good life," the doctor told them. "Different from how he was before. But he can still take pleasure in his family. His motor function will not be greatly compromised. Primarily, his injuries have to do with language and cognition."

There was a woman reading a magazine in the waiting room with Tom Cruise on the cover. A baby crying down the hall. At the water fountain, a mother was holding a child up to drink. Another child had spilled a bag of Cheerios on the floor. On the television mounted to the wall, *Let's Make a Deal*.

"The thing we all need to hold on to right now"—this was the doctor, still talking—"is that Toby could have died this afternoon. In certain ways, he did. You were very lucky your husband was able to bring him back with the CPR. Another thirty seconds—maybe less—we'd be looking at a whole different story. But it would be too much to expect a human brain to survive that long without oxygen and emerge unscathed."

No. No. No. No. Eleanor was shaking her head. Her whole body was shaking. Cam leaned in to put his arms around her. She pushed him away.

It had sunk in now. How this happened. The way she looked at him at this moment, she might have been confronting an assassin.

"You did this to our son," she said. Her voice a whisper.

Cam crumpled. Those red curls covering his face.

"I would give anything . . ." he said. "I would do anything."

"But there isn't anything you can do now, is there?" she said, her voice unrecognizable to her own self. Ice. "That moment has passed."

41.

we are the children

Toby's hospital room, three days after the accident. Toby on the bed, his arms at his sides. There was a tube going into his arm—glucose, because he couldn't eat—and a set of wires attached to his head that the doctor explained had been put there to monitor brain activity.

The four of them—Eleanor, Cam, Ursula, Alison—gathered by the bed.

"You might try talking to him," the neurologist who'd been brought in to consult on Toby's case suggested. "Even when we think nothing's going on in there, sometimes the sound of a familiar voice, a familiar piece of music, triggers something in the brain cells."

"I have an idea, guys," Ursula said. "Let's all sing to him."

She tried "Thriller" first. When that got no response, she tried another one—her thin, pure soprano just barely audible over the sound of the machines.

We are the world

"You remember this one, right, Tobes?" she said to him.

Eleanor studied the expression on her son's face as they sang to him. His full, beautiful lips, the constellation of freckles. The halo of red hair arranged on the pillow. Then she regarded her younger daughter. At that moment she understood what it meant to sing one's heart out.

". . . we'll make a better day, just you and me."

Nothing.

42.

ball. egg. dinosaur.

They put the violin away. In those first days after they brought Toby home from the hospital, Ursula had played his record for him, sitting him down next to the turntable and setting the needle on the familiar groove. "It's your favorite, Tobes. You remember this, right?"

If the notes reached some place in his damaged brain, nothing in his eyes or his strangely flaccid body gave indication of that. Toby stared blankly at Ursula, who stood next to the record player holding a ruler and waving her arms to the music, pretending to be a conductor.

"Will you just quit, for once?" Alison snapped at her. It wasn't like her to speak to her sister in this tone of voice. Ursula set down her ruler.

He walked, but differently. Toby moved slowly through the rooms of the house now, and in the yard where he used to fly past in a blur of wild energy. In the old days, he was always on the move: to the woodshop, the garden, the woods, always going someplace, always fast. Now he drifted like a piece of milkweed on a still afternoon. Mostly he just sat there, turning the pages of a book, if one was placed in his hands, or staring at the sky. Sometimes he just studied the tip of his shoelace or an ant crawling up his pants leg. The head of a dandelion or a piece of grass was enough to occupy him.

Eleanor spent hours turning the pages of one of their old baby books with Toby on her lap, pointing out the names of ordinary objects, colors. *This is a ball. This is an egg. This is a dinosaur.* When she couldn't take that anymore, she took down *Baby's First Hundred Words*—not much more advanced, but a little. *This is a farmer. This is a baker. This is a fireman.* Toby never objected to sitting there. But he never responded, either.

Very often, Sally would place herself next to Toby, her tongue on his leg or arm, breathing quietly and snorting when a squirrel or the memory of a good bone entered her dream. He seemed to like this, as much as anyone could tell what Toby liked anymore. His face, once so animated, was drained of expression. His features were as beautiful as ever, but the effect was all different without his jokes, his Michael Jackson dance, that big voice, announcing his arrival in whatever room he burst into. It was unclear to Eleanor whether he said so little because he no longer remembered words, or because he just had nothing to say.

When he spoke, it was usually about wanting something to eat, his request offered up in a high, soft whisper. Hearing him speak in the strange new voice, Eleanor sometimes had to walk out of the room so the girls wouldn't see her burying her face in her hands. Now and then, though, Ursula found her mother with her face pressed against the wall, or lying on the bed holding a pillow.

"Let's just be happy he didn't die, okay?" she said, stroking Eleanor's hair.

Darla brought lemon bars. Phyllis left a Bible on the table. Walt came by with his checkerboard. "I was thinking I could play this with your boy," he said.

"Don't get your hopes up," Alison said.

"It doesn't matter," Walt told her. "We'll have a good time sitting out in the sun, moving the pieces around on the board. It might be nice for him, and a help to your mother."

The one who really rose to the occasion, though, was Cam. Cam, who had never even taken one of their children to the dentist before and had a hard time keeping the names of their teachers straight from one year to the next, got on the phone, talking to doctors in places as far away as Denver and Atlanta, where they worked with children with brain injuries. He brought home photocopies of articles about innovations in brain rehabilitation from the state library and researched facilities where Toby could work on language, rebuild muscle tone. Cam's parents—never much involved—had offered to pay for treatment, but every place Cam contacted said the same thing after reviewing Toby's scans. Prospects for rehabilitation, with brain injury of this kind, were minimal. Expectations should be kept low.

Cam didn't let this discourage him. "Those doctors don't know everything," he said. "They don't know Toby." He sent away for a book by a woman who had invented a way to teach her brain-injured daughter to communicate with sign language and another book about foods that stimulated the growth of new brain cells, and then he cooked them. He joined a support group of parents of children who were brain injured—a term Eleanor was unable to utter. Tuesday nights, he made the hour-long drive alone to meetings.

Cam tried bringing Toby to the playground. He buckled his son into the toddler swing and pushed so gently that the swing barely rose. *One, one, Toby has fun.*

"Home now," Toby said, after Cam climbed with him to the top of the slide, trying to guide his newly limp body down. Toby had always loved the slide, and fought to stay longer on the playground every time they went there.

"Go home," Toby repeated. "Home."

Back in the kitchen, where they set him in his chair—his frog cup in front of him, and the Beatrix Potter bowl he'd always loved—he stared blankly out over the heads of the other children. Their amazing geologist. The boy destined for Carnegie Hall. The web-footed swimmer who might one day have swum the English Channel. The child who had told them he'd been a buffalo in a former life. The child who spoke to God.

Now he said nothing. Just reached for a piece of bread and silently chewed it.

43.

bad things, good people

Everything changed.

For Eleanor, the rooms of their home had become almost unbearable. As much as possible, she retreated to her desk now, staring at the blank page of her drawing pad. It was easier to put in long hours working than to spend her days with her son, confronted with the constant picture of what it meant that the boy she had raised and adored for four and a half years had disappeared, replaced by this odd little red-haired stranger.

She was angry now, all right. At Cam most of all. But there was a terrible secret she admitted to no one. She was angry at Toby, too.

There was nothing rational about this, but Eleanor had to work hard not to snap at him when he couldn't answer some simple question she asked or go up the stairs without getting on all fours, or when—this was the worst—she spoke to him and he looked through her as if he had no idea who she was. To Eleanor, it was as if the person responsible for the disappearance of her beloved son was this strange, silent imposter, cleverly disguised in a similar body—with the same flaming hair, but otherwise unrecognizable. She wanted the old Toby back, and though she told herself it made no sense, she resented the person now occupying his place at the table.

That fall, she set up a room for herself in the barn—the place Cam had once used for his woodshop. The place became her hideout. She would rather work all day at her drawing table in the barn—all day, and all night—and earn money to pay Phyllis than sit watching the boy flipping listlessly through the pages of a magazine or staring out the window at their empty bird feeder.

Ursula had always been the most tender one of Eleanor's children, but now she revealed a kind of compassion that had been largely hidden before, probably because until this awful moment, it hadn't been needed. Ursula was heroic. She became her brother's tireless defender and protector, with no consideration of the cost to herself. From the moment Ursula got out of bed everything she did and said seemed driven by two impulses: to help her brother and to make her family happy again.

She fixed pancakes for Cam and Eleanor—breakfast in bed—also muffins and cookies and bowls of popcorn, like in the old days, when they piled onto the couch to watch movies together. Phyllis did most of the housework now, but Ursula took on special projects—sitting with Toby on the floor for hours, reciting the numbers, pointing out shapes, reminding him of the names for things. She hung up all the clothes that had accumulated on the floor in Alison's room. She Dustbustered Eleanor's workspace. She arranged Toby's Ninja Turtles in interesting places—scenes intended to inspire her brother to play, only he never did anymore.

One night, Ursula set the table with candles and the plates they only used on Thanksgiving, with an artificial rose that appeared to have been taken from a cemetery in a vase at the center of the table. No special occasion, but there had been a segment on *Phil Donahue* that week about the importance of keeping the romance alive in marriage.

"You two need to have a candlelight dinner, like in the movies," she told Eleanor. She had put on a Dolly Parton tape and made sandwiches for the rest of them to eat upstairs so their parents could have privacy. She had been disappointed by Eleanor's choice of outfit for the special dinner, but—sensing her mother's reluctance to change into something fancier—ran upstairs to her room. She came back with a crown from her dress-up box.

"I guess we'd better act romantic," Cam said, as Ursula pushed the Play button so "I Will Always Love You" started—maybe their daughter had failed to recognize, this was a sad song—and left them to be alone. "We don't want to disappoint our daughter, right?"

After the accident, Cam had stopped showing up for softball games. For a while everyone figured he'd be back. That September—no Labor Day party that year—he told the team they'd better find a new first baseman.

He needed to spend more time with Toby, he told his teammates. But there was an element of self-punishment, too. What did it matter if a man made a brilliant catch on a long ball to right field and tagged the runner out on first, if he had failed to protect his four-year-old son from drowning?

Ursula did not announce this to any of them, but she had checked several books out of the library: a joke book, designed to liven up their silent dinnertimes; a book called *Love, Medicine & Miracles,* by a doctor she'd seen on *Phil Donahue* (a different episode); and a book from the Personal Growth section, located with the help of Mrs. Jenkins, the librarian.

The most helpful book, in Ursula's opinion, was *When Bad Things Happen to Good People,* written by a rabbi whose son had been born with a terrible disease that made him turn into an old man by the time he was Ursula's age, seven, which meant that he'd died when he was fourteen years old. This rabbi, a man named Harold Kushner, wrote the book to figure out how to stay happy after something terrible happens, and according to him this was possible.

As a second grader, Ursula found the book difficult reading, but she stuck with it—sounding out the words, working her way through the chapters late at night in her bed when everyone else in the family was asleep. After she finished it she wrote a letter to the author, Harold Kushner, in which she explained about her brother Toby, and how sad her parents were, and asked his advice—explaining first, regretfully, that they weren't Jewish, but she had a dreidel.

Harold Kushner had written back to say that a person didn't have to be Jewish to have a relationship with God. He suggested some parts of the Bible that she and her parents might find comforting, but when she tried to share these with the two of them, her mother had looked at Ursula as if she, too, were brain damaged.

"What kind of God would let something like this happen to Toby?" she said. She didn't yell at Ursula, but she sounded mad. "You're wasting your time with that book."

"Ease up, El," her father said. "Ursula was just trying to help."

Eleanor got up from the table. "Here's what you need to understand, Ursula," she said. "Some things that happen don't have any solution. Some things that get broken aren't fixable." She picked up Ursula's most recent library selection, *Love, Medicine & Miracles,* opened the door to the woodstove, and threw it in.

Crazyland alert.

"That was a library book," Ursula said quietly. She was a girl who prided herself on never once bringing library materials back late.

"It was a good idea, Ursie," Cam told her, after Eleanor left the room. "Your mom is just having a hard time right now."

After, from where she stood in the kitchen with Phyllis, slicing a roll of Toll House cookies and arranging them on the sheet, she heard her parents talking in the yard. Not really talking. They didn't do that so much anymore, except for working out things like who drove Toby to physical therapy and who picked him up.

"I'm just as sad as you are, Eleanor," her father said. "But we have to find a way to keep going. You can't go crazy on our children like that. Our daughter's just trying to help."

Ursula looked at the babysitter, who placed a hand on her shoulder. "All parents argue sometimes," Phyllis told her. "Don't worry." But she did.

At night, in bed, Ursula searched the pages of Harold Kushner's book for something that might apply: *What could a person do to help their father who believed he was responsible for the most terrible thing that ever happened in your family? Worst of all, what if your mother believed this also? How could you make everyone happy again, or just not so miserable?*

All she could think of was praying. She tried that, too.

By October, when the leaves on their big tree turned red, and after, when they fell, Ursula was still spending hours every day reading to her brother. Sometimes she told him jokes. She applied polish to his fingernails and his toenails and French-braided his hair, that nobody felt like cutting. Ursula held on to the hope that one of these days Toby might emerge, like Scuffy the Tugboat, through the fog, look her in the eye, and speak to her in that strangely husky man's voice of his—not just the one- or two-word phrases that came out of him now, but sentences and songs, like in the old days. Laughter.

Did you know I saw Mr. T on the playground?

I went over to God's house. We made spaghetti.

44.

call me Al

"I wish you'd give up already," Ali told her sister. "I'm sick of watching you wasting your time. Toby just sits there and he's not even looking at you. No offense, but it's kind of depressing."

Alison took a different approach from her sister's to Toby's transformation. Back in the old days—meaning before the accident; that was how they measured time now—she'd been the most enthusiastic of the family about going along with Toby on his wildest adventures—carrying on the long conversations in the language they'd made up, camping out in the woods, building a rope swing, rescuing a baby skunk whose mother had been run over by a car, dissecting a cow's eye—big as a pool ball—that her teacher had given her during their unit on the human body, taking apart an old radio Walt dropped off when he was cleaning out his garage. Ursula didn't love Toby any less than Alison did, but she was a more careful type, and she not only followed the rules laid out for her, she actually liked rules—where to Toby, and to Alison, little offered greater satisfaction than breaking them.

Toby had been the one in their family who shared Alison's love of everything mechanical—putting things together or (his specialty) taking them apart, and in the first days after the accident, Alison had kept trying to arouse a response from her brother. She spoke to him in their old secret language. She set a baby turtle in his hand, and a worm, and a piece of owl scat. She showed him Walt's broken radio with the suggestion that they fix it together, but he just sat there, staring at the objects she set in front of him. No glimmer of interest.

By September, Alison no longer spoke to Toby. She avoided all mention of his name. Passing through a room in which he sat, staring at a ball or a truck or wrapping his old pink ribbon around his finger, she seemed not to acknowledge he was even there.

"Can't you just pat him on the head or something?" Ursula said to her once. "You pet Sally more than Toby."

"Toby's not a dog," she said. "Toby's not anything anymore."

Another change took place in Alison's life that year, possibly touched off by the accident, and by a growing attitude of skepticism in her as to whether or not anything you thought was real in your life could actually be counted on, and the general pointlessness of everything.

Alison had never liked girl clothes and most of the other apparatus that went along with them—barrettes and bracelets, dolls, anything pink. But that summer seemed to mark a passage for Alison from simple tomboy behavior to living, as much as possible, like a boy. To Alison, it appeared, the position of son in their family stood vacant. Maybe that was part of it. Or maybe she just decided it was too hard putting on an act anymore.

At dinner one night, a couple of months *after* (no need to say after what), Alison made the announcement.

"You know that song Toby used to love so much?" she said, as Eleanor was wrapping up the leftover chicken, and she and Cam were loading the dishwasher. "I was thinking about it. When a person says they're born in the U.S.A., it's supposed to mean they're free, right? In this country, we're supposed to be who we want. Even way back when I was little, we were always playing that record with the pink cover."

She meant *Free to Be . . . You and Me.* For years, that was the family favorite on road trips.

"So I want to be free, Mom," Alison told her. "My real self."

"And you don't feel free now?" Eleanor asked her. "Did your father and I give you the impression you had to be someone you're not?"

"It's not your fault or Dad's," Alison said. "I just want my name to match who I am. From now on, I'd appreciate it if you'd call me Al."

Later that night, in the dark of their bedroom, Cam had reached for Eleanor. They had not made love since the accident. He placed his hand on her belly and stroked it.

"Here's where our babies came from," he said. "I will always love this place."

She lay there, not moving. She didn't speak. They lay in silence for a minute. Longer, probably.

"*Al*. Can you beat that?" he said. "Do you think it's a phase?"

He was trying it out. Saying the name. Getting used to this. He might worry very briefly about Alison, but it wouldn't eat away at him. He'd move on.

Cam was good at that.

45.

happy anniversary

Eleanor and Cam's anniversary fell six weeks after the accident. That week, Eleanor had traveled to New York, a two-night trip to meet with her newspaper syndicate. She had noted the day, of course, but though she called the children that night, she didn't ask to speak to their father.

After she greeted the children and gave them the presents she'd brought home for them (a pair of reflector sunglasses for Al, who didn't want you to look her in the eye anymore, a jewelry box for Ursula, a stuffed monkey puppet for Toby), Cam led her into their bedroom blindfolded. "Happy anniversary," he said, untying the bandanna over her eyes. He sounded excited. It took a moment for her to figure out what was different here.

In her absence, Cam had replastered the walls.

The color was a soft, creamy white, the texture like linen. The sun, coming in the window, made the room seem to glow.

This wasn't Sheetrock. Cam had applied plaster, the old-fashioned way, and covered the whole thing with a beautiful coat of milk-based paint he'd mixed himself. After he'd finished, he had set everything back in its place, and there was a new bowl on the dresser—a very small one, made from a burl she recognized, found on a camping trip they'd taken long ago, back when she was pregnant with Alison. A good size for holding a pair of earrings or a necklace.

He had not given her jewelry. The gift was the plaster, and it was a beautiful plaster job, a beautiful bowl. But that day all she registered was the emptiness of the bowl.

While she stood there taking it in, Cam stood quietly in the doorway. He moved closer and placed his hands on her hips. Maybe he touched her cheek. If so, Eleanor didn't notice.

"So when Darla asks what you gave me for our anniversary, I guess I tell her, plaster," Eleanor said. Her voice was flat. Hard.

"It's not an ordinary plaster job," he said, more quietly now. "I did it the old-school way. I thought you'd like it."

The truth was, she'd given him nothing to mark their anniversary that year. If Eleanor were honest with herself, nothing Cam could have offered her that summer would have changed anything. A stone rested on her heart. More than a stone. It might have been her son's entire rock collection, piled on top of her. So many stones, you couldn't even make out the presence of a woman's body underneath them all.

There was a Jazzercise class their babysitter Phyllis attended now and then at the YMCA where she used to teach. She brought Toby with her one time. The motions practiced by the women in Jazzercise were too complicated for Toby, and the loud music made him uneasy, but on their way out of the Y he'd spotted a bunch of old-timers doing gentle yoga, and something about that appealed to him. Phyllis told Cam and Eleanor, later, that he had stood in the doorway for a long time, watching, and when she suggested they might go home now, he hadn't wanted to leave.

Hearing this, Cam went to check out the class himself, and after, he brought Toby—the two of them the only ones under age seventy. He got a video of yoga postures and started working on them with Toby at home.

Cam's idea was that maybe, if he got his son's body moving in new ways, it might stimulate his brain. The good thing about yoga for a person like Toby—Toby, now—was how quiet it was. There were no explosive bursts of energy required. A person could move slowly through the poses, or just sit there in child's pose if he wanted. Or no pose at all. The music was soothing. Nobody asked anything of anyone else.

The two of them shared a mat together, Toby in front of Cam, with Cam manipulating his limbs into something approximating the poses. Toby never initiated a move, but he never resisted when Cam put him into a new pose. When he got comfortable enough, Cam brought him back to the Y to join the class.

One day in class during downward dog—it was fall now—an elderly woman near the front of the room had let out a fart. The others in the class ignored this, but something wonderful happened to Toby at that moment.

He laughed. This was not the big, hearty belly laugh from the old days when they watched old Laurel and Hardy movies from the library. But it was the first time in the months since the accident when anything he'd taken in had inspired that much of a response.

When they got home, it was the first thing Cam told Eleanor. He found her standing at the kitchen counter, chopping vegetables for dinner.

"You won't believe what our boy did at yoga," he said.

"Let me guess." She spoke in the hard, sarcastic tone that was her usual now with Cam. "Maybe he recited the first stanza of 'Where the Sidewalk Ends'?" That one had been his favorite Shel Silverstein poem, before.

"Or maybe he sang along with the words to a Dylan track." Her back remained facing him. Her knife made sharp, rhythmic clicks against the cutting board.

"A woman farted," Cam said. "Toby laughed."

"I guess I'm supposed to get excited about this," Eleanor said. She did not look up. She had not stopped chopping.

"It just seemed so hopeful," Cam told her. "If something like that can get through to him, other things can, too."

She sliced into a carrot, the knife coming down hard. Her face, a wall.

That winter was the coldest since the year of Al's birth. She was in third grade now. Ursula, second. Every morning a small, ten-seat bus pulled up at the end of their road—different from the one the girls took—to bring Toby to his special classes. All those days, back before the accident, he'd watched his sisters head out to school on the big yellow bus, asking why he had to stay home. Now finally he was getting on a bus, too. Just not the one they'd planned on.

She'd researched schools for children with Toby's kind of brain injury, and this one seemed like the best place within driving range.

But even Eleanor would have admitted that it was the time Toby spent with Cam, doing their yoga together, riding the tricycle Cam had got him on the bike path, and out in the woodshop, making birdhouses together—Cam cutting the wood, Toby sitting at the bench next to him, handing him a nail now and then—that probably accounted for much of Toby's progress.

He could speak in short, simple sentences now—*I want chips. Big truck come. Go home now*—though there was a lack of intonation to his voice, a flatness. He didn't dance or run the way he used to, but he no longer got down on all fours to climb the stairs as he had done in the first months after the accident. He had a funny, flat-footed gait and his body tilted as he walked. One time, when Eleanor had brought him with her to the girls' spring concert, a boy in Ursula's class had pointed to him and laughed. "Look, it's a zombie," he said.

Everyone started laughing.

"My brother just has a problem with his brain," Ursula told them. "You know what your problem is? Your heart."

The next week, when it was Ursula's time to give a report in school, she chose Toby for her topic.

"My brother used to be really smart," she told the class. "Then he fell in a pond. Maybe someday the doctors will figure out how to make his brain work better. In the meantime, he's still him inside.

"The thing you love isn't the person's brain," she said. "It's the person."

46.

nothing matters anymore

For the first weeks after Toby's accident, recognizing what Eleanor was going through, the newspaper syndicate ran old strips from *Family Tree* in place of any new material. After a month had passed, she got back to work, but her mind felt as blank as Toby's now appeared to be. She still filed the strip every Monday, but the story lines she came up with now had a forced quality to them, like episodes of some old sitcom she might have watched growing up.

One thing about the strip: Eleanor had always managed, within the structure of those five frames, to resolve the family stories she told, in pictures and dialogue, with some kind of hopefulness. But the story they were living now offered no humor, and no happy resolution.

She told herself she had to keep it going. This was their main source of income. Only she couldn't. The whole point had been telling honest stories about the life of a family, but the story that defined their lives now was the one she could never bring herself to tell. The beloved character of Jasper wasn't Jasper anymore.

At this point *Family Tree* was running in almost a hundred newspapers across the country. The strip paid their family's bills, but what had gratified Eleanor just as much was the way a community had grown up around the *characters*. Every week since it started appearing—more and more, as readership expanded—she'd open their mailbox to find it stuffed with letters from readers telling her how much her stories meant to them, how grateful they were that someone was talking about the kinds of things going on in the family she drew that nobody else talked about. Mostly, these letters came from women around Eleanor's age, raising families of their own and navigating their own complicated relationships, but others wrote to her, too, telling her how much the strip meant to them. She heard from a woman in her nineties who said, "You really bring me back to my own young days," and from a young woman who wrote to say that it was reading Eleanor's strip, week after week, that made her feel she wanted children.

"Who would think that a few simple drawings could tell a whole story?" she wrote. "But there's always so much going on in those pictures you draw."

"I had this idea that if I wanted to be a successful woman in the world, I had to set aside the idea of having a family," one reader wrote. "You make me feel that it might be possible to have both. Not easy, but possible."

There was a man in prison who wrote to her every few months. "I haven't seen my own wife and kids in five years," he wrote. "When I open up the paper and see the pictures you draw about Maggie and Bo and their kids, I like to pretend it's my family. That dad, Bo, is me."

For a while after Toby's accident she just left Jasper out of the strip, but people started sending letters asking what happened to him. Some of them were actually worried. Correctly, of course. She decided to bring him back.

After a dozen false starts, Eleanor finally managed to create a single frame. It was a picture of Jasper staring out the window, his eyes totally blank. Behind him stood his mother, Maggie. Eleanor herself couldn't have said how it was she'd accomplished this, but she had somehow managed, with a few strokes of her pen, to convey, on the mother's face, a look of utter and irredeemable devastation.

On the fifth day of having nothing further to show for her hours at her drawing table out in the studio, Eleanor called her editor at the syndicate.

"The strip is finished," she said. It used to be her joke, calling *Family Tree* "a non-comic." Now this was real. "Until I can find someone in the market for a tragic strip," she told Darla, "I'm going to have to find another line of work."

"What are you going to do about money?" Darla asked. Even before Cam—who would not have expressed any particular concern one way or the other—it was Darla with whom she shared her decision to end *Family Tree*.

"It doesn't matter," Eleanor said. It felt as though nothing did anymore.

She went back to her old freelancing—picking up one-shot jobs drawing logos. She called the textbook company she'd worked for, before the strip got picked up by the syndicate, to say she was ready to take on work again.

"I don't get it," her old boss at the textbook company told her. "I thought you hit the big time. I can't compete with the kind of money you must have been making with the syndicate."

"Never mind that," Eleanor told her. She had no desire to go into her reasons.

47.

shavasana

There was never this moment when Cam announced he was abandoning his woodshop. He had just stopped going out there. What was the point of creating one more burl bowl, when the shelves of his shop were filled with them—beautiful, but unsold?

Cam spent his days with Toby now—working him through the physical therapy exercises that never seemed to make a discernible difference in his motor skills, turning the pages of their *Baby's First Hundred Words* book.

"Show me the turtle, Toby," Cam would ask him. Sometimes he got it right. More often not.

For a few months, Toby and Cam had been attending their senior citizens' yoga class together. Every Saturday morning the two of them set off for the Y. Toby had his own mat now, next to Cam's. When their teacher announced warrior one, he took his position, same as he did for tree and fish and downward dog, happy baby, and *shavasana*. When the class was over, he said *namaste*.

"You should give it a try," Cam told Eleanor. "If there's anyone who could use an hour to chill out, you're it."

Maybe he said this out of loving concern, but she took his words as a criticism. The irony had not escaped her that in many ways what made it possible for her husband to mellow out at yoga class was the fact that his wife was home earning a living.

Eleanor no longer knew how to slow down or be still. She said she was too busy, but there was more to it. As long as she kept moving fast, she was okay. Those moments when she was not doing anything were the hardest. The last thing Eleanor wanted was to lie still on a yoga mat for ten minutes, or even one, alone with her thoughts.

48.

riding without a helmet

It was a Sunday afternoon. Cam had taken their children to the movies—a rerelease of *One Hundred and One Dalmatians*. Eleanor went out for groceries. She had just rounded the ice cream aisle when she heard a familiar voice calling out her name from the produce section.

"It must be my lucky day," he said. "Running into you here."

It was Timmy Pouliot. "You disappeared on us," he said. "The guys on the team all miss you and Cam."

He knew what had happened, of course. Everyone did.

"I could always count on seeing you up in the stands at our games," he said. "I used to ask Cam how he got so lucky to nab a babe like you."

Eleanor hadn't felt like a babe in a long time, if ever. Getting called that threw her off balance.

"Cam's been spending a lot of time with Toby," she told him. "There just wasn't room for softball anymore."

"We all feel terrible about your boy."

"Yeah."

He picked up a melon. Smelled it. "A person still has to have a little fun sometimes, right?"

"I guess."

He must have seen it on her face: how long it had been since Eleanor did anything remotely approaching fun. Maybe it showed, how long since anyone had kissed her. She studied an avocado.

"I should get some of these," she said. "My younger daughter loves guacamole."

He asked her, "You doing anything for yourself these days?"

She laughed.

"I'm buying you a beer," he said.

"I've got all these groceries." *Milk, eggs, butter, cereal, paper towels.*

"Do something dangerous," he said. "Abandon your cart."

Just like that, she did.

There was a bar across the street. He ordered IPAs for both of them.

"So, who are you dating these days, Timmy?" she asked him.

"Nobody at the moment," he said. "Nothing that matters."

"Every summer, you're with a different gorgeous woman."

"It's not about how they look in a bikini, you know?" he told her. "At some point you gotta get off the bike."

"I don't know," she said. "Riding away on the back of a motorcycle sounds pretty good to me right about now."

"Oh yeah?" he said. "Let's go."

She only had half an hour, she told him. Right about now, Cruella de Vil would be kidnapping the dalmatian puppies and taking them off to that castle of hers, to turn them into fur coats. In the old days she would have worried how it would be for Toby, seeing that. She would have had to tell him in advance that they were going to be rescued in the end. But Toby, now, would probably not even take in what happened on the screen.

"I'll get you back to your grocery cart in plenty of time," he told her.

Out in the parking lot, he realized the problem.

"Oh, jeez, I don't have a helmet," he said. "I've never been the helmet type, but you should be wearing one. With those kids and all."

She told him she preferred feeling the wind in her hair.

She put her arms around his waist. This was just standard practice for a passenger, she reminded herself. But it felt good just taking in the feel of his body this way.

"I never rode on a motorcycle before," she told him. With the engine running, she had to yell.

"You don't really need to hold on so tight. But I like it."

Her breasts had been pressing against his back. She loosened her grip. They were rounding a corner now, heading west out of town in the direction of the sunset. She leaned in.

"You're a natural," he called out over his shoulder.

She would have been happy to keep going, far from this place, toward the ocean or the mountains. But he took his promise seriously. They were back at the supermarket parking lot by the half hour mark. She hopped off the bike and arranged her hair, that had been blowing in all directions. She could feel her heartbeat.

"Next time, I'll take you to this road I know where there's this great boulder. From the top, you can see the world. We'd just need a couple hours."

"That was just what I needed," Eleanor told him. *I wish I had a river I could skate away on.*

"Call anytime," he said. He took a pen out of his pocket and took hold of her hand in a way that made her think, for a moment there, that he was going to kiss it. He uncapped the pen and opened her palm. He wrote his number on it.

After he dropped her back at the parking lot and drove away on his bike she retrieved her cart and paid for her groceries. Cam was in the yard when she got home. Her husband did not look up as she pulled the car in and lifted the groceries from the back.

Alison—Al—was upstairs, the place she spent most of her time these days. Ursula was playing Candy Land with Toby. She had taught him to work the spinner, but she moved his pieces for him. From the living room, she could hear her younger daughter's sweet, high voice, patiently explaining to her brother, not for the first time, why she had to move his piece all the way back to the Molasses Swamp. Not that Toby showed any indication he minded. Ursula just liked to pretend he would care who won.

Putting the groceries away, Eleanor allowed herself to think about the hour she'd just spent.

Timmy's body was completely unlike her husband's. More solid and substantial. Not as tall as Cam, but a burlier build, where Cam was lanky. If she had placed her hands on her husband's stomach, as she'd done with Timmy, she would have been able to feel every rib, but Timmy liked his beer.

She opened a bag of frozen peas and set them on the counter, put the water on to boil. Ursula came in the kitchen, in search of snacks.

"What's that on your hand?" she asked.

"A number I wrote down off a bulletin board," she said. "Some guy who sells cordwood."

After, it occurred to her that this was the first time she'd ever lied to one of her children.

That winter Cam enrolled in a program to become a physical therapist. There was a place in Boston with once-a-month weeklong immersion classes and summer intensives designed to get a person through the program in three years. He was thinking he could see clients out in the barn after he got his certification, he told Eleanor. Clear out his tools. Put in nicer floors maybe. Eleanor could keep her workspace out back. It didn't take up that much room.

"I want to be more of a contributor around here," he told Eleanor. "A good physical therapist can bring in a nice income. It could make a big difference. Take some of the pressure off you. And I might learn some new techniques for working with Toby."

"Whatever," she said.

Coco was off at school now—a place called the Center for Holistic Studies in Vermont, where they taught Reiki and massage and yoga, which Cam (Cam and Toby, she said) had inspired her to explore. Home on Christmas break, she stopped over to see them. She'd made tie-dye shirts for the children and bigger ones for Cam and Eleanor.

Coco thought the physical therapy idea was great, of course. Coco thought everything Cam did was pretty great, but physical therapy in particular.

"It's got to be a big advantage," she said, "having worked with your hands all this time."

"The yoga classes I've been going to with Toby really got me thinking," he said. "I could see the relationship between the body and the brain. Yoga's great that way."

"You should try it, Eleanor," Coco said. "It might help you to be not so stressed out."

"So now even my babysitter is giving me advice about how to relax," Eleanor said to Darla when she came over the next day. (There had been a bad scene with Bobby on Christmas Eve. The makeup she'd applied did not conceal the bruise.)

"Coco actually had the nerve to tell me I should be taking better care of myself," Eleanor told her. "The big eighteen-year-old expert."

"Of course she's right," Darla said. "That's what's so annoying. Same as you're right when you keep telling me to leave Bobby. Sometimes it just feels crummy, hearing the truth."

Eleanor did know, in fact, that she needed to have something in her life besides taking care of her children and paying the bills. But the idea of hanging out on a mat listening to a CD of *kirtan* chanting while performing sun salutations just didn't have any appeal to her. What she wanted to do, actually, was call up Timmy Pouliot and go for another motorcycle ride.

49.

zero gravity

That was the year Eleanor got her first computer, and they announced that a teacher was going up in space.

She'd always resisted technology—held on to her manual typewriter for years before finally buying her IBM Selectric. Back when she had her comic strip her editor at the syndicate was always urging her to upgrade. More significantly, maybe, Al, who'd been obsessed with technology as far back as kindergarten, when her grandparents sent them a Pong game for Christmas, had told her mother she should buy a computer from a new company called Apple. A Macintosh.

Everything was going to be about computers and programming now, Al told her. If you didn't accept that, you'd be living in the dark ages. Look at the *Challenger*! That's where the world was heading. Technology.

"Before you know it, Mom, computers are going to have graphic programs," Al told Eleanor. Movies, too, maybe, and ways of communicating with people without having to use a phone. On one of her visits to the library she'd found an article about a lab at Stanford run by a man named Terry Winograd—whom she now quoted regularly to her parents. "Pretty soon people will be able to talk to their phone and tell their stereo what music to play," she told Eleanor. She already knew she was going to study with Dr. Winograd at Stanford someday.

According to Al, computers were going to revolutionize the world. She herself preferred PCs, but for her mother's purposes, the Apple Macintosh was best.

"Just take my word for it," she said. "This is something I understand."

Finally, though it represented a big investment, Eleanor had ordered one of the new Macintosh computers. The box sat in her studio for two months before she had the courage to open it.

"You have no idea how much memory they can store on one tiny chip," Al told her. "It's like magic, only it's real. You'll see, Mom. This is going to change everything."

There isn't a computer in the world that can help Toby, Eleanor thought. But she didn't say it.

That fall it felt as though everyone was going off in different directions. Eleanor, working her long hours in the studio, was trying to come up with money. Cam was driving back and forth to Boston for physical therapy training and, weeks he was home, spending more and more time off somewhere—Eleanor never even asked anymore—studying his anatomy books in between drives to bring Toby to yoga. With Eleanor working so hard, Phyllis made most of the meals. Al just stayed upstairs in the kids' room, reading about programming and studying Mandarin. Days went by sometimes now when they didn't even have meals together anymore. The one thing Eleanor had said they'd always do.

Ursula was focused on the *Challenger* space launch. Christa McAuliffe lived half an hour from Akersville, in Concord. She had a husband and two kids, and a job as a high school science teacher, as well as a lifelong ambition to go into space. Except when she put on her astronaut suit, she looked like a regular mother. The happy kind.

They made a bulletin board about the *Challenger* in Ursula's classroom. Whenever you found an article in the newspaper about Christa McAuliffe or the other astronauts, you were supposed to cut it out and bring it in to add to the bulletin board. By Thanksgiving, the board had been almost filled up, and they weren't even going to launch the *Challenger* until January.

By November, the mission to space was all Ursula talked about. She knew the names of every one of the astronauts, but her particular focus was Christa McAuliffe. Christa just seemed so cheerful about everything—like Ursula herself, actually. In every one of the pictures of Christa on the bulletin board, she was smiling.

At Stop & Shop with Eleanor one time, Ursula saw a commemorative edition of *People* magazine with Christa McAuliffe on the cover. Eleanor didn't buy things like this normally, but Ursula said she'd rake all the leaves under Old Ashworthy plus empty the dishwasher for a month if her mother would buy the magazine. Eleanor had put it in her cart, though probably less because the deal impressed her than because she had no energy to argue.

Eleanor felt tired all the time now, though the feeling had nothing to do with staying up late or working harder than usual. It was a bone-deep weariness. When she tried to summon an image of something hopeful to look forward to, she came up blank.

For Ursula, nothing exemplified hope better than the *Challenger* launch.

At dinner, when the family gathered around the table, she talked nonstop about Christa. She knew the names of her children and that she had played piano when she was Ursula's age, and how she believed that everyone should have a dream and never give up on it. Ursula had seen a special on TV that showed Christa McAuliffe at the space center in Texas, practicing what it would be like not to have any gravity around. They showed her floating around a pretend space capsule doing somersaults in the air.

You would think a person's hair would look really crazy in a situation like that, Ursula pointed out, but Christa's hair had looked pretty much the same in the no-gravity space capsule model as it did in the other pictures on the bulletin board. Ursula found this difficult to understand, but Eleanor said that was a perm for you. It took more than zero gravity to mess it up.

Ursula wished she could be someplace where there wasn't any gravity. "When I grow up I'm going to be an astronaut," she told them at dinner.

"Good luck with that," her older sister observed, in the new, bitter tone of voice in which she delivered just about every remark. They all knew they were supposed to call her Al now, but they kept forgetting, which was one more source of irritation.

"You have to be wicked good at math," Al went on. "Plus, they give you a test where you do all these push-ups and jumping jacks. You'd never be able to pass."

"That's not what Christa says," Ursula told her. "Christa says if you just try hard enough and believe you can do it, anything's possible. Christa says, reach for the stars."

Al rolled her eyes and took a piece of chicken. Her hand extended across Toby's plate, as if no one was sitting there. Toby, observing the chicken passing by, studied his fork.

"Anyways, I got a B plus in arithmetic this report card," Ursula said. Also, she was doing sit-ups every night.

"You know how many people there are that try out for NASA? Like, a million."

"I think it's great that Ursula wants to be an astronaut," Eleanor offered. She still said the kinds of things normal mothers said to their kids, even though Ursula could tell it was mostly an act.

"I might just sign up to be an astronaut, too," Cam told them. "What do you think, El?" He held out a biscuit as if it were a spaceship and landed it on her plate.

She just looked at him. Her behavior had started to resemble Toby's. Whatever faraway place he occupied now, she seemed to have gone there, too. Or maybe a different one.

"You'd be a great astronaut, Dad," Ursula said. "You're great at everything."

"They have an age limit on astronauts," Al told her.

"Oh, well," Cam said. Come to think of it, if he went up in space he'd miss his family too much.

There was another reason why Ursula brought up the *Challenger* so much. It gave them something to talk about. She never remembered them having this problem before, but in the six months since the accident, they had less and less to say to each other. Maybe because so often it had been Toby who got the ball rolling, his silence now left them all at a loss for words.

A loss for words. Ursula couldn't remember where she'd heard that expression, but she understood what it meant now. You could lose your money, or your appetite, and one time she heard a woman at the post office talking about a man she knew who lost his marbles. But a loss for words seemed to her now the saddest of all.

There was this giant space in their family that Toby used to occupy, and even though he was right there in the room with them—more so than ever before, actually, now that he never ran off on his own the way he used to, climbing up on things and disappearing at museums and shopping malls—Ursula did everything she could to fill it. Not that her efforts worked very well.

It was as if their whole house was a zero-gravity chamber, Ursula thought. They were all floating around like astronauts, waving their arms, turning upside down or sideways, doing these normal kinds of things like eating Jell-O or getting toothpaste out of the tube, except the Jell-O just hung there in the air waiting for one of them to get a hold of it.

Nobody bumped into anybody. They spread out their arms, but nobody touched each other. The only difference was, when they showed zero gravity on TV, the astronauts all looked like they were having fun.

50.

a million pieces

All month, Ursula had been counting down the days to the *Challenger* launch. They'd canceled it twice on account of unusually cold weather at Cape Canaveral. Then came the news: the shuttle was launching. That morning, the astronauts were going into space.

Students at the girls' school were going to watch the launch in the cafeteria. They had all signed a card that they mailed off to Concord, where Christa McAuliffe lived, letting her know they'd be cheering for her as she blasted off the launchpad. Nobody would be cheering louder than Ursula.

Eleanor was packing the school lunches when Ursula came down for breakfast. She had on a light blue jumpsuit to match the jumpsuits of the shuttle crew. She told her mother she was too excited to eat. She'd eat after at the party they were planning at school for after the liftoff. Cam was heading out that day for an all-day physical therapy workshop. Watching him as he headed out the door, Eleanor was struck by what a beautiful man he was, and how long it had been since they'd touched each other. When he bent low to kiss Ursula and touch her cheek, Eleanor felt a strange little stab, remembering how that felt. She had been so angry for so long now, she had almost forgotten.

Eleanor wasn't done being angry at Cam. But she admired what he was trying to do with Toby. More than any of the other things they'd tried, it was the yoga that seemed to get through to him.

"Don't you want to see the *Challenger* go up, Dad?" Ursula asked Cam as he headed out.

"You can tell me all about it tonight," he said.

"This is the best day of my life," Ursula said as she headed out to the school bus. "I'm going to remember this forever."

Eleanor thought about the moon walk then. Neil Armstrong planting the flag. Matt Hallinan on top of her in the front seat of his car, after, whispering in her ear as he thrust his body into hers. *One small step for man.*

She stood in the doorway, watching her husband head to his truck. She wished she could make her heart open up.

"Cam!" she called out to him. She was thinking how good it would feel to put her arms around him, the way she'd done with Timmy Pouliot when she rode on the back of his motorcycle. She had almost forgotten what it felt like to have her husband put his arms around her. She wanted to say something—something loving, even; it had been so long—but she couldn't think what. They had drifted so far apart from each other. She didn't know how to get back.

Cam didn't turn around. Maybe he didn't hear Eleanor calling out to him. He drove away.

After the kids were gone—the girls to their regular school, Toby to his special one, Ursula hugging to her chest that morning's newspaper clipping with a giant picture of the *Challenger* and the words "Up, Up and Away!"—Eleanor took her coffee and bagel and headed to her office.

She put on a Joni Mitchell CD she loved, *Hejira*. It was her habit, when at her desk, to keep a single song on repeat so it became a kind of mantra for her. That morning, no doubt in recognition of the space launch, and the women taking flight from Florida, the song she kept playing was "Amelia."

The drone of flying engines, is a song so wild and blue. Alone in her studio, Eleanor sang along with Joni. For some reason she felt restless.

Eleanor turned on the new computer. She had finally gotten around to taking it out of the box—as gingerly, that first time, as if she were handling a grenade. Now she started every day at her desk by turning it on, slipping the disk in the slot, listening for the pinging sound that meant she could get to work (designing a company logo probably, or some letterhead). The smiling face appeared on the screen.

She stared at her glowing computer screen. For no apparent reason, except that this was the time of year her parents had been killed in the crash, she thought about her mother.

There was so much about Eleanor's life now that her mother wouldn't even recognize. Starting with this house and the three children she'd given birth to here—the one who seemed to live under a perpetual cloud of discontent, the one who just wanted everybody to be happy, and the one who had almost died and returned to them like a sad and silent little stranger.

Her parents, if they came back to life for a day, would barely recognize Eleanor now. They had known nothing of the books she'd published, the farm where she'd made her home, the tall, elusive, red-haired man—one-time goat farmer, first baseman, maker of bowls, and forts out of refrigerator boxes—with whom she'd fallen in love. They knew nothing of the fierce love she had for her children, her obsession with keeping them safe, the unspeakable grief she felt now over her failure to do that, and the wild yearning to reclaim a life for herself—how it felt that day on Timmy Pouliot's motorcycle, tearing up the two-lane with the wind in her hair—even as she dedicated her days, one after another, to the family waiting for her back at home.

What would Martin and Vivian make of the Macintosh computer in front of her—a device nobody could have imagined twenty years before? A granddaughter who didn't like wearing dresses, up in her room studying a whole other language called "programming." The shuttle on the launchpad in Florida and the children in school cafeterias all across America counting down—*ten, nine, eight, seven*—and the woman about to blast off into space? Strange to think that when Eleanor's parents died, Neil Armstrong had yet to set foot on the moon.

Reach for the stars, Christa said. This was Cam's approach to raising Toby—to believe that one day, if they just did enough sun salutations, his damaged brain would somehow restore itself. Words would come. (Did Alison's hero, Dr. Terry Winograd, have a computer program for that?)

Cam believed their son would learn to ride a bike. He would speak whole sentences. He would tell them what he was thinking again.

He'd have thoughts. Maybe he did now, Eleanor just didn't know what they looked like.

He'd fall in love someday with a woman who might love him back.

Ursula possessed a similar brand of optimism. She clung to the faith that if she just worked hard enough at it, she could make everything how it was before—or at least, make it all right. Maybe this was what had inspired her obsession with the *Challenger:* the way that space launch seemed to represent, not only to her but to everyone gathered that morning in Cape Canaveral to watch it, a belief in ever-broadening horizons, the triumph of hope at a time when, in her own family, it seemed in short supply.

Eleanor got to work then. Her current job was creating a series of drawings of famous American inventors and writing a capsule profile of each. This morning's assignment: Eli Whitney and his cotton gin. She wished she could care about Eli Whitney, but she didn't.

Sometime around noon, Darla called. "You were watching it, right?"

"Actually, no," she said. "I have all this work to do. I was just getting started on Thomas Edison. And if you want to know the truth, I'm a little maxed out on the *Challenger.* It's all Ursula ever talks about."

"Turn on your television," Darla told her.

Normally, she let the girls walk home on their own from where the bus dropped them off, but that day she and Toby were waiting, parked across the street from the bus stop, when it pulled up. The three children who stepped down first, before her daughters, all looked dazed, as if they'd just gotten off one of those really awful rides at an amusement park and wanted to throw up. Even Al, who had been walking around with a fuck-you look for half a year, appeared deeply shaken.

Ursula was the last one off the bus—the blue jumpsuit with the NASA patch on the pocket looking, now, like a bad Halloween costume. Her skin seemed to have turned a whole other shade since she left home that morning—she looked bluish, and strangely pinched, as if the air had been sucked out of her. She seemed, suddenly, very small. Crossing the street to the spot where her mother and brother stood, she looked like a very old woman.

"They blew up," Ursula said. Her voice was flat. "They blew up into a million pieces."

"Oh, honey," Eleanor said, wrapping her arms around her daughter. She, the woman who thought if she could just locate that Barbie shoe, she could protect her daughter from sorrow.

A picture came to her of that day in her dorm room back at boarding school when the teacher had come to the door to tell her about her parents' accident. And how, after, she had to keep going over the same odd, irrelevant details as if maybe, by doing that, she could make sense of what happened.

My roommate, Patty, had just made popcorn. I was working on a painting, but I'd taken a break. We were putting on nail polish.

"We saw it happen but at first nobody understood what was going on, not even Mrs. Ferguson," Ursula said. "When we saw the smoke, we thought it was supposed to be like that."

Eleanor got down low to put her arms around Ursula. She wanted to hold her older daughter, too, but Al pulled away, where Ursula pressed in tight against her mother's chest.

A surprising thing happened then. Toby might not understand the part about the shuttle explosion or the astronauts, but he did not fail to recognize that something terrible had happened. One look at Ursula's face and you knew that much. Now he patted her hair.

We were all watching on TV. We saw her kids in the bleachers. Everybody was cheering. Then it was like everything went crazy. When the rocket exploded, we all clapped. We didn't get it. Then we did.

The pieces fell in the ocean. They scattered everyplace. There wasn't anything left.

One more thing happened that day. In the scale of what took place over Cape Canaveral, this bore no consequence. But for their family it did.

After she picked the girls up from their bus, Eleanor took the long way home, past the waterfall.

The waterfall was not a place they usually went at this time of year, and passing it required her to abandon their usual route.

The falls seemed like a totally different place in winter than in the spring, when Eleanor and the children came down to launch their cork people, and later, when the weather warmed up and the fishermen appeared, when they'd lay out their picnic blanket and drawing pencils and books.

There was something about the way the ice formed over the rocks—the way the waterfall seemed to have been suspended in midair, in a column of ice, with sharp glacierlike forms rising up under the bridge in the very places where, a few months from now, they'd be launching their boats. Looking down from the bridge, a person's dark imagination might turn to what it would be like if she slipped on the ice at the edge and fell in. Maybe you wouldn't crack your skull on the rocks, but if not, you'd probably die of the cold before you could make your way out. Even in early summer, the water in this brook was heart-stoppingly cold.

But that afternoon, maybe because this had been the place they so often came in their happiest times, Eleanor wanted to sit there by the stone arch bridge for a moment with her children. Just sit there together, taking it all in. Maybe, she thought, on this day of terrible sadness, they'd find solace in this place they'd known so many happier times.

Somewhere deep down under the ice, trout slept, who would awake in springtime. That's what the seasons taught you. After every winter came spring. Even after great sorrow, a new day.

For Eleanor—and possibly the children, too—the waterfall was the closest thing she knew to church.

In the rearview mirror, she studied the faces of her children in the back seat. Whatever it was that Toby took in of the world that afternoon, and what he made of it, Eleanor had no clue.

Al's eyes were locked on a game of Donkey Kong. Ursula stared at her well-worn commemorative edition of *People* magazine, all those pictures of Christa as a little girl playing her piano, Christa and her children at Disney World, Christa at astronaut training school. Christa in her blue jumpsuit, waving to a crowd as she set out across the tarmac toward the space shuttle.

The memory came to Eleanor of how, when she was Ursula's age, she'd studied pictures in *Life* magazine of JFK and Jackie, in the moments before the assassination. As if they might contain some clue to the awful event about to take place.

Eleanor had imagined they'd have the place to themselves on a day like this. But a truck was pulled over at their spot—a familiar one. They were a hundred feet from the waterfall, but it wasn't hard to recognize the bright green 1972 Dodge that belonged to her husband.

On any other day, the unexpected sight of their father's truck pulled over along the side of the road would have prompted the suggestion from Ursula, "Let's go surprise him."

Not this time. Eleanor was the one—the only one—who had spotted Cam's old truck, but even from that distance, she took it all in. Not just the truck, but the rest.

Braking as hard and sharply as she did then was not a recommended move on icy roads. She could feel the wheels of her car seeking traction.

Another few seconds and Eleanor had managed to turn the car around. Icy as it was on this patch of road, she accomplished a screeching U-turn. Hearing the sound of the tires on the gravel road, the girls looked up and turned their faces to the window.

"What are you doing, Mom?" Al asked from the back. She looked up briefly, just long enough to see her father's truck. Ursula had taken her eyes from her magazine now to look out the window.

"What's Dad doing here?" Ursula said. "Maybe they canceled his workshop thing on account of the *Challenger.*"

Then Al again: "Why are we turning around?"

"I decided to go home the other way after all," Eleanor told them. "Maybe your dad needs to be alone."

Only he wasn't alone. Her children, with their heads bowed, hadn't seen it, but Eleanor had. There was another person on the bench seat next to her husband.

It was Coco. Easy to tell, from the back even, on account of that red beanie of hers and a scarf knit by Alison, a gift from the Christmas just past.

They had their arms around each other. They were kissing.

"When we get home, I'm making us popcorn and hot chocolate," Eleanor said. She would have liked to gun the engine, but the road was so icy, and she carried the memory still of a spin on this very spot, a winter far from this one, a baby in her belly and her husband back at their farm, stoking the fire, a time when it seemed their whole lives stretched before them, and the idea of a moment like this one would have been unfathomable.

They rode in silence then. Normally, Eleanor would have put on a tape, and they might even have sung along with it, but not today.

Passing Walt and Edith's house, she saw Walt outside, shoveling snow, and something possessed her to stop.

"I'll just be a minute," she told the children. She stepped out of the car, left the motor running.

"You look like you saw a ghost?" Walt said as she approached him. "That *Challenger* business got you upset, I reckon."

"My marriage is over," she told him.

"Oh, honey," he said. The same words she'd spoken to Ursula. He held out his arms to her, and for a short time—no more than thirty seconds, probably, on account of the children in the car, the motor running—she just stood there with her face pressed against his shoulder.

"I just had to tell someone," she said.

She drove very slowly the rest of the way home. Maybe it seemed that as long as they were still in the car, as long as they hadn't got to the house yet, she could stop time.

Cam didn't show up for dinner. Eleanor made a meal for the family, but nobody wanted to eat. For all the days leading up to the launch, Ursula had insisted on keeping the television on the news, but that night nobody turned it on. The girls went up to their room. Toby put on his Thomas the Tank Engine bathrobe, retrieved his meercat from her bed, and sat on the rug. Eleanor stoked the woodstove.

It was seven thirty when Cam walked in the door, bringing a gust of cold air with him. "Sorry about that," he said. "Guy on the road needed help changing a tire." Standing over the table, with his parka still on, he reached for a chicken leg off the platter and bit into it.

He must have been the one person in the United States of America who didn't know what had happened that day. He had come through the door, shaking snow off his boots, calling out to Ursula to tell him all about it. Meaning Florida. Christa. The *Challenger.*

"She's upstairs," Eleanor said. "She said she wants to be alone."

"Where's my future astronaut?" he called up the stairs. "Come down and give your dad a hug."

"I saw you with your girlfriend at Hopewell Falls," Eleanor told him, as he reached for a beer. Off in his truck all day away from the news, though not alone, he was thirsty. "Also, Christa McAuliffe is dead."

That night, after she tucked the girls in—Eleanor alone this time, though it was Cam who got Toby in his pajamas and settled him on his mattress in the borning room—Eleanor fixed a pot of tea and the two of them sat at the kitchen table. They waited until they were sure that everyone was asleep and kept their voices low, knowing how sound carried to the upstairs bedrooms. Cam's face, as he looked across the table at Eleanor, bore an expression she could not remember having seen before. She would have preferred despair, but what he offered looked more like eerily calm regret, and pity.

"We didn't mean for this to happen," he told Eleanor.

We. A new configuration, in which her husband had aligned himself with their babysitter. Years ago—when she was not much older than Alison, now—Coco had shown up in their kitchen with a loaf of banana bread to mark the birth of Cam and Eleanor's first child. Back in the fall, Eleanor and Ursula had baked a carrot cake to celebrate her eighteenth birthday.

Cam took a sip of his tea, rubbed his fine chin. His eyes, looking into hers, offered no excuses. This was supposed to be the moment when he'd put his arms around her and say, "What was I thinking? You're the woman I want."

"You know as well as I do that things between us have been bad for a long time now," Cam told Eleanor. She did know this, now that he mentioned it. Since that morning just over seven months ago when she'd knelt at the edge of their pond over the lifeless body of their son, she had not been able to forgive her husband. In many ways she'd left their marriage that day. Now he was the one departing from it.

"This isn't just about the accident," he said. "It's been a long time since we were in a good place together."

Eleanor studied his boot. Remembered, crazily, a night they danced the polka together in the Akersville town hall, the night they'd skated under a full moon as the ice below their feet made those weird, groaning sounds. *Expand. Contract. Expand.* She remembered a night, not so long ago—after Toby's accident—when he'd reached for her in the dark, and she had said, "Oh, God, not now."

"I have no desire for that anymore," she'd told him. "I don't know if I ever will, ever again."

"If there was anything I could do to fix it, I would," he told her. (And he had, actually. Tried. Yoga class at the Y. The plaster in their bedroom. Milk paint.)

Why was it a surprise that he had chosen to look for someone else—or that when such a person presented herself to him, as she had all those afternoons in their field, playing soccer, he would have leapt at the opportunity?

In Eleanor's eyes, Cam would always be the man who had left their son to wander alone into the pond that day. To Coco, Cam was still the handsome artist-hero she had loved since she was cartwheeling around the edges of the softball field, a man who could make bowls out of burls and forts out of refrigerator boxes and ice castles out of snow—a man who could make the most amazing catches on the softball field and kick a soccer ball farther than anybody. Who wouldn't choose to be with a young girl who could see you as a hero, over the one who had witnessed the moment of your greatest failure and never let you forget it?

"I'm sorry," he told her. "I'm in love with Coco. I know how you see me, but I'm not that guy. I just don't want to be married to you anymore."

51.

a marriage not long enough to bear peaches

After, when she could bring herself to think about those years (as, for a long time, she could not), Eleanor named the days when her children were little—she and Cam consumed by their care and raising, no doubt to the detriment of their marriage—as the happiest she had known. Later she would look back and realize how brief that stretch of time had been, that constituted the sum total of her marriage to her children's father, before everything fell away. It had been a handful of seasons, when you got down to counting—not even enough of them that they'd buried a dog together or seen their peach tree bear fruit. Thunderstorms on the porch, picnics in the field, science fair projects and art projects and trips to the ocean, snow days and sick days and summer evenings at softball games, winter mornings of pancakes with Reddi-wip squirted on top (Cam's idea, of course), shoveling out the car, trips to the dump, uneasy visits from the grandparents, times their checking account went overdrawn and other times—fewer of these—when some unexpected royalty check had shown up, and the two of them went out for dinner and looked into each other's eyes.

Did they hold hands across the table then? When they got home and paid the babysitter—the babysitter, there was a story—did they make love? Did they still love each other, or were they just too distracted by everything else to even ask the question, too consumed with everything else to even consider the question, were they happy?

Later, she would wonder if maybe it was never that good in the first place. Maybe all that time, she'd been kidding herself. When you looked closer, maybe trouble was always there, lurking under the sweet pictures of their lives together. Maybe trouble was always everywhere, and what mattered was what you did about it. Some people hung on and kept bobbing down the stream. Some went overboard.

Later, when Alison began turning away from her—Alison and then Ursula, never Toby, thank God—Eleanor wondered if any of it had been real, after all. Maybe she'd been a bad mother, without even knowing it. Maybe nothing she'd once believed was true.

Scenes came back to her in the night. Not of the good times, but of others.

She'd found an old piece of hamburger meat in the back of the refrigerator one time, left so long that when she took it out it turned out to be teeming with maggots. This was the picture that came to her now.

Milk gone sour. The blood in Matt Hallinan's car. The sound of the abortion doctor's voice, coming from the machine in his neck. Mr. Guttenberg, standing in her dorm room. *There's been an accident.*

She was back in Crazyland now. The room was spinning. Everything wrong that ever happened, that she had chosen not to consider, swirled around her like whiteout conditions in a blizzard, so bad you can't see the road five feet in front of you anymore, and the only thing for it is to pull over, only maybe you can't.

She was gunning the engine. The hunt for the Barbie shoe, the *bûche de Noël,* but ten times worse.

She thought about the time her station wagon had broken down on a muddy road with four children in the back (hers, and Toby's friend Jack) and she had knocked on someone's door in town to call Cam, only he didn't pick up, and when she'd finally made it home with them all, on foot, it turned out he was playing the Talking Heads so loud he hadn't heard.

"You have to hear this song," he said, as she walked in the door. He didn't even say anything, just started playing "Creatures of Love."

She had just looked at him.

There was the time when she thought she was pregnant again, and they knew they couldn't afford it, and she had stayed up all night crying. They were still trying to figure out what to do when she had the miscarriage—blood all over the kitchen floor, as she was mopping it. They had sat up together most of that night, holding each other. "I guess we really wanted that baby after all," he'd said.

Not that they'd try again.

The steak on his breath the night Alison was born. The way he'd looked at Timmy Pouliot's girlfriend at their Labor Day party. A time—such a small moment, but it had stayed with her; had she imagined this?—when, with his arm draped across her body in the dark, a few months after the birth of one of their children (Ursula? Toby?), he had gathered up the loose flesh of her belly and said, "Maybe somebody needs to cut down on the butter." A look on his face when she stepped out of the tub.

And then no look at all. He didn't watch anymore when she pulled her dress over her head or dropped her towel to the floor.

They had argued about stupid things—who cleaned the vegetable bin in the refrigerator, whose job it was to check Ursula for head lice, and when they found them, whose job it was to spend the next six hours picking out the nits. They'd sworn this wouldn't happen to them, but days had gone by in which they exchanged little more than the details of who was picking up which child at which friend's house, or what to bring home from the store. There had been a time when she'd loved it that Cam was an artist, and loved how excited he could be, finding a great piece of wood or creating from it some amazing salad bowl, never mind that nobody was ever going to buy it.

Then it changed. Then, when he embarked on some new and amazing project—a rock cairn, a bed in the middle of the woods planted with moss, a wind chime made from old spoons—a vague sense of irritation overtook her.

Why didn't he get a job?

She remembered a night, not so far back, that until now she had chosen to forget.

Eleanor sat at the kitchen table, paying bills. Too many of them, as usual. Once again, she was going to have to figure out which to pay, which to put off for a month.

Cam was doing pull-ups on the bar he'd attached in the doorway going into the living room. She studied that perfect chest of his, those chiseled abdominal muscles. She set down the calculator.

"Don't you ever think about money?" she said.

It was November—always a hard month, with the days suddenly short and dark, once they'd set back the clocks. The ash tree was bare, its leaves swirling outside the window, and all of winter still ahead of them.

For a moment there, he had looked confused. They were having a nice evening up until then. He was, anyway.

"It's no fun thinking about money," she said. "But someone around here has to."

The grin disappeared. A different expression came over him. He stood in the doorway, bare chested. Like a man waylaid, unarmed, in an alley. No escape possible. For a surprising length of time, he just looked at her.

"You care so much about money? I'll give you money," he said, his voice low and filled with contempt, a voice she'd never heard before. He disappeared from the room for a good ten minutes then, into his woodshop. When he came back, his pockets were stuffed with pieces of paper the size of dollar bills, except that instead of the face of George Washington or Ben Franklin on the front, the face was an ugly green caricature of her own.

The bills fluttered down over her head and onto the kitchen floor like wedding confetti, but not. Twenty of them at least. More likely fifty.

"Here's that money you're always so goddamned eager for," he said. "All that beautiful cash you love so much."

Even in the middle of this, they both understood not to wake the children. He spoke in a voice she didn't recognize, a terrible whisper. Not a whisper so much as a hiss.

"You happy, Eleanor? Happy now?"

Later, he had apologized. Cam was good at that, always ready to make peace, quick to admit when he'd been wrong. Cam was good at letting go of the bad parts. But the memory of that night—his face as he scattered the pretend money over her as she wept—had stayed with Eleanor. Until that night she had not known he was capable of so much coldness or, call it what it was, so much quiet rage. Maybe that's what happened when someone who had once been in love with you wasn't anymore.

Part 2

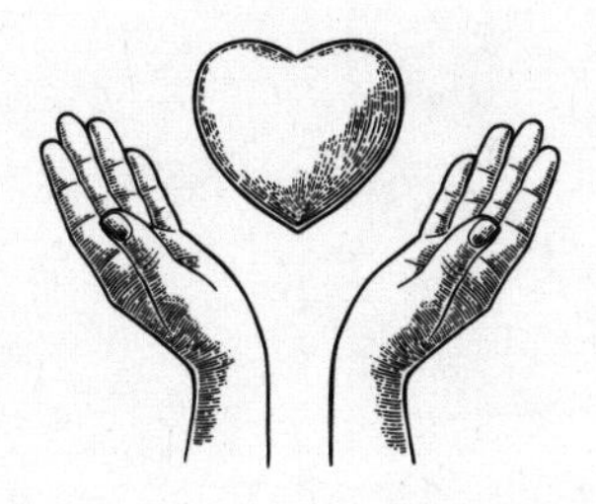

52.

faulty O-ring

February was when Eleanor had always brought out the box of supplies for making valentines—origami paper and wallpaper samples and doilies, glitter and stickers and stick-on rhinestones and stacks of old magazines and seed catalogs to cut up. Every year their creations got more elaborate. The previous Valentine's Day, Ursula had used a glue gun to attach interesting shells around the edges of a heart-shaped box that had once contained her grandparents' annual gift of holiday chocolates, with a different note in each of the spaces that used to hold a chocolate—every one of the notes for her mother. Al, never into fanciness, had cut pictures of all different kinds of tomatoes out of the Burpee seed catalog and stuck them on an old cigar box for Cam to use, to store fishing lures and the car keys he was always losing. Toby, before the accident, used to pick out stones from his collection that he'd cover with red poster paint and ice cream sprinkles. One year he had glued hearts all over his naked body and told them the valentine was himself.

Things were different now. By the first week of February they would have been working every night on their cards, but this year Eleanor had not gotten around to putting out the usual abundance of craft supplies—just a stack of construction paper left over from the previous year and a couple of dried-up markers.

It was an odd moment to engage in a celebration of love. In the week since she found out about Cam and Coco (if she hadn't seen them that day, when was he going to tell her?), the five of them (Cam, Eleanor, the children) had carried on with their routines much as before, though a heaviness hung over the household, and even Toby seemed to pick up on it. He was even quieter than usual, and more listless. The formerly pink ribbon remained permanently wrapped around his pointer finger, its frayed tip twirling inside the soft pink opening of his ear.

Eleanor figured the girls would attribute the mood to what happened to the *Challenger.* The morning after the explosion Ursula had taken down all the pictures she'd hung in her room. When she took out the trash that afternoon, Eleanor found the commemorative coin Cam's parents had sent from Florida, with the date January 28, 1986, engraved on the front along with the profiles of the astronauts.

A week or so after Eleanor had seen Cam and Coco together, he came to her as she was putting away the leftovers from dinner. The children were asleep. The house was quiet.

Ever since that first night, the two of them had barely spoken to each other. Now he put a hand on her shoulder, in a way that almost made her think he was going to tell her the whole thing was a huge mistake and ask her forgiveness.

"I don't know what I was thinking," he'd say. "You're the woman I want to spend my life with. We made this family together."

"Can we talk?" he said.

They sat on the couch by the woodstove. He must have bought a bottle of wine on his way home. He poured her a glass, then one for himself. Always, in the past, on those occasions when they'd bought wine, she'd set the cork aside, for cork people. This time, she just studied it, unable to imagine where any of them would be when the snow melted.

"You know, this doesn't have to be a tragedy," he said to her. "We have so much to be grateful for. Three wonderful children."

She took a sip of her wine and looked into his eyes, trying to understand what he was saying.

"If I had it all to do over, I'd marry you again," he said. "You've been a wonderful mother to our children."

That was it? Her face must have betrayed how she took in what he said, because now he amended it.

"And so much more."

Eleanor still just sat there, unable to speak.

"The important part is that we stay friends," he said. "I know we can do that. I have nothing but respect for you, El."

This would have been the moment she'd say the same thing back to him, only she couldn't.

"Let's promise each other we'll never speak unlovingly of each other to the children," he said. "If we can do that, I think they're all going to be fine."

She brought the wineglass to her lips and sipped deeply. She studied his face. Even now it still struck her by surprise sometimes what a handsome man he was, but for the first time she took in the fact that maybe he was no longer quite as handsome as he had been. His skin looked pale. He needed a haircut.

"Sure," she said. "That makes sense."

The next week, Eleanor announced a family meeting. She fixed the most comforting meal she knew, mac and cheese, and told the children they didn't have to finish their broccoli to get dessert. She made brownies, their favorite.

Watching the three of them around the table as they ate their meal (and first, as they sang grace, always the same song, "Simple Gifts"), she studied their faces, memorizing the sight of them. Hard events had taken place before this, and—less than a year earlier—a truly terrible one. But always before, their family had weathered them together. This was the last night their world would be intact.

They had recently lived through a national disaster, of course: they had witnessed the spacecraft bearing their hero as it broke into a million pieces in front of their eyes. They had survived their brother's accident and the long, sad chill that set in after, registered the tension between their parents—even noted, perhaps, that their parents seldom touched each other anymore, or met each other's eyes, even.

For all of this, they would still have said (or not even said it, because this was simply a fact of their lives, as real as the seasons—real as the earth under their feet or the fact that they would always live together at the end of this dead-end road) that they had two parents who loved each other. Maybe Ursula—the self-designated rescuer, their tireless cheerleader and mascot—worried about whether they were happy, and what to do if they weren't. But even their parents' increasingly apparent irritation with each other (their mother's with their father, at least) was acceptable, so long as they were together.

Their family—the circle made by the five of them as they held hands, singing grace around the table or touching fingers around Old Ashworthy—was the thing they had always believed they could count on forever. When they sat down to dinner that night, this was as much a fact of their lives as the air they breathed. By the time they went to bed all that would have changed.

After the brownies, they cleared away the dishes together, folded the napkins, and carried the trash to the compost pile under the beam of Al's high-powered flashlight. For the first time since the *Challenger* explosion, Ursula was talking about future plans—tryouts for the talent show, her book report on *Betsy and Tacy Go Downtown*, a new girl who'd just joined their class.

"They used to live in San Diego but her dad decided to leave his old job but maybe what actually happened, according to her, is he got fired on account of he drinks too much, and they couldn't bring her dog because they don't allow dogs at her apartment building but she's hoping they can get a hamster," Ursula was saying. Listening to her younger daughter tell the story, Eleanor thought about film footage they'd all watched a hundred times now, of the astronauts, smiling and waving as they headed toward the space shuttle that morning. No clue what was coming.

She felt like a sniper. About to pick off an unsuspecting pedestrian, out walking her dog.

"I was telling Juniper"—this was the new girl; she had hippie parents, evidently, perhaps fellow devotees of *Spiritual Midwifery*—"about the fort Al and me are going to build," she said. "I was thinking we could invite her over and maybe have a sleepover." There was also a fundraiser coming up at their school next Saturday with a three-legged race. The parents against the kids.

Ursula actually looked happy again. Like her old self, almost.

Eleanor shot a look in Cam's direction. They could still change their minds. Maybe they didn't have to go through with this after all. For a moment, she allowed herself to imagine an alternative to the scenario she'd been dreading. What if, even as they stood here on the precipice, about to jump, they might choose instead to turn back, descend the mountain, and make camp by some quiet stream? Begin again. Do better this time.

Only they couldn't. From the set of Cam's jaw, the cool, even way he took his seat in the rocker by the fireplace, she knew he was resolved in his choice. This was Cam: a man who, once he made a decision, never looked back.

At this very moment, maybe, he might be thinking about Coco. (And how, later, after their family meeting was over, he'd go out to his shop and call her. "I might not be able to see you for a while," he'd tell her. "Till things settle down.") He would have explained to Coco that this was the night they were telling the kids, and he'd be needing to give them a lot of extra attention in the days ahead.

A picture came to Eleanor of Coco, off in her dorm room in Vermont—her long, beautiful legs folded under her, her beautiful long hair falling down her shoulders. A look of concern on her face. "How did the kids take it?" she'd ask.

"Of course it was rough," Cam would say. "But you know my kids. They'll be okay. They love their mother. But they love you, too."

Eleanor imagined the next line. Cam's voice, whispering low. *Not as much as I do, of course.*

"The children will be fine. All they want is for us to be happy."

It wasn't anything they'd planned, but the children had positioned themselves on the couch in the order of their birth. They had brushed their teeth and put on their pajamas.

"Okay, guys," Ursula said, having reclaimed her role as family cheerleader. "Mom and Dad have something to tell us."

That night even Toby had an air of expectancy. Some big and surprising piece of news must be coming. A winter camping trip, maybe, or a new building project. Ever since visiting her friend Pamela, whose parents had a farm, Al had been lobbying hard for their family to get pygmy goats.

"You used to have one, Dad. Mom told us all about it. Opal, that you brought to the craft fair with a flower in her collar the day you and Mom fell in love."

Maybe this would be the moment their parents would say, "Okay, then, let's do it. Goats. But no more than six of them."

The three of them sat there, each with their brownie, waiting for the family meeting to begin. Whatever the big news was that they were about to receive, they were ready.

Good morning to you. The first song Eleanor had taught to Alison. *We're all in our places, with bright shining faces.*

Eleanor started it.

"You know we love you more than anything," she told them. "We're so proud of the three of you. You're the best kids anyone ever had."

Blah blah blah, she might as well say. *Blah blah blah blah blah.*

"But your father and I . . . we haven't been . . . we've come to the decision—"

Eleanor hadn't come to any decision. Cam did.

"It has nothing to do with the three of you." This was his contribution.

Slow motion.

She watched their faces as they took in the words. A gradual crumbling. Like one of those time-lapse films of an avalanche, with the sides of a mountain caving in on itself, collapsing, until all that was left was a heap of snow. Somewhere in there, the word: "divorce."

"We still care about each other," Cam told them.

Blah blah blah.

"We'll always be your parents. Everything that matters is going to stay exactly the same."

Lie.

"Your mother and I just need a little space."

Needing space. Where had Eleanor heard that one before?

"The important thing is, we love you so much."

So if you love us so much, why would you do this to us? If you care about us more than anything, how could you let this happen?

"We know you probably feel very sad right now," Eleanor said. "That's natural. Maybe you have some things you'd like to ask us. Or just things you want to say."

They had nothing to say, in fact. Then Ursula got up from the couch. "It's time for *Cosby,*" she said. There was a happy family for you. The Huxtables.

Al had no interest in television. "I guess you're done, right?" she said, when Eleanor had completed her speech. "So, can I go now?" She picked up her programming book and headed to her room. A minute later they could hear the sound of her Mandarin tape, and Al repeating the phrases.

Ursula's eyes stayed fixed on the television—an episode in which Rudy Huxtable stole a pack of gum from a convenience store and her father, Dr. Huxtable, as portrayed by Bill Cosby, made her return it. Toby sat on the floor next to her, stacking blocks.

Eleanor was just clearing away the mugs from the hot chocolate she'd made for them when it happened. The reaction they had been bracing for, from the one of their children who would have seemed least likely to deliver it.

Toby. He shot up from his spot on the rug, as if a high-voltage electrical current had surged through his body. Or maybe it was more like magma, rising up from the center of the earth, finally reaching the surface and spewing hot, flaming lava in every direction. He knocked over the blocks. Then he flung himself on the ground. He let out a howl so primitive and raw a person might think it could only have come from a desperate animal, shot through the heart.

"You're going to be all right, Tobes," Eleanor said, kneeling on the floor next to him, not so differently from that other time, when she'd found him in the pond, though this time he fought back. With a force no one would expect from a five-year-old, he pushed her arms away, yanked her hair, kicked her in the stomach, the breasts. He lay there howling. In all the months since his pocketful of stones pulled him to the bottom of the pond, he had barely displayed a shred of emotion. Now came a torrent. Under other circumstances, this might have seemed like a hopeful development.

It lasted several minutes. When he was done, his body went limp. Eleanor picked him up and carried him to bed.

"It's going to be okay, Toby. I promise. We'll all still love each other."

He said the same four words, over and over. The same ones Eleanor herself, though in possession of a vastly greater vocabulary, felt like speaking herself.

I want my family.

Later, she would always connect the end of her marriage with the *Challenger* explosion. As with that one, there had been warnings. That faulty O-ring. Nobody paid attention, was all.

One difference Eleanor had always recognized between herself and Cam: he had an amazing capacity to sail through life, even in difficult times, or awful ones. There was an ease about him, with which he shed old sorrow, always with the assumption that some new joy would replace it. Cam didn't suffer injury or grief or anxiety as Eleanor did. He would not have spent a moment worrying over the loss of a Barbie shoe, and he seemed equally adept at sidestepping worries over a girl who bullied Toby on the playground, the looming specter of a tax bill they didn't have the money to pay, letters from Alison's teacher telling them that Alison—Al—appeared depressed.

"Maybe we should take her to a counselor?" Eleanor said.

"Or take her out for an ice cream cone," he'd answered, grinning.

Sometimes Cam's refusal to saddle himself with sadness or worry seemed like a gift, and a trait Eleanor wished she could emulate. Sometimes it left her feeling as though the weight of the world sat on her shoulders alone. Maybe the same thing that made him so enviably carefree also resulted in his maddening obliviousness. Life just didn't seem so earthshakingly serious to Cam.

He wasn't nostalgic about their past. "Why do I need to look back?" he said. "We're in the present." Old history, old injuries, pain, losses—they never stayed with him. Where everything that ever happened to Eleanor—her lonely childhood, her parents' accident, that summer in Matt Hallinan's car, and all the summers after, and all the other seasons—all that remained alive for Eleanor. Eleanor remembered everything and never let it go.

It was the gift, or curse, she brought to her artwork, too. She remembered perfectly that moment when the police car had appeared in the driveway with Charlie's body lashed to the top. The picture remained clear enough that had she chosen to, she could have drawn it. She could still hear the sound of Mr. Guttenberg's voice on the other side of the door the night he came to her dormitory room to tell her about the crash.

Most of all, the image she could never get out of her brain was of her son, facedown in the pond. And Cam, who was supposed to be watching, running down the hill.

It was that moment, and a thousand smaller ones leading up to it, that had hardened her heart. She might tell Darla that it was the affair with Coco that ended her marriage to Cam, but Eleanor knew it wasn't, really. Cam's falling in love with someone else was the symptom, not the cause. In Eleanor's eyes, Cam would always be the one responsible for the worst thing that ever happened in their lives. What ended her marriage was her inability to forgive him for that.

It didn't matter how many times he told her how sorry he was and how determined to become a better person, or that he—the same man who had once asked where they kept the diapers—had dedicated himself to the full-time job of overseeing Toby's rehabilitation. It was still hard for Eleanor, just looking at his face—a fact noted by Ursula, who observed one day, at breakfast, "Mom, why do you always look in a different direction when Dad's talking to you?"

Ursula never missed anything.

53.

beyond valentines

Valentine's Day came and went, without the usual whirl of craft projects and strawberry desserts. Only Ursula followed through in delivering cards that year, and only to her parents. "Love!," she wrote, in letters so big they barely fit on the paper. Less a celebration than a plea.

Cam and Eleanor still lived under the same roof, but barely spoke to each other now. If Cam bumped into Eleanor, passing in the kitchen, he said, "Excuse me." Eleanor, seeing him walk in the door now, as she stood at the sink, stepped away to another room. It was as if just breathing the same air hurt.

Someone was leaving. Someone was staying. The situation was clearly terminal. They were standing around waiting for the last breath of their marriage. They were beyond valentines.

After the discovery of Cam's affair, and his announcement that he didn't love her anymore, Eleanor might have told him to move out. She would have had legal grounds for that. Moral ones, anyway.

But that would have meant staying on in a place where every room offered reminders of the life they didn't have anymore. More than any place on earth, this was the one that had represented her safe harbor. Since the days of their children's births she had pictured them getting married here someday, grandchildren running through the field. Someday, far from now, she had imagined her ashes and Cam's scattered under the great tree. But the idea of staying alone with the children, in the house where they had been born, overlooking the field where two parents no longer married to each other had spoken their vows, seemed impossibly sad.

She had made her home on this farm. She could not imagine a

home she would ever love as much as she had loved this one, and because this was true, it hardly mattered where she located herself next, except that it had to be somewhere her children could feel safe. She had found something she'd never known before, living on this dead-end road with the father of her children—a sense of home. But she saw no way of staying on here now, when every room—and the field beyond, and the vegetable garden, and the studio, and the pond (that, most of all)—triggered memories of the life she didn't have anymore.

She remembered as clearly as if it had been yesterday that first afternoon she saw the house with the old Realtor, Ed. The wide-board floors. The beam where, every Fourth of July, a few generations of Murchisons had penciled in the heights of their children and fired off the miniature cannon afterward. The little knoll at the foot of the field where Cam and Eleanor and their children had planted a row of firs to serve as their Christmas trees for the next thirty years.

This year, same as always, they'd tromped through the snow together to chop down their tree and put it up, as always, in the corner opposite the fireplace. She had chosen her children's gifts so carefully this past Christmas, as she always did—as if locating a Cabbage Patch doll for Ursula or getting the Commodore 64 for Al would ensure their happiness. (Toby was another story. Toby didn't care what you gave him anymore.)

Then came the next part: how, with her three children watching, standing frozen among the newly opened presents, the twinkling lights, she had picked up the platter holding the precious cake she'd spent the last three hours constructing and smashed the whole thing into the trash.

So much for protecting your children. So much for ensuring their happiness.

If Cam had been the type to hold on to old injuries, as Eleanor did, he might have blamed her forever for that one, but she was guessing that if you said to him now, "That was pretty awful, what your wife did that time with the *bûche de Noël,*" he might not even remember.

Eleanor remembered everything, and it was the fact that she did that made her know: she had to leave this place.

Her lawyer told her not to do it. But if she was sure she had to leave the property, he told her, they'd need to hire an appraiser, settle on a figure as to its current market value. Once they had this, they'd know the figure Cam had to come up with to buy her out. Fifty percent of whatever the farm was worth.

How was anybody supposed to calculate that one? What was her home worth? Everything, if a happy family lived in it. Otherwise, nothing.

She knew this, too: whatever figure an appraiser came up with for the farm, there was no way Cam could buy her out. Cam earned almost nothing. Their savings—though he'd be entitled to half—amounted to a little over a thousand dollars.

With her syndicated strip gone, she was just getting by on her freelance jobs, and Toby's school and speech therapy had wiped out the money she'd saved from her days as a bestselling author of children's books. There was no way Eleanor could afford a house of her own without the money from the buyout. Still, the thought of selling the farm—even if she never got to live there again—was like imagining a death.

The agreement they came to gave Cam nine years to figure out how he might buy out Eleanor's share of their farm. Meanwhile, he'd assume the mortgage and Eleanor would rent a place somewhere else. "I'm not endorsing this," her attorney told her. "Frankly, I think it's a lousy deal for you. Nine years. Your ex-husband's a smart guy. Maybe he'll come up with something. Either that or his parents will kick the bucket and he'll inherit some cash. Or maybe they'll bail him out."

The document they drew up left it that when Alison turned eighteen Eleanor and Cam would have the farm appraised. At that point Cam would be obligated to pay Eleanor half of that figure, to take over full ownership of the property. Failing this, it would be put on the market.

"Not that it's my business, but you need to promise me," her attorney said. "The day your older daughter turns eighteen you're demanding full payment on the buyout. If your ex-husband can't do it, you put up the For Sale sign."

Eleanor signed the document. So did Cam.

"I don't understand why you and Dad have to do this," Ursula said. Speaking of the divorce.

Ursula was always the negotiator, the peacemaker. As for Al, she seemed to have shut them all out. When she got home from school now, she headed to her room and barely emerged, except when called for meals. This left Ursula to be the children's spokesperson.

"Can't you two just sign up for some counseling?" she said. "You could go on a romantic vacation together, just the two of you. Al and me could take care of everything. Phyllis could drive us places. And Coco can come over on weekends when she's home from college and play soccer."

They all loved Coco. She'd make things right. That's how the children had seen her before. And still did.

54.
why would you blow up our life?

Eleanor had assumed the next thing to happen, after they delivered the news of their divorce, would be an announcement to the children, from Cam, that he and Coco were a couple now. As much as she wanted to spare their children pain, maybe Eleanor looked forward to that moment. The girls would hate Coco then. They'd be angry with their father. As angry at him as Eleanor was.

But the announcement never came.

Maybe Cam was right that telling the children about his relationship with Coco at this point would be too hard for them. But the result of his not telling them made for a different kind of trouble that fell on Eleanor's shoulders.

Because Eleanor was the one moving out, they saw her as the one responsible. Their mother was leaving their father. That's how it looked, and Cam said nothing to disabuse them of this idea. And Eleanor, though she wished she could explain, believed that by doing so, she would become that person she vowed never to be: the bitter parent who poisons her children against their other parent. She and Cam had promised each other they'd never speak ill of each other. Adhering to the promise meant, for Eleanor, holding her tongue about Cam having fallen in love with their babysitter.

Now there was this: having told Eleanor he was in love with Coco, suddenly she was nowhere to be seen—off in Vermont, attending her school for holistic studies, evidently. From a conversation Eleanor had with her mother, Betsy, when the two of them ran into each other at the food co-op, it was clear to Eleanor that Coco's parents knew nothing of her relationship with Cam, either. She was eighteen now, but Eleanor doubted that Betsy and Evan would be happy if they knew their daughter was involved with a man almost twenty years older, a father of three.

Al was the first to express her anger toward Eleanor. Eleanor had been making one of those speeches parents getting divorced deliver to their children, that she and Cam still cared about each other and that nothing was the children's fault, and nobody was going to love them any less. She went so far as to suggest things might be better for the three of them without the tension of their parents' fighting.

Eleanor hated the sound of her own voice, saying these things. But not as much as Ursula did.

"I don't want to hear it," Ursula said, covering her ears, when Eleanor had launched into her most recent attempt at reassuring them.

"You'll see," Eleanor said. "We're going to make this work. The most important thing will always be you three."

"If we're so fucking important," Al said, "why would you blow up our life?"

(She said "fucking." She used that word. She must have known that under the circumstances, Eleanor was not about to give her a hard time for using bad language. This was the children's moment to give her a hard time. As hard a time as they chose.)

"I want you to tell me your feelings," Eleanor said, another time. The four of them had been driving somewhere—Al's basketball practice, probably—and for fifteen minutes, nobody had spoken a word.

"You're leaving our family," Ursula said—all the usual softness and love absent from her tone. "How do you *think* we feel?"

"You need to tell them the truth," Darla urged Eleanor. "Don't you see you're protecting this guy? The jerk cheated on you with the fucking babysitter, and still you're letting him look good to your kids. Like you're the bad mother and he's the poor innocent victim you abandoned."

"I don't want to turn our children against their father," Eleanor said.

"So they turn against you instead."

"That won't happen. That couldn't ever happen."

"A lot of shit starts coming down, once people that used to love each other don't anymore," Darla said. "They start rewriting their history. I probably do that myself. There must have been a time when I actually loved Bobby, but I can't even remember why anymore."

"Our children love us both," Eleanor said. "That won't ever change."

55.

a new mattress

Long before this, in the aftermath of a different hard time in her life, Eleanor had set out to buy a house. Two weeks after Cam told her he was in love with Coco, she set out again in search of a home, though this time she'd be a renter.

Once, this would have seemed unimaginable for a person who loved swimming or skating in their pond and growing tomatoes and looking at the stars, but that was before. Now she headed south to Boston—a place to which she would have said once she'd never return. Close enough that the children could go back and forth. Far enough away that she might manage to start fresh.

She figured she'd find a condominium. Simpler than a house. Easier upkeep. Cheaper. The first three she looked at were no good; Eleanor recognized this the moment she walked in the door. But the fourth was perfect—recent construction, a little bland, but with a tiny yard and enough space that each of the children could have their own room. The kitchen was small, but the children could do their homework there while Eleanor made dinner, with space for a couch where they could watch movies. There was a sunny dining room where she'd put a big table where they could lay out their valentine-making supplies every February and a bay window for the Christmas tree.

She wasn't going to love this condo the way she had loved their farm, but she didn't need to. And in certain ways—particularly those having to do with the children—this place offered advantages to life on the farm. At the special school Toby had attended near Akersville, children with totally different kinds of disabilities were placed in the same too-small classroom. Where they'd be living now, there was a school whose entire focus was on children with brain injuries like Toby's. A bus would pick him up every morning and bring him there.

The plan was for the children to stay put until the end of the school year. Eleanor would come to see them on weekends. The rest of the time she'd get the new place set up for them to move in when summer vacation started. That way, by the following September, they'd be accustomed to their new home.

The girls would have to change schools, naturally, but they'd have better teachers, more opportunities. Where they'd be moving, they could walk by themselves to the library. There was no pond, of course, but there was a big public pool and in winter, an outdoor skating rink and a much more competitive basketball team for Al. Eleanor would get a family membership at the Museum of Science.

These were all the aspects of the move Eleanor pitched to Al and Ursula (less so to Toby, though he was there in the car when she laid it all out).

"Your friends can come over without their parents driving them," she said.

"What friends?" Al said. "We don't know anybody in Brookline."

Eleanor didn't kid herself. None of the attractions of city life she suggested replaced what they were losing, and the children all knew it. Who their mother had been in their lives, until now, was the person Al, Ursula, and Toby had counted on to fix things. Who she was now was the person who broke them.

About the particulars—the requirement, far into the future, that their father buy out Eleanor's share of the farm they shared—she said nothing. The main thing was that the children would still have the farm in their lives. They'd go there on weekends. Even though she would no longer be there herself, Eleanor knew this was a good thing.

The owners of the condo Eleanor chose to rent had moved to Florida to be near their grandchildren, and the place was available for as long as she wanted. The first week of March (cork people season, but not this year), she rented a U-Haul truck. Walt helped, but there was surprisingly little to be done in the end. Eleanor didn't want to dismantle her children's home, and she didn't want much of the old stuff anyway. Mostly, she assembled the furnishings she needed from secondhand stores and a bunch of things the former owners didn't want to bring south with them.

She bought a new drawing table—a smaller one—and turned a small storage room into her studio and plugged in her Mac. Pulling her car in the driveway of the condo, she did not say, "I'm home."

A few days after the move, Eleanor drove back to their farm one more time to pick up the last couple of boxes (a few clothes, her cookbooks, a couple of muffin tins) that hadn't fit in the U-Haul. It was late morning, a Tuesday, all three children in school. Cam was out in the yard bucking firewood.

"Those look heavy," he said. "I'll give you a hand."

He followed her into the house. In the kitchen, she took in the sight of a pan of homemade Rice Krispies treats on the counter (not part of her repertoire or, in the past, her children's, and Phyllis was not a baker). An unfamiliar pair of women's skates hung by the woodstove.

"Coco's been here," she said.

"She was home from school on a break. The kids wanted to see her."

His voice was flat, revealing nothing.

The full moon. Black ice. The sound of cracking beneath her skate blades.

She had left the box of clothes in the closet. To reach it meant passing through their old bedroom.

"I'll just be a second."

All those years, through the births of three children and a thousand times they'd made love on this bed (every day, at first, then less)—the nights in which one or another of their children, and usually all three, had ended up there next to them—they'd always meant to get a real mattress but never did. All those years, they had slept on the futon from Cam's cabin, back in his Vermont days.

There was a new mattress in their old bedroom. A good one, from the looks of it.

Eleanor stood at the side that had been hers, looking out the window. From this spot, when in the late stages of labor with their daughters—and, that last time, with their son—she had looked out to the branches of the old ash tree, reaching leafless across a winter sky. There was a spot on the ceiling she'd focused on during contractions, where, when she'd first moved into this house, before she and Cam got together, she'd stuck a single glow-in-the-dark star.

It was still there.

She remembered the first night they spent together, when she'd tried to count the freckles on Cam's chest, but gave up. His pale naked skin in the candlelight seemingly lit from within.

A winter night. The sound of a basketball game coming from the other room, oranges tumbling off the bed, the world, or just her body, ripping in two.

We have a daughter.

Sixteen months later: *We have another daughter.* She had loved it that he registered no trace of disappointment at the news. He was not one of those men who required a son.

And one more time, another baby. The picture came to her of the moment, in the bathtub this time, when Toby burst into the world—Toby, the one of their children born so fast they had cut the cord and wrapped him in blankets before the midwife made it down their road. Before they even knew the sex of this baby, Cam had called out, "This one's a redhead." Those damp curls. Fists, punching the air. *A boy.* They had told themselves they didn't care about the sex, but when they saw, Cam said the words, over and over, "I don't believe it. We have a son."

She remembered the pronouns. *We have a daughter. We have a son. We.* This part—the part where he'd speak of the two of them as a single unit—would change. Had already.

There had always been a quilt on this bed. Double wedding ring, stitched by Cam's grandmother. But today there were only sheets.

She stood there looking out the window at the familiar view. The tree, the field below it. The stone wall. The pond she would give anything to have never built. She didn't hear Cam enter the room.

"I was stripping the bed," he said. So many phrases took on new meaning now.

She looked up to see her husband—she had not stopped thinking of him that way yet—standing beside her. He touched her arm.

Later, driving back to her new home in the unfamiliar town where she slept now, she tried to reconstruct the event that had taken place at the house with Cam that afternoon. He must have put his arms around her, but that embrace had nothing to do with lust or longing. The way he touched her was more of an acknowledgment of shared grief, like the comfort one person offers another when there's been a death in the family.

Cam had wrapped his arms around her. She didn't so much return the embrace as she collapsed against his body. If he hadn't caught her she might have dropped to the floor.

He was the only other person on earth who remembered everything that had happened in this house. How could it be that a person could be both the source of your greatest sorrow and the source of your only comfort, all at once? That afternoon he was both.

Neither of them said anything. He pulled his shirt over his head—the same way he'd done all those years back in his Vermont cabin that night, the first one. She unbuttoned her blouse, let her tired, well-nursed breasts fall free, not even caring anymore what they looked like in the daylight because he already knew, and anyway, no further need existed to be what she was not, to him: an object of desire. The day would come when they'd be strangers, but this hadn't happened yet. Who each of them was that day, to the other, was the only other person on earth who understood what had been lost.

They unzipped their jeans and stepped out of them, let their clothes fall to the floor and faced each other, less like a man and a woman than two parts of the same whole, two halves of a marriage coming apart. Unlike that first time, there was no shred of illusion on his part or hers that what was happening here held any promise for the future. They were honoring their shared past, was all. In an odd way, she believed she was paying homage to their children. The place they came from, where they began.

"I think we should have lots of babies together," he'd told her once.

"I want to make a family." Well, they had done that. Now came the unmaking part.

She knew his body as well as her own. He could have said the same of hers. She knew where the birthmark was that he used to call North Dakota. He knew where the stretch marks were from that first pregnancy, and the two that followed.

"We both get to be the parents of this child," she'd said. "But my body is wrecked. And you look like some marble statue at the Metropolitan Museum."

"You're beautiful to me," he'd told her. At the time she believed him. At the time he probably meant it.

His body had barely changed since the day they met. One look at Eleanor's and you would have known this was a woman who'd given birth. Now he was in love with a skinny girl with small perfect breasts and a flat stomach and legs that went on forever—a girl who believed he hung the moon.

A memory came to her.

They were in Maine, on a family trip on which Coco, twelve years old at the time, had accompanied them—to help entertain the children and make it possible for Eleanor and Cam to go out alone for a lobster dinner and a glass of wine now and then. At a rest stop on the highway, heading to Acadia National Park, Coco had gotten her period for the first time. She'd taken Eleanor aside, embarrassed to have gotten blood on her shorts. "Don't worry," Eleanor said.

She'd taken Coco to the ladies' room. The two of them shared a stall, Eleanor squatting beside Coco as she sat on the toilet, teaching her how to insert a tampon.

Eleanor's lovemaking with Cam that final afternoon had not lasted particularly long. Nothing happened that stood out as different in any way from a hundred other times their bodies had come together in this way, except for the knowledge that they were saying goodbye. They would never be in this place together again. They held each other but did not kiss.

After she'd put her clothes on again, she picked up the box she had set down before—the one with her cookbooks, which she would seldom if ever use again. *The Tassajara Bread Book.* (Homemade sourdough slathered in butter that they fed each other by the fire, naked.) Julia Child, *Mastering the Art of French Cooking.* (Consulted one time only, the night Patty came to dinner. Coquilles St.-Jacques. Chocolate mousse.) *The Silver Palate.* (Chicken Marbella, for years, her standby when her in-laws came to visit.) So many ways to mark the passage of time in a marriage, the seasons of love.

Neither of them said anything as she walked out the door, after. Where would you begin? Where would you end?

56.

I will always love you

Sometimes, waking up alone in the new condo, she would forget where she was, reach for a door that would have been there if she were back in their old bedroom, or—not yet familiar with the layout here—find herself bumping into a wall she hadn't expected.

It was strange for Eleanor, after her years of caring for young children, to find herself living as she did over those first months after moving out—alone in a city condominium, with nobody to cook meals for or ask: Have you done your homework? Have you practiced your clarinet? For the first few weeks after she moved, she called them every night, but there was an uncomfortable awkwardness to their conversations, and sometimes even the sense that the girls were going through the motions, impatient to get off the phone and back to their lives.

One time, when Eleanor called, Ursula told her that Coco was there. Home from school, she'd stopped by for a visit. She'd fixed them a stir-fry dinner in a wok, with a kind of noodles she'd brought from Chinatown.

"Coco's taking us to *Disney on Ice*," Ursula said. She'd seen ads on television since she was little and always wanted to go.

"We even got Dad to come. Even though he's not the Disney type."

"Coco's around an awful lot these days, huh?" Eleanor said.

"She misses us," Ursula told her. "Phyllis still babysits. Coco's just our friend now."

Cam hadn't told them the rest. Whatever went on between him and Coco—weekends the children were with Eleanor, probably—he kept from them.

Eleanor asked Ursula something about her social studies report then. She had been working on a project about Helen Keller. Maybe the two of them could go to the library when they got together over the weekend.

"Maybe," Ursula said.

She had to go. It was her turn in Monopoly. She didn't want to keep everyone waiting.

"Coco made popcorn balls," Ursula told Eleanor. In the background, the sound of laughter.

Alone in the Brookline condo, Eleanor spent her days on a series of Easy Reader books she'd signed up to write and illustrate, on the presidents. (She'd been assigned the biographies of Woodrow Wilson and William Howard Taft. Could there be a more boring president?) Shutting her computer down at the end of the long days at her desk, she painted the walls in the children's bedrooms in the colors they'd picked out with her—buttercup yellow for Ursula, green for Toby, and an awful shade of purple that Al insisted on.

"Did you ever consider that surrounding yourself with four walls the color of an eggplant might be kind of depressing?" Eleanor asked Al.

"It's not the color of my walls that's depressing," Al said. She spoke in a low, faintly sarcastic snarl. More and more these days, this was her tone, to Eleanor at least. She wondered if Al did the same with Cam. The one time she'd tried to bring this up to him, his response had been clipped, dismissive.

"You have your relationship with Al, I have mine," he told Eleanor. "How your children speak to you is their business, not mine."

She told herself it would be better once the school year ended and they moved into the new place with her. She bought a foosball table and a trampoline. Other than a few things she'd bought that she hoped would be fun for her children, there was little furniture in the place, still. Her shoes on the floor made a hollow, echoing sound as she walked through the rooms.

Friday afternoons now, Eleanor drove up the highway to pick up her children—her first time returning to their old place as a visitor. The three of them were standing outside waiting for her, their bags lined up beside them in the driveway. The message was clear enough: Cam, though not in evidence, didn't want her coming inside what had once been her home.

When they got to the condo, she showed them their rooms. "I didn't know mine would be so purple," Al told her.

"It'll be fine. Once you put up a bunch of posters, it won't show so much."

All spring, she made the trip to Akersville on weekends. Eleanor took the Friday afternoon pickup. Cam took Sundays, bringing them home to the farm.

Because the condo wasn't set up for cooking yet, and none of their things were there, on their weekends with Eleanor they went out for hamburgers at the diner mostly, or bowling. When Al's baseball season started, Eleanor made the long drive to her games when she could and the longer drive home. She sat on the bleachers with the other parents—one or two of them old friends from softball summers watching the Yellow Jackets, and mothers of children in Al's class whom she'd known since their children were babies—women whose children had played at their house over the years, women who'd worked with her selling Avon products to raise money for the class trip to the science museum.

They all knew her name, and some of them greeted her. (They knew the story, too. Or thought they did: That Eleanor was the one who'd moved out of their house. That Cam had stayed. That the children were living with him.)

Beyond an occasional clipped greeting, few of them spoke to her now. Maybe the women thought she'd set her sights on their husbands. Maybe they imagined divorce was contagious. Or she was just a reminder of everything they didn't want to happen to them.

Cam showed up at Al's games, too, of course—never with Coco, though one time, on her way to her old house to pick up the children, she'd seen Evan and Betsy walking along the road. Their brief conversation when she'd rolled down the window to greet them—Betsy's observation that it must be easier getting first-rate help for

Toby, now that she lived near Boston, Evan's report on the ins and outs of Coco's life at the Center for Holistic Studies—made it clear to Eleanor that Coco's parents still had no clue of the relationship between their daughter and Cam. The way they had spoken with Eleanor that day conveyed a combination of regret and wariness. She noted a small, strange chill in their tone toward her. In the story they had constructed, it appeared, Eleanor was the one who must have decided to end the marriage, with Cam, the lonely abandoned husband, left to hold down the fort.

Another time, in June, right before school got out, Eleanor had run into Coco herself at the house—out in the yard, kicking a ball around with Al. Coco had actually waved when she caught sight of Eleanor, as if she forgot for a minute the most recent chapter in their long history. As for Cam, when he showed up on her doorstep to pick up the children on Sunday afternoons, he might have been the pizza delivery man for all he spoke to her now.

After he left, she walked over to Coolidge Corner to buy herself an ice cream cone. Sitting on a bench outside the ice cream parlor, she could hear someone's car radio tuned to a country station, and Dolly Parton came on. "I Will Always Love You."

A couple of teenagers came out of the shop carrying a giant banana split, the girl dressed in short shorts like Daisy Dukes, the boy in a tank top, though he looked like a person who had only recently begun shaving. When the girl got ice cream on her chin, he licked it off her while, on the radio, Dolly sang that part that always got to Eleanor.

Bittersweet memories. That's all I'm taking with me.

One of those older couples walked by, who had probably been married so long the husband didn't need to ask his wife what flavor she wanted, or if she wanted a sugar or waffle cone. The wife stayed outside on the other side of the bench, waiting, while the husband made his way up to the window to get their cones.

"We always get maple walnut," she told Eleanor.

Eleanor finished off the last of her cone and walked the five blocks home. But home had a whole different meaning now. Home was a neat, bland condo in Brookline with Corian countertops and vinyl tile floors. No dog. No hooting owl. No stars. No small warm bodies climbing in next to her in the middle of the night. When she woke in the morning, with nobody there but her own self, the bed felt vast as the ocean.

57.

Crazyland dead ahead

She had always been careful about drinking. She never wanted to be like her parents. But one time, she'd bought a bottle of Jack Daniel's—the brand her father had favored. She had four shots that night. Pouring herself another, she dialed Cam's number.

"You alone? Or is your girlfriend there? Maybe she's babysitting?" She spoke the word as if it were an obscenity.

Crazyland, dead ahead.

"Stop it, Eleanor. You don't want to do this."

"So when are you planning to tell them the truth?" she asked him. "Maybe you're waiting for Coco's twenty-first birthday? If so . . . that's a long time."

"The children have gone through a lot of changes," Cam said. He spoke in the calm, even tones of the narrator on a nature video, or Mister Rogers.

"It's pretty convenient, from your perspective," Eleanor told him. "Keeping them in the dark about the reason for the divorce. Leaving them with the impression that I'm the one who bailed on our family."

"Nobody bailed on our family," Cam said. (Mister Rogers again. Soft music—Kate Bush, she thought—in the background.) "We just grew in different directions."

"And yours led you straight to an eighteen-year-old girl." She was gripping the phone so tightly that if it were a kitten, it would be dead. Her heart was beating hard. "How do you think your old friends Evan and Betsy might feel, if they knew?"

"I wish you didn't have to be so bitter, Eleanor. It's not good for our children. It's not good for you, either."

"And you're so damned concerned about me, aren't you, Cam?

High on the list of your priorities, right after getting a new mattress and family trips to *Disney on Ice* with Coco."

The sound of her voice, speaking to him, had a new, hard edge. Not unlike what was happening to Al, it occurred to Eleanor. Even Ursula. Maybe this was what divorce did to people. It made them mean.

"I guess you occupy the high ground here," she said.

"I'm going to hang up now."

"Namaste." The way she spoke the word was nothing like how a yoga teacher would say it.

58.

code of silence

The children moved into the Brookline condo with Eleanor that June, the weekend after school let out. That night she took them out to dinner in downtown Boston—to a Chinese restaurant where the paper place mats let you figure out what animal year you'd been born in. Alison was the year of the snake. Ursula was—a happy discovery—the year of the horse. Toby, year of the monkey. Eleanor, to her chagrin, was also born in the year of the snake.

They got a pupu platter and drinks with paper umbrellas, and after, walking home, they stopped for ice cream. Eleanor felt like a tour guide, pointing out all the stops. Here was the Y where they could go swimming—even in winter, imagine. Here was the craft supply store and the funny little store, on a side street, run by a man who sold comic books and action figures. *Look at this, Toby. Castle Grayskull in the window.*

They stopped to look at the posters at the movie theater. A movie called *Ferris Bueller's Day Off* looked like something Al would like. She was the choosy one. Ursula liked everything. Or used to.

"Oh, boy," Eleanor said, studying the poster. "This one looks really funny." There was an unnatural brightness in her voice as she spoke to them, a false air of gaiety. She was like a person on a first date, but with her own children.

Slowly, things got more like regular life around their house. New regular life. The children started school. They got to know other kids. Al joined the basketball team. Mornings, the bus picked Toby up for the school Eleanor had enrolled him in for children with cognitive issues, and twice a week he worked with a tutor who helped him with reading—an expense Cam's parents had offered to cover.

Toby had a friend, a boy named Jacob with Down syndrome. One day he came over and the two of them spent all afternoon looking at Toby's rock collection.

But the children were different now. They were older. Part of it was that. But they displayed an unfamiliar self-protectiveness around Eleanor, a wary distance. They didn't climb into bed with her anymore at the new house—and maybe, she considered, that old tradition would have died out by now even if she and Cam had stayed together. But in other ways, too, she could feel them pulling away. Carrying their clothes in brown paper bags (Eleanor had provided them with small suitcases, but they seemed to prefer the paper bags), they moved back and forth between the houses of their parents as if they were navigating a demilitarized zone between enemy territories, the only constant in their lives now each other.

Maybe this had been a formal decision on their part, though more likely, it was instinct that told them to behave this way: the three of them (Eleanor chose to include Toby here) adhered to a strict code of silence with one parent, where the activities of the other were concerned. What happened at one house was never reported in the other.

Or at least—maybe this was more accurate—they hardly ever told Eleanor about what went on in her old house with Cam. What they told Cam about life in their mother's condo was unknown to her, though there was little to tell.

Now and then they'd mention a visit from Coco, times she came home from school for the weekend—an outing, a dinner—but nothing Eleanor observed suggested they viewed her as anything more than a family friend who liked to stop by and play Monopoly or go ice-skating with them on the pond.

Eleanor didn't see Darla as much as she had when she'd lived in Akersville, but they talked a lot on the phone, though at odd hours, never when Bobby was home—Bobby being Darla's primary topic of discussion. One night when he was drunk he'd yanked her arm so hard it came out of the socket, and she ended up in the emergency room, again, though when the nurses asked her how it happened, she'd lied. Another time, when Eleanor stopped by Darla's house on her way back from delivering the children to Cam's for the weekend, she'd seen a bruise on Darla's arm. Darla had put foundation over it, but the purple showed through. To Eleanor, anyway.

"You have to leave him," Eleanor told her.

"You know what kind of a dump I could afford for Kimmie and me?"

"You'd still be better off. You think this is good for Kimmie, seeing her father beat you up?"

"It's not that bad," Darla said. "He mostly only gets out of control when the Red Sox lose."

"So if they make it to the playoffs, your marriage problems are over?" Eleanor asked her.

"If I get hit by a bus, my marriage problems are over," Darla told her.

59.

a waterbed

It was March again, and with a warm front coming in, the snow had mostly melted. In the old days, this would have been the weekend for Eleanor and the children to make their boats and their cork people and launch them in the brook, but they were with Cam. After she dropped them off at the farm, she pulled up alongside a pay phone and called up Timmy Pouliot.

Eleanor had not seen Timmy again since that day at the Stop & Shop, their unlikely motorcycle ride.

The truth was, Timmy Pouliot had been on her mind for a while. Sometimes, alone in her bed back in Brookline, she allowed herself to think about him—how it had felt on the back of his motorcycle that day, her arms wrapped tight around him. She imagined other things, too. Timmy kissing her, peeling her clothes off her body. She pictured the tattoo on his arm, with his father's name on it. Pictured him naked in the bed next to her.

That afternoon, before setting out on the drive to Akersville, Eleanor had written his number on a piece of paper before she left Brookline. Dropping her dime in the slot, she could feel her hand trembling. Maybe he wouldn't pick up. Most likely he'd be out on a date.

He answered.

"I was remembering how much you always liked my chocolate chip cookies," she said. "I just made a big batch. I thought I might bring you some."

He sounded surprised, but not in a bad way. He gave her the address of his apartment.

It was a third-floor walk-up above the video store. The kind of place only a young person would live, or someone with hardly any money. Timmy Pouliot was both.

There was a bumper sticker on the door that said "Save Water, Drink Beer." From another apartment on the same floor, Eleanor heard an album she thought might be Led Zeppelin, and from somewhere else, the sound of an unhappy baby and a woman yelling at the baby to shut up. Someone had hung up a poster in the hallway of a naked man under a yellow raincoat and the words "Good Boys Always Wear Their Rubbers."

Eleanor imagined what she must look like standing there—out of breath from the stairs, a thirty-four-year-old woman with a do-it-yourself perm, wearing lipstick for the first time in a couple of years, holding a tin of chocolate chip cookies. She had squirted perfume on herself, and it came out faster than she expected, so the smell of it seemed to fill the hallway. If she hadn't already knocked on the door, she might have changed her mind and gone home.

She thought about what would happen when he opened the door. She imagined handing him the cookies. She imagined kissing him.

Were women supposed to carry condoms now that there was this terrible virus going around that nobody knew anything about except that it killed you? She had no idea of the rules these days, not that she ever had.

His face, when he opened the door, looked so happy to see her. She had forgotten how blue his eyes were, and more so, the intensity of his gaze. He was in his housepainter pants and a T-shirt, and his hair looked as though he'd just come out of the shower. She held out the cookies.

"I didn't want to eat these all myself," she said.

"Not that you have anything to worry about," he said. "I always thought you had a killer body."

He invited her in. There was a big-screen TV and a recliner chair and a beanbag, also a bong, and a couple of empty pizza boxes.

"Jeez, I should've tidied up," he said. "I'm not that accustomed to entertaining guests."

She sat on the beanbag. It was difficult knowing where to put her legs.

She had changed clothes a couple of times before making the drive, Ursula noting with surprise that she had makeup on. She had also dug through her underwear drawer in search of a pair of underpants that weren't stretched out from one or another of her pregnancies. She had also needed to make the cookies.

He offered her a beer. She took it. He already had one going.

"So how are your kids doing?" he asked her. "I mean, I know it's been difficult with your little boy. But the main thing is, he could've died, right? Cam saved his life. I'd hope I could pull it together to do something like that. Keep my wits about me."

Eleanor just sat there. She couldn't speak. But Timmy kept going.

"Not that you'd ever want something like that to happen in the first place, naturally. But if it did."

"My kids are pretty good," she said. "Everybody's doing okay, considering."

Except her daughter who pretty much lived in her room all the time. Her son who had been trying to master the first five letters of the alphabet for three months, and hadn't managed yet. Her former husband, former woodworker turned yoga devotee and physical therapy student, in love with their babysitter, though nobody was supposed to know about that. With the exception of Ursula—good, steady, dependable Ursula—every member of their family, including Toby, was basically unrecognizable from the person they'd been not even two years earlier, but Ursula wasn't the same, either, since the *Challenger* exploded.

"We're already talking about the new softball season," he said. "We were just saying how much we're going to miss Cam the Man on first base. I haven't seen the guy in over a year."

Eleanor raised the beer bottle to her lips. It had dawned on her finally that Timmy Pouliot didn't know that she and Cam weren't together anymore.

"That husband of yours is a lucky man," Timmy said, biting into a cookie. For as long as she'd known him, he'd had a way of looking at her. A kind of yearning. He had it even when he was thirteen, that first time she'd met him at the waterfall when they'd talked about Van Gogh and he told her about his father's suicide.

"Tell him hello from me, would you? We all miss him."

Whatever Eleanor had imagined might happen when she went to

Timmy Pouliot's apartment, it wasn't this. Sitting on the yellow plastic beanbag, breathing in the too-strong smell of her own perfume mixed with the faint scent of pizza and marijuana, she realized she had not constructed any specific pictures of what might happen once she showed up here. She had not gotten any further than the idea of putting on the mascara, delivering the cookies. But she had worn her one pair of decent underwear.

"Too bad he couldn't come over, too," Timmy said. "I really admire Cam. I hope someday I can be as good of a dad to my kids. If I have kids."

His mouth was full of cookie, and it looked like it had been a couple of days since he'd shaved. He wasn't handsome like Cam, but he had a kind face.

She put her head in her hands for a moment before looking up, looking him straight in the eye.

"I didn't actually come here to talk about my husband," Eleanor said.

She was jumping off the ledge now. She was falling. She didn't even care. What did it matter anymore if she looked totally stupid and crazy? She didn't even care if she looked to him like a terrible mother.

"I guess you hadn't heard," she said. "Cam and I separated last winter. The divorce will be final any day now."

"Oh, jeez," he said. "Holy cow. I always thought you two were, like, the perfect couple."

Once, maybe.

"Those kids. It must be rough," he said. "If there's anything I can do—"

She looked at the beer poster, the pizza box. Through a beaded curtain, the bed.

"I was thinking I'd like to have an affair with you," she told him.

It looked to Eleanor as though Timmy was having trouble processing her words to him, the same thing that was true when she spoke to Toby. For a moment his face took on a similar baffled expression.

"Oh, man," he said. "Oh, man. I wasn't expecting that."

Already, she was apologizing. "I don't know what I was thinking," she said. "I was just a little crazy for a moment there."

He reached out then and touched her hand. "You're not crazy."

"I'm sorry," she told him. She was trying to get up out of the beanbag chair now, but it wasn't easy. "You must think I'm some kind of pathetic idiot."

He moved over toward her then so his face was even with hers, on the low chair. He touched her face.

"I'm the idiot here," he said. "A beautiful sexy woman that I've been nuts about since I was in seventh grade shows up at my apartment to say she'd like to make love with me and I start talking about softball, and what a great guy her husband is. Ex-husband."

He kissed her. That first kiss was oddly tentative, like the kiss a junior high school boy might deliver, but the next one was different.

"I never did this before," she told him. "Not since I got married." Not much before, either.

He was running his hands through her hair now, kissing her neck. His body, pressed against hers, felt hot, vibrating, almost.

"I don't know what to do," she said.

"I do," he told her.

He had a waterbed. There were all these motorcycle magazines on top of it. Those, and a Stephen King novel, *It*. He swept them onto the floor.

"Come here," he said.

Eleanor had a rule about Timmy Pouliot. Starting with the way she spoke of him, though the only person she mentioned him to was Darla. But when she thought about him—and she did, a lot—she never thought of him as Timmy. Always Timmy Pouliot. It put him in a different category from the other people in her life—her ex-husband, parents of her children's friends, Toby's speech therapist, other former softball teammates of Cam's. She spoke of him the way a person would speak of a movie star or a politician or some famous athlete—some character you knew about, and observed from afar. Admired, maybe. But she wouldn't have thought of him as a friend, or even—even after they had sex—as a lover. Timmy's apartment was a place she could go, now and then, where she got to step out of her life for an hour or two, and instead of taking care of everyone else, she was the one who got taken care of.

After that first time she'd paid a visit to Timmy Pouliot's apartment, she figured it had probably been this onetime deal, but a few weeks later he called her up. "I was just thinking about you," he said. "Who am I kidding? I'm always thinking about you."

The first thing he did when she got there was to run her a bath. Eleanor didn't know anything about how people conducted love affairs, but she guessed this was unusual. Timmy Pouliot had recognized that she was a woman overdue for tender care, and it turned out he was very good at providing it. After that first time, he always had bath salts for her, also lotion, and candles, which he lit for her while she soaked in the tub. He had asked if she'd like to be private for her bath, but she liked his company, so he sat on the toilet with a beer and they talked.

It got to be a thing she did Friday nights, after dropping off the children. Going over to Timmy Pouliot's apartment for her bath, followed by lovemaking on the waterbed, was something she looked forward to all week, but never counted on. Now and then—if the children were with their father for some school holiday, and once in the middle of a weekday when they were all at school, when it had come to her that this was the anniversary of her parents' accident—she made the drive unconnected to a drop-off or a pickup, just to see him. She played music loud as she drove, and didn't even mind the time it took getting there. Time in the car on the way to Timmy Pouliot's apartment always felt peaceful to Eleanor, but also exciting. She loved how he touched her. But equally, the part that came before. The bath.

This was not exactly the kind of bath they featured in the pages of women's magazines, in articles she'd read and occasionally even illustrated about "me time" or "Create Your Own Spa Vacation Right at Home"—though he always lit a candle for her, cinnamon spice, and put on one of the few tapes he owned that wasn't heavy metal or country. There was the giant New England Patriots towel hanging from a hook on the door, and on the shelf above the tub, a can of

Right Guard and another of shaving cream, a jock strap looped over a hook on the door, and a poster tacked up that appeared to have been there awhile—the classic shot of Farrah Fawcett, from so long ago Farrah's swimsuit was totally faded.

He always tested the water temperature on his wrist, as a person might do bathing a baby. He had wine chilling for her, and he had bought a special sponge—a loofah—that he used to rub her back.

That first time, she'd been careful to keep certain aspects of her body concealed from him. She held in her stomach when she got up from the bed. She didn't like how her breasts sagged now. Then there were the stretch marks.

"You don't have to be shy with me," he told her. "I think you're beautiful. You had kids, that's all. You're a mother."

After that Eleanor felt a surprising absence of self-consciousness taking her clothes off around Timmy Pouliot. She had seen plenty of his girlfriends over the years, with their perfect bodies. But he always made it plain that he loved looking at her, and that nothing about Eleanor's naked body altered any of that.

Walking out to her car after—sometimes at midnight, sometimes later, the night air so cold on her face it stung—and on the long drive back to Brookline, she told herself that what she had with her former husband's former softball teammate, these Friday night visits, represented no more than a small oasis of comfort where she'd allowed herself to touch down, just for now.

It didn't mean anything.

All that summer and into the fall, on Fridays after dropping the children off at Cam's (it was odd, still, speaking of their old house this way), Eleanor drove to the apartment building with the video store down below. She parked on a side street and walked up the two flights of stairs to Timmy's apartment. Sometimes she could hear the water running in the bathtub before he even opened the door.

She had questioned what was in it for him, having this woman seven years older than he was coming over to his apartment and getting into his bathtub, but she came to accept that in some odd way, he enjoyed their times together. She might talk to him while she lay in the water, tell him stories about her week. Sometimes she'd just lie there while he sat on the edge of the toilet drinking his beer, and sometimes he'd tell her about something that happened on the job that day, or a problem he had with his car, or a fishing trip he'd taken with his brother, or an evening he spent at his mother's house with her new boyfriend, who was pretty much a jerk but she seemed happy with him so he let it alone. It was not unheard of, at these moments, for Timmy Pouliot to recount the story of something that happened with one of his seemingly endless succession of beautiful young girlfriends. He knew Eleanor wouldn't be jealous, and she wasn't.

Sometimes they'd skip a week. She didn't want to use it up, or leave him thinking she expected anything from him, which she didn't.

Every time she left the apartment and made her way back down those two long, dark flights of steps, Eleanor considered the possibility that this might be the last time she'd find herself here. Sooner or later he'd get a girlfriend again. It was never hard for Timmy Pouliot, getting a girlfriend. At some point, he'd marry one of them.

"I met this girl," Timmy said. She was in the tub at the time, with the glass of wine he'd poured for her. Softball season starting up again. He was sitting in his usual spot with his beer. "It doesn't mean anything. We just hang out. She likes Harleys."

After that, Eleanor knew not to come by for a while. Then one night came the call. November now. They had just turned back the clocks, so it got dark around four thirty. She was getting ready to bring the children to Cam's when the phone rang.

"You in the mood for a bath?" They started up again.

She never spent the night with him. But one night she had stayed later than usual. After they made love, she had fallen asleep. When she opened her eyes it was close to morning.

"You should have woken me up," she said.

"Why would I do that?" he told her. "I figured you could use the rest. Plus I like watching you sleep."

She surprised herself by how easy it felt, being naked with Timmy Pouliot. She loved his body—solid and thickly muscled, where Cam was lean. The first time he'd touched her naked skin, Eleanor had been startled by the roughness of his hands. "I know," he said. He must have registered her reaction. "That's what being on the road crew and grunt construction work does to a guy." He told her he'd pick up some kind of lotion.

When she dressed to go, there was never any discussion of when they'd see each other again. She didn't invite him over for a meal or bake him one of her pies. They never went out for dinner together, or to the sports bar he frequented. Though he had taken her on his bike that time, the experience was not repeated. Their whole relationship, whatever it was, was played out in the two rooms of his apartment—two places, his bed and his bathtub, and nowhere else.

"My mom was getting after me the other day," Timmy Pouliot told her one time. Lying side by side in bed, as usual. "She wanted to know when I was going to settle down with someone. Have kids."

"And when will that be?" Eleanor asked him. Maybe this was the moment he was going to tell her he didn't think she should come over anymore. *It's been great. Need to move on.*

"I told her it would have to be the right woman," he said. "These girls I always end up running around with. It won't be any of them."

Eleanor lay there next to him on his Patriots sheets, saying nothing. She was studying his strong, broad chest, the scar on his right hand from a time when he was just starting out as a carpenter and he'd almost lost a finger to a table saw, the tattoo with the name of his dead father on his bicep, his appendix scar, the one on his thigh from an accident on his motorcycle when he was sixteen. Sometimes, when it rained, he walked with a limp, though most people would not have noticed this.

She knew his body so well, as he did hers.

"Maybe you need to start hanging out with a different kind of woman," she told him.

"Well, look at me," he said. "I am, aren't I?"

He should find someone younger, she told him. Someone who might have kids with him. Someone who didn't spend her days caring for a brain-injured son. She started putting her clothes on.

"You know you're my dream girl, right?" he said to Eleanor.

She laughed.

60.

never a good time

Driving down the road to their old house to drop off or pick up the children, the words would come to her that she always used to whisper to herself when she rounded the last bend: "I'm home." But this wasn't her home anymore. She no longer spoke them.

She was not welcome inside their old house anymore, evidently. On Sundays, if it fell to her to pick up the children—as it did sometimes, when Cam was off on one of his physical therapy trainings and Phyllis was babysitting—the three of them were always outside waiting for her when she pulled up. If it was too cold for them to stand outside, Cam must have instructed them to keep an eye out for her, out the window, because they ran out very fast, as if to avoid the possibility that she might get out of the car and come in to get them.

She hardly ever saw Cam, but when she did, it caught her up short. He was cordial, but there was nothing in the way he behaved with Eleanor now to set her apart from some woman waiting on him at the hardware store or the bank. A person seeing the two of them together as they were now, meeting—very briefly—on the steps of the house where their babies were born, would never know these were two people who used to love each other, used to make love.

Those times in the driveway, watching her children disappear into their old house—the chill that lingered from the way she had become, to her ex-husband, a person he greeted no differently than he might a vacuum cleaner salesperson or a stranger canvassing for a political candidate—she took comfort where she found it. In ten minutes, she'd be climbing the stairs above the video store.

She had figured the visits to Timmy Pouliot would end when winter came. He'd lose interest, maybe, find a girlfriend his own age.

But when the snow melted (cork people season, not that Eleanor and the children made those any more), she was still coming over, and in summer—the season she pictured him with some adorable new twenty-one-year-old on the back of his bike, they still had their Friday nights. Not every week, but more often than not.

After that first time she'd invited herself over, when she'd been so nervous—and Timmy so clueless—her visits felt like the best part of her week. Of all the things going on in her life—worrying about Toby's brain and Al's moodiness (call it what it was, depression), being mad at Cam, missing her house, missing the stars and the sound of the waterfall down the road, watching the changes in her children, figuring out how to pay the bills—this was the simplest part. Walking into Timmy Pouliot's apartment and letting him unbutton her jacket. Stepping out of her jeans and into the bathtub.

He always poured her a glass of wine when she got there. "Tell me what's going on," he said. Mostly what Eleanor had to report had to do with her children, but Timmy always seemed interested.

There was this one Friday night, almost a year since Eleanor had started going over to Timmy Pouliot's apartment. She must have looked even more worn out than usual. It was winter, and the drive to Akersville had taken a particularly long time. When she walked in his apartment, he had taken one look at her and said, "I know what you need." He'd given her a massage. Then, as always, the bath.

Darla came to see her in Brookline. She'd only been to Boston a few times in her life—long ago on a school field trip to the Museum of Science and once, with Bobby, to Fenway Park.

On their big Boston weekend, Darla and Eleanor went out for breakfast and had croissants and cappuccino, a new experience for Darla. They brought Toby to the Children's Museum and after, crossed the Congress Street Bridge to visit the Tea Party ships—Eleanor explaining the story of the settlers throwing the tea overboard, Toby more interested in the granola bar Eleanor had given him, and after he was finished with it, the wrapper.

Seeing him, as she did, every day, it was hard for Eleanor to pick up on changes in her son, but to Darla, who hadn't spent time with the two of them in months, Toby was doing better.

"I have to hand it to Cam," Eleanor told her friend. "He's the one, when I felt hopeless, who started bringing Toby to yoga. That was the first time after the accident that he seemed interested in anything."

"Cam's not a bad guy, really," Darla said.

"I know," Eleanor said. It would have been easier if he were.

They rode back to Eleanor's place on the T, another first for Darla. That evening, they left Toby back at the condo with the girls and went out for dinner in the North End. They had real pizza, not the kind you got in Akersville. Darla loved the North End—the markets selling fresh pasta, the smell of garlic, the street musicians at Faneuil Hall.

"When I get the cash together to leave Bobby, this is where Kimmie and I are coming," Darla said. She had researched mortuary schools in the area. There were two.

When Darla had said this in the past, Eleanor always encouraged her, but this time what she expressed was simply impatience.

"You're always talking about this and you never end up doing it," Eleanor said. The words came out sharper than she'd intended. She could see, on Darla's face, a flicker of hurt.

"This isn't a good time."

"There's never a good time," Eleanor told her.

61.

just like in *The Sound of Music*

Somewhere along the line—from Darla, who cleaned Betsy and Evan's house—she learned that Coco had graduated from her holistic studies training. She was gone then—off in Hawaii attending a course in what her mother had called "higher-level healing modalities." Word came back that she'd met someone there at an acro-yoga retreat. "It sounds serious," Betsy had told Darla. Hearing the news secondhand, Eleanor had felt a rush of relief, though she could not have said why.

Then, suddenly—more than a year later now—there was surprising news.

"Coco's back," Toby announced. They were in the car on a Sunday afternoon, making the long drive back from Akersville to Brookline after the weekend with Cam. From the back seat, Eleanor could sense the uneasy silence from her daughters. Ursula had poked Toby—a signal to keep quiet. But Toby wasn't having it.

"She lives at our house now," Toby said. "They told us on the way home from ice cream."

"Coco and Dad are getting married," Ursula said. They must have designated her to announce this.

Eleanor knew they were all watching her closely. Or the girls were, anyway. Possibly even Toby understood this was a big moment.

Eleanor kept her eyes on the road. "When did this happen?"

"When Coco came back from Hawaii they realized how much they missed each other when she was away," Ursula said. "It's like in a movie: they knew each other practically her whole life but it just hit them they were in love."

Eleanor could hear the cautiousness in her younger daughter's voice, the air of tension in the car from the others—even Toby. The children hardly ever spoke of what happened at their father's house, but Ursula had made the decision, evidently—more likely, she and Al made it together—that their mother needed to be told about Coco moving in, Cam and Coco getting married.

They knew they were headed into dangerous territory, but she was going to find out anyway. They must have figured it was better to tell her now—and while they were at it, Ursula was doing her best to make it clear to Eleanor that she and her siblings were fine about what was happening. More than fine. Happy. The last thing any of them wanted would be to suggest that their father was doing anything that had upset them. Their mother had enough grievances against their father. They weren't about to contribute any others to the list.

Eleanor had learned this over the years: children of divorced parents were like citizens of two hostile countries, observing the laws and customs of each, depending on where they were at the moment. Crossing borders, going through customs. Shedding the language and clothing and manners of one culture when they entered the other, doing the same when they crossed back. Having to keep their story straight, depending on where they were. Their one source of continuity, each other.

"He said it just happened, when she came back," Al added. The fact that now Al was contributing information struck Eleanor as out of character. Maybe she wanted to emphasize to Eleanor that the romance between their father and Coco was a recent development. Maybe some part of her had actually considered the possibility that it wasn't.

"It's just like in *The Sound of Music,* where the girl starts out being a nun that's just helping out with the family, and then one day the dad figures it out that they should get married," Ursula said.

Except that in this case, unlike that of the von Trapps, the children's mother hadn't died. She was alive and well—alive, anyway—in a Brookline condo. Coco was not much of a singer. Other than that, she was evidently assuming the role of Julie Andrews.

"It's really good Dad fell in love, finally," Ursula said. "He was so lonely in the house by himself all that time."

Eleanor gripped the steering wheel tightly. She could feel her chest tightening. "How about Coco's mom and dad?" she asked. "How do they feel about this?" Most parents would not consider it cause for celebration, hearing their daughter's announcement that she was marrying a man twice her age, only a few years younger than her father.

"Coco said at first they needed some convincing," Ursula said. "But once they saw how happy Coco was, they said it was fine with them. I guess that makes Betsy and Evan kind of like our grandparents."

"That's really great," Eleanor told her. "You kind of came up short in that department, before."

"Dad said you might be mad," Ursula said. She was probably still waiting for the Crazyland moment.

"Why would I be mad?" Eleanor adjusted the rearview mirror, studying Al's face, and Ursula's. Toby's, she knew. "We got a divorce. He can do what he wants."

"That's what I said," Ursula said. "It's not like some stranger we never met is moving in. We love Coco. You love her, too, right, Mom?"

They got married six weeks later—a small gathering, just Evan and Betsy and the children, Eleanor gathered—though nobody mentioned it until after, and might not have said anything even then if Toby hadn't told about the cake they had with two miniature people on the top, and chocolate frosting, his favorite.

Every Friday now, when Eleanor drove out to the farm to drop off Alison and Ursula and Toby she'd see Coco's little yellow VW Bug in the driveway, and once, when there was laundry hung out to dry, she noticed a row of tiny bikini underpants clipped to the line. Coco had planted petunias, but in that way that a person does who's a first-time gardener. A single row of plants, twelve inches apart, like soldiers.

The children said very little more to their mother about Coco after that, but when they got home at the end of weekends at the farm now, and they unpacked the contents of the backpacks, there were craft projects (not the kind Eleanor might have thought up;

these came from store-bought kits, mostly: potholders with happy faces, key chains with identical googly-eyed puppies) and little Tupperware containers full of healthy-looking cookies of a kind Cam would never have gotten around to making. Sometimes, when they unpacked, Eleanor would spot a new shirt with a unicorn on the front (this would be Ursula's) that said "Dreams can come true," or a vial of some kind of herbal remedy for Toby that was supposed to help new brain cells develop.

Al returned home one Sunday with a pair of Doc Martens Coco had bought for her at the mall—the shoes she'd been wanting all year. Once, undressing Toby for bed, she had found a press-on tattoo of a goat with the word "Capricorn" circling it. Coco might as well have taken out a Sharpie and written the words "Coco was here."

He's not your son, she wanted to tell Coco. *Don't scribble your graffiti on him.*

62.

dream girl

Dark as it was at Timmy Pouliot's apartment—with a smell always hanging in the air of other people's dinners, the sound of other people's babies crying, the faded Farrah poster—it was the place where Eleanor most consistently found comfort. Stepping in the door, Friday nights, after dropping off her children, she could feel her whole body soften. She closed her eyes, and when she opened them, he'd be there holding her, his face buried in her hair.

"Take off your shoes," he said. She took off everything.

She loved that moment when he'd hold out the towel for her, as she stepped out of the tub. Later, on his saggy waterbed, he'd lay his head on her belly and kiss her stretch marks.

"I know you," he had said to her once.

She knew him, too—not just his body, though that, too.

Often, when she got to his apartment, he'd be playing Guns N' Roses, but he also loved Hank Williams and Vince Gill. He had a sweet voice, and he was teaching himself the guitar. He'd written Eleanor a song that he called "Dream Girl."

Now he stood on the bed—his body swaying a little on account of it being filled with water. He wore nothing but a bandanna, and he had a belly on him, but not much of one. A sweet smile. That tattoo of his dead father's name, "Brian." The tattoo artist should have written "Bryan," but making the change would have cost too much, so he just left it. Sometimes, lying next to him, Eleanor traced her finger over the letters.

A person who didn't care about Timmy Pouliot might have said this was a pretty bad song, but for some reason it made her cry. He only knew a couple of chords. The lyric featured "love" and "skies above." The refrain had to do with Eleanor being his dream girl.

"I never wrote a song before," he told her. "I guess you inspired me."

After, as she hit Route 93 South back to Brookline, Eleanor thought about what it would be like if she invited Timmy Pouliot over for dinner some night, to have dinner with her and her children. They knew him slightly from Yellow Jackets games. But they would never in a million years picture him as someone who could be their mother's boyfriend.

Toby wouldn't mind, of course. Toby liked everyone, but a guy on a motorcycle, more so. Timmy would take him for a ride. Slow enough not to worry her, and with a helmet. Most people to whom Toby showed his rock collection would take about sixty seconds to look at it and then say something like "Wow, impressive," but Timmy would study each rock and ask where it came from, ask Toby which one was his favorite, at which point Toby would bring out his best find, a piece of granite with a very small garnet embedded in it.

Ursula, meeting Timmy in this unexpected role of boyfriend, would be baffled, then disappointed. She'd recently started making suggestions to Eleanor about men she thought her mother should date—the widowed father of a boy in her class, whose gaze seemed fixed on the floor every time she met him at some school event. Their neighbor down the street, Barry, who wore beautiful suits and had a poodle. Barry was clearly gay, but Ursula loved his dog.

To Ursula, Timmy would appear poorly dressed and scruffy. "What's his job, anyway?" she would ask. Ursula would like her mother to marry someone with a house at the Cape, or a mansion, or a boat. Either that, or British royalty. Observing Timmy's choice of transportation (the motorcycle or his ten-year-old Subaru), she would conclude, not incorrectly, that Timmy was poor.

Al would be mortified by the way Timmy looked at her mother, and the way he touched her. Which he would do, for sure. He couldn't help it.

"I promise I won't do anything totally nuts," he would say to Eleanor, if she invited him to their home. "But you can't expect me to keep my hands off you all night. I have to at least kiss you."

She would push him away when he did that. But not very hard.

63.

Mr. Fun

Many times over the months and then years after she and Cam parted, Eleanor reminded herself what they had told each other, told themselves: that they would never speak ill of their children's other parent. Cam probably managed to keep to his side of the bargain. He seemed to go on with his life as if Eleanor had never existed. She, on the other hand, brooded over their story until she questioned even the good parts of their marriage, or the parts that had seemed good once.

Maybe they had only appeared to be happy, back in the old days. Maybe Cam never loved her, he just liked living on the farm and everything that went with it. Maybe all those years she'd said it wasn't a big deal that Cam spent so much time off making bowls and playing softball, it had been eating away at her, and she was just now waking up to her anger.

Eleanor didn't know what was real anymore. The story she'd lived—the one she had told in her *Family Tree* strip—felt like fiction now.

In the old days, when they were married—the early years, anyway—she had said it was okay that she made most of the money. They each did the things they were good at. They were a team. But with the syndicate money gone, and the pressure to come up with enough to pay for the braces Al needed, and for Ursula's braces, and for Toby's rehabilitation sessions—nobody there to shovel the snow or fix the dishwasher when it gave up the ghost—the absence of a contribution from her children's father began to wear more heavily. She had no doubt that even with his new income as a physical therapist, money was even tighter on his end, particularly since he now had to come up with the mortgage payment. And still, Cam seemed to move through the world (as little as she saw of him in it) with the same easy, relaxed air he always had.

She called him up one night—rare event—to say that Ursula wanted to take guitar lessons. Al had bitten into a Brazil nut and broken a tooth. A doctor had recommended special shoes for Toby, to help with his balance issues.

"I can't do everything on my own," she told Cam. "You need to chip in."

On the other end of the phone, she heard him sigh. "I don't know what to tell you, Eleanor," he said to her. His voice sounded far away, as if he were in some yoga pose—the one they did at the end of the class, where you just lie there chilling out—and she had crashed into the room playing some kind of awful music, with the volume cranked up high.

"I'm sorry you're so hung up on money," he said. "For your own sake, I hope you learn to let go of your anger."

She could feel it happening: the bitterness taking hold of her. She no longer minded if her children heard her on the phone to him, the speeches she made about how hard she worked, how much it took to support a family. Maybe she wanted them to hear this, as if, hearing her, they would recognize how unfair he'd been, as if she could make them stop loving their father. Why would any loving parent want to accomplish such a thing?

"Of course you're the cool one," she said—loud enough to be heard in the next room, where they were doing homework. "Mr. Easygoing, Mr. Fun. See how much fun it is to pay for braces."

Only he would never know that.

This conversation took place on the phone. But she could see him on the other end of the line—knew, even, the place where he'd be sitting, at the old trestle table he'd built from a tree that had come down in a storm one time, his hair tied back in a ponytail, maybe, feet on the old velvet footstool that had belonged to his grandmother. There would be a fire in the woodstove, and Coco fixing some extremely healthy dinner for the two of them. Out the window, icicles, and snow drifting down over the bare branches of their old tree.

She could picture Sally at his feet, having one of her squirrel-chasing dreams. There had never been any question, when the two of them split up, which of the two of them would get their dog.

"Maybe I could be mellow and easygoing, too," Eleanor told Cam now, over the phone. (Crazyland alert. She was heading in that direction.) "If I didn't have to support three children."

Whatever their father said in response, the children couldn't hear it. Only the shrillness in their mother's voice, a sound nobody hated more than Eleanor herself.

On the other end of the line, Cam said something about the farm. How hard he was working now to take care of it, on top of physical therapy classes and working with Toby.

"You're quite the hero, all right," Eleanor said. "Maybe you forget who it was that bought that farm in the first place. Who paid the mortgage all those years while you were off at craft fairs charming the pants off some girl or other."

He must have put down the phone at that point. Ursula stood there.

"I wish you wouldn't be so hard on Dad all the time," she said. Al had already headed up to her room. Toby, on the floor, kept his eyes on the controls of his video game—something about lining up jewels so all the matching colors filled a row, not that he ever got them to do that.

64.
goodbye *Goodnight Moon*

It was August, and the girls were off from school. (Not Toby. For Toby, school was a year-round event, not that it seemed to be doing much for him.) Ursula was trying to show Toby how to tie his shoes. Al was stationed at her usual spot—the Commodore 64, having recently discovered a sound chip that could re-create songs in three-part harmony. She had just successfully programmed it to play a tinny version of "Fast Car." Now Tracy Chapman's words appeared on the screen—"Starting from zero, got nothing to lose"—as a bouncing snowflake followed along.

Eleanor loaded the dishwasher as the three of them ate breakfast, and Ursula's conversation turned to a yard sale they were planning to hold at their dad's farm the weekend after next. Normally, even this amount of information would have been more than they'd share with their mother. But Ursula had been explaining how she intended to send the proceeds to Ethiopia for the babies who were starving there. They'd seen pictures in a magazine.

"That's great," Eleanor said. "So what are you planning to sell?"

She had made waffles that morning, feeling guilty at having spent the whole day before at her desk, sending out pitches for work.

"Tons of stuff," Ursula said. "Dad said we might as well get rid of all the old books we outgrew. There's got to be a hundred."

She could see their covers, and the shelf in the borning room where they were kept. *Blueberries for Sal* and *Babar* and *Caps for Sale, The Story of Ferdinand* and *Miss Rumphius* and *The Little House. Goodnight Moon,* and, in the later years, *The Borrowers, Matilda, James and the Giant Peach.* And a few hundred others. It seemed to her that the story of her years of raising children in that house was contained in the pages of those books.

"You can't sell our books," Eleanor said. She was trying her calm voice.

"We don't read them anymore," Al said. "Even Toby isn't interested."

Eleanor set the plastic jug of maple syrup on the table. Maybe she slammed it down.

"My teacher says we should try not to buy so much plastic," Ursula offered. Changing the subject, or trying to.

"Dad's syrup comes from trees," Toby said. He was speaking sentences, finally. She could have been happy about this, but that wasn't what she was taking in at this particular moment.

"Your dad does everything right," she said, in the bitter tone of voice she nearly always adopted when the topic came around to Cam.

"Who are you anymore, anyway?" Al said. She got up from the table.

"I'm serious. *Who are you?*"

It was a question Cam had asked, too. It was a question Eleanor asked herself.

The children were heading out on a camping trip with their father that weekend. This was the unit now: Al, Ursula, and Toby, a little tribe who trudged back and forth along the same stretch of road from the home of their birth, with their happy, carefree dad and his new wife, to the condo inhabited by their angry and resentful mother. No experience in their lives to date had bonded them more powerfully than their parents' divorce.

Saturday morning, Eleanor woke with a plan. If she were planning a bank robbery she might not have felt any greater level of adrenaline coursing through her body.

She set out early for the farm. The temperature had been over ninety all week, and she thought if she went early she might escape the worst of the heat, but by eight thirty, when she arrived, the temperature was right back up there.

Pulling into the driveway, she saw Coco's VW Bug. As her car pulled up in front of the house, Coco appeared at the entrance to the porch. Evidently Cam had chosen to go camping alone with the kids. Maybe Coco had some massage appointments scheduled. Maybe a twenty-year-old needed a break from parenting.

Except for one time—just long enough for a quick wave—Eleanor had not seen Coco since her split from Cam. The last time they'd spoken was in her kitchen, baking together—back when she paid Coco a dollar an hour to look after her children.

Now Coco was wearing a very short dress, more like a nightgown. Maybe it was one. Through the fabric she could see Coco's tiny breasts, her dark nipples. Those long legs. Bare feet. Beautiful toes, with nail polish on them. Eleanor imagined her lying on the grass with Ursula (Toby, too, maybe, but definitely not Al) applying polish to each other's toes.

"I came to pick up some things," Eleanor said, approaching the door. "It won't take long." Coco followed after her, as if all one hundred and ten pounds of her could have any effect on barring Eleanor's entrance into the house she'd bought when she was the age Coco was now.

Eleanor had brought a box of green plastic trash bags with her—the extra-large, heavy-duty kind.

"I'm not sure Cam wants you to come in his personal space anymore," Coco said. But nobody could have taken her seriously, saying this. Her voice was soft and tentative, and the way she spoke the words—her inflection going up at the end of the sentence—was more like a question.

Eleanor brushed past her, headed for the borning room.

She knelt on the floor by the bookcase. Someone—Cam, probably, but maybe the girls—had already taken the books off the shelf. They had been stacked in the corner, awaiting sale.

This was my life. Eleanor didn't say the words out loud, but she was thinking them.

She allowed herself to look, for a moment, at the cover of the first book she picked up. *The Little House*—the story of a cottage built on a piece of land in the middle of a field with nothing else but trees in all directions, and how, page by page, a town and roads and then a whole city grew up around it until the little house was almost swallowed up. It struck her now as a sad story, though at the time she had not viewed the book this way, and neither had her children when she read it out loud to them.

The Poky Little Puppy. Stone Soup. Frog and Toad Are Friends. One Morning in Maine. D'Aulaires' Book of Greek Myths—the one whose illustrations of Zeus had once reminded her of Cam. They were all here. *Charlotte's Web,* naturally. When she read certain parts from that one out loud to her children, Ursula would cover her face with a pillow. *No no no no. It's too sad.* But when Eleanor put the book down, it was always Ursula who begged her to keep reading.

Coco had followed Eleanor into the house. She stood in the kitchen, a few feet back, as if whatever it was that possessed Eleanor might be contagious. "Maybe you should talk to Cam about this first," she offered, but even as she spoke the words, she must have recognized their futility.

Eleanor had started out setting the books, one by one, into the first plastic garbage bag, but she was flinging them in the bag now—all the beloved stories, familiar covers, characters who had been, for her children, as real as friends—a half dozen at a time. Picture books and chapter books. *Where the Sidewalk Ends. Madeline. A Chair for My Mother. Sylvester and the Magic Pebble.* Baby books, books of poems, books about rocks and minerals, the solar system, dinosaurs. All those wonderful Laura Ingalls Wilder stories they loved, about the homesteading family off in the woods, a little like them. Only not.

When the first bag was filled, Eleanor started in on the next. She was sweating now, only in part from the heat of the day. Coco stood a few feet back, saying nothing.

In the end, it took four garbage bags to contain all their children's books, with a few stragglers that didn't fit.

The bags were so heavy she couldn't lift them. One by one she dragged them across the kitchen floor that she'd mopped a few thousand times. Coco still stood there, watching.

There had been a time when Eleanor and Cam had sanded this floor together, by hand. Here was the place where the slant of the floorboards was so extreme, Toby could let go of a truck and it went by itself.

She remembered how, when Alison was just crawling, she had cut out pictures of babies from magazine ads for Pampers and taped them onto the inside of the low cupboard doors for Alison to see while she sat there. Her first word, spoken to the image from the Pampers ad, when she opened the cupboard, had been "baby."

When she had all the bags in the back of the station wagon, Eleanor went back in the house one more time for the handful that still lay on the floor. As she passed through the kitchen with the last of the books, Coco pointed to a paperback in Eleanor's hands and said in a whisper, "I gave Toby that one."

Eleanor studied the cover. Coco was right.

It was a stupid book, the kind she would never have bought for their children, a pop-up whose main character was a cartoon character from television, with buttons that made noises when you pushed them.

"Then you should keep it," she said, holding out the book. Her voice carried a tone of magnanimity. The image she summoned for herself was of Princess Diana, extending her hand to an AIDS sufferer. Diana—regal and beautiful and, like Eleanor, wronged by her husband—visiting the site where land mines exploded, offering comfort and compassion to the victims.

Coco stood there holding on to the one last book. At some point during the heist, despite the heat, she had put on a sweater. Eleanor recognized it as one of Cam's. Maybe Coco had realized how easily a person could see through her nightgown.

"Have a great day," she said, as Eleanor got in the driver's seat and turned the key. As she made her getaway, she took in a last glimpse of her ex-husband's young wife, barefoot in the dirt. Standing in the driveway in her nightgown, still holding the pop-up, along with a paperback copy of *The Berenstain Bears Visit the Dentist*. Another of her contributions to their library, evidently.

As Eleanor drove back down the road, her car was so weighed down that its belly skimmed the gravel. She should have driven slowly, till she reached the tar, but she flew out of that place like Cruella de Vil with her carload of dalmatian puppies. When she got home, she saw the oil pan was punctured. Later, when she got the repair bill, it came to three hundred dollars.

Later, Eleanor told Darla the whole story of the raid on their children's books. The friendship was unequal that way. Eleanor told Darla everything. For Darla, though she made joking references to Bobby's impossible behavior, there remained areas Eleanor knew she wouldn't go—bruises covered with makeup, visits to the emergency room she didn't mention. Darla told Eleanor about Kimmie's recently acquired habit of pulling out her hair, but when Eleanor tried to raise the reasons why she might be doing that in the first place, Darla went silent. They could talk about what Cam did, but seldom if at all about Bobby.

"I'm glad you're not with him anymore," Darla said, speaking of Cam. Darla did a better job of defending her friend than she did defending herself.

"You know the funny thing?" Eleanor said. "I know Coco must have told Cam what happened when I came to take the children's books, but he didn't say a word about any of it."

"If I tried something like that with Bobby," Darla said, "you'd be shopping for a funeral arrangement."

Cam wasn't the type to display anger, least of all to Eleanor. In some ways, his anger would have been easier to take, because a person who is angry at you is at least acknowledging your existence. But Cam drifted along like a cork person. The kind that somehow, miraculously, makes it all the way down the brook without getting caught in the weeds.

65.

you don't live there anymore

It was not the marriage that killed the last of the good feeling between them. It was the divorce.

At their children's school performances and soccer and basketball games now, they sat on opposite sides of the bleachers, opposite corners of the room. When Cam arrived with Coco beside him, Eleanor could feel her body stiffen, but he always looked happy and relaxed. Once, when the two of them had attended the 4-H fair in Akersville where Ursula and Toby were displaying a pumpkin they'd grown, Cam's face had lit up at the sight of their old friend, Harry Botts, on the other side of the room, with his entry in the annual pie contest. But Cam had not greeted Eleanor. Ever since the day she had come to refer to (though only in her head) as the Great Children's Book Heist, his gaze passed over her as though she no longer existed. Beyond exchanging information concerning drop-offs and pickups, the two of them no longer spoke.

Somewhere over the course of those months, their old dog Sally had died. Eleanor found out months later, when Toby mentioned they were getting a puppy at their dad's house, and Eleanor asked how Sally was dealing with having another dog around.

"I wish you'd told me," she said when she learned the news.

"Dad took care of it," Al said. They had buried Sally's body under the ash tree.

"I would have wanted to be there," she told her daughter. She had loved Sally, too.

"You don't live there anymore," Al said. "You moved, remember?"

The terms of Eleanor and Cam's divorce specified shared custody, the children to spend weekends and school vacations in Akersville, along with most of the summer. The farm was the place where the children could play outside on their own and be with their new dog, camp out in the tree fort, swim in the pond.

The pond. Eleanor didn't want to look at it, but the children still played there, catching frogs and swimming out to the raft. Even Toby. Toby most of all, probably, because he remembered nothing of the awful day. All he knew was that he loved splashing in the water, and that there was no place on earth he loved more than the farm where he'd been born. That was how all of them felt about the place. Including the person who no longer lived there.

The document that Eleanor and Cam had signed, drawn up by their lawyers, carried the stipulation that Cam would buy out Eleanor's half of the property when Alison turned eighteen. Doing that—against the advice of her attorney—had been Eleanor's way to postpone an awful moment. They had a ways to go yet before Al's eighteenth birthday, but the question hung in the air. What was going to happen when they reached the date for the buyout?

Cam had no money, and no likely prospect of saving up any. The only logical alternative Eleanor's attorney had presented: putting the property up for sale.

It was an awful thought, even to Eleanor—to Eleanor as much as any of them, probably. She had loved that property before any of them. Three long winters, she'd lived there on her own.

"You're going to need that money," the attorney had told her, back when they'd worked out the divorce agreement. "A single parent making a living the way you do can't afford to walk away from her most significant asset. Wait till you see what it's like when you start paying for college. Correct me if I'm wrong, but from all appearances, you're the one who'll be footing the bill."

Maybe, at the time they drew up the divorce decree, Eleanor had allowed herself to believe that someday Cam would earn the money to pay her for her share of the farm, but if so she'd been dreaming. From the poster she'd seen up at the health food store, Eleanor gathered that Coco was teaching yoga at the farm part-time now. Cam was still working on his physical therapy license, and doing massage therapy on the side. But it was impossible to imagine that even with their combined incomes, he and Coco could come up with a lump sum sufficient to buy her out.

In Eleanor's life, too, money no longer flowed in as it once had. There were fewer jobs from her editor at the textbook company these days, and the royalties from sales of her Bodie series had largely dried up. She still took freelance jobs when they came her way, but when money was really tight, she picked up work as a substitute teacher in the Brookline school district.

She sent out a proposal to her old editor at Applewood Press. A few weeks later, a letter arrived, informing her that her editor had retired three years earlier. Nobody there knew her anymore. The form letter they sent thanked her for her interest. They were not considering queries at this time.

An idea came to her. That weekend, when the children were at Cam's, Eleanor set herself up at her desk with her drawing pencils and a stack of white paper. She spent two solid days making greeting cards. By Sunday afternoon, when it was time to pick up her children, she had created over a dozen. Monday morning, she mailed them to the Sweetheart company in Indianapolis.

Two months passed with no money coming in. Eleanor made stacks of bills now: the ones she had to pay, the ones she could put off. Somewhere along the line, Cam's parents had discontinued paying for the tutoring, and Eleanor cut Toby's sessions back.

Now his tutor called her in for a conference. For Toby to make progress, he needed more than two sessions a week, she told Eleanor.

That afternoon a call came from Indianapolis, the greeting card company. The creative director liked her submissions. Of the fourteen designs she'd sent them, they were buying eight. "That's highly unusual, by the way," he told her. "All of us here think you've got a great future in greeting card design."

Ten days later a check arrived with enough to pay for Toby's tutoring and cover the next two months of rent on their condo. She sent off over a dozen more greeting card designs the following month and sold every one—three for birthdays, five for anniversaries, one for bereavement, and one each for Father's and Mother's Day.

For some reason ideas for Mother's Day cards did not come as easily to Eleanor as the cards for birthdays and anniversaries did, the condolence cards, the thank-yous and Easter blessings. Eleanor had a hard time coming up with pictures and snappy lines about the bond between a mother and her children. She had too much to say about that one, too much feeling to put into a greeting card.

Maybe loving her children too much was her downfall—the weight it placed on the three of them, knowing that for their mother they represented everything of greatest meaning in her life. No question their father loved them, too, but without the heavy sense of obligation her devotion seemed to carry with it. Cam's sense of well-being did not reside, as hers did, in how the children were feeling that day. (Three children! Exposure to heartbreak, tripled!) If they were having problems, as surely they would, he would not suffer their pain in the way Eleanor did.

Young as they were, the children must have sensed this in their mother, and it seemed to leave them with a certain brittle edge of protectiveness where she was concerned. It was enough for a person to be responsible for his own happiness. No child wanted to be responsible for his mother's happiness, too.

She kept it together most of the time, but she knew this, and so did her children: when you tried too hard all the time, and worried all the time about making things perfect for your children, every so often you reached the breaking point.

Eleanor recognized all of this without being able to change any of it. There was always that territory of Crazyland out there, just over the border, where she might find herself at any moment if she wasn't careful. Always, just around the bend in the river, rapids to pull her down.

66.

a new human being

The first thing Eleanor had loved about Cam—more even than his handsome face and the bright red curls encircling it—was how he loved babies. The words he'd said to her the night they met: "I want to make babies with you." Not "have" but "make." Choosing to have a child represented an act of construction, embarking on a shared work of art.

"A cheap thrill," he called their children. For him, maybe, that had been true.

"I can't believe it's possible for two people to get together and come up with something as great as this," he'd said, a few days after Alison's birth. "It's like the best-kept secret, having a kid."

Not such a secret, exactly, Eleanor had pointed out to him. Plenty of people throughout history had figured this out before they did.

"I'm not talking about sex or reproduction," he said. "I mean, getting to be parents. Having this baby show up, that the two of us made by ourselves, without hiring any experts or going anyplace or spending anything besides a few bucks for the prenatal vitamins." (Well, they didn't just *show up,* she might have said to him. Anyone who described it that way had probably never experienced childbirth.)

Back at art school, Cam said, everyone used to talk about heading to New York City, getting gallery representation, having a show. It struck him as ironic—some kind of big cosmic joke—that all this time, they had this amazing capacity inside their own bodies to create something so much more important than any sculpture they'd build, or anything they'd ever put on a piece of canvas. A new human being.

"We made a person," Cam had said to Eleanor, the day of Alison's birth. "It's the ultimate creative act."

A few months after Cam and Coco's wedding came the news. The girls must have known for a while, but kept it to themselves, recognizing that it would hit Eleanor hard. It was Toby—for whom no filter existed now between what you thought and what you said—who finally told her.

"Coco's getting fat," he said one day, when she'd picked them up at the farm that Sunday. She'd stayed in the car till they came out, as usual. No glimpse of Cam or Coco at these moments.

Coco, fat? This was hard to imagine. In the back seat, Eleanor could feel the tension in Ursula as she jabbed Toby, the code that meant *Say no more.*

"Last I looked, Coco was pretty skinny," Eleanor said. She delivered the words like a friendly defense of her former babysitter, but there was strategy in what she offered, of course.

"Skinny legs," Toby said. "Fat stomach."

"Maybe she's going to have a baby," Eleanor suggested. If she kept her tone level and calm, they might tell her the rest.

The girls didn't bite, but Toby did.

"Baby brother," he said. "Maybe sister. I hope it's a boy."

From the back, she could feel the girls draw in their breath, waiting for an explosion—that part of Eleanor capable of spinning out into Crazyland.

"That's wonderful," she told them, her voice level. "Whatever sex it is, you're going to love being a big brother, Tobes.

"And you'll love it, too, girls," Eleanor went on. Hands steady on the wheel, ten o'clock and two. Eyes on the road. "I know you'll be wonderful big sisters to the new baby, same as you already are."

Silence. The three of them just sat there: hear no evil, see no evil, speak no evil.

"So, when is it due?"

This must have served as a signal to Ursula that all was well. Or at least, not as bad as she might have anticipated. "October," Ursula told her. "Dad said we never had a leaf season baby in our family before."

Our family. Not Eleanor's. But theirs.

"And you'll have all Thanksgiving vacation to get to know the baby," she offered. "Perfect timing."

67.

the last bath

It was Friday night, five days after she learned about Coco's pregnancy. It had been a few weeks since Eleanor had stopped by Timmy Pouliot's apartment, but that morning she'd called him. "I was hoping I could see you." She didn't usually put it that way, but the news of Coco's baby had left her wanting her bath.

It was all so familiar to her—as, once, her home with Cam had been. The Farrah poster and the beer signs and the upstairs neighbors' baby (now a toddler) that never stopped crying. That night, it suddenly all seemed pathetic. Her ex-husband was remarried to a beautiful young woman and training for a new career. They were having a baby. And what was she doing with her life? Designing greeting cards and taking a lot of baths under a poster of Farrah Fawcett in an apartment full of pizza boxes, with a man who listened to heavy metal music and played horseshoes.

She remembered a movie she saw back in her brief days at college, *The Last Picture Show.* Specifically, she was thinking about the character of the lonely, sex-starved coach's wife, played by Cloris Leachman, who has an affair with a boy on her husband's team, played by Timothy Bottoms. At first he's excited to be having passionate sex with an older woman, but later the relationship is nothing but an awkward embarrassment. Cloris Leachman is pleading with him not to leave her. He walks out the door, with Cybill Shepherd waiting for him.

"I'll be forty before you know it," Eleanor told Timmy from her place in the tub.

"Is that supposed to sound old?" he said.

"How would I ever introduce you to my children?" she said. The words had come out faster than she intended. She could see their effect on his face.

"You're ashamed of me," Timmy said. "I guess it comes down to that. Your ex-husband doesn't worry that his kids will stop loving him because he's shacked up with a twenty-one-year-old. But you still feel like you need their okay?"

He was right about that. But Eleanor knew she wouldn't get off as easily with her children as Cam had with Coco. She could see Al's face, sizing up Timmy Pouliot. Ursula would be more kind, but privately, she would judge him. She'd judge Eleanor too. What Ursula wanted was a normal life, free of drama. A regular boyfriend, the kind who wore a suit and tie and carried a briefcase and drove a minivan, not a Harley.

"You don't need a woman with three children," she told him. "You should have your own kids. With someone young."

"And what makes you so darned sure you know what I need?" he said.

"You know it's true. You'd love to have kids."

"You've got kids. I could love them."

He was fighting for her. But she believed she saw something else, too. Part of him knew she was right. He was letting go.

"We need to stop." Until she spoke, she hadn't planned on saying this. There was a terrible sound to her words, as if the act of speaking them made it true.

She was in the bathtub when she told him. Timmy Pouliot was kneeling on the floor next to her, running a washcloth over her back. When she got up, so did he.

He held the towel out for her, same as he always did. But there was something different about the way he looked at her this time. As she stepped out of the bathtub, he seemed to be memorizing her body.

They made love one more time. She wasn't sure, but she thought he might be crying. She dressed quickly. She was on the highway ten minutes later. Not that it mattered now, but it occurred to Eleanor, driving away that last time, that she had probably loved this man.

68.

not their half brother

She carried on as before. A mother of three children did not have the luxury of doing otherwise. What she'd been doing with Timmy Pouliot all those Friday nights was nothing but an escape from her real life. She couldn't afford that. She told herself it was better, spending her Friday nights getting caught up on the laundry. And anyway, she should focus her attention on her kids. They gave her plenty to worry about.

Since the separation Eleanor had watched a transformation in Al. Back when they'd first moved to Brookline, and Al enrolled in middle school there, she had taken herself to a barbershop in town where she'd had her hair chopped off short as a boy's and razor-cut around her neck and ears. Something about seeing her older daughter's tender pink skin, exposed for the first time since she was a baby, felt to Eleanor like a wound as raw as if her own body had suffered it.

This was always her problem, of course. That her children's sorrows became hers. She felt their pain so deeply, she hardly registered her own. It was funny (but not very) to remember the time she'd once wept over a scratched-off chicken pox scab.

There was a harder part. In the old days—meaning, days Eleanor was with Cam on the farm, when her children were going through something difficult, they'd come to her to talk about it. There had been a time, not so long past, when they had viewed their mother as the one able to fix whatever trouble it was they encountered. Sometimes, as with the death of Christa McAuliffe, there was no fixing possible, but she could comfort them. They looked to her for that.

More and more, they didn't. Toby might turn to her as he always did—climb on her lap, ask for a back rub—but she recognized a change in her girls. It was small things, mostly—a certain sharp, critical way Al looked at her across the table when they had dinner, Ursula's uncharacteristic silences. Much of the time now her daughters treated her with chilling politeness. Eleanor could hear the way they spoke with their father, when he called them up during the week—their easy laughter, their readiness to recount stories they had not mentioned to her. Once, when she had walked through the room in the middle of one of their phone conversations with Cam, Ursula had abruptly fallen silent, as if Eleanor's very presence in the room constituted an intrusion on something precious and intimate. They had secrets from her. Secrets they shared with Cam.

Most evident to Eleanor were the looks on their faces when her station wagon pulled down the road to drop them off at Cam's on Friday afternoon. She hadn't even turned off the ignition before the three of them were opening the car doors, racing toward the house.

"We're home," Ursula called out.

Then there was Coco—her belly just beginning to show under her apron—or Cam, opening the door in his brown work jacket and the hat Al had knitted him for his birthday two years ago, that he evidently wore even in the house. Eleanor knew that Ursula probably waited until the four of them were inside to express the full measure of her joy at being reunited with her father. (Coco, too, probably.) But driving away one time, Eleanor could see them all through the window: Cam bending low to hear what Ursula was telling him, Al hugging her bookbag and some CD—punk, for sure—that she wanted to play for her father. Toby, loping over to the spot by the woodstove where their new puppy, Buster, was lying, to scratch his belly and lie down next to him. Coco in the rocking chair by the woodstove, probably. Good spot for a pregnant woman.

They spent Friday night to Sunday afternoon with their father—their father and Coco—but Toby saw Cam on Wednesdays, too, when Cam drove to Boston for Toby's physical therapy classes. After, they'd attend the restorative yoga class in Cambridge that Toby loved. It would be nine o'clock by the time Cam dropped him off at the house.

"I miss my dad," Toby said, as he climbed the stairs to bed. "I miss my home."

The yoga was helping. Or something was. Toby's motor control had improved dramatically since the two of them had been going to classes and working together, just the two of them, weekends on the farm.

The children never said much about this, but Cam had evidently completed his physical therapy training. Darla had told Eleanor about an ad that appeared in the *Akersville Gazette* that spring, announcing that Cam and Coco were opening a joint practice—physical therapy and massage—in what used to be his old woodshop. A friend of Darla's had consulted with Cam about a back injury and reported that her session with him had been amazing. This was not a surprise to Eleanor. Cam always had a natural, intuitive sense about the workings of the body. What he'd done with Toby in their long afternoons together in the woodshop, going through exercises he'd designed, had done more for their son than anything he had received at his expensive school.

At some point the girls announced they were all vegetarians now. Then vegan, like Cam and Coco. Ursula still liked to bake, but what she produced in the kitchen now, and the snacks she brought home from her weekends at the farm, featured oats and carob and chia seeds. Most recently, when Eleanor had set one of her key lime pies on the table, the girls had told her no thanks. Only Toby still cleaned his plate.

Coco was one of those women (having known her since she was in grade school, it was still hard for Eleanor to think of Coco as a woman) who looked beautiful pregnant. In her own pregnancies, Eleanor's whole body had been overtaken: her ankles swelled and her face got puffy. Even her fingers had looked fat.

Eleanor laid eyes on Coco for the first time during her pregnancy somewhere around the sixth month—pulling the car up to her old house to bring the children for their summer vacation. She looked like some farm maiden, in from the garden, with an apronful of fresh produce. Or just one perfect watermelon. Her breasts had filled out a little, but from behind you wouldn't have known she was carrying a baby in that long, slim-hipped body of hers. She looked twenty-two years old, and she was.

It was August the next time Eleanor returned to Akersville. The children had been spending the summer there, which had made it possible for Ursula to perform in a kids' summer theater production of *Oliver!* Eleanor was just taking her seat when she spotted the two of them—Cam and Coco—off to one side of the auditorium, talking with a couple she recognized from the softball team, back in the old days—Peggy and Bob Olin, parents of Gina, the pale, strawberry blond child they'd all watched slowly dying over a single long softball summer. Except for the day of Gina's memorial service, Eleanor hadn't seen the Olins since. Peggy had disappeared from the bleachers, and not so long after, so had Eleanor.

But here they were now, the four of them, greeting each other like long-lost relatives and appearing to be in deep conversation. Maybe they were discussing their tomato crops, or the pros and cons of synthetic decking. Maybe Bob, a contractor, was offering his thoughts on some home renovation project Cam had embarked on. Or Cam was advising Bob on exercises for his back.

It felt like a hundred years ago that Eleanor sat on the bench next to Peggy at games—a barely pubescent Coco off on the field with the children, blowing bubbles and performing cartwheels—as Peggy held forth about the Adelle Davis diet while Gina and Ursula played in the dirt.

After Gina died, one of the other softball wives said she'd heard Peggy was drinking a lot, and there were rumors of Bob having an affair, but they must have worked things out, because here they were now, come to see their other daughter performing in the show, just as Eleanor was. They were holding hands, even. Eleanor had forgotten about Gina's big sister. Checking the program, she saw that Katie Olin was playing Oliver.

There was something about the sight of the four of them—Peggy and Bob, Coco and Cam—standing there talking and looking so easy and happy. Eleanor couldn't take her eyes off of them. Then Peggy took off her sweater. Eleanor watched as Bob lifted it gently from his wife's shoulders. Sometimes it was the smallest things, like this one, that caused a stab. It had been so long since anyone had helped her off with her sweater, or anything close.

Timmy Pouliot helping her into the bathtub. But that was over.

With the sweater removed, it was clear: Peggy was pregnant, too—about as far along as Coco, from the looks of her. Eleanor watched as the two of them compared each other's bellies, laid their hands on the places where at that very moment their babies were probably kicking.

Not so many years ago, Peggy and Bob had buried their younger child, but they were going for it again. That was the thing about a pregnancy. It represented hope that the future might offer something that the past had taken away. Another chance.

How long did Eleanor stand there, taking it in? The four of them were laughing about something—one of those pregnancy symptoms like how you get up five times in the night to pee, or an unlikely craving for ramen noodles or Eskimo Pies. A person could not have guessed, observing the two of them—Peggy and Coco—that only a handful of years earlier, one of them had spent a season at Boston Children's, watching her child fade away. Not so long before that, Coco was teaching Gina how to execute a cartwheel.

Eleanor could still remember that last summer she spent sitting with Peggy—Gina bald and close to skeletal in her wheelchair, the blue veins visible under the translucent skin of her naked skull, Toby—Toby as he was then—looking baffled and worried when she'd ignored his offer of a mozzarella stick. Everybody always wanted to play with Toby, but Peggy and Bob's daughter was already leaving the world by then. The other children sensed it. Other than Toby, they'd all hung back.

Within the space of a couple of years, Gina would be dead and Toby would be sitting on the couch with a look on his face as blank as the screen of Eleanor's computer when she first turned it on. Now here they all were again—one character gone, another two on the way, the cards shuffled, deck redealt.

The show began. From up on the stage, Katie Olin was holding out a bowl and looking hungry.

"Please, sir, may I have some more?" she said.

Eleanor kept her eyes on Ursula, the fourth orphan to the right. She wondered if Peggy Olin, seeing Ursula, was imagining who Gina would be now if she had lived, whether she'd be up there on the stage with her sister and her friend. Sometimes, observing other people's non-brain-injured nine-year-old sons, Eleanor caught herself trying to imagine who Toby would have been at this age. But there was nobody remotely like him, so that never worked. Toby had been a shooting star.

Cam and Coco's son, Elijah, was born that fall. Cam called to tell the children the news. That afternoon, he drove to Brookline to pick them up to meet their new brother.

Their brother. That's how they spoke of him. Not their half brother. Watching the car pull away, containing the three people she loved best in the world, going off to meet a person who would be part of their family now (theirs, not hers), she felt like a woman lost at sea. There had been a shipwreck, and the rescue boats had circled around and managed to pick up the survivors. Except for Eleanor.

69.

no more onions in the bed

Growing up, Eleanor had lived in a household where the only touch seemed to occur behind closed bedroom doors, between her parents. She had craved affection, and finally—for a while there—she'd gotten it. For close to ten years, Eleanor had not known a night without a human body pressed up against her own. Not only Cam's skin against hers, but the warm and occasionally damp presence of her children wandering into their bed at midnight—small sojourners bearing their blankets and pillows—a stuffed meerkat, the piece of ribbon Toby liked to wind around his pointer finger when he sucked his thumb, the other end twirled inside the pearly shell of his ear. For a while there, Alison had insisted on bringing into bed (first her own bed, but later in the night, the bed of her parents) a doll she'd named Onion Head, made out of a sprouted onion, with a kerchief tied around the bulb of the onion that served as the doll's head. Over the weeks, the onion had acquired a smell so rank that Cam had finally laid down the law.

"I draw the line at sleeping with onions," he said, but in the end they let Alison into their bed anyway.

No more onions in the bed. No more anyone.

All those nights that Eleanor lay on the old futon—the same futon where in days past she'd given birth—with the hot breath of one child or another on her face, their hands on her belly, her breasts—silky hair tangled into her own, no inch of her body unclaimed, not even her brain, because she could never stop thinking about them or anticipating what they'd need next.

"I'm possessed," she told Cam. "By children."

Sometimes now, alone in her bed at night, Eleanor ran her own hands over her skin just to remind herself what it felt like, being touched. The thought had occurred to her that if she never experienced warm human touch again she might just wither up. Stroking your own skin wasn't the same as the touch of another person. A familiar body, a familiar person. A person you loved, who loved you back.

If she and Cam had made it through, now might have been the moment they started having more sex again, but as it was, nothing was a clearer reminder of what had been lost than the unoccupied space in her bed. She filled it with pillows and books and a sketch pad, where, when she woke in the middle of the night—as she did a lot these days—she could scribble down ideas for greeting cards.

One time, late at night, in her bed, she'd written a long letter to Cam. "I just want to talk about our children sometimes," she wrote. "We might not be married, but we're still parents together." No response.

This was probably the worst part: the silence. It seemed as though everything that had happened between her and the man she once loved, and still shared three children with, had melted away, or that it had never happened in the first place. All those years they were a family seemed to have been wiped from the memory of the man who used to be her husband as surely as if it had been Cam, not Toby, who'd ended up facedown in the pond that day with his brain deprived of oxygen, the memory of every beautiful thing gone.

Who could say what Cam thought about that time? Eventually he had made a whole other life for himself, and except for the fact that the marriage he went on to make, with his new partner, his new child, took place on the same piece of land, under the same roof, where the two of theirs had played out, all memory of their old days seemed to have been erased. It wasn't just that the two of them turned out to have no future together. More surprising, for Eleanor, was the obliteration of their past.

There had been a time when Eleanor craved nothing so much as ten minutes alone. "I'm having Quiet Time," she told her children, setting the timer and pouring herself a cup of tea (or, later, wine), pulling her stool up to the counter with a copy of *Redbook* magazine that was probably two months old, to study some article about giving yourself an avocado facial, or ten interesting things to do with garbanzo beans.

Now it was always Quiet Time in Eleanor's world. Her children still needed her—more than ever, maybe, but for driving and cooking and rounding up the materials for science projects and signing forms and finding lost sneakers. They needed her for writing checks.

When they were four and three, or seven and six, Eleanor had known everything there was to know about her daughters' lives. Now whenever they returned from their father's house—the place they still referred to as home—their wariness accompanied them into the Brookline condo; they moved through the rooms like double agents, their gaze conveying distrust. Their mother had let them down once, by her failure to stay married to their father. She was the one who'd left, wasn't she? What would she do next to upend their world?

Some of it was a function of their ages, no doubt. In the old days, when they emerged from the tub she'd wrap a towel around each one of them, tight as a mummy, take them onto her lap, kiss them behind their ears, their necks, their toes. In their new life with their mother in the Brookline house, they didn't want her in the room when they took their baths. Their bodies, that were changing so rapidly now, were hidden from her. Worse, though, so were their thoughts.

The truth was that even if their parents had stayed together, that perfect life they knew, growing up on the farm, would have had to change. But as it was, the girls attributed every bad thing to Eleanor's departure. All their lives she had been the one who'd made it her mission to protect them from disappointment and hurt. If they experienced, now, a level of disappointment that went so much deeper than the loss of a toy or an embarrassment at a T-ball game, it must be Eleanor's fault. It was Eleanor—the one who'd promised to protect them always—who had let them down.

They never said this. They didn't even know it, probably. But Eleanor could see the silent disapproval on their faces, the way they looked at her as she set the cereal on the table or called out, as they headed to school, "Did you remember your math homework?" They viewed her with a nearly perpetual air of mild irritation and occasional contempt.

You promised us one kind of life. You switched it out for another. They never said this, but their faces revealed the thought.

They blamed her for their parents' divorce. They blamed her for the life they led now, shuttling back and forth between two houses.

Her worst offense—she knew this—was her bitterness toward their father. Most of the time she held her tongue in front of them on the topic of Cam, but now and then—mostly when she was tired, or she'd had a glass of wine or two, when her own father's ghost seemed to inhabit her—she said things she'd regret later.

"If your dad contributed," she said, "you could go to summer camp." "If your father contributed, we could get you a new bike." "If your dad contributed, I wouldn't have to work so hard all the time."

If their dad contributed, maybe she'd be a nicer person.

They tuned her out, like a radio station playing music from the fifties.

More and more now, Al stayed in her room. Even Ursula—sunny, cheerful, pliant, chatty Ursula, the peacemaker, though she still presented herself in the world as the easiest, most trouble-free of any child anybody ever met—seemed to have acquired an unfamiliar edge, a way of responding to whatever Eleanor said or asked that met the requirements of civility with little left over in the way of warmth.

At the house Cam shared with Coco now, everything was different, a whole other life. Things happened there that Eleanor would never hear about.

Goats, camping trips, yoga, the death of the family dog. A baby brother. A child she had never laid eyes on, about whom she knew nothing because that's as much as they said about him.

Whatever it was they felt about this new character in their lives, Eleanor could only guess. Her children were becoming mysterious to her, like someone you went to school with once who you meet up with at a reunion twenty years later and barely recognize.

She saw, in her mind, those boats they used to make that they brought to the brook every March. The ones that disappeared in the culvert, the cork people who drifted away. This was where her children were now. Not quite out of sight, but heading there. Even Toby, doing his sun salutations and downward dog, lying on his yoga mat in happy baby pose, barely registered her presence sometimes when she came in the room. When she picked him up after a weekend with his father, his eyes stayed locked on his Game Boy. Al, bent over her homework or her computer programming manual, answered her questions with the fewest syllables necessary. Even Ursula seemed to be playing a role now when she got in the car—her smile tight, her brisk hug like the greeting a candidate might offer up on the campaign trail.

Now Eleanor wondered if all of Ursula's old sweetness had ever been real. Maybe she had been quietly resentful all along. Maybe her famous goodness had been her clever tactic. It was easier to be very good than troublesome. Maybe her cheerful demeanor had been an effective way for a girl to keep her mother out of her hair. All that time Eleanor had spent worrying about Alison, worrying about Toby, when all along, maybe the one she should have been focused on had been her perfect middle child—her compliance a strategy for keeping her mother at bay. *Keep smiling, and they'll never know what's really going on.*

"What do you say we go for a bike ride?" Eleanor said to Ursula one time in April, a precious Saturday when the children were with her, not Cam (he was attending a workshop on spinal issues), and the whole day stretched before them. Precious now, in a way they never used to be.

"Thanks, but I better do my homework," Ursula said—her politeness more chilling than anger might have been.

She still put her dishes in the dishwasher without being asked and read Toby his beloved truck book five times in a row without complaint, still cleaned out the crisper drawer, still brought home perfect report cards. But when her official responsibilities in the family had been met she disappeared into her room, much as Al did. When Eleanor asked about school, or friends, her answers were clipped and monosyllabic, like her sister's. Mostly she avoided her mother's gaze, but when their eyes met, hers betrayed nothing of what went on behind them.

Even before the divorce, Al had announced that she would no longer answer to her old name. But only after the divorce had she insisted on the buzz cut. Now she wore nothing but jeans and army boots and baggy shirts meant to conceal her small but developing breasts. The year after Eleanor brought the children to live with her in Brookline, Al got her period—a piece of news she delivered to Eleanor with a determined brusqueness, the week after the event took place.

"You don't need to give me some big talk or anything," she said. "I know everything. I'm taking care of it."

70.

the reason for every single bad thing

A year or so after Eleanor moved out, she had received a call from the counselor at school expressing concern about Al. "Of course, we might also see this kind of behavior even in a child from an intact family," she said. "But we need to consider closely the detrimental impact of recent changes in your family dynamic."

The counselor quoted an expert, a psychologist named Dr. Judith Wallerstein, who'd conducted an in-depth study of children of divorce. The findings weren't good. Name virtually any psychological issue a person might suffer from, down the line; according to Dr. Judith Wallerstein, the children of divorce were more likely to suffer from it.

"Alison resists having anything to do with the other girls at school," the counselor told her. "She wants to play sports with the boys, but they don't want to include her. She doesn't have friends. She doesn't seem to want them."

"Al," Eleanor corrected her. "Our daughter goes by Al now."

When they'd done a square-dancing unit in gym, the counselor told Eleanor, Alison—Al—had refused to participate. For women's history month, when the girls were supposed to choose a famous woman from the past and dress up as that woman to deliver a report on her, Al had requested that she be excused. "I don't like putting on dresses," she said, though in the end she agreed to portray Babe Didrikson Zaharias.

Eleanor sat in the counselor's office, trying to take in what she was saying, though her mind kept wandering to a plant on the windowsill, desperately in need of water, and the photograph on her desk displaying a smiling husband and two happy-looking children. An "intact family."

Did Al exhibit evidence of distress around issues of her gender before the divorce, the counselor wanted to know? The implication was clear enough: It had been Eleanor and Cam's decision to end their marriage that triggered their daughter's current struggles. Eleanor's decision, from the sound of it. (There it was again. A reminder, from the counselor, that it had been Eleanor who'd moved out of the family home. Al had told her as much.)

It was a terrible thought for a parent: that she might have ruined her child's life not just in the present, but far into the future, as Judith Wallerstein's findings seemed to predict they would.

Did divorce have to be the reason for every single bad thing that went on in your child's life? Didn't the children of those "intact" families the counselor was talking about have problems, too, now and then? And if she and Cam had subjected their children to irreversible trauma by their failure to stay married, what were they supposed to do about that now?

So Al was depressed. Ursula was polite, but wary—like a distant relative come to visit, on her best behavior. Then there was Toby. Gentle, loving Toby, who could sit on the floor for a few hours making a ball out of rubber bands or examining a Rubik's Cube with no particular goal of lining up the colors. Toby, who liked drawing rows of parallel lines and untying his shoelaces and humming songs from their *Music Man* soundtrack. The old Toby had loved Michael Jackson, but when they showed him the "Thriller" video now, it just scared him.

He spoke more now—short sentences, constructed like telegrams—and thanks no doubt to all the work Cam did with him, he could run, in his funny, lurching way. And he seemed, if not precisely happy, content anyway. He loved his sisters and most of all he loved his new baby brother, Elijah.

Before the accident, Toby had a dislike of clothes with buttons. After, he appeared to have forgotten about that, as if he had forgotten who he was: A boy who played the violin once. A boy who danced naked and peed outdoors in winter so he could spell his name in the snow. A boy who reported on his conversations with God and said once that he loved Eleanor's toes so much, he wanted to marry them.

One day, when Toby was nine—having lived almost as long with the damaged brain as he had with his healthy one—something had possessed Eleanor to put on their old recording of the Wieniawski Polonaise that he had loved.

The record was all scratched up from all the times his four-year-old self had played it. Maybe she held out the crazy idea that after all these years some old synapse gone dormant after his time in the pond would have regenerated itself. Did Eleanor really believe this might be possible? Maybe she just wanted to hear that piece of music again, herself, and summon the memory of the child who used to play it. The first twelve measures, anyway.

Toby, hearing the record now, displayed no reaction, except to be slightly annoyed by the intrusion of music. Except for *The Music Man* and the theme song from the Toys "R" Us commercial (featuring that maddening line "I don't want to grow up, I'm a Toys 'R' Us kid"), he seemed to prefer silence most of the time. That or humming. He sat in lotus position a lot, a function of his time with his father at yoga class, staring at some object—a rock, a pencil, a stick of wood—and turning it around in his hands.

He liked *Mister Rogers* and televised golf tournaments. He liked laying toothpicks in rows on the rug, or side-by-side paint samples that Eleanor got for him at the hardware store. Small, simple, repetitive activities.

One of the few aspects of who he was now, at nine, that had endured from his life before the accident was his habit of picking up rocks wherever he went and carrying them in his pockets. Though there appeared nothing distinctive in the specimens he collected, he resisted any suggestion of paring down his collection. Rocks filled his room—lined the walls and windowsills. Most of them were indistinguishable from each other, except to Toby, who knew every one.

71.

I want to go home

Out on the highway, heading north to Akersville to pick up her children after a weekend with Cam, she'd spotted him: Timmy Pouliot on his Harley. In Massachusetts, the law required a helmet, but the minute Timmy Pouliot crossed the line back into the Live Free or Die state, he always took it off.

That's how she knew she must be in New Hampshire now.

There was a woman on the back, of course. Timmy Pouliot always had a woman on the back of his bike. No doubt she was young and no doubt beautiful.

Eleanor only caught a glimpse of the two of them. Timmy Pouliot was going faster on the bike than she was in her old Subaru. She figured he wouldn't have noticed. But as he passed, he raised one hand very slightly, the way Harley riders did, seeing another person on a bike, only there was nobody on a bike around. He must have been waving at her.

A feeling washed over her then. Regret, possibly.

There had been more than a few reasons Eleanor had believed she had to break things off with Timmy Pouliot as she had. But above all others was the fear of her children's disapproval.

Now look. Her children disapproved of her anyway.

The children raised the subject at dinner on a night they'd just come home from their father's house. She'd made spaghetti carbonara, one of their favorites. Cam was a vegan now, as was Coco, and the girls had given up meat and even dairy-based foods now, too, but spaghetti carbonara—the most comforting meal she knew—had been their tradition, and even after they shifted to the new vegan diet at Cam and Coco's, they made an exception for this particular dish.

Eleanor set down the platter and took her seat. Except for rare occasions, they had abandoned their old tradition of singing their song, "Simple Gifts," before beginning the meal.

"We have something we need to talk to you about, Mom," Al said.

It had seemed like a good sign, Al saying this. They wanted to talk, for once. Eleanor was ready to listen. She waited as Al took a long breath.

"Toby wants to live on the farm with Dad," Al said. "We all think it's a good idea."

She was picking out the prosciutto. Next to her, Ursula scraped the cream off the noodles.

Eleanor steadied herself. Toby? Move? Who was this "we" her daughter spoke of, who'd evidently agreed on what a good idea this was before mentioning it to her?

"I'm his mother," Eleanor said. "He needs me."

"It's just too confusing for Toby, going back and forth all the time," Ursula chimed in. "And he gets more help from Dad than at that expensive school you're sending him to. Dad works with Toby all the time. The physical therapy and the yoga are really helping."

"Then there's Elijah," Al added. "You should see how those two get along with each other."

She had not seen this, of course. She had not seen anything that went on at their father's house.

Ursula now: "Dad thinks it would be better if Toby could stay put. Al and I think so, too. And Coco."

Eleanor steadied herself. She could hear, in Ursula's words, how carefully she'd prepared them. She had probably practiced this moment in her room and discussed it with her father. ("Your mother's not going to like this," he would have said. "But it'll go over better coming from you.")

"It always takes him a whole day adjusting from one place to the other one. Plus, he really loves being around the goats."

"Goats," Toby said—the first time he'd weighed in. "I got four goats, Mama." This was news to Eleanor, too.

She turned to study her son—the only one of the three of them who seemed to be enjoying the carbonara. "How do you feel about going to live at your dad's, Tobes?" Eleanor asked him.

"I love you, Mama," he said. "But I want to go home."

She didn't have to ask her son where home was. Or any of the three of them. It didn't matter whether she bought a trampoline, an air hockey table, or a Commodore 64 computer. Her son wanted to live on the farm with his father.

Eleanor knew how much Toby loved Elijah—the one person in the family whose developmental level remained below his own, though the days were numbered when that would remain true. Every Sunday night when he returned from his father's house, Toby talked about Elijah. Soon enough Elijah, young as he was, would be able to do things Toby could not, but for now Toby could hold him and line up blocks on the rug beside him and the two of them could play—and unlike all the other people in his life, for Elijah, playing with Toby was never a chore. Of course Toby would want to be with Elijah. Every day, if possible.

She wanted to throw her glass against the wall, but she set it down as gently as if it were fine crystal. She got up from her chair and knelt beside Toby. He was arranging his peas in a circle and humming. "I'd miss you a whole lot if you move back to the farm," she said, "but I want you to be happy."

"I want to be with Lijah," Toby said. "I like my home."

Eleanor couldn't argue with that. She understood the feeling. Even now, even to Eleanor, the farm remained the place she loved more than any other.

Toby must have recognized this was hard for her. He patted her on the arm and laid his head on her shoulder.

"Don't worry, Mama," he said. "You can come see me when I go live with my dad."

Toby had a particular way of arranging his rocks, and it troubled him when one was out of place. In preparation for the move back to Akersville, the girls labeled every rock with a numbered sticker so they could re-create the lineup in the upstairs bedroom at Cam's house he'd share with Elijah now.

"I'll bring him down to see you on weekends," Cam told Eleanor when she brought Toby to the house.

For a few weeks, they tried this. But Toby didn't like leaving Elijah, or his goats.

Mostly, now, when Eleanor and Toby spent time together it was in Akersville. She took him bowling a couple of times, with bumpers in the gutters so he'd knock over some pins. (There was no further need to require that he recite the No-Cry Pledge. He didn't care whether he knocked over any pins.)

Darla—who had recently begun attending Cam and Toby's yoga classes, mostly as a way of trying not to let life with Bobby get her down—reported that everyone in the class loved Toby.

"Cam's incredibly patient with him," she said. "In spite of everything, I've got to hand it to the guy."

After he moved back to the farm, Eleanor made a point of calling her son up most nights just so he could hear her voice. She always asked him about his day, without expecting much of a response. *Played with goats. Little brother. Veggie burgers. Coco. Dad.*

"Come see me at my house," he told Eleanor. He didn't really want to come to her home in Brookline anymore, but he never understood why she couldn't come to his.

72.

my mother just hit me

Sometime that fall, Al picked up a Guns N' Roses CD. It was called *Appetite for Destruction* and the cover featured skulls on a cross. A year before, Al's artists of choice had been New Kids on the Block. Now all she wanted to listen to, for hours every day—up in her room with her computer manuals and her Commodore 64—was "Sweet Child o' Mine" and "Welcome to the Jungle," with an occasional dose of the Indigo Girls.

That night they'd had one of their arguments—something to do with Eleanor's request that Al write a thank-you note to her grandparents for the back-to-school gift they'd sent her, a dress that looked like something Shirley Temple might have worn in one of those old black-and-white movies they used to watch together after they got their VCR, on snow days, snuggled up on the couch with the popcorn.

"Why should I thank people for a present I hated?" Al said. "I'll never wear that dress. I threw it out already."

"It shows they were thinking about you," Eleanor told her. "It's the thought that counts." She hated the sound of her own voice saying this. She was starting to sound like a greeting card.

"It shows they don't know me at all." Al stabbed her fork into her tofu. "If they paid any attention they'd know I hate dresses." Especially a dress with lace ruffles down the front and buttons shaped like hearts.

The truth was, Eleanor didn't have much affection for Cam's parents, either. But she believed in good manners, and part of that meant writing thank-you notes.

"You want me to be fake?" Al said. "Maybe I want to be real for a change."

Al did not say to her mother that for her, just going off to school in the morning felt fake. The person she was inside bore almost no resemblance to the one people perceived her to be, named Alison. Ever since she was four years old, and maybe even before this, she had been telling her parents this. Nobody listened.

She got up from the table. She carried her plate into the kitchen and jammed it in the dishwasher.

A minute later, from up in her room came the sound of Guns N' Roses, the voice of Axl Rose screaming "Welcome to the Jungle . . . I wanna watch you bleed." Louder than normal, even.

Eleanor stood at the foot of the stairs and called up to Al to turn down the music. No change in volume. She climbed the steps, knocked, then opened the door to her older daughter's room.

"I asked you to turn down the music."

No response. Eleanor might as well be invisible. The same way Cam had treated her for years now. That was what set her off, probably.

Eleanor knew, even as she did this, that she would regret it later, but she couldn't stop herself. She advanced into Al's room. She didn't just turn off the music. She unplugged the boom box, whipping it off the table with enough force that she knocked over Al's stack of Mandarin tapes and her collection of Japanese comic books.

She carried the boom box out of the room, into her own bedroom, and threw the machine in the closet.

Al had followed her mother into her bedroom. "Fuck you!" she screamed. "Bitch!"

Eleanor turned around to face her daughter. She could feel her own blood pumping and her heart beating fast. She had never struck one of her children, but now she raised her hand, palm open, and slapped her daughter across the face.

The two of them just stood there then, facing each other. In her daughter's eyes, she could see no trace of anything resembling affection. Eleanor could barely breathe, but there was an eerie calm to Al as she crossed the room, picked up the telephone extension, and dialed.

"I thought you should know, Dad," she said. "My mother just hit me."

He was there in under two hours. By that time, Al had packed a bag full of her things (not the brown paper she used on weekends, but an actual suitcase this time). Also the boom box Eleanor had briefly confiscated, her *Introduction to Algorithms* book and her Mandarin tapes and all her CDs, her Commodore 64 and her precious Doc Martens. By the time Cam's truck pulled up, she was out on the sidewalk with her things, waiting for him.

Cam did not get out of his truck, but Eleanor could see from the window how he embraced their daughter when he reached her. He held her that way for at least a minute. Then they were gone.

She left a message on his machine. ("We need to talk. I was wrong. But Al was out of line, too. It's important, when things like this come up, that we can still present a unified front . . .")

He did not return the call.

There was school the next day. Eleanor figured Cam would bring Al there, but sometime in the morning a call came from the office.

"Your daughter didn't show up. We just wanted to make sure you knew."

"You'd better call my children's father," she said.

The next night Cam called her: "Al has chosen to remain here at the farm," he said, in the way of speaking he'd adopted with her since the divorce. Quiet, calm, betraying no evidence of emotion. "She'd like to go back to her old school. You can make an issue of it if you choose, but we're hoping you won't turn this into a battle. She's old enough to make her own decisions."

Crying was never a good idea with Cam. Neither was yelling into the phone, or slamming the receiver down. At times like these she always ended up sounding like a crazy woman.

"I hope you get help, Eleanor," he said. "I pray you find peace."

It always worked this way, that after she hung up, she thought of all the things she wished she'd said to him, instead of what she did. Which was nothing.

It was May when Ursula made her decision to leave Eleanor's house and go live on the farm, too, with her brother and sister. She waited until seventh-grade graduation. Once Al made the move, it was probably inevitable that Ursula would follow.

"Toby needs me," she said. "Plus, Coco needs help with the baby." And Betsy was teaching her how to sew.

By the time school started in the fall—eighth grade for Ursula, ninth for Alison—the visitation schedule had been flipped. The parent they visited on weekends was Eleanor now, but more and more, their activities got in the way of those visits, too. Field hockey and basketball games, soccer and 4-H. Ursula was helping Toby raise rabbits, along with the goats. Then Cam's old friend Jeremy gave them an old horse he'd bought in the classifieds, before it occurred to him he had no place to put her. Once Midnight showed up, and the chickens, the children hardly ever came to Eleanor's anymore. There was always some job to take care of back on the farm.

She called them up most nights, but often, when she did, they'd be in the middle of some game with Elijah, or tending to the animals.

"Can we call you back later, Mom?" Ursula would say.

Sometimes they did. More often they didn't.

There had been a time when Eleanor craved quiet so much she had sent Toby to the borning room for ten minutes of peace. Now her house felt like a tomb. Toby's Legos and rock collection were gone, along with Ursula's Judy Blume books and hair products, the glitter she tossed in the air every morning as she walked out the door to school to make herself sparkle, the bottles of nail polish lining the bathroom sink. She missed Al's wardrobe—black shirts, black pants, black socks—scattered on the floor of her room, her collection of underground comic books, along with odd Japanese snack foods, exotic fly-eating plants. Weirdly, Eleanor even missed the sound of Guns N' Roses blasting from Al's bedroom.

Eleanor hadn't played her old vinyl records in years, but now she set up the turntable again and took out the *Blue* album. It felt almost as if she were back where she'd started (same sad songs, the same Boston suburb, even).

I wish I had a river I could skate away on. It was almost as though that other whole life—her real one—had never happened.

73.

perfect Christmas

Cam used to say Eleanor became a crazy person for the entire month of December, and she probably did, though in the scale of problems, going overboard for your children at the holidays didn't seem like the worst problem a person could suffer from. It didn't take a great therapist to recognize the origins of this particular obsession. All you had to do was look at the photograph albums from Eleanor's childhood—the stiff, formal annual Christmas card portrait of Eleanor and her parents in front of a tree covered with one color of ornaments only (blue one year, gold the next). Martin and Vivian always had a drink in their hands, even in the pictures. Eleanor, in that year's holiday dress, sat soberly on her stool, not so much smiling as turning the corners of her mouth up. Her mother didn't like giving her paints because they were messy, so she got dolls and ski equipment. Never the dog she asked for every year.

Eleanor had spent her children's whole childhood obsessed with doing Christmas differently. Ever since they were very little—but old enough to understand the concept of the gift inside the wrapping paper, and not just the wrapping paper—Eleanor had seen the presents she chose for her children as a way of acknowledging to them the things she loved and valued about them, all the aspects of who they were that only someone who knew them as well as she did would recognize. The best presents were the ones that only someone who paid as close attention as she did would know to put under the tree.

For Alison, one year, it had been a pogo stick. She never asked for one, but Eleanor remembered a time, in Boston, when they'd watched a subway busker perform an act on a pogo stick, and Alison, not yet six years old, had stood transfixed, watching him. Very shyly, and only once, Ursula had expressed the dream of becoming a fashion designer. That was the year Eleanor drove three hours to a department store in western Massachusetts that was going out of business and getting rid of its mannequins. She'd bought one, the same size as Ursula. Driving home in a snowstorm with the naked, bald-headed child mannequin stretched across the back seat, she pictured how her daughter would dress up the mannequin—the wonderful, crazy outfits Ursula would create for her. She wasn't wrong about that.

For Toby—the old Toby—it was always easy. Geodes and crystals. Books about birds and insects and planets. For Cam, there had been a year when Eleanor tracked down an African drum, and another year when, broke as they were that season, she got him an antique pocket watch.

That was the year Cam gave her the wooden hat. From a distance, it looked like a regular cowboy hat, but when you got close you realized it was made from a single maple burl, though he had worked the wood so finely, with such care, that it was very thin and amazingly light. Cam had never been one for big romantic gestures, but he'd burned an inscription into the inside of the hat. *My cowgirl.*

In the years since the divorce, they'd alternated holidays, but this particular time—even though it was Eleanor's year, but knowing they would want to share the holiday with Elijah—she'd let the children stay with Coco and Cam.

Their Christmases hadn't always ended up so magical, of course. Not just the *bûche de Noël* year, but others, Eleanor spent so much time—also thought, also money—trying to make everything perfect that by the time the actual day came, she was exhausted. More than once, she had gone to Crazyland then. After it was over, and they'd taken the tree down, a terrible sadness came over her. It was about that vast space she never seemed able to breach, between the dream of a happy family Christmas and the reality of what happened when she tried to pull one off.

Then came the divorce, the every-other-year holiday meals that left her with the perpetual sense of coming up short. It wasn't just

Cam's absence they felt now, though that was enough. As difficult as the visits had been with his parents, now that they no longer came for Christmas, Eleanor missed them. More accurately, she missed the feeling of being part of a big family, or even a medium-size one, with all kinds of personalities (even the irritating ones) gathered around the table, reminiscing about long-ago holidays—overcooked turkeys, ugly holiday sweaters. At other people's houses—the houses of the people with big families—there would be presents wrapped in ten different kinds of paper, three kinds of pies, charades and caroling by the fire, ending the evening with popcorn and a video of *It's a Wonderful Life*. Eleanor knew, from Darla, that just having a big family was no guarantee of a happy holiday. Still, she couldn't let go of the feeling that she was letting her children down for her inability to provide for them a family like the ones in the greeting cards she was so good at creating.

At the Brookline condo, Eleanor tried, once, inviting other people over to join her and the children—a ragtag bunch of casual acquaintances who didn't have another place to go—but the evening had felt a little sad, with everyone making uneasy small talk and exchanging candles and soap. Partway through the meal that year—whose guest list had included a teacher from Toby's school, on a one-year visa from the Czech Republic, and a neighbor from their condominium development, and a woman she'd met in line at the DMV, Ursula got up to call her father. He must have put Elijah on the phone, because then the three children all gathered around, laughing and saying the kinds of things a person says to a thirteen-month-old.

"I wish we could see our baby brother," Ursula said when she returned to the table. The woman from the DMV line had asked Ursula if she had any hobbies. The teacher from Toby's school, who'd drunk a surprising amount of punch, knocked over the gravy onto Eleanor's lace tablecloth. The condo neighbor was telling them his theory that the world would be coming to an end at midnight, December 31, 1999.

After that, Eleanor decided not to try making Christmas at her house anymore. Even on the years when she was legally allowed to have the children with her, she let them go to Cam and Coco's. That's where they wanted to be.

The year the children moved back to the farm with their father, Patty invited Eleanor to come to New York City for a holiday dinner at her apartment in SoHo with her new husband and their baby. (Philippe was long gone. This was Greg, a stock trader.)

Patty's father had died the previous summer, but her mother, Alice, would be there. "Mom still asks about you all the time," Patty said. "And we might even rate a visit from my brother, the congressman, though between the twins and everything going on in Washington, he's spread pretty thin."

Matt Hallinan had been getting a lot of press lately, Eleanor knew. She'd seen an article that spoke of him as "a rising star in the new Republican Party."

Eleanor wrote back to thank her old friend for the invitation. But she'd have to pass.

74.

the three amigos

Back in October, she'd bought a copy of an alternative newspaper published in Vermont with personal ads on the back page, accompanied by a 900 number you could call to leave a message if someone whose ad you read seemed interesting. (Or maybe, simply, if nothing in the ad contained any immediate deal breakers. The bar was low.)

There were no photographs attached in these ads, and most of the time they contained only basic information. People who ran them paid by the word, which kept most of them short, though now and then she'd come upon a very long ad that must have cost its author a lot of money. All Eleanor could learn from virtually every ad she read was that the man who'd placed it was easygoing, considerate, romantic, and liked to play golf.

Sometime in early December, she had seen one that looked different from the others.

Russell looked to be a few years older than Eleanor—early forties, probably. He was divorced, with two sons, eight and ten years old, who lived with him full-time. Whatever it was that might have explained the disappearance of his children's mother was more than a man could explain in a personal ad, but Eleanor gathered that he was on his own with his children now. In the one and only sentence he'd provided about himself, he said he liked hiking and bird-watching. "I think I'm a nice person," he wrote. He'd been an Eagle Scout. He still lived by that code, or tried to.

One of the things about a personal ad, particularly one as simple and brief as this one, was the way it allowed whoever it was reading it to fill in all those things that were left out with a picture of how she'd like the person to be.

Sometimes, just having a fantasy got a person through a few days. She recorded a response to his ad (LovingSingleDad), with a suggestion that he send her a note telling her more about himself. Two days later a letter arrived. Maybe she detected a hint of desperation in his eagerness to meet up, but who was Eleanor to find fault with a person for occasional feelings of despair?

Christmas was coming. She was going to be alone for the holiday for the second year in a row. She figured they could make a date. She'd get to put on a nice dress for once, and maybe high heels.

She gave him her phone number.

Eleanor had always believed you could tell more about a person from his voice than from his photograph. Russell's voice was low and soft, and he chose his words well, as not everyone did, even in the ads they published, let alone in conversation.

"Would you consider having a date?" he said. It was a little difficult for him, leaving his boys. But maybe she'd be up for coming over?

"You're probably doing something on Christmas," he said.

She wasn't, actually.

He didn't ask how it could be that she had no family to spend the holiday with, though some people—hearing this—might have concluded that Eleanor was a loser. He just asked if she'd like to come for Christmas dinner with him and his boys. It was a crazy idea, spending Christmas with a man she'd never met, and his two children.

She said okay.

He lived in a very small town in western Massachusetts, an hour and a half from Boston, not so different from where Eleanor had lived on her old farm. The directions Russell gave her were extremely thorough. Included in these directions, recited over the phone while she wrote it all down, was every landmark a person might look for at every turn in the road, as if he worried that one wrong turn might doom any possibility of a future for the two of them.

He wanted to know if she was allergic to any foods. He was not much of a baker, he said, but his grandmother had a great recipe for corn bread that he made every year. He wanted to know whether she liked marshmallows on her sweet potatoes or preferred them plain. His sons liked the marshmallow kind, but he was thinking of making a second, smaller pan without the topping.

That sounded good, she said. She had never been a marshmallow fan.

"I told the boys all about you," he said. (What could he have said? He knew almost nothing about her. Same as she knew nothing of him.) "They're so excited you're coming."

Even without children in the house she woke early on Christmas morning. Making her coffee, she thought about her three children—off at the farm, with Cam and Coco and Elijah and the grandparents. Drinking her coffee in her strangely quiet kitchen, she looked out at the snow. She could see, through the window of her neighbors' house across the street, the blinking lights of their tree and her neighbor Mrs. Winstead in a bathrobe handing out gifts. In the house next door someone was playing the same Alvin and the Chipmunks Christmas album they always used to put on Christmas morning, loud enough that even through the windows she could hear the Chipmunks' rendition of "Up on the Housetop."

She called Akersville. Her ex-father-in-law, Roger, answered. Odd how it worked: one year a person's part of your family, the next, his voice sounds like some loan officer at a bank turning down your application. "I'll put the kids on," he said.

Al came on first. She had gotten a camera and a new winter jacket. Socks, books, another of the dresses Cam's mother seemed determined to give her that she would never wear, and a pair of pink fuzzy slippers. Cam's mother, Roberta, was always giving Al pink items, as if that might suddenly remind her she was a girl. Al turned these over to Ursula, just as now—as swiftly as possible—she handed over the phone.

Ursula was more talkative, though not as much as she used to be. Her good cheer, that Eleanor had always taken for granted, now carried an air of affectation.

She provided a list of her presents, which included a Walkman and a sweater she'd asked for and a pair of high boots. She offered up a recitation of their activities over the last few days—a cookie party with her old friends from softball days, a snow sculpture contest, caroling with Coco's parents. Cousins, even! Their father's brother had paid them a visit from Texas, with his three kids. Eleanor could hear, in her voice, the care Ursula was taking to make sure that nothing she said sounded too great, even though, to Eleanor, it did, and the truth was, this made her happy for Ursula more than sad for herself.

"There's probably a lot going on there," Eleanor said. "You should get back to the fun. Let me talk to your brother."

Talking with Toby over the phone was always difficult. Maybe it was hard for him, not seeing a person's face, to connect with the words she was saying, or offer any back.

"Coco made waffles," he told her. "With syrup from our trees."

Back to the Game Boy.

Sometime around midmorning Eleanor made the pie she'd promised to bring to the holiday dinner of Russell and his sons: apple.

She put on the Joan Baez Christmas album that her family used to play when she was growing up. After, she changed into a red dress she hadn't worn in a very long time—a little out of fashion with its padded shoulders, but her hosts were unlikely to mind.

Russell's directions got her to where he lived twenty minutes ahead of schedule. Eleanor pulled over a block away and sat with the motor running until it was three o'clock. It occurred to her that she should have brought something for his sons, but she didn't even know their names.

They lived in an old house that had been converted to apartments—theirs on the second floor. Climbing the steps, she thought, momentarily, about Timmy Pouliot. He'd be with his big French Canadian family, of course. His brother, his brother's daughter, who she remembered from softball, his three sisters and his mother, whom she'd never met, but knew from the photograph Timmy Pouliot kept next to his bed.

The bed, she knew.

Russell's sons answered the door. The older one wore thick glasses, and the kind of haircut a boy gets when his father, economizing, tries to cut it himself—a bowl cut. He was very thin, his pants held up, but just barely, by a fake leather belt. He was wearing a clip-on Christmas tie that lit up when you pushed a button, which he did.

The smaller brother was only slightly less thin. No glasses, but when he stepped forward to greet her she saw that he had some form of cerebral palsy. Mild, but recognizable.

"I'm Arthur," the older one told her. "This is my brother, Benny. His umbilical cord was tangled up around his neck when he was born. That's why he walks a little funny. He's not retarded or anything."

This was old news to Benny. He paid no attention to the health report. "We bought a turkey," he said. "Usually we go to the Ramada for Christmas but my dad said since we were having company we'd make a feast at home."

"We got two kinds of dip," Arthur added.

Someone had decorated the entrance with a "Merry Christmas" sign and a cutout of Santa in a disco outfit. Eleanor would not have noticed if the older brother, Arthur, hadn't pointed this out, but they had hung a bunch of mistletoe from the ceiling.

"Stand here, okay?" Benny said. "That means my dad gets to kiss you." His speech was a little difficult to understand, but Eleanor figured out what he was saying. Until now, she had not actually laid eyes on her host, but now she saw him, standing a little uneasily a few feet behind his sons—a pale man of average height and narrow, sloping shoulders wearing a red-and-green sweater with a reindeer on the front and a bow tie. He had a regretful air about him, as if he already knew he was a disappointment, but maybe his sons would win her over.

"Don't worry," he said. "I wasn't going to do anything like that. The boys are just excited you're here."

Benny led her in—the picture coming to mind of Ricardo Montalban's small sidekick, Tattoo, on *Fantasy Island,* escorting that week's guest stars off the plane and down the plank leading to the island.

Russell was no Ricardo Montalban, but he had clearly worked hard to set the stage for her arrival. There were carnations on the table, and though it was daylight out, candles already lit. He had a record playing, the Carpenters' *Christmas Portrait.*

Russell asked how her drive had gone. Arthur asked what kind of car she had, and concealed his disappointment when she told him Subaru.

"My brother really loves Dodge Chargers," Benny told her. "He was hoping you had one. But that's okay."

Russell had bought wine, and now he poured her a glass. Red, a little sweet. "I'm not really much of a drinker," he said. "But it's a special occasion." Eleanor handed Russell the pie. The boys gathered around to admire it, as if what she had brought were a rare and exotic treasure. This may have been their first homemade pie.

"You're pretty," Benny said. "We were talking about it before you got here, since we didn't know what you look like. Arthur said the important part is if you're nice but it's an extra bonus when someone's pretty."

He turned to Arthur. "Doesn't Eleanor look like that girl on the commercial for Diet Coke? The one with the brown hair?" He spoke her name. Not everyone you met did that.

Arthur gave Benny a look. "Don't mind my brother," he said. "He's a little crazy."

"Not really," Russell said. Maybe he was worried she'd believe this. Also, he didn't want to hurt Benny's feelings.

She had only been in their apartment five minutes, but already she understood this: Russell was looking for a wife. Even more, Russell's sons wanted a mother, and he would do what he could to find them one. If she were up for it, the two of them could be married by Valentine's Day probably.

"Do you have kids?" Benny asked.

"Three. They're with their father today."

A worried look came over Benny. Maybe she was another one of those mothers, like his own, who had left. "We haven't seen our mom since I was a baby," he said. "It turned out we weren't her cup of tea. She wanted to ride around listening to the Grateful Dead."

"There was probably more to it than that, Benny," Russell said. "Your mother loved you. She just had some problems being a mom."

"Do you have problems being a mom?" Benny asked Eleanor.

She told him she didn't. She could have said more, but this was not the moment.

They arranged themselves at the table. Benny made sure Eleanor was sitting next to his father. Arthur held her chair out for her.

"You taught your boys good manners," Eleanor said.

"Eagle Scout," he told her.

Russell carried in the turkey. From the silver plastic platter on which the meat was arranged, it appeared to have been purchased, precooked and presliced, along with disposable plastic bowls of cranberry sauce and gravy.

"I found this great place that makes everything ready to go," Russell said. But he'd made the sweet potatoes and corn bread from scratch.

"It's called Stop & Shop," Arthur pointed out.

They loved her pie. They loved everything about her. Over the course of the meal, the things Benny complimented Eleanor on included her hair, her necklace, her shoes, her baking, her appetite, and—when he showed her a patch he'd recently earned at Cub Scouts and asked if she could stitch it on his shirt for him—her sewing ability along with (related to this) good eyesight, as proven by her ease in threading the needle.

She was sitting at the table sewing on the patch when it came to her what this reminded her of: Peter Pan and the Lost Boys. She was Wendy.

A wave of terrible sadness came over her then. These were children without a mother, and she was a mother without children. It should be perfect.

More than anything—more even than a man who loved her—Eleanor wanted this back: the life of taking care of children the way she used to, living in a family, sharing meals like this. (Well, not like this one, but other meals. The good kind.) But it was not something you could find in the pages of the classifieds, this family life. She wanted it with her own children, not the two sweet, pale strangers who sat across the table from her, their eyes full of unconcealed longing. And in the seat next to her, the sweet, gentle Eagle Scout who would probably love her forever, if she gave him the opportunity, which she would not.

She had planned to leave as soon as she had stitched on the patch, but when she handed the shirt back to Benny he said they had a surprise for her.

"Let's do our act for Eleanor," he said to Arthur. They had worked up a scene from the *Three Amigos* movie.

His brother looked uneasy. "I don't think so, Benny. She probably doesn't want to see it, and anyway, it's kind of lame."

"Artie's just saying that," Benny told her. "You should see my brother's Steve Martin imitation. My dad does the Chevy Chase part. I'm Martin Short."

Now Russell was the one looking embarrassed. "I only do this because they need a third person," he told Eleanor. "I'm not very good at being funny. When I make people laugh, it's usually unintentional."

"Come on," Benny said. With that odd, slightly spastic gait of his, he was clearing a space in the middle of the living room now, his floppy puppet arms flailing. Arthur got up out of his chair to join him.

"You too, Dad," Benny said.

The three of them stood before her then, taking their positions, their best imitation of three men doing their best imitation of cowboys.

Benny started it off. "Hey, you slime-eating dogs," he said, facing the invisible desperados.

"Hey, you scum-sucking pigs." This was Russell's line. He delivered it with unexpected feeling.

"You sons of a motherless goat." Arthur now. His Steve Martin impersonation was more impressive than Eleanor would have anticipated. He even executed a dance step, more or less.

For a second there, Benny stepped out of character, addressing Eleanor. "Here's the part where one of the bad guys says, 'And who are you?' You can be him. You can do that part."

"And who are you?" Eleanor asked them.

"Wherever there is injustice, you will find us," Benny said as Martin Short, the hero mariachi. "Wherever there is suffering, we'll be there."

The next line was delivered in unison. Clearly they'd done this before. Though if Eleanor had to guess, she would say this might have been the first time they had an audience. The first time they performed it for a woman, anyway.

"You will find the three amigos!"

They took a bow. Eleanor clapped. If this had been an audition—and in some ways it was—you would have to admit they'd done a good job.

There was one more thing they needed to do before she left, Benny told her. (It was always Benny taking the lead. Russell and Arthur were probably accustomed to this, and grateful for it. Without Benny as the emcee, this would have been an excruciatingly quiet gathering.)

"Do you want to see something really special?" he asked her. Who would say no?

He took her hand. A little unsteadily, he led her into a small, dark room at the end of the narrow hallway.

This was the bedroom of a man for whom a bedroom is nothing more than a place to sleep: a mattress on the floor with a faded spread pulled up over a single pillow. A pile of laundry waiting to be sorted at one end of the room. A plastic storage crate containing a great many white tube socks. On the bureau was a framed black-and-white picture of a geeky-looking wedding couple—the bride wearing glasses, with a broad bucktoothed smile, the groom bearing a strong resemblance to Russell, a younger, more hopeful one.

There was another picture—Russell with a crew cut, wearing a Boy Scout uniform. He was probably around fifteen at the time.

"You wouldn't believe all the things our dad knows how to do," Benny told her. "Astronomy. Leatherwork. Insect studies. Kayaking. Animal husbandry. Archery. Cooking. Any kind of knot you want to make, he can do it."

For a moment then, crazily, Eleanor imagined herself in this bed with Russell—a place she would never be. She imagined his soft, pale, naked body on the mattress above her. Her hands extended behind her head as he demonstrated a particularly elaborate knot that left her powerless to resist him. Benny and Arthur asleep in the beds in the next room, happy in the knowledge they'd found themselves a mother.

Now Benny led her to a bookcase at the far end of the room, piled high with papers and folders, plastic bags full of receipts, an instrument case that suggested it housed a trombone, stacks of old comic books. More tube socks.

"We never showed this to anyone before," Benny told her, taking down a wooden box. He set it on the bed as a person might some sacred possession. (A Fabergé egg. The last remaining copy of the Gutenberg Bible. A homemade apple pie, hers.) He opened it.

At first what she saw looked like a jumble of rocks, not so different from Toby's, back at Cam's house now, though his collection could not be contained in a single box, or even ten of them.

"They're arrowheads," Benny told her. His voice was hushed, as if someone might be listening in and, if so, might steal the precious box. "My dad found them in the woods all over Ohio when he was a kid. There's two hundred and forty-six in here. My dad says some of the arrowheads in this box are probably five hundred years old."

She sat there studying the contents of the box. Nothing she might have said at this moment seemed adequate.

"It's okay to pick one up," Benny told her. "Now he brings us along to look for more. Every weekend we go on an arrowhead-finding adventure. We never brought anybody along, before, but you could come."

"That sounds like fun," Eleanor said. There was no need to tell them, here, today, that she would not be joining those expeditions.

"Someday, our dad will probably donate our collection to a museum," Benny told her. "The Smithsonian or someplace like that."

He reached into the box. The arrowhead he chose to lift from the pile appeared to be familiar to him. He probably knew every one. He placed it in Eleanor's hand.

She wrapped her fingers around it, letting herself take in the sharpness of the stone. She pressed it against her skin, hard enough that it almost hurt.

"There's nobody else like our dad," he said. "He's the best."

She studied his face. He could not have tried any harder to win her.

Later, driving home, it was the feeling of that arrowhead in her palm that she thought about, the sharpness of the point, every edge chiseled by someone who'd been dead for hundreds of years. Somewhere along the line—maybe after a battle, or a hunting expedition in the wilderness—that particular arrowhead had been buried in the dirt. A few hundred years later—what do you know?—along came Russell and his sons, with their trowels, to dig it up and bring it home and set it in the box with their other treasures.

"You know, some Indian brave killed a lot of deer with this arrowhead," Benny had told her, with reverence in his voice. "All you have to do is shoot one of these straight into the heart of your prey, and he's a goner."

75.

the advantages of forgetting

Her children never wanted to come to Brookline anymore, and Eleanor no longer pushed it. Every Saturday now, she made the trip to Akersville to see which of her children she might persuade to go out for lunch with her or—if the weather was good—on a picnic. Mostly, the one who'd be up for this was Toby. In winter, they'd make snowballs and line them up in rows. In spring he liked to go to Agway and look at the baby chicks in the incubator or, when it wasn't the season for chicks, to study the tools. In summertime, he wanted to go to some lake or other. He didn't swim, but he liked to put his feet in the water.

"Webbed foot," he said, when Eleanor untied his shoes for him. He liked the feeling of the mud on his toes.

A man in town had a collection of old Mack trucks in his yard that Eleanor and Toby liked to check out. It didn't matter if they'd been there the week before. He was always happy at Sorley's Truck Museum. They'd climb into the cabs of Toby's favorites—an old dump truck from the forties and a snowplow and a fire engine—to work the manual windshield wipers, and after, he would sign the guest book Mr. Sorley had set up in the yard, tied to a post, with a pencil alongside. The names went back almost thirty years. Not many people visited the truck museum anymore. Mostly, the names in the visitor's book were theirs.

Sometimes she took Toby fishing at a spot below the waterfall, the same place where, years before, they used to launch their little homemade boats bearing the cork people. The same place she'd first met Timmy Pouliot when he was about the age her son was now.

One day, sitting next to her by the water, Toby had set down his pole suddenly and looked at her with a kind of intensity in his gaze that she had not seen since before the accident.

"Boats," he said. "We put boats in the water."

It was like the runoff after the spring thaw—the way a pine cone, or a boatload of cork people, that had gotten wedged among the weeds suddenly came dislodged, and once it did, how the water carried it, bobbing and tumbling, over the rocks. A memory buried in the mud of Toby's damaged brain had returned to him. Memories being, for Toby, the rarest commodity.

"That's right," she told him. "We made little people out of corks with toothpicks stuck in them and put them in paper boats to be the passengers. You thought up names for them all. We ran alongside the brook watching them go. There was this one called Bob. Another was Elvis."

A look came over her son's face, as if a door had opened somewhere, that had been shut for a long time.

"One time," she told him, "your boat tipped over and all your cork people fell out. You had them belted in with rubber bands, but they fell out anyway. Your sisters and I tried so hard to comfort you, but you cried all the way home."

"Cork people," he said dreamily. "Nobody sees them anymore, but the cork people are still down there someplace." In eight years, this might have been the most he'd ever said.

It was like what happens when the clouds covering the sun part all of a sudden to let the light through. Just for a moment. That was how it felt seeing Toby as he was at that moment, when the memory returned to him. It occurred to Eleanor that everything that happened was inside him still. Just deep underwater. Water, or mud.

Toby went back to his fishing then. Whatever glimpse he had been given, for that one brief moment, of their long-ago lives, it was gone again—the memories of Bob and Crystal and Elvis, Betty and Pamela and Harriet.

Sometimes, Eleanor reflected, it might be better for a person to remember less.

76.

the last Cubs fan

At the supermarket sometime in late winter—a quick stop to pick up groceries on her way home from seeing the children—shopping in the way Eleanor did now, one small meal at a time—a familiar-looking person caught her attention. Familiar, but not.

He was standing in the canned-foods aisle: a tall figure, so gaunt it would not have been difficult to imagine his clothes falling off his body onto the linoleum. At first she couldn't see his face—just thin fingers reaching up for a can of soup. But even from the back, she recognized something about him. The slumping shoulders, maybe. Thin wisps of hair sticking out under a baseball cap—an odd choice, for this time of year.

It took a minute to place him. It was the cap that did it—a red C in a blue circle, rare for a person making his home in Red Sox country. The fingers were so much thinner now, but she had seen that hand before. Reaching for a softball.

Harry Botts had been a Cubs fan. A Chicago native, he had chosen, as his team, one with a worse hard-luck story than even the Red Sox. Eleanor remembered how, years ago, Harry had talked about his team back home and his eternal hope for a pennant.

It had only been three years since Eleanor had seen him. In the old days, he'd been a little chubby. He was skeletal now. When he turned around, hearing her call out his name, his skin seemed to be stretched over his skull like a sheet that doesn't fit the bed, and it was mottled with odd-looking black splotches.

She knew what it was. The disease everyone was so terrified about. AIDS.

Some people said you got the virus from touching a person who had it. But there was no way, seeing her ex-husband's old teammate like this, that Eleanor wasn't going to put her arms around him.

"Oh, Harry," she said. No point asking, "How've you been?"

"You recognized me," he said. "Most people don't."

"How many Cubs fans do you think there are in this town, anyway?" she said.

"One, for now," he said. "Maybe one less in the near future."

He was carrying one of those baskets you use, shopping, if you were only picking up a few items. All he had in it: Jell-O and five cans of Campbell's soup.

"I don't get out much," he said. "Just laying in supplies."

"Not a lot of protein there," she said. "Let me take you out to dinner. Buy you a steak."

He shook his head. "I have these sores in my mouth," he told her, indicating the contents of his basket. "This is about as much as I can handle."

"I'm so sorry," she told him. "Is there someone helping you?"

"My mom," he said. "Kind of ironic, actually. She was the whole reason I came here. To get away. But when she figured out what was going on she flew in from Illinois."

After he got sick, Harry had tried to keep the record store open for a few months, he told her. But even when his health was good he never had that much business. Once word of his illness got out—*my situation,* he called it—nobody came in the store anymore. He had sold off the last of his inventory a month or so back.

"Selling old vinyl records was my big dream," he told her. "That and the Cubbies taking the pennant, and playing with a bunch of guys on a softball team."

"Two out of three, anyway," Eleanor said. "I'll never forget that amazing catch you made. Nobody who was there that night ever will."

"That was something, wasn't it?" he said. "I can still remember what it felt like when that ball landed in my glove. I was just so amazed, all I could do was stand there."

"We were all so happy."

"I was a pretty terrible ballplayer," he said.

"It's funny how things work," Eleanor observed. "At the time, you think it's about whether or not you win the game. After, you figure it out. That part doesn't even matter anymore. The great thing is, you caught that ball."

77.

reply hazy, try again

Back when her attorney drew up the settlement papers in the divorce, the date they'd arrived at for the buyout of their farm had seemed far away, the idea of their oldest child going off to college, unimaginable. The official deadline for Cam to buy out Eleanor's share of the farm—Al's eighteenth birthday—was just two years away now, but it was clear that Cam would never come up with the money. Eleanor just hadn't been able to bring herself to call the lawyer. Meanwhile, though Eleanor hadn't set foot in her old house since the day of the event she still thought of as the Great Children's Book Heist, her name remained on the title, alongside her ex-husband's. The idea of forcing Cam to sell the property—knowing what that would mean to their children—filled her with dread.

It was late in February, a few days after Al turned sixteen, and Eleanor had picked Al up from school to bring her to the DMV for her driving test. In the car on the way over, she'd tried a few times to get Al talking—about school, basketball, a science project she was working on. Al had told her recently about a program she hoped to attend that summer where they taught advanced skills in computer programming, a concept as remote from Eleanor's world as professional wrestling or bungee jumping.

"It costs a thousand dollars," Al told her. "But I know I'm going to make a lot of money someday as a programmer. When I do I can pay you back. I'm going to have my own computer company."

Eleanor wrote the check. She took on a job for a commuter airline that needed drawings depicting the correct manner to attach one's oxygen mask in the event of a loss of pressure in the plane. When the airline liked that one, she did a second series of drawings, illustrating evacuation on a body of water. Her two least favorite jobs ever.

The computer school Al wanted to attend was in upstate New York. "I still don't get the idea of sending a kid off to a place where she's going to spend all day sitting at a computer terminal," Cam said, when she picked Al up to drive her there. This represented more than his usual level of communication. All business, as usual.

"It's what Al loves, Cam," Eleanor said. She had volunteered to bring Al to camp chiefly because she knew Cam never would, but she had also been looking forward to time with her daughter in the car. She'd bring Ursula and Toby along. They'd make a family trip of it.

Al had the headphones on for much of her drive. But somewhere around the New York border the batteries on her Walkman ran out. Ursula was reading a magazine. Toby, in the front seat next to her, had been holding his Magic 8 Ball, turning it around in his hands, studying the fortunes, not that he could read what they said. Ursula did that for him.

"Are we going to stop at McDonald's?" he asked the 8 Ball.

"*Cannot predict now.*"

"Will I ever get a pet monkey?"

"*Signs point to yes.*"

"I wanted to talk to you about something," Eleanor said to them. She had been thinking about this ever since the Vermont border. Now felt like the moment.

"It's looking like your father might not be able to come up with the money to buy out my half of the farm," Eleanor said—her voice even, no evidence in it of the anxiety she felt addressing this topic. "I hope he can, but it's a lot of money for him. He might not manage it."

"What are you talking about?" This was Al speaking. Instantly on her guard. All three children had learned long ago that conversations in which their mother got onto the topic of their father and money meant trouble. No doubt Al was wishing she'd brought an extra set of batteries along on the trip so she could get back to playing music on her Walkman.

"I'm going to need that money," Eleanor said. "For you guys."

"We don't care about clothes and trips," Al said. "None of that stuff matters."

"I'm talking about paying for college, and your brother's schooling," Eleanor said. She could have mentioned computer camp but knew that if she did, Al would only say she didn't really want to go anyway. She would not put it past Al to jump out of the car. As it was, her older daughter just stared out the window.

"Money, money, money. I'm sick of money," Ursula said. "I just want to be happy."

"I just want to go to McDonald's," Toby said.

Deep breath. Eyes on the road.

"So . . . it's possible . . . if your dad can't pay the money . . . that we'd need to put the farm up for sale."

There was no good place to deliver this news. She'd chosen the car because there was no way for the three of them, taking in the words from inside the station wagon, in the middle of the New York State Thruway, to walk away from her.

"You can't sell the farm," Al said. "That's not okay. It's horrible. We won't let you."

"You didn't even ask what we think." This was Ursula.

"I hate the idea of selling the farm as much as you do, honey," Eleanor said. "But I might not have a choice."

"Oh, *right,*" Al said. Her voice dripped with contempt.

"School costs a lot of money. Everything does. Right now I don't even own the home I'm living in and I want to have a place of my own someday. But the main thing is you guys. Your education. Your security."

"We don't care about school," Ursula said. "We don't care about any of that other stuff."

"You can't make us leave the farm. And Dad and Coco and Elijah and Buster." Al again.

The tree fort. The animals. The woodshop. Their moss bed, and the lady's slippers. Old Ashworthy. The pond.

It was probably just as well Eleanor had to keep her eyes on the highway. If she had been able to look at her daughters' faces, she knew what she would see.

"You make me sick," Al told her.

"Honey . . ." she said. Honey what? What could she say that would make her children feel any differently? Nothing.

"I can't believe this. I just can't believe it. You're crazy. You're mean." This was Ursula.

It was Al who delivered the final blow, the one that flattened her. She spoke from the back seat, her voice hard and low—no yelling, just a deadly whisper.

"If you make our dad leave our house we'll never forgive you," she told Eleanor. "We'll hate you for the rest of our lives."

Al put the headphones back on. Her Walkman might be dead, but she would shut her mother out anyway.

There was nothing to say after that. With the exception of once, a half hour later, when Eleanor asked Ursula to take some quarters out of her purse to pay for the toll, and another time, when Toby asked Al to read what the Magic 8 Ball told them in answer to the question "Is God real?" ("Reply hazy, try again"), they rode the rest of the way to computer camp in silence.

The appraisal on the farm came in at just over three hundred thousand dollars, meaning that to buy her out, Cam needed to pay Eleanor half that figure. There was no way he'd manage even a tenth of this—no way he could pay her anything. There had been a time when his father might have helped him out with money, but Eleanor had gathered, from the children, that their grandfather had suffered a stroke and required round-the-clock care now. All of the family money was spoken for.

Computer camp lasted a month. If Eleanor had supposed her daughter might have softened her position by the time she came home, she was mistaken.

Four weeks after dropping Al off at camp, Eleanor drove west again to pick her up—this time, without the other children. Getting in the car, with her Walkman and her duffel bag, Al said nothing until they were out on the highway. Then, surprisingly, she took off her headphones.

"Are you still going to try and make our dad sell our farm? Because if so, I'll find my own way home."

The next day, Eleanor called her attorney. "I want to sign off on my rights to the farm," she said.

Silence on the other end of the line. She paid two hundred dollars an hour for moments like these.

"Do you know what you're saying, Eleanor?" he asked her. "You're walking away from a six-figure asset. You understand that, right?"

That wasn't the half of it. She drove over to his office that afternoon to sign the paperwork.

Her old home was gone that swiftly. A visit to the lawyer's office. A signature on a piece of paper. She was out the door in ten minutes.

The farm at the end of the long dead-end road wasn't hers anymore.

After it was done, she called Timmy Pouliot.

"I know you've got a girlfriend," she told him. "But is there any chance you could take me out on your bike for an hour? Strictly friends. No need to lend me a helmet." She wanted to feel the wind in her hair.

"Let's go fast," she told him.

78.

like dating your own children

If Eleanor had expected Al or Ursula to express gratitude for her decision to sign over the farm, she would have had a disappointment in store, but she knew better. The girls didn't seem to pay much attention to what she'd done, though if she had taken the other course of action presented to her, they would have had plenty to say, and none of it good.

"You're nuts," Darla told her, when she heard about Eleanor signing over the farm.

"I couldn't bear having my daughters hate me," she said.

She had told Cam her decision on a weekend visit to Akersville to bring Toby to the truck museum.

"That's a beautiful gesture," he told her, carrying a bushel of zucchini in from the garden, Elijah running alongside him. He barely broke his stride. Of all of them, the one who seemed to recognize best what it had meant to Eleanor to give away her rights to the property was Coco.

"You don't know what this place means to us," she said, taking Eleanor's hand.

"Oh, I do, actually," Eleanor told her. "The same thing it meant to me."

Not long after she signed over the farm, at one of Al's baseball games, she had spotted her old neighbor Walt, sitting in a folding chair, a blanket over his knees.

"I hear those two ended up with your farm," he said to her. "Don't know how that happened. Just figured I'd express my regrets. I know how hard you worked, taking care of that place. All you put into it."

"Oh, well," Eleanor said. "A home is only as good as the life you live inside it, right?"

"Still," he said. "I remember how it was, you moving in all by yourself. What were you, nineteen? Twenty?"

"Too young to know better."

"Damn shame things worked out like they did," he told her. "That's probably why Edith and I stayed together all those years. If I tried to leave she might have got her hands on my truck."

"There would be a heartbreaker for you." Eleanor managed a laugh.

"Next time," he said, "stay married. It might not be what you expected, but you get used to it."

She studied his face. It occurred to her that all these years, in his quiet Yankee way, her neighbor had probably been in love with her. Not that he would ever have done anything about it, besides delivering a cord of nice dry almond wood now and then, back when she lived alone on the farm, and plowing her driveway when snow fell.

"Or just stay single," he offered. "Safer that way."

Her time with her children seemed to be contracting. Weekdays alone in Brookline, she worked, mostly, though now and then she went out to dinner or a movie with a friend. She was volunteering at a soup kitchen, where she'd made friends with a nice group of fellow volunteers.

Weekends she drove to Akersville to see the children, when they could work her into their increasingly demanding schedules. More and more often, they couldn't. Even Toby was busy now, with 4-H. He was raising goats for the annual fair and helping Cam out on the farm, building a new pen.

Even in the best-case scenario, their times together were short. They'd get a meal at Friendly's or bowl a few frames at Moonlight Lanes, but they hardly ever got to spend the kind of time together that Eleanor loved best—when there was no particular activity going on. Times they just got to be in the same place, breathing the same air.

The one she talked about this with was Darla, of course. "When they come to Brookline," she said of her children's increasingly rare visits, "they're always either just taking their stuff out of those paper bags of theirs or gathering it all up again to go away," she said. "It's impossible to get a rhythm going. The truth is, they don't want to be there. They prefer their dad."

"That's the one good thing about being married to an obvious asshole, instead of a nice guy who just got tired of being married to you," Darla said. "With an asshole for a father, my kid is always grateful to have me around. She has no alternative."

The main thing was, the condo where Eleanor lived now had never been her children's home. Not really hers, either, though she lived there.

She remembered times, long ago, when it was a snow day and they all got to hang around all day in their pajamas, making popcorn and watching all three Herbie movies in a row or sitting around the table making their valentines or their paper boats, the day Ursula invited all her friends over to make miniskirts on Eleanor's old treadle sewing machine, the time they had a skating party on the pond with a bonfire.

Now she needed to create a major event to get them together with her. When a big check arrived for a Father's Day card she'd designed that became a big seller, she took them all to a Club Med in Florida for a week. They had a good time, but she realized something on that trip: that what she did now to make a good time possible seemed to require joining up with a group somewhere—another family, or a whole lot of them, as if the unit of herself, on her own, was not enough. She needed to throw in trapeze school and snorkeling and surfing lessons and karaoke nights. She wanted to make every day wonderful, and the pressure to do this often created the opposite result.

"It's like I'm dating my own children," she told Darla. "And it's always a first date."

One spring vacation, she rented a cottage on a beach in the Bahamas for the four of them, making the flight out of Boston in a blizzard and arriving to torrential rain and an infestation of sand flies. They spent the week playing card games and going out to eat a lot. Except for one day, it rained all week, and when the sun came out, Toby and Ursula got sunburned. When they went home, everyone seemed relieved.

"I miss my brother and my goats," Toby said, in the car on the way back from the airport. "I want to go home."

Home meaning the farm. That part never changed.

79.

what it meant to be real

She read the news in the paper: Harry Botts died. No mention of his cause of death. "At home . . . following a short illness . . . survived by his mother . . . a lifelong fan of the Chicago Cubs . . . formerly a proud member of Akersville's long-standing softball team, the Yellow Jackets."

The old team, disbanded now, all showed up for the funeral: Cam and Coco were there, of course. Also Sal Perrone (long divorced now from Lucinda, who'd moved to Arizona with their children), Peggy and Bob Olin with their very young daughter (a strawberry blonde), Bonnie and Jerry Henderson, the Pouliot brothers.

Eleanor was past forty now. It had been a few months since Timmy Pouliot had taken Eleanor out on the Harley that last time. Catching sight of him in the pew a few rows ahead of her, she could hardly remember what it felt like, stepping into his dark little apartment, letting him peel off her clothes, lowering herself into the tub he'd run for her. No man had seen her body in a few years now.

Harry's mother sat in the front row—a well-dressed woman, wearing gloves and the kind of hat that identified her as definitely not from New Hampshire, her face ravaged. In the row behind her were a couple of men Harry had evidently known from a group of amateur Gilbert and Sullivan performers he was part of in Boston. One of them looked almost as thin as Harry had that day Eleanor ran into him at the supermarket. Everyone in the church knew what that meant.

Harry had asked that a friend of his from Chicago read the poem "Casey at the Bat." A Unitarian minister read out loud from *The Velveteen Rabbit*—a passage Eleanor remembered from back when she'd read that book out loud to her children. Toby in particular had loved this one—about what it meant to be real, and how it didn't matter how beat-up you looked, or if your ear fell off, if you were loved.

Harry had definitely looked pretty beat-up that time Eleanor saw him buying groceries, and he probably looked even worse by the end. She hoped he had felt loved. It made her sad that she didn't know if he had, or anything about what that part of his story had looked like.

They ended the service with the hymn "Morning Has Broken," that most of them probably knew from the Cat Stevens version. Eleanor remembered an end-of-season softball party at the farm—buffalo wings, potato skins, homemade cider and doughnuts—and how she and Harry had danced to a Cat Stevens record, *Tea for the Tillerman*. What a good dancer he'd been.

"You and Cam are so lucky," he'd told her. "You've got this beautiful farm, those beautiful kids."

He had grown up in Oak Park, he told her. His parents had a huge house, right down the street from one designed by Frank Lloyd Wright. "But they were never happy," he told Eleanor. "And I could never tell them who I really was. They don't even know me."

Maybe his mother did now, finally. A little late.

She thought about her own children. She used to say she knew every inch of their bodies. But more and more, they were a mystery to her. What had it meant that Ursula had seemed so relentlessly happy and hopeful all the time—until she wasn't anymore? Why did Al stay in her room, all the time, and why was she so angry? Who were these people she'd given birth to? What if, like Harry Botts's mother, it turned out she never really understood who they were?

She didn't stay around for the reception. She didn't feel like catching up with all those wives she used to know from their days together on the bleachers, didn't feel up for the uncomfortable looks married women give to the single—part pity, part fear. There had been a time when they had shared the most intimate details of their lives (marriage, sex, childbirth, the hunger for a life beyond the kitchen and the bleachers, the death of a child) but they were strangers now, or something worse. For the women who had stayed married—and so far, all of the other women in this room had—someone like Eleanor, whose marriage had ended, was as threatening a presence as a man with AIDS had been. Her face might as well have been covered by Kaposi's sarcoma. She was that untouchable.

To many of those at the church that morning, anyway, but not all. As Eleanor was heading out to her car, Timmy Pouliot approached her. She had thought she'd make a swift getaway without seeing him—what could either of them say in this place?—but he ran up and put his arms around her. What did it matter who saw them? On that day it didn't.

Much had changed, but not those blue eyes of his.

"I miss you," he told her.

"I miss myself," she said.

80.

The Cork People

Long ago, when she was growing up—only child of two parents so involved with each other they frequently seemed inconvenienced by her presence—she had acquired the habit of finding escape in the pictures she made.

Something happened when Eleanor began to draw. She left the world for a while and stepped into a new one. Again, that fall, she took out her pencils. Two decades had passed since Eleanor had worked on a children's book, or any story at all. Now this one consumed her. Alone at her drawing table with no children to look after, most days, she plunged so completely into the lives of her characters that she almost forgot her own.

At first she started with drawings—random images of a young mother and her children, the three of them closely modeled on her own. She drew them on one of their walks to the falls, drew a small boy looking out over a bridge as his cowboy hat got blown into the water, and another boy—an older one—standing on the banks of that same brook with a fishing pole, a little farther downstream. There was a dog who looked a lot like Sally, and a girl, like Al, who had cut her hair very short and only wore pants, and another girl who loved ruffled dresses and hair ornaments. The images of the children were never the problem. It was bringing the parents to life that got in Eleanor's way, so she left them out of it.

In the story that came to Eleanor, the parents were off somewhere, doing their jobs, probably. It was that time of year that's not quite spring yet, but you know it's coming. (Snow melting. Runoff.) So the children decided to make some boats, and some cork people.

Once she had that part, the story came easily. But it wasn't really about the children. It was about the cork people, attached by rubber bands to their various small boats, launched into the dangerous waters that looked a great deal, in Eleanor's drawings, like Hopewell Falls.

From then on, the story was about the adventures they had, the places their boats took them, from the brook to a small river, to a larger river, all the way to the ocean and beyond. The cork people made it to Africa, and to the South Sea Islands, New Zealand, and the Maldives. They faced dangers, of course—sharks, oil tankers, cruise ships, giant waves, even a spoiled child who found one of them washed up on a beach in Florida and wanted to bring him home with her as a toy. (Imagine a cork person, shut up in a fancy dollhouse!) But he'd escaped. The cork people in Eleanor's story—as the months passed, a whole collection of stories—always made it through.

At some point it occurred to her that the children who'd launched the cork people in the first place needed to be brought back into the story. It turned out there was a magic rock at the falls. (Toby would like that part.) When you rubbed it, you got very small, just the size of a cork person, though lacking a cork person's useful powers of flotation. For this reason, the children—who had climbed into one of the boats themselves to follow their cork people—were constantly in jeopardy. More than once, it was one of the cork people who rescued them.

The story was a happy fantasy. The children got to be in charge of their own lives, without the troublesome interference of parents. Every day for them was a wonderful adventure in which nobody ever told them what they couldn't do. In Eleanor's story, they encountered danger and adversity, but they always overcame it. At the end of every one of their treacherous but thrilling escapades, the children grew back to normal size again, put the cork people in their pockets, and headed back home to their farm—just in time for dinner, it turned out. Their parents, setting the food on the table, had somehow failed to notice they'd been away. (That was parents for you. Their children might be off having these whole other lives, and all the parents would want to know was "Did you do your homework? Did you brush your teeth?")

Never mind the parents. Now that the children knew about the special rock, and had made friends with their cork people, there would always be more adventures.

She worked all winter on her book, and into the spring. With the children gone, Eleanor was able to work on her story with almost no interruption. Apart from her increasingly infrequent Saturday trips back to Akersville, she spent the days at her drawing table.

As long as she kept working she felt happy. She particularly loved working on the character she based on Toby. Those hours she spent at her drawing table, it was as if she had the old Toby back.

It was all she wanted to do that winter—to lose herself in a story other than the one she was living. At some point, it seemed to her, these characters she'd created took on lives of their own, and all she was doing was telling about what she watched them doing, in her head. And she loved taking herself back to her old farm—still her favorite place in the world and the one where she'd been happiest.

She titled the book *The Cork People*. In May she mailed her manuscript to an editor who'd sent her a note long ago, asking if she had any new projects in the works.

No word for a couple of months. Then came a letter from the editor, beginning with an apology. "I hope my silence won't be mistaken for any absence of enthusiasm," she wrote. "I just didn't get to your manuscript until four days ago.

"All of us love what you've done here," she told Eleanor. "We'd like to offer you a contract."

The initial advance for *The Cork People* was considerably smaller than what she'd been paid for her Bodie books, but before the first book about the cork people had even come out Eleanor's publisher asked for another one, and this time the advance was a large one. A few months later the publication rights were sold to a lot of other countries Eleanor had never been to. They'd be sending her on a European tour in addition to all the major U.S. cities.

"I don't ever have to write one more sappy line for some anniversary card," Eleanor told Darla the day she announced to the creative director at Sweetheart Card that she would no longer be submitting designs. "I didn't have it in me to think up one more poem about how great it is to have a grandmother," she said. "Or one more way for somebody to talk about the fact that a person died without ever using the word 'death.'"

The Cork People was published the following fall, with sales so strong it went back for a second printing within weeks, earning more money than Eleanor would have made by selling her half of the farm.

"You can buy your own damn farm now if you want," Darla told her.

She wasn't interested in other farms.

After Cam and Coco took over formal ownership of the property, they had put up a sign at the end of the long dirt road leading to the house with the name of their physical therapy, massage, and retreat center, "Healing Hands." Now when Eleanor drove there to pick up the children or deliver them back to Cam, she passed the sign, along with a second one that said simply "Namaste."

The girls hardly ever came to Brookline for the weekends now, though she sometimes managed to wrench one of them away from the farm—for a Beastie Boys concert one time, and another time, when she got tickets to see Madonna. Mostly the girls wanted to be where their friends were.

Toby never wanted to be anyplace other than the farm. From the stories her children recounted of their lives there, she knew that Elijah was old enough now to climb the ladder up to the tree fort the girls had built long ago in Old Ashworthy. The two of them—Toby and Elijah—spent whole days up there, playing games and looking at books. Elijah was reading now, as Toby was not. They both loved rocks. Elijah had taken up the guitar, and sometimes the two of them made up songs together. Or Elijah made up songs, and Toby hummed along, clapping his hands, though seldom in time with the beat.

Toby—the person he was now, anyway, and he'd been this person for most of his life—preferred familiar things and places. He had not gotten used to Eleanor's house, or the small yard out back, the presence of all those cars driving by, and neighbors, the streetlights shining in his window at night. Nights he stayed over, he'd wake up early and come into her room. "Can I go home now?" he said. "Lijah needs me. I got to feed my goats."

She didn't argue.

Al, when she visited Eleanor's (there was that word again, "visit"), spent most of her time on the phone with Garrett, a boy she'd met at computer camp, and a girl named Siobhan, from her school, who also wore a buzz cut and, after junior year, only answered to the name Steve. Sometimes the two of them talked so late into the night that Eleanor would find Al passed out on her bed, the phone still in her hand, the sound of nothing but a dial tone, suggesting that off in another house, miles away, Steve or Garrett had probably fallen asleep in the middle of their conversation, too.

One time, driving Ursula home from the orthodontist, Eleanor had asked Ursula about Garrett and Al's relationship.

"Are they boyfriend and girlfriend?" she said.

"Oh, God," Ursula said. "Did you really think Al would have a boyfriend? Are you living under a rock?"

"I was just asking," Eleanor said.

"Al's gay, Mom. She's the most obviously not-straight person I ever met. If you want to know who Al's got the hots for, it's Steve."

The news should hardly have been a shock, only it was. Up until then—crazily, perhaps—Eleanor had never viewed all the things about Al that had been different from other people's children as indicative of her sexuality. Al was simply different from other kids. Now, hearing her sixteen-year-old explain this most basic information about her own child left Eleanor feeling like an idiot, and—worse—a bad mother. Here she was, a woman obsessed with meeting her children's needs even before they named them, and in this most basic and essential way, she'd failed to see her daughter for who she really was.

She was also sad, and worried for Al. You didn't have to harbor any moral judgment on a person's sexual orientation to recognize that being gay was unlikely to make life easier for her daughter. It had not yet occurred to her that maybe the hardest part, for Al, was not her sexuality. It was trying to conceal who she was. Her life might actually be a lot easier and happier if she were able to present herself to the world as the person she had probably been all along.

"The great thing about Al," Ursula said, "is she also doesn't care all that much what anybody thinks about her, or if she's doing what they want. She's not one of those people who's always worrying what everybody thinks and how they're doing."

Ursula didn't add, but she might have, that she wished she could be more like her sister in that regard.

81.

can you forgive him?

Eleanor had read about a man in Maryland, Dr. Evans Almendinger, who ran a place called the Institute for Human Potential, where they worked with brain-injured children. The idea was that if one part of a person's brain had been damaged or maybe even ceased to function altogether, some other part of his or her brain could be trained to take over some of the tasks normally handled by the injured portion. Now, with the money from the sale of *The Cork People,* she could bring her son to the institute.

Dr. Almendinger was not a physician or a neurologist. In the book he'd written, *Triumph over Brain Injury,* he spoke of children he'd worked with in other parts of the world who'd experienced injury and trauma from war or other disasters but, through their work with Dr. Almendinger, managed to live active, productive lives. One story in particular had captured Eleanor's attention. In India, some years back, when he was on some kind of medical mission, a woman had come to him carrying her nine-year-old daughter, who'd been unable to walk or speak since a near-drowning accident that took place when she was three years old. For six years, the child had mostly lain on a mat, only vaguely responsive. Then the mother brought her to Evans Almendinger.

He taught the mother a series of exercises designed to reprogram the girl's muscles. They created a series of flash cards for the girl. At first it seemed preposterous to imagine she'd respond, but slowly, miraculously, she had begun to do so. By the time Dr. Almendinger left Mumbai, the girl was walking and talking and doing math.

Eleanor knew better than to run any of this by Cam. For Cam, the yoga practice he and Toby had established the year after the accident, and the physical therapy routines he'd designed for their son, were all Toby needed. And it was true, Toby had made real progress, especially physically. Cam had no interest in hearing about anything more.

Maybe the thought was too painful, that more might be possible. The more you hoped for, the greater the disappointment when it didn't work out. Or maybe—more likely—Cam was just more able to accept life as it was. But if Eleanor wanted to bring Toby to Maryland, and Toby was okay with it, he wouldn't stand in the way.

"It's your money," Cam said. "If you want to spend it chasing after some so-called experts, and it's okay with Toby, that's your business."

Three weeks later—with Al working as an intern at a computer start-up, Ursula waitressing at a hotel in Ogunquit—Eleanor and Toby headed to Maryland. Because Toby was afraid of flying, Eleanor drove, seven hours, for their consultation with Evans Almendinger, but after it was over she called up Darla to report on the meeting. (Not Cam. Eleanor had learned, long before this, that Cam no longer wanted to discuss their children with her, or anything else.)

"You know, I told myself a long time ago I wasn't going to chase after any more miracles for Toby," she told Darla. "But this man makes so much sense."

In the printed materials sent to her from the center he ran, the head of the clinic was referred to as Dr. Almendinger, though it was unclear what kind of a degree he possessed. Eleanor didn't actually care. Conventional medicine had so little to offer her son. If some outlier got results, she wasn't about to ask for his credentials.

The institute was housed in an old private school that had closed down years before. Clients were expected to stay at a motel down the road. "You won't be spending much time there," Dr. Almendinger's assistant, Gillian, explained to Eleanor when she checked in. "You'll be in training sessions every waking hour."

They met with Dr. Almendinger first, so he could evaluate Toby. He shone a light into Toby's pupils and tapped his knee with a rubber mallet—all the usual routines. But he also wanted to talk with Toby. He showed him a ball and tossed it to him. Toby didn't catch the ball, but he actually tried, which was unusual for him.

Every day for a solid two weeks Toby and Eleanor attended trainings together. The idea was not simply to provide help for Toby during their time with the staff, but for Eleanor to learn the kinds of exercises she could do with him when they were back home. At first Toby couldn't do most of the things they showed him in their training sessions, but he didn't object, either, and after a few days he began to enjoy being around the other children in the program. Until now, his main companion had been Elijah—though more and more, even Elijah, loyal as he was, had been moving out into the world, playing with his friend Abner from kindergarten. Though Toby had attended special schools for years now, along with all the tutoring, none of the training he'd received before came close to what they found at Dr. Almendinger's clinic.

During their time in Baltimore, Eleanor made friends with a few of the other parents—a couple who had flown there from Denver with their mildly brain-injured daughter, and another whose twin sons had both suffered from oxygen deprivation at birth.

Nights after the children were asleep, the parents sometimes gathered on the balcony at the motel—close enough that they could hear their children if they woke—to share their experiences. It was the first time in all the years since the accident, Eleanor realized, that she'd had the chance to talk about what it had been like for her, after.

"His father was supposed to be watching him," she told the others. "He didn't notice when Toby wandered off."

"Can you forgive him?" one of them asked her.

"If you notice," Eleanor said, "I came here alone."

On their last day in Baltimore, they had a graduation for the eight children in attendance for the program and the parents who'd brought them. When it was Toby's turn to get up, he recited a poem, "Fog," by Carl Sandburg.

"The fog comes on little cat feet," he began. Just the idea of Toby saying that line would have seemed, to anyone who knew him, impossible two weeks earlier.

"It sits looking over harbor and city, on silent haunches—"

He paused. Looked out at the dozen or so people assembled in the room, all but one a stranger until a few weeks ago.

Eleanor held her breath. A dreamy look came over Toby's face, as if he was considering the scene. The fog. The harbor. The catlike haunches.

". . . and then moves on." Then came the most surprising part of the evening. Toby broke into the most radiant smile. Except for rare times with Elijah, or alone in the goat pen (but Eleanor was seldom present for those), she had not seen her son look so happy and proud in years. But she saw something more than joy on his face. At that moment, for an instant anyway, she saw the old Toby again.

Back at the motel, their last night, Eleanor wished she could tell someone what had happened. She knew Al didn't like talking about Toby anymore. She preferred pretending he didn't exist. Ursula would have been happy to hear the news, if she hadn't been at her job. No way to reach her.

The one she really wanted to call was Cam. She didn't, of course.

She called Darla.

82.

crazies out there

Most people Eleanor knew in Brookline were married—and even more so, in Akersville, when she made her regular trips back to attend her daughters' school events. Very possibly they were married unhappily. They might even be cheating on their partners or they just never had sex—with anyone—anymore. But they showed up in twos at school events and Al's or Ursula's games, which were the main social events on Eleanor's calendar besides conferences with the team of therapists who worked with Toby and, on her rare trips to New York, meetings with her editor.

A new way of meeting up had come along, Match.com, that allowed you to read the profiles of other single people online and email back, instead of the old system of using a 900 number. Sometimes now, if she couldn't sleep, Eleanor scrolled through the listings of men in her age group. She told herself she'd like to find a man with some nice, comfortable professional career—no more yoga and burl bowls—but when she answered the ad of some lawyer type, or the emergency room doctor with whom she had a few phone conversations, or the Tufts professor who was an expert in trade with Asia, the worlds they inhabited felt far from her own.

The men in Boston talked about good restaurants and Celtics tickets and golf, knew nothing of trout fishing in a fast-moving brook or how to whittle a slingshot. For all the bitter resentment she felt now toward Cam, she liked it that he knew the names of birds and stars and how to build a good fire and pick up a snapping turtle, and that he fixed things himself instead of hiring people to do it. She liked it that he stacked his own firewood and knew how to prune fruit trees. He owned ice skates and actually used them.

Alone in her Brookline condo, Eleanor couldn't stop herself from turning on her computer and studying the ads. Now and then she'd give her phone number to some man whose profile displayed no obvious red flags, but most of the time, if he called, the sound of his voice and—more so—what he said, was enough to discourage any thought of leaving a message of her own back. But now and then someone whose ad she'd responded to would sound promising, briefly. She still allowed herself to believe that somewhere out there was the partner she was looking for.

It was never the profiles of the serious, stable professionals that spoke to her, in the end. She was moved, every time, by the men whose life stories revealed sorrow and trouble. Even when they didn't write openly of some tragedy or loss in their lives, she had a sixth sense for recognizing a person who had lived through hard times.

Widowers, men recently fired from their jobs. A man who'd been diagnosed with MS, a recovering alcoholic. Vietnam vets (so many of those). There was a man who had lost his wife and child in a boating accident. She left him a message and they ended up meeting at a pizza place off the highway outside of town, where they spent the evening talking about his dead son, and later, parked in the front of his car—Eleanor in the passenger seat—he wept in her arms while she held him. She had kissed him when they parted, but with no thought of seeing him again. He'd just needed someone to listen, and that night she'd been the one.

One profile she responded to led to a date with a mortgage broker named Ken who eyed her up and down as she approached the table at the bar where they met and said, as his greeting, "Great legs. You should see some of the dogs I've met."

More than once, she'd meet a man for coffee who spent their whole (brief) date telling her about how his ex-wife and her divorce lawyer had screwed him over. Men who lived with their mothers, men who complained about child support, a man who was about to strike it rich, if she could just loan him a thousand dollars. (He'd invented a whole new kind of bicycle helmet—a soft one, that could be transformed into a belly bag. "Isn't the whole point of a bike helmet that it should be solid?" Eleanor asked him. "Are you always such a negative person?" he said, getting up from the table. Leaving her with the check.)

One man Eleanor met online turned out to have been recently released from prison on domestic abuse charges. She had coffee with a man (a few of these, actually) who was still married but separating any day now. One of her dates explained to her, partway through their (also brief) date, that he never went anywhere without a concealed weapon. "There's a lot of crazies out there," he told Eleanor.

There were good men, too, who could have broken her heart if she'd let them—not out of passion, but sorrow. One whose wife had died in a fire. "I'll never be okay," he said, "but I have to keep living." One whose time in Vietnam left him unable to sleep more than an hour at a stretch. The night they met he asked her to marry him.

"I think, if you were next to me in bed, I could finally get through the night," he said, clutching her tight as a gun.

There was a man with a stutter so bad it was difficult to understand what he was saying to her. "I stutter," he told her, "but I never stutter when I sing."

There was a man who turned out to be homeless. He'd logged in to the dating site from the library. When they met at a restaurant, he urged her to order the steak, but said he wasn't hungry and requested tap water. He had money enough for one meal, evidently. Unlike some of the others, he insisted on paying for hers.

And more: A man—also married—whose wife was tired of sex and gave him permission to have girlfriends. A man who was married and wanted to bring her home to his wife, so the three of them could get together. A man who believed there was a plot to murder the surviving Beatles, one by one. He was trying to get a message to Ringo Starr, to warn him.

There was an artist with whom she spent one extraordinary four-hour dinner—talking and laughing and sharing intimate stories that allowed Eleanor to believe this might actually be something good, which was followed by another three hours of wild necking in the restaurant parking lot. She never heard from him again.

There was a very handsome man—romantic, unnervingly poetic in his emails to her, a truck driver who told her in their first phone conversation that he listened to opera on long drives and, when certain arias came on the classical station, could not help himself from weeping. The voice of Kiri Te Kanawa, in particular, traveled straight to his heart. When Eleanor met him at the restaurant the first and only time, and he stood up from the table to embrace her—tears in his eyes—he revealed himself to have a hunchback so extreme he was nearly doubled over.

"I know," he said. "Not what you expected, right?"

The new online sites made it possible to check in at any hour of the day or night, type in your zip code, and find out who might be out there, awake at 3:00 A.M. like you, searching. You could study their pictures, read their profile, send them a note, hear back, all without even meeting for coffee.

Sometimes, briefly, these men sounded promising, though on those rare occasions when Eleanor actually agreed to meet up with one of them, they generally turned out to be older, fatter, shorter, or crazy. She began to wonder what it said about her that she was there meeting them in the first place.

She'd go home and renew her vow to give up on her search, knowing she had to write a note to the person she'd met that night, offering the gentlest possible explanation for why she would not be pursuing a relationship. She'd put the blame on herself. She was confused, she told them. She had issues.

"Fucking cunt," one wrote back. "You don't look as good as your picture in real life by the way. I didn't want to date you anyways."

83.

I would have taken good care of you

It was a Saturday afternoon. Eleanor was driving back from a visit with Toby. As she passed Walt and Edith's place, she noticed Edith's car was gone—she was off selling Avon, probably, or visiting the grandchildren. Walt's truck was out front, though, and Walt underneath it, replacing some part, no doubt.

Maybe it was the knowledge that she wouldn't have to experience the air of disapproval Eleanor always encountered in Edith's company that inspired her to stop that day. All those years she'd lived on the farm, a week never went by, and seldom more than a day or two, that Walt didn't pay her a visit. Now almost two years had gone by since she'd seen him last.

The familiar work boots stuck out from the front end of the truck, and the cuffs of his pants. "That old Dodge just never quits, does it?" she called out to him. It was the same thing she might have said of Walt himself.

"What do you know?" he said, as he pulled himself out from under the chassis. "I thought you were gone for good."

He stood alongside the truck, taking in the sight of her. Except for that one time, right after she'd discovered Cam and Coco together at the falls, he had never reached out to put his arms around her. An old Yankee, that was Walt. A married man didn't go around hugging other people's wives, or their ex-wives, either. If he had an affection for a person, as Eleanor knew he did for her, he might drop by with a half dozen ears of Silver Queen corn, or pop over to till up a flower bed. He kept his hands busy with tools.

"I was in the neighborhood," she said. She had been in the neighborhood plenty, of course, over these two years. Something had kept her from saying hello. Maybe she was afraid, if she did, that she might cry, and that would have been hard on Walt.

"You moving back to the old place?" he said. "It's about time."

"Not moving back," she told him. "Just stopping by to see the kids."

"You should come back," he said. "You bought that place. It's your home."

"It was. Not anymore."

If he took this in, he made no indication. "When are you coming back?" he said. More insistent this time.

"Cam lives there now," she told him. "Cam and Coco. They have a son."

"I'll help you move. We can use my truck."

She had recognized, when she first laid eyes on Walt, how much he had aged—his hair mostly gone now, except for a few thin white wisps around his ears. Now she noticed something else—a vacancy in his eyes, not unlike that of her son before they'd started work at the clinic in Baltimore. Walt's body looked surprisingly solid and strong, but she understood now that his mind was betraying him.

"Those damned newcomers that moved into your house," he said. "They're not even mowing the field like we used to. Whole place is going to seed."

"They're not exactly newcomers," Eleanor told him. "I used to be married to Cam, remember? Coco's from down the road. Evan and Betsy's daughter."

"I don't care who they are," he said. "I don't think much of those two. They got themselves a bunch of goats. Crazy animals. Tearing up your garden."

He was wearing his same overalls, and the checked wool jacket he had favored since the first time she met him. His face was thinner now, and though it appeared that he'd shaved, he'd missed a few places, and there was a piece of food—mayonnaise, maybe—on his chin. He wasn't okay.

Slowly then, like a man in a dream, he reached for her. His fingers touched her hair and stroked it, as a lover of horses might stroke a horse's mane. Eleanor stood there, unable to move.

"Pretty," he said.

"I should be going, Walt," she told him.

"That old woman isn't home," he whispered. "We can go inside. I want to take off your dress."

"Oh, Walt," she said. "That's not a good idea."

A look of sorrow and confusion passed over his face. He reached for her breasts. He was fumbling at the buttons on her blouse. "I always wanted to touch you," he said. "That bastard that was always hanging around. He wasn't good to you. I would have taken good care of you."

Both his arms were around her now, his face buried in her breasts. He had pushed her against the side of the truck, the full weight of his body pressing down, and he was breathing hard. Whatever else was lost, he still had the grip of a man who'd worked all his life hauling and splitting wood, running farm equipment, moving rocks. His hands on her skin were rough. His breath was hot on her neck.

This was not the first time in Eleanor's life that she'd felt a man's weight holding her down.

"I love you," he told her. "I want to kiss you all over."

"No, Walt," she said. "You need to let me go."

His mouth was on her neck. His large hands were locked on her shoulders. Eleanor might have been scared, but what she felt, more than fear, was a terrible sadness.

"Get off me," Eleanor said. She spoke in the voice a parent might use with a child, when she discovered him doing something that was not simply forbidden, but dangerous—a voice she had employed with Toby many times, back in the old days. "Get off me, right now."

He did then. Recoiled, like someone who's touched a live wire. Or simply like a person who has suddenly remembered he's been dreaming and come back, reluctantly, to the world where the things a person dreams no longer remain possible.

"Let me give you some tomatoes," he said. "The Early Girls came in great this year."

Two months later came the news, from Darla. "Your neighbor Walt drove his truck off the road last Tuesday," she told Eleanor. "Hit a tree. Died instantly. There's a memorial service on Saturday." Eleanor was due to fly to California that day, and sent her condolences.

84.

car wreck in Paris

The same week Eleanor learned of Walt's death, a very different kind of loss struck her, though this one had involved a person she had never met. She was at her drawing table, working on the sequel to *The Cork People,* when a voice interrupted the radio program to announce an accident in Paris. A car carrying Princess Diana and the man with whom she was spending the weekend—not her husband; he'd been out of the picture for a while now—had crashed in a tunnel. Diana was dead.

Eleanor took the news harder than made any sense. What connection did she possibly have with a British princess, the mother of a future king? But she had always loved Princess Diana—the idea of her, anyway, the mother she imagined her to be to those two little boys, close in age to her own children. Most of all, the struggles in her marriage that Diana had talked about so openly (never mind the obvious differences) somehow spoke to her own.

For the next three days, she kept the television on, following every stage of the grieving across Britain and the world. She watched the funeral, of course, and the procession that preceded it—the two motherless princes (one of whom Ursula used to say she'd marry someday) making their way down the wide avenue from Buckingham Palace behind their mother's coffin, as thousands of people lined the streets to catch a glimpse of them; the stoic, anxious expression on the face of Diana's former husband, whose lover probably awaited him in a castle somewhere, when it was over. Elton John at the piano (the only one visibly weeping). The queen, in her hat. The endless display of photographs of the dead princess. Her hair. Her clothes. Her trips to Africa. Her dance with John Travolta. Her haircuts. Her too-thin body. Her sad and lovely smile. The expression on her face when she looked at her sons.

Like Eleanor, Diana had tried so hard to be a good mother, whatever that was, though no doubt she had fallen short in many ways. This had connected them.

85.

the life of some whole other person

A film company in L.A. bought the rights to *The Cork People*. They were turning it into an animated TV series. Another check arrived, bigger than the earlier ones.

Once every six weeks, Eleanor and Toby made the trip to the clinic of Dr. Almendinger. After years in which Toby could only manage the simplest phrases, he could tell them stories now. He had made a friend at the clinic—Kara, the brain-injured girl from California. When they went bowling, he could knock down some pins, and he cared about his score.

Her son was seventeen years old now; his voice had changed, and his body was filling out. He still carried rocks in his pockets, still loved goats. When he grew up, he said, he wanted to be a strawberry farmer. That, or breed rabbits, though only for pets, not meat. He would live on his father's farm forever, that much was sure. Except for his trips to Baltimore with Eleanor, to Dr. Almendinger's clinic, there was no place else he wanted to be.

If you had told Eleanor, twelve years earlier, that she'd be spending one week out of every month in a fluorescent-lit classroom, doing puzzles with her teenage son—lining up stars, triangles, rectangles, and circles by color, matching the animal with the sound he made, reading *Hop on Pop*—she would have called that a picture of tragedy. But Toby's accident and the years that followed had taught her patience.

Very slowly—in increments almost too small to measure—Toby was doing better. He might never live on his own or hold a regular job, but he could catch a ball, and crochet a potholder for the woman he considered his grandmother, and write a postcard to his little brother. Sometimes, sitting on the couch with him, watching a cartoon together—or dropping him off at the farm after one of their Baltimore trips, watching him burst out of the car and run to Elijah, who would be waiting for him at the door—Eleanor would see on her son's face the most radiant smile, unencumbered by the ambivalence or wariness of her other two children. Nothing about him but his red hair resembled the person he had been before, but in some ways, he had become, of the three of them, the one in possession of the greatest capacity for joy, and the one who provided the greatest joy to those who loved him.

Al was off at college, spending most nights in a computer lab, building programs—a whole other language Eleanor could not understand. A couple of years had passed since she'd come back to see any of them, not even to the farm.

Ursula, at college in Vermont, was interested in nothing but her boyfriend, Jake. To someone who didn't know her well, it would have appeared that Ursula was an unusually cheerful and easygoing person, but Eleanor recognized something else in her. She was wound tight as one of those rubber band balls Toby liked to make—always busy, always taking care of everyone around her, but harboring a generally well-concealed resentment of this role. Even if she was the one who'd chosen it.

The success of Eleanor's book provided plenty of money, but changed very little. It seemed to her as if she were a cork person herself, who had gone over the waterfall. Not at the bottom of the brook just yet, but off in the weeds, just barely visible, as swift and icy water raced past. She had made it through some rough patches.

At age thirty she had imagined she knew where she'd be for the rest of her life and what she'd be doing there. Now, the future looked like some vast body of water with no shoreline in sight.

The producers of the animated series *The Cork People* invited Eleanor to a screening for the first episode—a first-class ticket, a suite at the Beverly Hills Hotel. Eleanor invited Toby and Ursula to come with her (no point asking Al, she was barely communicating), but air travel made Toby nervous and Ursula didn't want to be away from Jake.

No doubt there was more to it. There seemed almost a direct relationship between how attached Eleanor's children had been to her in the old days and how distant they had grown in recent years.

For Eleanor, the distance that existed now between herself and her daughters was a grief greater than anything she'd known, including the deaths of her parents, and in her worst moments, she had pointed this out to them, not that they needed reminders. Their father was the one, not she, who'd found someone he loved better. But the way the story of the divorce had taken shape in their minds, she remained—after all these years—the one her daughters saw as responsible for the breakup of their family.

Eleanor knew some of the reasons why, of course. She was the one who remained angry, and she could no more conceal it than a person with a port-wine stain can cover it with foundation. The red part kept bleeding through. There was almost a smell to her bitterness. She knew this without being able to contain it.

She had not succeeded in keeping the promise she and Cam had made to each other that night, in the first days of their separation, when they'd agreed they would never speak badly of each other to their children. But of all the critical and angry remarks she'd let them overhear, and had directly addressed to them, she had never told her children about their father's affair with Coco—the kiss at the waterfall, Cam's announcement that he was in love with Coco, and his declaration to Eleanor that night that he was done with their marriage. For a long time she had believed he'd tell them himself, and by the time she realized he never would, the damage was done. If she told them now, they'd see her as trying to alienate them from their father. And maybe they'd be right.

Here was the irony. The thing Eleanor had done to hold on to her children's love—signing over, to their father, the farm that meant more to her than any place on earth—was the thing, more than any other, that made it possible for her children to keep her at a distance. She could fly them to Club Med with her, fly them to Hollywood, or not—but the farm was home to them and always would be. And she was no longer welcome there. All those years she spent reading picture books and constructing cork people, picking out library books, helping with science projects and making valentines and Halloween costumes, driving to games—it all felt like the life of some whole other person than the one she was now.

86.

the red carpet

She called Darla. "Come to L.A. with me," she said. "You can be my date at the screening. We'll take one of those cheesy tours of stars' houses and go to Grauman's Chinese Theatre and Venice Beach. We'll go shopping on Melrose Avenue."

"You know how much I'd love that," Darla told her. "But I can't. I've got even bigger plans for that weekend."

In all the time they'd been friends, Darla had hardly ever had plans.

"I'm finally doing it," Darla said. What she'd been talking about since the day Eleanor met her. She was moving out.

She could only talk for a minute. Bobby was passed out on the couch, but you never knew with him when he might come to, mad as a bear with his foot in a trap. Her voice was low, but excited.

"I put a deposit down on a place outside of Arlington, close enough to mortuary school that I can take night classes. My cousin Ricky's coming down from Maine with a U-Haul as soon as Bobby leaves for work."

No explanation necessary. The only way for Darla to get out of the house the two of them had shared all those years was to do it fast, while he was gone, and be out of there before he got home. The only person she could tell, besides her cousin and Kimmie, was Eleanor.

"This is the best news," Eleanor said. "I'll be back in five days. We can go yard-saling, find stuff for your place."

"Just so long as we steer clear of Akersville," Darla told her. "If Bobby knows where I've gone he'll come after me. You know what he's like."

The L.A. trip went fine. Everyone loved the *Cork People* series. Eleanor got room service at her hotel and sat by the pool a lot. On Melrose Avenue—shopping alone—she bought Darla a housewarming present: a T-shirt that said, "*No.* How Is That for a Boundary?"

Eleanor was in a taxi coming home from the airport when she heard the news on the radio in the cab: a woman had been shot and killed at a gas station outside Arlington as she was filling her tank.

Darla Ferrell. Age forty-nine. Her estranged husband the apparent gunman. After shooting his wife, he'd turned the gun on himself. Both of them were dead at the scene.

Eleanor must have let out a cry, because the taxi driver turned around to ask if she was all right. She couldn't answer.

When Eleanor got home, she didn't unpack. She had been a young woman who lost both parents in a single night. She knew that story, though this one was worse.

She needed to find Kimmie, and when she did, she would tell her the only thing a person can offer at such a moment, that nobody had said to her all those years back.

"I'm here."

87.

I won't be coming home

Three years earlier, when Al was a senior in high school, she'd applied to MIT, CalTech, and Stanford and got accepted at all of them. She chose Stanford for its proximity to Silicon Valley but most of all for its affiliation with her longtime hero, Dr. Winograd. That September, when Eleanor brought her to the airport (one suitcase only), had been the moment when her daughter had first indicated the changes that were coming, but at the time, she hadn't understood their magnitude.

"You might not be seeing me for a while," Al told her that day. "I need to be on my own to figure everything out."

By second semester she had designed a program in a language she'd created. Before school got out, she'd been hired on at a gaming company in Menlo Park and because they were working on some huge deadline, she'd written to say she couldn't come home to New Hampshire for the holiday. Or to Brookline.

The year Al left for college was the start of her gradual disappearance from their lives. When spring semester ended, she touched down at the farm—and, for an afternoon, in Brookline—but then she was back on a plane to San Francisco for the rest of the summer. She'd been hired on by a different company this time.

For the rest of her years at college, Eleanor saw Al only once or twice a year. She doubted Cam did much better. They did not speak again about what Al had told her that day at the airport, when Eleanor put her on the plane for California that first time. But slowly, she came to understand.

All her life, Al had felt she inhabited the wrong body. After years in which Eleanor had totally missed all the abundant indications Al offered them concerning her feelings about her sexual identity,

Eleanor understood this, finally. When she thought back to Ali's struggles—as a six-year-old, presented with dresses she didn't want to wear; as a second grader cast in the role of a dancing princess at Cinderella's ball; as a high schooler, secretly in love with another girl and unable to speak of it—Eleanor felt the deepest regret and shame. How could she have failed to notice? Her child must have been in great pain. And she, the mother, had been so consumed with her own sorrows—the disappearance of the old Toby, the end of her marriage, the loss of the farm—she'd failed to notice.

When Al graduated from Stanford, she returned to the farm for the longest stretch of time since she'd left for California that first time—two weeks. After, she'd be heading to England to begin a program in—weirdly—medieval studies. Nothing to do with computer programming and engineering. Al's studies wouldn't begin for a couple of months. The idea was she wanted to settle in, get comfortable in this new place.

"Could you have chosen any graduate program farther away?" Eleanor said, when Al announced the choice of Oxford over Harvard and Yale.

"Maybe that was the point," Al said.

Eleanor drove Al to the airport. On the sidewalk in front of the airport, the two of them faced each other for a few moments. Even Al—who had remained, over the course of their brief visit, more evasive than at any other time in their relationship—appeared to recognize this as a moment in their lives that needed to be honored.

"I won't be coming home for a long time," Al said. Not for the first time. "I mean, not back to the farm or anything."

She barely ever came home anyway, Eleanor pointed out. This was nothing new.

"I mean, you won't see me for a long time. A really long time, possibly."

"What do you mean?"

"Don't take it personally," Al said. "I just have some things I need to work out. It's easier without my family around."

They were standing together at the departures drop-off at Logan airport. Cars pulling up, passengers getting out. Young mothers with babies and strollers. Grandparents with golf clubs or walkers. Teenagers carrying surfboards, carrying backpacks. Couples in love, or thinking they were.

"I need to be around people who didn't know me before." Al's face looked, suddenly, both very young and at the same time much older.

"Before what?" Eleanor asked her.

"Before I transition."

It took a moment for Eleanor to understand what Al was saying.

"This isn't some quick decision, Mom," Al told Eleanor. "I've been thinking about this a long time. I've done the research. I won't be doing it all at once, but I know what I want. What I need to do takes some time."

Later, Eleanor would remember this moment. She was not just sending her daughter off on a plane. She was saying goodbye to her daughter.

"I always knew I was meant to be a boy," Al said. "It's not like you did anything wrong. It has nothing to do with our family. It has nothing to do with you."

How Al looked at that moment was beautiful. Her voice—Eleanor still knew no other way of speaking of this—was firm, but for once, there was no anger as she spoke.

"It's okay, Mom," Al said. "This is the opposite of a tragedy. I know the next stage will be hard, but I'm clear about my decision. I'm getting on with my life, and when I do I'll be a lot happier."

Al stood very straight as she spoke. Studying her face, Eleanor felt the shift come over her. Al was not beautiful. She was handsome.

"Got to go," Al said.

"When will we see you again?" Eleanor asked.

"I don't really know," Al told her. "When you do, I'll be different."

"That's true of us all, all the time," Eleanor told her.

Her daughter turned to the door. *Daughter.* A word that would not apply much longer.

"One thing stays the same," Eleanor called out. "I'll always love you."

"Same here," Al called back.

88.

happy, or close enough

Two years into the hormone treatment that ultimately led to the final surgery and Al's gender reassignment, he sent an email to the family (his siblings, including Elijah, as well as Cam and Eleanor, also Coco) informing them that from here on out, the pronouns employed to speak of the person he was—the person he had always been, he was just claiming it fully at long last—should be "he," "him," and "his."

"You don't need to worry about me," he wrote. "I'm happy. I have a great job at a start-up in Seattle that pays a ridiculous amount of money, and I'm learning how to sail. I met a great woman, Teresa. We're in love."

But he didn't come home—not to Brookline, and not to the farm, either.

"It'll happen," he wrote. "I miss you all. This just isn't the right time."

As sad as it made Eleanor to think of Al disappearing from their lives for an unspecified period of time—a long one, from the sound of it—she recognized something in Al's voice (a deeper voice, but recognizable) that hadn't been there for as long as she could remember: a firmness, but a lightness, too. This was a long time coming, and no doubt a lonely struggle, but he had made his decision.

It was an adjustment, but Eleanor had experienced plenty of those. And it had come to her, taking in the words in Al's letter, that this was what good news looked like. What did a parent want more than for her children to be their true selves, live their fullest lives? Al was doing that, finally.

Not long after Al sent out his email to the family, Ursula sent an announcement of her marriage to Jake—her high school sweetheart, the first boy she ever kissed—shortly after her graduation from UVM. "It was either put on a big wedding, or put the money toward the down payment on a house," she told Eleanor. "We chose the down payment."

Eleanor called her right away. "I would have paid for a wedding," she told Ursula. "Consider it going to the down payment fund."

The house they found was just outside of Burlington, Vermont, where Ursula worked at a day care center and Jake coached soccer at a high school within biking range. It seemed to Eleanor that the experience of making a home together had the effect of softening the faint air of disapproval she'd felt from Ursula ever since the divorce from Cam. Maybe the wound of seeing her family broken up as it had been, back when she was seven, no longer seemed so raw to Ursula, now that she was in the process of building a family of her own.

Ursula called Eleanor more often now—a big improvement on how things had gone in the years before this. Most Sunday afternoons, she'd call—to talk about work, or her garden, or one of the home renovation projects she and Jake were undertaking on their place, an old cape not so different from the one in which she'd been raised.

At least once every six weeks, Eleanor made the drive to Burlington to see Ursula and Jake. After all those years in which Eleanor had walked on eggshells with her younger daughter, it felt as though she'd gotten her back—not the old, relentlessly sunny Ursula, but a more authentic version, probably, a young woman who stayed up late with her mother as she wept over the murder of her best friend, and talked with her about the lessons she'd learned from clients at the center where she worked who were going through gender reassignment surgery similar to Al's. Eleanor could talk with Ursula about her times with Toby at the center in Baltimore, and about her experiences in the strange, alien world of Hollywood. One topic only remained off-limits—Eleanor could feel this without Ursula's saying it. They never mentioned Cam, or Coco, or the divorce. Ursula had witnessed way too much of her mother's bitterness toward her father. They both understood it was best to steer clear of that territory.

89.

no big drama, no sleepless nights

The *Cork People* TV series was a hit. The network ordered thirteen episodes and hired Eleanor to come on as a story consultant. She still lived in Brookline, mostly, but she sublet an apartment in Silver Lake and flew out to L.A. every six weeks to advise on the show.

At a gallery opening Eleanor attended in Santa Monica a few months after she'd taken on the television work, she met an art dealer in his late sixties, Peter, who invited her for a drink, which led to dinner. The next time she came to California, he invited her to go to Ojai with him for the weekend. Then, even more incongruously for a person like Eleanor, she accompanied him on a trip to Hawaii.

None of this bore any resemblance to how she had spent the first five decades of her life, but Peter was a smart and interesting man who seemed to appreciate her company and, unlike many other men his age in Los Angeles, did not set his sights on some twenty-five-year-old. He expressed affection for her drawings. In addition to art (mid-twentieth century prints and photography his specialty) he knew a lot about wine and architecture and Irish wolfhounds. He wasn't bothered by the fact that they only saw each other once every six weeks. It suited them both.

Peter did not move Eleanor the way Cam had, or Timmy Pouliot. But he was good company, and kind, which at this point in Eleanor's life mattered more than the qualities of being handsome, sexy, exciting, or wildly romantic. His business took him regularly to London, and he invited her to come with him. With the exception of one brief trip to promote the British edition of her book a couple of years back, she'd never spent any time exploring there, but she had loved visiting the Tate and going to the theater every night.

After London, they flew to Venice. Then Paris. She thought about Darla, how much she would have loved hearing about their trip—Darla, who had never traveled farther from northern Maine and New Hampshire than Boston. Once, and once only, she had started telling Peter about her friendship with Darla—how she'd sold her motorcycle to buy a double-wide trailer, and hidden away her earnings from cleaning people's houses to save up for mortuary school. She could see, on Peter's face, as she talked about her friend, a blankness. He had no frame of reference for a person like Darla, or a place like the one Eleanor had lived all those years and still missed. It was best to keep that part of her life separate from her California world.

The good thing was, no heartbreak existed in her relationship with Peter—no big drama, no sleepless nights. He had a daughter in her forties, but she lived in Argentina and hardly ever came to California. California! Every time her plane touched down at LAX, and she looked out the window at palm trees, it amazed her that she had a life, even a part-time life, in a place like this. And what was California, anyway—*their* California, anyway—if not a place where the sun always shone, and your biggest problem was getting through the freeway traffic?

It probably said something about what Peter and Eleanor shared, and what they didn't, that he never came to Boston—let alone New Hampshire—or asked to meet her children. In an odd way, that made it easier. Too much had happened to start over now. How could she ever explain everything? Better not to try.

Peter knew that Toby had issues with his cognitive development, of course, and that Al didn't come home. He'd heard about Eleanor's visits with Ursula and Jake in Vermont. But how did you explain having given birth to a child you had considered to be your daughter, who told you that everything about the first twenty-two years of her life had felt like a performance? ("What did you think you were performing?" Eleanor had asked her, that day outside the airport. "The act of being female," Al said.) How did you explain what it was like finding your four-year-old son facedown in that pond you'd built—

standing in the hospital corridor as the doctor spoke the words "irreparable brain damage"?

How could you explain to a man who owned a house in Pacific Palisades and another in Ojai about all those years you spent starting every day making two columns on the back of an envelope: *Money coming in. Money going out*? Bills that could wait. Bills that couldn't. Taking a pen to a piece of paper and in the time it took to sign your name, giving away forty acres of land on which you once believed you would live forever.

How could you explain to a man like Peter what it meant to love a piece of land as Eleanor had loved that one? Better to let it all go, say nothing, start over fresh on a whole other coast, at the wheel of a rented forest-green BMW convertible.

Only—what was a person supposed to do with all that history? Who would she be without it? How could she ever be known?

For a little over three years, Eleanor split her time between the Boston condo and Peter's house overlooking the Pacific Ocean. When she was out west, she drove to Pacific Palisades on Friday nights to spend the weekend with Peter. Sometimes they went to an art opening or a fundraising event for one of the many cultural organizations Peter supported, on whose boards he occasionally sat. Sometimes they went out for dinner, or took a weekend trip to his house in Ojai, or to Big Sur maybe. Carmel. London.

One Friday she called him to say she thought she'd stay home that weekend, if he didn't mind. She needed time for herself. As she anticipated, he expressed no concern or dismay.

When the next weekend approached, she realized she didn't feel like going to see Peter then, either. On the third weekend, when he sent a text to tell her he'd been called away to Beijing on some kind of business, she felt only relief.

They had a few dinners after that, and one more weekend away together, at which time they agreed that the relationship had run its course. The astonishing thing, for Eleanor, was that no tears were shed, no rancor expressed on the part of either of them. It stunned her how easy it had been to end things, and how sad it was that this was so. Maybe a person only had a certain amount of wild, obsessive attachment to offer up over the course of her lifetime, and Eleanor's had been spent already. (Most of it for Cam, in their early days. And, though she hadn't realized this until it was over, for Timmy Pouliot.)

She might have viewed the ease of her breakup with Peter as good news, but it made her sad. It was a surprise to discover that among the emotions she missed, one was a particular kind of deep grief that can come only from the deepest variety of love.

When the series ended, and her responsibilities as a script consultant were over, she gave up her furnished sublet in Silver Lake and returned to Brookline, full-time, with no regrets.

90.

I met somebody

For a few years there, Eleanor used to invite Darla's daughter, Kimmie, to join her for Christmas, and for a couple of years the two of them had shared a meal of Chinese food and a double feature of Blockbuster holiday films. But Kimmie was married now, with a baby. Off in Las Vegas, of all places, making a new life, the way her mother always wanted. Remembering what it had been like for herself, when she was young, to navigate life without parents, Eleanor made sure to call Kimmie now and then—on Darla's birthday, and her own. But Kimmie had made the choice Eleanor recognized well—to immerse herself in the marriage she'd made to a man who appeared to bear no resemblance to her father, and to being a mother.

These days Eleanor spent her holidays alone, or someplace warm that had a pool. There had been that one sad holiday she'd shared with Russell, from the personals, and his two sweetly hopeful sons. The three amigos. Maybe that one Christmas cured Eleanor of any future attempts to insert herself in anybody else's holiday celebration. She must still have, somewhere in the back of her cupboard, the big roasting pan she used, back in the days she cooked the holiday turkey. But she hadn't taken it out in years. Wouldn't even know where to find it now.

In the early days after her children moved back to the farm, Eleanor went on many dates, then fewer, then none. One time, when Darla was still alive, she had made the observation, about some online dating site to which she'd paid a rare visit, that the same profiles were there, of men she remembered from ten years back. A few had changed their pictures, and their ages were different now, of course, but they looked familiar. She had actually gone out with a few of them.

"Pretty sad, huh?" Eleanor had observed to Darla. "They're still knocking around after all these years."

"And you've been on there yourself long enough to know," Darla had pointed out.

Eleanor hadn't given up her membership on Match.com, but she didn't spend long hours reading profiles there, either, and on the increasingly rare occasions when a message popped up ("Hey babe! Nice smile"), it went unanswered. If you were over fifty years old, and you admitted you were, your dating prospects were probably not great.

Even Timmy Pouliot wasn't as young as he used to be. She had run into him only once since that night at the bar, and he seemed different. For the first time in all the years she'd known him—since he was thirteen years old—he hadn't greeted her with the look she'd known since the day they first met at the waterfall. He was distracted, looking over her shoulder, as though he were keeping an eye out for someone.

"I hear they made a TV show of a book you wrote," he said. He would have watched it, only he didn't get cable.

He asked how her kids were doing. She asked about his brother and his mom.

"Still trying to marry you off?" she asked.

"I met someone, actually," he told Eleanor. When she asked for details, he'd seemed reluctant to offer them. Maybe that meant he'd met someone he actually loved. Someone other than her.

91.

a teenager in the house

Flipping through the Sunday paper one morning, Eleanor's eyes fell on an article about an exhibition opening at the natural history museum affiliated with Harvard. A major bequest had been made, of what was said to be the single most substantial collection of arrowheads assembled in North America. Oddly enough, the individuals responsible for the gift had not been wealthy collectors or archaeologists. It was a pair of brothers in their early twenties with no particular background in Native American history who had chosen to donate the arrowheads to the museum as a way of honoring their father.

"Our dad worked at an insurance agency all his life," the older of the brothers was quoted as saying in the article. "But this was his passion from when he was a little kid, and he passed it on to us. Just about every weekend, growing up, we'd drive to some crazy place, nowhere near anything, and take out our digging tools. It was like a treasure hunt.

"The way he talked about those arrowheads made us think about the people who'd made them and what their lives might have been like. He taught us to recognize the beauty in those little pieces of stone.

"My brother has cerebral palsy," the older brother said. "So you might think this would have been hard for him. But our dad never let him believe there was anything wrong with him. He hiked along on all those trails on our digs, same as I did."

There was more in the article, but Eleanor was stuck on the photograph of the two pleasant-faced and slightly geeky young men, standing beside a glass case (one of many, evidently) housing a part of the collection they'd amassed, along with a plaque commemorating their father. Russell.

"Our dad died last year," the older brother, Arthur, explained. "Our mother left when my brother and I were really little, so it was always just the three of us, but he worked so hard to make it okay for us. Going off on those digs on weekends, he made us feel like we were on this amazing adventure. He used to call us the three amigos."

One night she picked up the phone to hear the voice of a teenage boy. It took Eleanor a minute, placing him.

"It's Elijah," he told her. "'I'm calling from our farm."

She had seen Elijah often over the years, times when she picked her children up to bring them someplace. As a little boy, he had reminded her of Toby, as he'd been before the accident, though he was taller than Toby, with the lanky build of his father, where Toby's body was shorter and more compact. Elijah had not inherited Cam's red hair. In coloring, he took after his mother.

She had always liked Cam and Coco's son. Whatever bitterness a person might harbor toward her ex-husband or the woman he'd married, for whom he'd left her, none of it was Elijah's doing. He always appeared, to Eleanor, like an interesting child and a kind one, where Toby was concerned, most of all. The irony had not escaped her that, having always hoped for a child who played guitar, this one—though not her own—actually did.

When he was younger, Elijah had been able to offer Toby something none of the rest of them could. He had admired Toby and looked up to him as his big brother. When, somewhere around age four, it must have become clear to him that of the two of them, he was the stronger one, he'd become Toby's fiercest and most loyal protector—the job that had fallen to Ursula, once. If a child made fun of Toby at a 4-H fair or on a trip to the bowling alley, Elijah stepped in. If Toby was lonely, Elijah played with him. Long after the age when he'd outgrown them, he played Hungry Hungry Hippos and Operation with his brother, accompanied him on his rock hunts, and sat with him in the dirt, acting out fights between his triceratops and Toby's T. rex. When, in sixth grade, he'd started a rock band, he'd enlisted Toby to play the bongos. In his fashion. In high school, when the band started going out on gigs, Elijah never failed to bring Toby along, where he stood on the stage, shaking the rhythm eggs, or in the front row, singing along to the songs Elijah had written. He knew them all.

When Elijah called that night to speak with her, Eleanor assumed it must have something to do with her son.

"Did something happen to Toby?" she said. Her stomach tightened.

"Toby's fine," Elijah said. "I called to ask a question. It doesn't have anything to do with Toby. You know I've got this band. The Goonies. We started out just playing at school, but we've been getting gigs. For pay."

Eleanor had heard something about this. From Toby, actually, so the details had been a little hazy, but amazingly, Elijah's band had been hired earlier that winter to open for a reasonably well-known Boston band—well known to people of a certain age, though unknown to Eleanor.

The gig had gone better than any of them had expected. Afterward, the lead guitarist of the headlining band had asked Elijah if he was interested in joining them on gigs, playing rhythm guitar and providing backup vocals.

This was a serious professional band. It was a great opportunity.

The problem was rehearsals. The band met every Sunday to practice, and they already had a bunch of gigs lined up for Fridays and Saturdays at a club in Boston. Elijah could get a bus into the city, and another one home on Sundays. But gigs ran late. If he was going to do this, he'd need a place to stay.

"You'd like to stay over at my house those nights?" Eleanor said. She had plenty of space. Al's room and Ursula's and Toby's. None of them occupied.

"You'd be very welcome," she said.

"My mom thought you might not like me asking," he told her. "But I figured, the worst you could say is no."

"I'm happy to have you stay here," Eleanor said. "I always hoped someone in the family would play the guitar. Until you, nobody did."

He showed up every weekend after that. She told him, the first time he arrived with his guitar case and his backpack, not to worry about thinking he had to socialize with her. "Consider this your place to crash, no obligation," she said. "I'm sure you have better things to do than sit around the kitchen drinking tea with me."

But strangely enough, Elijah seemed to like having tea with her. Many nights after band practice, when the guy who played drums, Oliver, dropped him off, the two of them—Eleanor and Elijah—would end up at the kitchen counter sipping cups of lemon ginger tea and talking about music, or school, or a girl he liked, even. He spoke about the frustrations, for a boy his age, of living so far out in the country, when what he really wanted was to be playing rock and roll with his friends.

"The farm's such a beautiful place," Eleanor said.

"I guess," Elijah said. "There just isn't that much going on. Unless you're into yoga and goats."

One time when he came in, she was just serving herself some left-over beef stew she'd made the night before.

"I don't suppose you'd want any of this," she said, guessing he was vegetarian like his parents.

"Are you kidding?" He reached for a plate.

That summer, when school got out, he moved his stereo in, and his amp. Big sneakers sat by the front door again, the way they used to when she had teenagers in the house. (Not so many of those times. By the time her children were teenagers, they'd been occasional guests at best.)

Sometimes now, from the room where he stayed (Al's, but Al didn't come here anymore), she could hear the sounds of unfamiliar music. Hip-hop and rap, more often than not. Singers whose names she didn't know. Lyrics that made little sense, but it didn't matter. Guitar riffs he was practicing, late into the night, which never bothered Eleanor. She had longed for, and missed, the sound of a teenager in the house.

92.

another mother moves out

The year Eleanor turned fifty-three, on what had become their regular Sunday afternoon call, Ursula told Eleanor she had some news.

"You're going to be a grandmother," Ursula said.

The next day, Eleanor ordered her a copy of *Spiritual Midwifery*—still in print after all those years. "I know this will seem like the ultimate hippie book," she wrote, in the note accompanying her gift. "But back when I was pregnant with you, I found a lot of wisdom in these pages. Mostly, I'm just so excited for the two of you. There was nothing that ever brought me more joy"—this was true, though she could have added the words "or more sorrow"—"than raising the three of you."

Ursula's impending parenthood seemed to have brought her closer to her mother. In addition to their regular Sunday afternoon conversation, Ursula called Eleanor every few days with a question, generally related to pregnancy. After all those years in which her daughter had kept her at arm's length, hearing her voice on the other end of the line now asking about water birth, or the pros and cons of letting the new baby in your bed, felt like a wonderful and unexpected gift.

The summer after his sophomore year in high school back in Akersville, Elijah rode the bus to Boston—and the T, to Brookline—to see Eleanor. "I've got this crazy idea to run by you," he told her. "It's okay if you say no."

He wanted to ask if she'd consider letting him move in with her. School never really worked for him, he told her. When you got down to it, all he cared about was making music. But if he lived in the city, he could get a job to pay for lessons and audition for gigs. He'd pay her rent, he told her.

"Forget about rent," Eleanor said. "But what about school?"

He told her he'd study on his own time and get his GED.

Elijah moved into Al's old room the next week. He was taking guitar lessons twice a week from a Berklee graduate and landed a part-time job at a music store. Within a couple of months he'd picked up work performing in clubs around the city every weekend. More often than not, in the evenings, she'd hear the sound of Elijah upstairs, practicing.

She was working at her drawing table one night when he came in with a mug of tea for her. He asked if they could talk.

"My parents are having problems," he said. "My mom's moving out."

All these years, Eleanor had felt bitterness toward Cam and Coco for how happy their lives had looked to her—having the three older children around, and another of their own, their garden and Coco's massage practice, and the big, loving gatherings she heard about—bonfires and dance parties, holiday meals. In her mind, at least, she had constructed a picture of the life they led together as a close approximation of the one she'd imagined once for herself and Cam. They seemed to have everything she had wanted, back when Ed Abercrombie first brought her out to the farm.

Now, hearing Elijah's news, she registered nothing but sorrow. Nobody who'd lived through the end of a marriage could wish that on anyone else, not even the person partly responsible for the breakup of hers. Most of all, she felt sad for Elijah. And for her own children, of course, who loved Coco, and no doubt counted on their father's marriage as the one model they could look to of an enduring relationship between a man and a woman.

"I'm sorry," Eleanor said. It was not for her to ask what happened, but Elijah volunteered.

"My mom fell in love with someone else," he said. "She told my dad and me last weekend."

It might have looked to Eleanor like a form of perfect justice, Coco leaving Cam in the same way Cam had left her. Very likely whoever was replacing him was younger, as Coco had been when she moved into Cam's life.

Observing him stacking wood out by the barn the other day when she'd been out to the farm to see Toby, she had been struck by how old he looked. He was still a handsome man, but he had looked tired. Hearing this news now, she was surprised to discover she felt sad for Cam, too.

"I can't believe my mother took off with some idiot she met at a bar," Elijah said. "What was she doing in a bar, anyway?"

93.
she doesn't count to ten

That weekend, the call came from Vermont: Jake, telling Eleanor that Ursula had gone into labor. All that night he called with updates, as Ursula had evidently instructed him to do. When he called to say they had a baby girl, Ursula wanted to get on the phone with her mother.

"Come meet Louise," she said.

Fifteen minutes later Eleanor was packed and on the highway, headed to Vermont to meet her granddaughter, her heart exploding in a way she had not known was still possible.

She'd planned to stay at a hotel nearby, but Ursula surprised Eleanor by suggesting that she stay at their house. She could help with meals and laundry, and hold the baby when Ursula took a shower.

"I don't want to get in the way," Eleanor said.

"You won't," Ursula told her. "Jake and I want you here. Me in particular. It's the kind of moment when a woman wants her mom."

As someone who'd given birth three times, without her mother, Eleanor understood.

Later, Eleanor replayed those days—three of them, all told—for signs of the trouble that followed, but in her memory of that early, precious time taking care of Ursula and getting to know Louise, she couldn't remember a single moment that had felt wrong, or difficult. Ursula was breastfeeding Louise, so Eleanor wasn't needed to feed the baby, but in all the other ways, Ursula had seemed grateful for her mother's presence. Now that she had a baby of her own, she had a new and limitless interest in the stories of her own birth and those of her siblings. The two of them—Eleanor and Ursula—sat by the woodstove, discussing every moment of Ursula's labor—the minutiae that were lost on Jake—in a way that nobody but her mother could have cared about as much as Ursula did.

Up until this point, they'd been getting takeout and snacking on food Ursula and Jake's friends brought by, but on the third night, Eleanor offered to cook them dinner. She had expected Ursula to ask for a vegan dish, but her daughter said, actually, what she'd love was Eleanor's spaghetti carbonara.

They were sitting around the table—Louise in Eleanor's arms, to give Ursula a chance to eat her meal more comfortably. Jake had opened the bottle of wine Eleanor had brought them. Ursula wasn't drinking, but Eleanor and Jake had nearly polished it off.

"I can't wait for Dad to meet the baby," she said. "I'm hoping Louise can cheer him up. He's been having such a hard time, since Coco left. It's such a crummy thing what she did, cheating on him like that behind his back. I don't think I can ever forgive her."

Eleanor wrapped her arms tighter around the baby. She had some things to say about a person being unfaithful in a marriage. She knew she should keep them to herself.

Look at Louise, she told herself. What else mattered, but that she was in the home of her daughter, holding this baby? All she needed was here: those rosebud lips, the nose that even now resembled Ursula's, the feel of her chest rising up and down, the wonderful smell on the top of her head that every newborn baby she'd ever met had, but only briefly, the feel of Louise's quick little heartbeat under the flannel blanket, her fingers wrapped around Eleanor's as she slept.

"I just can't believe Coco would do something like that to Dad," Ursula said. Maybe it was having given birth so recently that allowed her to speak of her father as she was doing, when normally she'd been so careful never to bring up his name. Maybe she just thought things were so much more comfortable with Eleanor now that the subject of Cam was no longer off-limits.

"One day he thinks everything is good," she said, "and the next day, Coco's telling him she's fallen in love with some guy."

Eleanor could feel the old familiar tightness in her chest, her heartbeat accelerating. She remembered what Ursula used to say—

Ursula at age six, age eight, always the peacemaker. Trying to keep everyone happy. *Take a deep breath, Mama. Count to ten.*

"I always loved it, how Dad and Coco got together the way they did," Ursula was saying. "After all those years of being our friend, helping out with us, coming over and cheering us all up after you two split up. Then finally one day it hit them, they'd fallen in love."

Not quite. But look at the baby. All that mattered here, her granddaughter.

Jake reached across the table to Eleanor, holding the wine bottle. "We might as well finish this off, El," he said, refilling her glass.

"It always seemed like the most beautiful story. Coco coming back from Hawaii and the two of them suddenly looking at each other and realizing they were in love."

"It was a little different than that," Eleanor said. She looked at her precious daughter. She could still see, in Ursula's face, at twenty-eight, the child she'd been at seven, the day they'd sat down to tell the children they were getting a divorce. Ursula, thinking they were about to learn their parents had agreed to get baby goats.

Eleanor reached for the wine. Just one more sip. That didn't mean she was headed to Crazyland.

"Your dad's going to be okay," Jake said to Ursula. "We don't know the whole story, either. Maybe he wasn't into her anymore, either, by the time Coco hooked up with this other guy. For all we know, it was mutual."

Ursula wasn't having it. "You don't know my dad like I do," she told Jake. "It was bad enough, seeing how broken up he was after my mom left," she said. "Now here he goes, all over again."

"It wasn't like that exactly," Eleanor said. With the baby in her arms this way, she said the words quietly. "With your father and me. I didn't leave him. He left me."

The minute she spoke the words, she knew it was a mistake. Across the table, Ursula shot her a look. This was the Ursula Eleanor remembered, from all those years of being the object of her younger daughter's quiet, carefully disguised anger. That harsh, judging gaze. But worse.

"What are you talking about? You're the one who moved out."

Eleanor took a deep breath, as if she were about to go underwater for a very long time. A dive to the bottom. She had passed the point of no return.

"I moved out because your father had fallen in love with someone else," Eleanor said. "If someone in that story had their heart broken, it wasn't your father."

"You left us. You left him to take care of everything. I remember how he was then. Even after Toby's accident, Dad wasn't as sad as he was when you left. I don't know how he would have survived if Phyllis and Coco hadn't helped out."

Coco helped out. You bet she did. Eleanor was no longer sure if she thought the words or said them.

"Your father . . ." Eleanor said.

Don't go there.

She did.

Later, what she would remember was Ursula across the table, taking in her words. Three days earlier, she'd given birth, but there may have been no expression on her face, in labor, to equal the pain Eleanor saw in the way Ursula looked at her now.

It was too late. Eleanor was in Crazyland.

"All this time, you actually thought that your father lived like some kind of sad monk after your heartless mother abandoned him? And Coco, the loyal family friend, was just coming by to make popcorn balls and play Monopoly? And then finally, when she turned twenty-one, the two of them suddenly looked at each other and slapped their hands on their foreheads and said, 'What do you know? We're in love.' You really think that's how it happened?"

Jake had gotten up from his chair now, heading in Eleanor's direction. He lifted their daughter from Eleanor's arms. Returned to his place beside his wife.

"Your father was fucking the babysitter, Ursula," Eleanor said.

Whatever it was that happened after she said that, Eleanor no longer remembered. Only that Ursula was rising from her chair, no trace of love in her eyes. Jake was standing there holding Louise.

"I can't take one more minute of your bitterness about my dad," Ursula said. "You want me to stop loving him, but I never will."

It felt to Eleanor as though the ground was giving way. It felt as though her heart might stop beating, or—the opposite—explode. The room seemed to be spinning. All she could see was the face of her daughter. No sign of love there.

"Don't come back. Don't ever come back. *Don't plan on seeing your granddaughter ever again.*"

94.
even better than you thought it would be

Eleanor had learned this a long time ago: Even with the things she would have said were unsurvivable, she survived them. Not without great sorrow and cost. But she kept on with her life.

For a few weeks after her return from Vermont, Eleanor spoke to nobody. She couldn't eat. Most nights she was in bed by eight thirty. All she wanted to do was close her eyes and shut out the world.

A woman she knew from Pilates, who'd heard about Ursula's pregnancy and the trip to Vermont to meet the baby, stopped her on the street a few days after, to ask for the details.

"There's nothing better than being a grandparent, right?" the woman said. "As much as people tell you how great it's going to be, until it happens to you, it's hard to imagine."

Eleanor just nodded.

At first Eleanor held out hope that things might get better with Ursula. She called, but Ursula didn't pick up. She wrote her daughter a letter, of course, and then another. She woke in the middle of the night, imagining what she'd say to Ursula if she got a chance to speak to her, but she never did.

A year after Louise's birth, she sent a stuffed elephant for Louise, a necklace for Ursula. Like all the other gifts, they went unacknowledged. Six months later, when the second Christmas passed with no word once again, Eleanor told herself she had to let go of hoping things would change. The loss of her daughter and her granddaughter was eating her alive, or would if she let it.

She looked for good things where she could. Her times with Toby. Her work. And, oddly, Elijah. The child she had not given birth to, whose gigs she attended now and then (where she was invariably the oldest person in the room), but only if they started earlier than ten o'clock. How had it happened that the child who brought her greatest joy, at this point in her life, was Elijah, the son of her ex-husband and the woman for whom he'd left her, who lived in her daughter's old bedroom and sometimes, late at night, sat in the kitchen and talked about life.

She understood now that stupid expression "Life goes on." It did, actually. As time passed, it became harder to remember, sometimes, why she had seen as so important all those things that no longer mattered at all. Old arguments, ancient injuries, faded away. She knew, of course, the reason why she and Cam had parted, but now she wondered: Did any of that make any sense? What if they'd worked it out? Carried on, with the same losses and regrets, but hauled them along with them, side by side, instead of breaking everything apart. Was anybody really better off? Maybe they'd just substituted one brand of disappointment for another. Imagine if, that night she'd confronted Cam about the affair with Coco, he had told her he was sorry. What if he'd said, "Let's keep our family together"? What if she herself had set her bitterness aside?

"Intact family." The words the teacher at Alison's school had used, referring to what other families were, that hers was not. What was the opposite? *Broken home.*

Now it was all behind them, of course. They'd moved on. Another stupid expression, Eleanor thought. As if they were navigating a game board, landing on Marvin Gardens with a hotel on it. Passing Go. Or—in a different game—sent back to the Molasses Swamp to begin all over again. They had made other lives, with all these other unlikely aspects neither of them would have imagined once: Yoga. Greeting cards. Physical therapy. Hollywood. Elijah.

Eleanor and Cam barely knew each other anymore. It was all about the next generation now—the survivors of the divorce. Their children, and their children, and someday, the ones after that.

Sometimes Eleanor would run into one of her old friends from softball days when she was back in Akersville for a visit with Toby.

When she did, the conversation nearly always seemed to turn to grandchildren.

Pictures came out. Stories of family vacations together. Babysitting the grandkids while their parents—those children who'd played in the dirt together long ago, nights at the ball field—went out for a date night. Mostly what the women said—the wives from long-ago days on the bleachers—was how wonderful it was being a grandparent. The best time of life, maybe, because you got all the joy of the children without all the struggle. Now and then, they'd complain about how tiring it was, times they were on duty with the grandkids for a whole weekend, times the kids dropped them off unannounced. But even when they seemed to complain, it was apparent to Eleanor how much they loved even the hard parts. The best thing ever, they kept telling her.

A little over a year after Louise's birth, she ran into Jeannie Owen, the one of their group who had not been out of maternity clothes in all the seasons they'd shared the bleachers at their husbands' games. Jeannie had taken out her phone to show pictures of her recent visit to Hampton Beach with her daughter Paulette's youngest.

"Your kids give you any grandkids yet?" Jeannie asked. The idea being, apparently—to Jeannie, at least—that grandchildren were a gift children bestowed on their parents. A gift bestowed, or withheld, depending.

"Ursula has a little girl, Louise," Eleanor said. "They live in Vermont."

"Best thing ever, right?" Jeannie said. Here it came again: "As great as everyone tells you it is, until it happens to you, you can't even imagine."

"Just great," Eleanor said, as Jeannie scrolled through the pictures on her phone, displaying images of the various babies, toddlers, and preschoolers her children had provided for her. "The grands," she called them. She was so busy showing them off, she never got around to asking Eleanor for pictures of Louise. Just as well. Other than the ones she'd taken that first day Louise came home from the hospital, she didn't have any.

Her own life as a grandparent was small and simple. Every few weeks, from when Louise was less than a year old, Eleanor sent a her a postcard—an art reproduction from a museum she'd visited, or a picture of a baby animal, with some small observation of the kind a child might enjoy, assuming her parents showed it to her. (Louise was three years old now. How did that happen?) Now and then she sent Louise a drawing she'd made for her—a picture she made of Louise—as she imagined her—doing some interesting activity, though this was difficult. She didn't even know Louise. Was she the kind of little girl who liked pictures of ballerinas, or kittens, or monkeys? Elijah had shown her a few photographs, but Eleanor didn't actually know what Louise looked like.

One of the things Eleanor had learned about being a parent whose child has shut you out of her life was that people formed judgments about you—much as they'd done when she'd moved away from the farm, and all the softball wives assumed she'd abandoned her family. Even if you had seemed, up until then, like a normal and reasonable person, this fact about yourself—that your own child had felt the need to ban you from seeing your grandchild—was sufficient to call your whole existence into question.

For this and other reasons, she had learned not to speak of Ursula's choice to cut her out of her life. That didn't keep her from grieving it daily. Or holding out hope—the thing Ursula, in particular, had been so good at—that someday things might be different.

95.

the White House in his sights

For a few years now, Eleanor had been aware of Matt Hallinan's career in Washington. During his first term in Congress he'd made a name for himself with a speech on the floor of the House of Representatives about traditional family values and the importance of prayer in the schools. The story he'd told that day—something about his grandmother baking bread, and a puppy, and going hunting with his dad—had made such a stir that he'd been invited to speak at the Republican National Convention back when he was still in his thirties.

Eleanor had gathered from Patty's annual Christmas letter that after his many terms in Congress as an increasingly vocal voice of "family values," Matt had recently been elected to the Senate. Patty acknowledged, in the letter, that her brother's politics seemed a little far to the right for her taste. But it was all just politics, she said. "You know my brother," she wrote at the bottom of the letter, in the part of her message meant for Eleanor alone. "All he really believes in is money and beer."

Eleanor was washing the dishes when Matt Hallinan's voice came on the radio as that week's guest on a show called *Talk of the Nation*. "There's been a lot of talk about Senator Hallinan lately," the host of the program announced. "Some movers and shakers in Washington are mentioning him as a contender for the number-two spot on the ticket, next time out."

Matt would be in his late fifties now, but Eleanor knew from the Hallinan family Christmas card that she still received every year that he was still reasonably fit, with a smiling wife and a couple of attractive clean-cut blond children. If he were chosen to run on the Republican ticket for vice president, of course, he'd be in a great position for the top spot, down the line. "So what do you think about that idea, Senator?" the host asked him. "Is the White House in your sights?"

If Darla were still alive, this would have been the kind of moment that would have inspired Eleanor to pick up the phone and call her, knowing there was at least one person on the planet who would understand the feelings that suggestion brought forth in her, the image of President Hallinan. As it was, she just picked up a Brillo pad—scrubbing harder than necessary.

"I'd be honored and humbled," he said. "I'll serve the American people in any way I'm called to serve. If that includes the White House, so be it."

The host of the program was asking him something about his political philosophy now.

"Some people may call me a dinosaur," he said. "But for me, it all goes back to the traditional values I was raised on. Love of country. Love of family. Love of God.

"Americans are losing sight of the strong moral values of our forefathers," he went on. "Drugs. Divorce. Gays in the military. Children left in day care while their moms collect welfare and unemployment. Liberals are turning us into a nation of crybabies. We've got men who wake up one morning and decide they're going to be a woman, women deciding to be men. You never know who you're going to run into anymore, when you walk into a public restroom."

"Of all the issues facing America today," the host asked Matt Hallinan, "what, for you, is the most serious?"

"We've got thousands of babies being murdered in our country every day," he said. "Sometimes I can't sleep at night, just thinking about them."

Hearing his voice—surprisingly familiar, after all these years—had a more disturbing effect on Eleanor than she would have anticipated. She was back in the summer of 1969. The front seat of his car.

Matt Hallinan's breath on her face, his fingers pinching her nipples. Her skirt around her waist, her underpants around her ankles.

And later, the trip to Poughkeepsie. The back room. The five hundred dollars. The silent drive back to her dormitory as blood soaked the sanitary napkin between her legs.

It was a call-in show. More than once, they'd announced the phone number. "If you've got a question or a comment for our guest," the host was saying, "now's your chance. Come on, listeners, let Senator Hallinan hear from you."

Eleanor stood frozen at the sink, staring at the radio. She pictured Matt Hallinan as he had been all those years back, a bored frat boy going to summer school and figuring out how to cheat his way into law school.

"Crybabies." Maybe that was the term Matt Hallinan chose for every human being who ever acknowledged pain or struggle about something other than his team not making it to the Super Bowl.

She thought about Toby, bent over the Richard Scarry book, working so hard to relearn the words for every single thing he used to know. Harry Botts, sharing a beer with Jerry Henderson after a game—Jerry laughing, as he took a swig. "You don't have AIDS or anything, do you?" Darla and all those years of cleaning houses, hiding her cash in a secret bank account to make her getaway, and finally managing to pull it off. Packing that U-Haul with everything she was able to salvage from her old life for the new one she'd believed she was just beginning. Only taking as much as she could get out of the trailer while Bobby was at work. Standing at the gas pump as she had that night and turning around to see him standing there—the man she'd been trying to get away from for over twenty years, Bobby. With a gun he'd picked up at a Walmart.

Most of all, Eleanor thought about what Al must have endured—Al, presented with his grandmother's annual gift of a ruffled dress, Al, making the decision to transition from the sex he was born with to the gender he was meant to be. For a moment there, she took in the full weight of Al's courage. She felt something like physical pain, imagining how it would be for her son, hearing Matt Hallinan's words now.

Another picture then: Matt Hallinan, pushing her underpants down around her ankles, whispering into her ear. *One small step for man.*

"We're waiting for your call," the host said again. Eleanor picked up her phone.

She drew in her breath. This time it wasn't the old pattern—that familiar feeling she always got, entering Crazyland, of stepping off the edge of the world. Eleanor was surprisingly calm as she dialed the number. No doubt hundreds of people were calling in. She'd never get through.

A minute later, there was a voice on the other end. "You've reached *Talk of the Nation,*" the woman said. "Where are you calling from?"

"Brookline, Massachusetts." She gave her first name, all they asked for.

"And do you have a question for our guest?" Before she had time to consider this, she was on the air.

"You should remember me, Senator Hallinan," she said. "The summer I was sixteen, I stayed with your family and you used to give me rides to work. I thought you were like a big brother."

Off in the studio someplace in Washington, she could feel his discomfort. Matt Hallinan must have been thinking fast, figuring out how to finesse the situation, but Eleanor wasn't done talking.

"At that time," she said, "you were trying to figure out a way to get out of going to Vietnam. As I recall, you were going to hire someone to take an exam for you, to get into law school. But that wasn't the main thing I remember about those rides, Matt. It's what happened in the car . . ."

He was trying to cut in now. "I don't know who this person is," he said. "I guess you get a lot of crazies on this show."

"I was your sister Patty's roommate at school. I think you know that. My parents had just died in a car accident."

From her kitchen in Brookline, Eleanor spoke into her cell phone. Her voice was steady.

"This caller doesn't seem to have a question," Matt Hallinan was saying. "Let's move on to someone who does."

"Matthew Hallinan raped me that summer," Eleanor said. "When it turned out I was pregnant, he took me to have an illegal abortion."

The host of the show had stepped in now. "These are serious charges you're making here . . ."—she must have consulted her notes—". . . Eleanor. Do you have anything to say in response, Senator Hallinan?"

"This caller is obviously a nutcase," Matt Hallinan said.

The line went dead, but Eleanor had said what she had wanted.

Long ago, she and Darla had made a pledge. Darla would leave Bobby. Eleanor would settle her score with the man who'd raped her in the front seat of his parents' car. She had just done that.

Within ten minutes of Eleanor's call to *Talk of the Nation,* her phone rang. It was a producer on the program, calling to say a reporter from CNN had heard Eleanor's call and wanted to speak with her. They weren't giving her number out without her authorization.

The reporter called five minutes later. "I need to know, before anything else, if you are prepared to go on the record with your allegation concerning Matthew Hallinan," she asked Eleanor.

No doubt most people would have told her to consult an attorney first. (She was the daughter of one. All these years after his death, she knew what he would have told her.)

Eleanor recounted her story for the reporter. The summer in Rhode Island. The rape. The abortion.

"And you were how old at the time?" the reporter asked.

Sixteen.

Within a week of the CNN story, four other women had made statements concerning experiences of sexual assault at the hands of Senator Matthew Hallinan. Eleanor was asked to appear on the *Today* program. Though he declined an invitation to address the allegations himself, a spokesperson from his office appeared to say that the charges were baseless.

The next week, the *New York Times* ran a picture of Matt Hallinan at a fraternity party, in his law school days, hoisting a flag made from women's underpants and carrying a sign that said, "No Means Yes." Shortly after, Senator Hallinan announced that out of a desire to spend more time back home with his family in Rhode Island, he would not be running for a second term in the Senate.

A letter arrived from Patty. "Good job ruining my brother's life," she'd written.

Eleanor didn't write back.

96.

crash

Cam called—an event so rare Eleanor didn't recognize the number when it showed up on her phone.

"Elijah's with you, right?" he asked.

"He's at a gig," she told him. "A new band wanted to try him out. He's so excited."

She was so startled to hear Cam's voice that it took her a moment to realize the rest. She could make out the word "accident." The word "truck." Ambulance. Emergency room.

"It's Coco," Cam said. Except for the day of Toby's accident, she had never heard him sounding this shaken. "She was on the back of some guy's bike and a truck hit them."

Her first thought was of Elijah. Eleanor was not his mother, but the news of injury to the woman who was struck her like a physical blow. She pictured this boy she'd come to love, hearing the news. His mother, injured on a highway, airlifted to Boston, awaiting surgery.

"They called me from the hospital," Cam said. He was actually crying. "Even though we aren't married anymore, my name was still the one on the card in her wallet."

Coco was alive. Concussion and a fractured jaw. Massive internal injuries. Also a broken pelvis. One of her legs was pretty mangled. The doctors weren't sure they could save it.

For a moment all Eleanor could hear on the other end of the line was the sound of the man she used to be married to, crying about the woman he used to be married to. All Eleanor could do was listen.

"I was so mad at her for what she did," he said. "But I didn't want her to die. If things had just stayed how they were, none of this would have happened." That was always the truth, wasn't it? If things had just stayed how they were.

The truck driver was drunk, he told her. The motorcycle they were riding ended up on the whole other side of the highway.

Somewhere in there Eleanor thought to ask, "What about the guy driving the motorcycle?" Coco's boyfriend, the man for whom she'd left Cam.

DOA.

It wasn't until the next day that she read, online, the newspaper story about the accident, with a photograph of the mangled motorcycle Coco had been riding on and the name of the man who'd been driving it. *Timothy Pouliot.*

Sitting at her desk, her hands shaking, she googled his obituary.

All this time, Timmy Pouliot had remained, in Eleanor's mind, a perpetual boy, but he'd been forty-eight years old. Survivors included his mother, Ruth, a brother, Ray, three sisters, Carol Anne, Jill, and Anita. Twelve nieces and nephews.

Eleanor studied the photograph in the newspaper. Black and white, it failed to convey Timmy's most striking feature. The extraordinary blue of his eyes.

She thought about a night a few years back, not the last time she'd seen Timmy Pouliot—when, she now guessed, he must already have been seeing Coco, and panicked at the sight of Eleanor—but the time before that. It was in a sports bar near Fenway Park. She'd run into him on one of those awful dates she kept going on for a while with men she met online. Timmy must have come into town to see a Red Sox game.

She was heading to the ladies' room, counting the minutes for the evening to be over, so she could say goodbye forever to Phil, the orthodontist, who looked ten years older and forty pounds heavier than his picture on Match.com. She had just spent an interminable ninety minutes listening to him talk about dental implants. All she wanted was to get back home.

Leaned against the bar watching the postgame wrap-up, he had spotted her. He'd been alone. Funny how, that night, he had no longer been Timmy Pouliot to Eleanor. Just Timmy.

It was getting close to off-season, that time of year when Timmy found himself between girlfriends. His face lit up when he saw Eleanor.

"I didn't think you hung out in places like this," he said to her.

"I'm on a date," she told him. "But not for long."

"I would have brought you here," he told her. "If you'd let me. I would have brought you someplace nicer."

He set his bottle down on the bar. Behind him on the screen they were playing game highlights. The Red Sox slaughtering the San Diego Padres. He'd always looked so young, but that night he didn't.

"I would have taken you anywhere," he told her.

She had studied his face then as if for the first time. All those Friday nights she'd spent in his apartment, times he ran a bath for her and sat on the edge of the tub or the toilet seat, listening to her stories about what was going on with her marriage, what was going on with her children, what was going on with the farm—sometimes just letting her cry, and after, when he held her, and they made love. Looking back now over those times, she realized they had been the best times she'd ever known with a man.

It had never occurred to Eleanor that Timmy Pouliot could be anything other than a sweet boy who used to play softball with the man she used to be married to, who had swept her away on his motorcycle when she needed to disappear.

"You were always my dream girl, you know," he said to Eleanor that night at the bar.

"You need to find somebody your own age and have a couple of kids with her," she told him. "And anyway, I'm not your type."

"What type would that be, exactly?" he'd asked her. "Did you think there was some set of rules out there to tell you how love works?"

She did, actually. All these years, she had supposed there was a rule book out there on how things were supposed to go in relationships. She just never got a copy. She had been so busy assuming she got everything wrong that she totally missed it when the possibility was revealed to her that maybe there had been something very good going on, or something good enough, anyway, right in front of her. Or two flights up. On a waterbed.

97.
invitation to a wedding

Elijah called the next morning. Evan and Betsy were there at the hospital with him, and Toby, who had insisted on being there with his brother. At first it had appeared they'd need to amputate Coco's leg, but in the end they managed to save it. A team of surgeons put two metal rods in her. Then came another surgery for her broken pelvis and broken jaw.

When Elijah called Eleanor again a few days later, the news was better. His mother was going to be all right, more or less. No more cartwheels. She'd walk with a limp, but she'd walk.

"I guess I won't be coming to Brookline for a while," Elijah told Eleanor. "My mom's going to need me."

He stayed with Coco at her parents' house after she got out of the hospital. Six months later, she moved somewhere in upstate New York with a girlfriend of hers who ran a spa and gave her a job. She couldn't stay on her feet long enough to give massage, but she could sit at the front desk. The band that had just hired Elijah got a recording contract, and he moved to L.A.

Cam remained on the farm with Toby, of course, working with his physical therapy clients. Eleanor hardly ever went to L.A. anymore, though she flew out once, when Elijah's band opened at the Hollywood Bowl.

Ursula and Jake were having another baby. Eleanor heard this from Toby and Elijah, who visited them in Vermont sometimes, but Eleanor herself heard nothing from her daughter. The more hopeful news was that after more than five years in which there had been no communication other than a card on her birthday and one on Mother's Day, Al had started calling Eleanor up, checking in with her, talking about the software company he'd started and his life with Teresa, asking about hers. The first time he'd called, out of the blue, they had spoken only briefly—the conversation uneasy. Then he was calling more. She knew the name of his dog, and that he and Teresa had taken a trip to Oaxaca, and that his start-up was doing so well, he and Teresa were buying a building outside Seattle. One time he asked Eleanor if she'd send him the recipe for her spaghetti carbonara. "We've tried making it, Mom," he told her. "But it never turns out as good as yours."

You could say this was a whole new person she was getting to know. Or you could say he was the person he'd been all along—just happy, finally. What mattered was, he'd found someone he loved, someone who loved him, and they were getting married. Families didn't always look the way you pictured them. And even if they did, that was just about never the real story.

"Don't you think it's about time we saw each other?" Eleanor asked him one Sunday. "Soon, I promise," he told her. Three days later, the invitation to his wedding arrived.

98.

together again, whatever that means

The ceremony was set for 2:00 P.M. on a Saturday in late June. The card announcing the event included directions to the farm. As if Eleanor needed them.

That morning she checked the weather on her phone. There were predictions of thundershowers and lightning, and out the window, the sky confirmed the possibility. Eleanor's old self—the one who had actually tried to control her children's universe and spare them all pain—would have felt anxious at the thought of rain falling on Al's wedding day, but she wasn't that person anymore. Or at least, whatever aspects of that old habit endured, she recognized their pointlessness. A parent could no more protect her children from sorrow and loss than she could keep the sun from setting, or rising again the next day.

She took her time getting dressed. Best not to overdo it, particularly if rain fell. Likewise, though she had noticed, a few days earlier, that her hair was overdue for coloring, she left it as it was. There would be people at this gathering ready to view her as a wealthy outsider, gone Hollywood. There would be other women in attendance with graying hair and unfashionable dresses. She'd rather fit in the best she could than stand out, and though, when she reflected on seeing Cam again, she felt an impulse to look good, she knew they were beyond all that. This was Al and Teresa's day.

Years had passed since Eleanor had seen Al, but she wasn't worried about seeing him now. Their conversations over the last year or two had become more frequent and more relaxed. Al, as he was now, seemed a lot more comfortable in his relationship with her—probably because he was more comfortable with himself—than he had been when she'd seen him as Alison.

He was not the only one who'd changed. More and more over the years, without anyone suggesting this, Eleanor had found herself avoiding the words "she" or "her" when speaking of Al. This was awkward sometimes. But in her mind, Eleanor understood now, as well as a person could for whom the concept of transitioning to a whole other gender had been, until recently, utterly foreign. She was the mother of two sons and a daughter. Her oldest child was a man.

The more difficult part about the day ahead, for Eleanor, lay in the prospect of seeing Ursula again. And Louise. Except for pictures Elijah showed her now and then and a family Christmas card with nothing but the words "Happy Holidays from Our Family to Yours," Eleanor had not seen her daughter or granddaughter since Louise was three days old. Unlike Al, who had been calling every week, Eleanor had not heard Ursula's voice in three years. She had no idea what words might come out of her daughter when she saw her today.

So here she was again, on all these familiar roads she'd traveled before, once as a girl in the front seat of a Realtor's car, once in the front seat of a U-Haul truck with Walt, moving her possessions to a new home in Massachusetts. Later again, as a divorced woman on her own, heading back to drop her children off on a Friday night.

She turned on the radio. Every station on the dial seemed to be playing nothing but Michael Jackson songs. Then she heard the news. He had died—Toby's favorite singer, before he didn't have a favorite singer anymore. Though it was Michael Jackson who dominated the news, the broadcast also reported the death of Farrah Fawcett—the woman whose face had smiled down at Eleanor every time she took a bath in Timmy Pouliot's tub. She was so young in that picture. But not as young as Michael Jackson, on the radio now, singing "ABC."

Downtown Akersville was barely recognizable from the place she'd driven into over thirty-six years ago. (The Watergate hearings on the radio. Phyllis Schlafly, sounding the alarm bell that the Equal Rights Amendment would destroy the lives of American housewives. And "Tie a Yellow Ribbon Round the Ole Oak Tree." "Bad, Bad Leroy Brown." "Killing Me Softly.")

There had been no stoplight in town back then, and no need for one, but there was a nail salon and two different pizza parlors on Main Street now and—this struck her as funny—a dry-cleaning establishment, the business her ex–father-in-law had offered to set his son up in, that might have offered more in the way of an income than selling hand-turned wooden bowls. (How many parents, like Cam's, failed to recognize who their children were? She had been guilty of this herself for way too long, with her oldest child, her daughter who always wanted to be her son.)

She passed the lake where they'd gone skating, back in the days before they built the pond, the field where she used to bring Toby, which used to be full of the old Mack trucks he loved to climb, the town dump, where she and her children scavenged for treasures, the bowling alley in whose parking lot they used to recite the No-Cry Pledge.

As she got closer to the farm, Eleanor's car was joined on the road by others—more than the usual number of vehicles for these parts, on account of the wedding, probably. There would be locals in attendance, Eleanor figured—old neighbors she'd recognize from years before when everyone was young (but not the one she would have wanted most to see, Walt). Also a couple from Seattle, friends of Al and Teresa, who had brought their infant twins, and some high-level programmers from the start-up where Al had previously worked in Silicon Valley. Teresa's family was there in force, of course. A large group of them had rented an RV to make the trip east from Texas, a sticker on the back: *Dios te bendiga*.

The last half mile of road was lined with signs letting guests know they were getting close. "Don't give up, you're almost there." "Look out for snapping turtles." The old "Deaf Child" sign still stood at the corner, having been there since the first time Eleanor ever visited the farm, though whoever that deaf child had been was probably in her forties now.

Then came the turnoff for the road Eleanor knew so well. The "Cam and Coco" sign had been taken down, though the one remained that said simply, "Namaste."

Someone had strung *papel picado* across the entrance to the property. From farther down the road, Eleanor could make out the sound of Latin music—an unlikely mix, but that's what happened when a marriage took place: it didn't just connect two individuals, it brought families together.

One of the things Eleanor had always loved about the dirt road leading up to the house was the strip down the middle where grass grew. Driving very slowly now, Eleanor reached the place on the road where the house came into view, and the particular spot where she used to say, out loud, "I'm home." Silent now, she drove the last stretch to the field where they'd set up signs, "Park Here." Elijah, in a suit he probably got at a thrift shop—too big, but the sleeves were short for him; he had his father's long-limbed build—directed traffic. Eleanor took a deep breath (cleansing breath? Was that what they called it here?) and pulled into the designated space. She stepped out onto the grass.

There was the house, looking better cared for than she remembered. Tubs of daisies and brown-eyed Susans had been placed on the granite slab by the front door—Ursula's touch, probably. To the right of the driveway lay the pond, with lupine in bloom around the edges, from seeds Eleanor and the children gathered on a long-ago trip to Maine.

Memory took her back to the summer Buck Hollingsworth had spent digging the hole. Every morning at seven he got to work, scooping dirt out as her children danced around the edges, naked in the mud, watching as the hole slowly filled with water over the course of one glorious summer. (Two of her children did this, anyway. Maybe Alison's self-consciousness had come from a feeling Eleanor hadn't understood at the time. That the body she inhabited never felt like the one she was intended to have.)

Now came another picture, the one that never left her. *Toby, facedown. Ursula screaming. Cam running toward their son, then pumping his stomach. The siren. The ambulance pulling up. And from Toby, nothing.*

There was a band playing now. Men with large guitars and black suits singing in Spanish—an unlikely scene, unlikely sound, to encounter in this place. A crowd gathered at an outdoor folding table, getting their drinks. Margaritas, maybe. She could use one.

Walking up the path to the tent they'd set up for the meal after the ceremony, Eleanor saw for the first time the new structure Cam and Coco had built a few years back for their physical therapy and massage practice, with the living space above it—more energy-efficient than the old house. There was a deck looking out over the field. Gardens. A chicken coop. Toby's beloved goats.

Inside the tent, they had set up tables—a vase of flowers on every one, and on each a small Mexican retablo. It was a good idea that they'd be eating under cover; the sky was darkening, and in the distance, Eleanor heard the rumble of thunder.

The first one to greet her was Elijah, who'd evidently flown in a couple of days earlier from L.A., where he was living now. Eleanor had heard from Toby that Elijah was getting lots of work. "My brother's a rock star," Toby told her.

Elijah put his arms around Eleanor. "Al's out on the porch getting ready," he said. "He asked me to bring you back to say hello before the ceremony. Ursula's there, too, with Louise."

It was probably a good thing that there were all these people around—some from down the road, some from Texas and Mexico, some from Seattle and Silicon Valley, along with one or two of Cam's relatives. Young women with pink hair. Young men wearing dresses. Stout Latin men with silver belt buckles. Nerdy millennials, instantly identifiable as programmers. She spotted Darla's daughter, Kimmie, who'd flown in from Las Vegas with her new baby.

"If only . . ." Eleanor said.

The two of them stood there for a long time then with their arms around each other. No need to say anything more.

Kimmie had just taken off to change her daughter's diaper when Eleanor spotted Al. He was surrounded by his best men—Teresa's brothers, and Toby—adjusting their boutonnieres. She opened her arms. "I want you to meet Teresa," he said. "But we have to wait till after. Tradition, you know."

Eleanor made her way over to the porch. Through the screen door, she saw Ursula, pinning a sprig of bachelor buttons on her brother's lapel. Her older brother. Al. Also Elijah, and two young men who must be brothers of the bride.

Eleanor stood outside the door to the porch, which allowed her the small, simple pleasure of getting to see her children looking happy and relaxed, as at least one of them—Ursula—was unlikely to be when she encountered her mother. It might all change when she stepped in the door, so for a moment, Eleanor just stood there watching this young woman she'd given birth to, soon to give birth for the second time herself. Whatever else was true, one thing did not change. She would always love this child, and her children.

Then there she was—Louise, racing past Eleanor and bursting in the porch door to join them all. Her granddaughter didn't know her, of course. To Louise, Eleanor was just another wedding guest.

Now she leapt into Toby's lap and ruffled his hair. "My Toby," Louise cried out. "I was looking for you everywhere. Let's go see the goats."

Toby had always loved babies and young children. (The old Toby, and even more so, this one.) "We can go after, okay, Lu?" he told her.

Through the screen, Toby spotted his mother before the rest of them did. For this one child of hers, no conflicted emotions existed. Just joy. (Here was his mother. This was good news. Simple as that.) His face broke into a smile, as it always did when he saw her. "Mama," he said. The rest of them looked up.

"What do you know?" Eleanor stepped onto the porch. "All my children in one place. When was the last time that happened?"

She just stood there for a moment, taking in the sight of them. *Her family.* This had been the thing she wanted more than anything else, all her life, and she had gotten it. Just not as she'd imagined.

In many ways, Al was the least changed of the three. His gender had altered, but not his unyielding refusal to say or do anything that felt inauthentic. Now he reached out to embrace his mother, and for a long moment, the two of them just stayed that way. There was no need to say anything.

Ursula hung back, her silence heavy in a way her older brother's was not.

It had always been Ursula who had felt a need to put a cheerful face on everything, like one of those yellow stickers kids used to attach to their notebooks. That endlessly loving, hopeful, perpetually smiling person Ursula had been no longer existed, any more than the wild, exhausting, impossible, and endlessly lovable red-headed son did.

Ursula had been Eleanor's easiest child, until she became the hardest. And for a while, it had seemed to Eleanor that she'd never get over the last words Ursula had spoken to her, never survive the loss of her daughter, and of Louise.

But Eleanor had suffered that loss so long now, the wound of Ursula's words to her that day had repaired itself. Not healed—never that—but she had learned to live with the injury, much as Coco had no doubt learned to walk again. With a limp.

"Hello, Ursula," she said.

It occurred to Eleanor that they were standing in the spot where Eleanor used to set Ursula in her Johnny Jump Up, to keep her entertained while she planted her bed of zinnias outside the porch, that first May after her birth. The spot Eleanor used to pull up, every Friday afternoon (in a different decade), to drop the three of them off with their father.

"Mom." Ursula hadn't exactly smiled when she caught sight of Eleanor, but just hearing her say the word was more than Eleanor had received from her daughter in three years, more than she expected anymore. Well, she no longer expected anything.

"How was your drive?" Ursula said—the question people asked, Eleanor recognized, when they didn't know what else to say.

"This is your granny, Lulu," she told the little girl.

Ursula set down the boutonniere. A little stiffly, she put her arms around her mother, close enough that Eleanor could feel her daughter's pregnant belly pushing against her own. Whatever pain and hurt Eleanor had suffered—and there'd been an ocean of that, for Ursula, too, no doubt—didn't matter at the moment.

"I missed you." *That doesn't begin to convey it,* she might have added. But she'd leave it simple. They were here now.

"This is Louise."

"Would it be okay if I picked her up? Some children this age aren't wild about strangers."

"You're not a stranger," Ursula told her. "I've shown her your picture." She handed the little girl to her mother.

"It's okay, Lulu," she said to Louise. "She won't hurt you."

They'd set up the chairs in the meadow, the same spot where Eleanor and Cam had been married so long ago. Five or six rows of chairs, facing out to the meadow where the peach tree stood, where—thirty-two years before—they'd attempted to bury the placenta of their firstborn child, only the ground was frozen.

Scanning the rows of guests, Eleanor picked out the faces she recognized. There was Bonnie Henderson—the one of the wives who never let any of them forget how many orgasms she had with Jerry, particularly nights he hit a home run. The two of them had split up back in the nineties. "But what do you know?" she told Eleanor—she and the old pitcher from the Yellow Jackets, Rich McGann, had fallen in love after Rich's wife, Carol, realized she was gay and Jerry reunited with his high school sweetheart at his twenty-fifth high school reunion. "You wouldn't believe the sex," she told Eleanor, of her new life with Rich. "Every night of my life, I thank God for Cialis."

The front row of chairs, on one side, was filled with members of Teresa's family. The bride's father wore a dark suit, his stout and beautiful raven-haired wife, a lacy suit with an enormous corsage. If they were having a problem with their daughter's choice of Al for her husband, their faces betrayed nothing. The bride's mother, Claudia, dabbed her eyes with a hanky, same as the mother of any bride might, marrying any groom. (The good news was, this one made a great deal of money. More important, he would be—here was one thing Al would have retained from his days as Alison—a deeply loyal person. When Al made a promise, he kept it.)

Eleanor and Louise were standing next to an unfamiliar-looking young woman—one of Al and Teresa's friends, evidently, who'd flown in from the West Coast. Her name was Heather.

"Can you even believe how beautiful this place is?" she said. "Al told us about his dad's farm, but I never pictured how totally awesome everything would be. I mean, I come from total suburbia. It must have been so cool, growing up here. The old farmhouse and the studio and everything. The pond."

"It's a nice place, all right," Eleanor said.

"And it's just so great how Al's dad created all this. He must be an amazing person."

Eleanor studied Heather's face briefly. She was probably not even thirty. No doubt she was exceedingly good at designing computer programs.

This might have been the moment when Eleanor stepped over the line. She could even feel the familiar tightening in her chest. Her heartbeat quickened. Her face felt warm. It would be so easy to go to Crazyland now.

Only, she didn't. Crazyland was a far-off country now. Holding firmly to her granddaughter, she knew this: she would not be visiting that place again.

The Mexican band had started playing again, and she spotted Cam, walking very slowly down to the spot where the chairs and the arbor were set up. He was wearing a suit jacket Eleanor recognized—the one he'd worn when they got married, and when they'd gone to the bank to take out a loan for a new furnace, and she'd been worried they'd get turned down. He'd worn it again when they went to court to sign the divorce decree.

She couldn't see his face, only the back of his head as he reached the spot where the ceremony was set to take place. He was talking to Ursula, and to the two people—a woman, and a man who was clearly a priest—who appeared to have been enlisted to offer a blessing. They were looking at the sky, assessing the likelihood of rain, from the looks of things. The sky had been steadily darkening, and from the east they could make out the sound of thunder, closer now. There was a feeling in the air of a storm on the way.

Cam turned around briefly then, and for a moment, Eleanor wondered if this was not him at all, but his father, Roger, except Roger was dead. Cam's body appeared to have shrunk that much; he looked that old. Always a lean man, he seemed close to skeletal now, his neck too thin for the shirt he was wearing, so a wide gap was visible between skin and fabric. You could have slid your whole hand in that space.

But the part that shocked her was Cam's face. He was still a handsome man, but his cheeks were sunken. His skin had a gray cast to it, and his eyes bore the look of a person who has seen something visible only to himself. Something hard. He had always borne an air of detachment, but he seemed now to be someplace else altogether.

A bell sounded, signaling the time for whatever guests were still milling around to take their seats for the ceremony. Eleanor's newfound granddaughter clung tight, studying Eleanor's bird necklace, and for Eleanor, that was all that mattered. She studied the little girl's face, with no impulse to locate in it a resemblance to her own three children. This was a new person; who she looked like was nobody but her own self.

Up until now, it was the Mexican band that had played for them, but now, from two speakers facing out to the assembled guests, came the recording of a song she actually knew. "A Simple Love," by Melissa Etheridge. From the direction of the goat pen, the bride made her way across the field, preceded by Ursula and the other bridesmaids. Louise, still in Eleanor's arms, and seeing Ursula at the front of the procession, waved and called out, "Mama." She showed no signs of concern that it was Eleanor and not her mother holding her.

The bride, Teresa, had reached the spot in front of the assembled guests where Al stood, waiting for her in his dark blue suit—his hands folded in front of him, his eyes full of love.

The woman officiant welcomed the group—first in Spanish, then English. The woman—a friend of the bridal couple, ordained for the day—read a poem by Wendell Berry called "The Country of Marriage." Off in the distance, the darkening clouds caused the assembled guests to look up at the sky again, but the rain was holding off.

Teresa's brother Mateo read Sonnet 17 by Pablo Neruda. *"Te amo sin saber cómo, ni cuándo, ni de dónde . . ."*

Ursula read Elizabeth Barrett Browning. "How do I love thee? Let me count the ways." Eleanor looked over toward Cam as their daughter spoke the words. Hard to say if he remembered another wedding in this spot, another voice—his own—speaking the same words long ago.

The priest asked them if they agreed to a long list of promises, which they did, and pronounced them husband and wife. For a surprisingly long time, they kissed.

From where she stood at the back of the assembled guests—Louise nuzzling her neck and making bird sounds inspired by her necklace—Eleanor studied the face of the man she used to be married to, seated in the front row—present at the births of her children, absent at the moment their son entered the pond. They were back on the exact piece of land where they'd started out their marriage, thirty-three years earlier.

Here she was, in the place where the best things that ever happened in her life had taken place. Also the most awful. Always before, when she came back, the thought of all that had felt crushingly sad. But they'd survived, in one way or another. And the fact that this was so seemed now, suddenly, like a kind of miracle.

Al was in love. Toby had his goats and his chickens. He had his home on this farm. (And he could read now, and drive the tractor, and call up his classmate from Dr. Almendinger's clinic, Kara, to talk about the new episode of *Glee*.) Whatever bitterness Ursula still carried toward her mother, and no doubt she did—many people had issues with their mothers—it appeared that they might actually be speaking to each other again. More than that, maybe. With luck, Eleanor might actually get to be a grandmother to Louise, and the new baby none of them had met yet.

A thought came to her. Not a thought at all so much as a feeling. It was time to forgive her children's father. And to ask for the same.

This was when they heard it—that sound, like an explosion of gunpowder, followed by a terrible cracking, a long, deep groan, like a piece of the earth breaking apart. Then came a crash, when whatever it was that broke fell to the ground. The sky lit up, then darkened. Now the rain came down. Whole sheets of it. So much rain it was hard to see what was going on.

"Oh, God," someone cried out. Someone else: *"Dios mío."*

"It's okay," Eleanor whispered to Louise, who was holding on to her very tightly now, but not crying. "I've got you." From the top of the hill where the house sat they heard an enormous crash, the loudest yet.

Already drenched, they headed up the hill to survey the damage.

99.

one of the great things about rocks

At first, after it had fallen, all anyone could take in was the sight of the felled ash tree, Old Ashworthy, struck by lightning—now lying across the front yard, branches splayed in all directions.

"Some tree," Toby said. With one minor variation, this was the same thing Charlotte the spider had written, in her web, of Wilbur the pig, in his all-time favorite book from his childhood.

They all just stood there, too stunned to say anything more. Then they noticed the rest.

Old Ashworthy had been a tree of such height and breadth that for a few moments the sight of it toppled had obscured what lay beneath. Now, through the vast expanse of broken branches and leaves, they recognized the house, or what was left of it. Through the tangle, Eleanor could make out pieces of roof, and the dormer and a couple of shattered casement windows. The chimney was still standing, but everything that surrounded it had been crushed: roof demolished, walls flattened, furniture smashed, shards of Fiesta ware dishes and pieces of furniture. A single beam that had spanned the length of what was once her kitchen—spaghetti carbonara every Sunday, their tradition—upended so it was pointing skyward, like an arrow.

After they'd taken it all in—the splintered trunk, the splayed branches, the tangle of limbs and leaves, and everything that lay beneath all that, which was an entire house, demolished—beds, tables, chairs, dishes, dresses, books, old records and CDs, summer hats and winter boots, flyswatters, electric fans, a hot water bottle, a Cabbage Patch doll, a sink, a waffle iron, a one-quarter-size violin—after they took it in (but really, who could?), a surprising thing happened.

A person might have expected that the one to step forward and say something at such a moment would have been Cam. Or possibly

Al. Ursula, maybe—forever the caretaker. The one who had designated herself as the fixer of all things broken.

But it was Toby who spoke. In his usual slow and slightly off-center way, he loped toward the mountain of broken pieces that used to be their home, placed himself in the center, and—peering intently—bent down to retrieve something. To anyone who didn't know him, what he held out to show the assembled guests would have appeared to be nothing but a random rock, only it wasn't. It was a particular rock, as they all were in his collection.

"You know one of the great things about rocks?" he said. "They don't break."

Even then, nobody else could say anything. If the damage had been less, this might have been the moment to rally the group in some kind of cleanup effort, but they were way beyond that possibility. This was a bomb site. This was the end. Mount Saint Helens, after the eruption. The *Challenger* exploding. The World Trade Center after the towers fell. The mangled vehicles after the accident that killed Timmy Pouliot and left the woman on the back of his bike—Elijah's mother—with a couple of steel rods in her leg.

Al had his arms firmly around Teresa. Jake was doing the same for Ursula. Eleanor held tight to Louise. Then Cam took a few steps to join Toby and put his arm around his son. Thin as he was, he still possessed an air of strength that Eleanor remembered from long ago. This, more than anything else—more than his handsome face, his glorious red hair—had drawn her to him. It should not have come as a surprise to Eleanor that the loss Cam chose to remark on first was not that of the house, a fact she loved about him, even now.

"This was a really great tree," he said.

Later, they would remark on all the ways it could have been worse. Because Cam had recently constructed the new building on the property, most of the family's essential possessions (surprisingly few) had not been in the house at the moment the tree came down on top of it. Cam's lifetime collection of unsold burl bowls was safe, as were the children's artworks from back when they were young, his mother's double-wedding-ring quilt. What was lost had been all the things nobody actually used anymore, but hadn't gotten around to throwing out.

"Thank God I gathered up all the photograph albums last summer and brought them to Vermont," Ursula observed. Eleanor experienced a small moment of gratitude that her daughter had evidently cared about the record of a childhood and a stretch of years that had included her.

Later, the topic came up of homeowner's insurance (the coverage which, someone pointed out, would probably allow for the construction of a more modern and energy-efficient structure: Marvin windows, granite countertops, that kind of thing). Someone else mentioned the name of a guy with an excavator—the son of Buck Hollingsworth, the backhoe operator who'd dug the pond so many summers back, the children's hero, who had invited Toby into the cab of his machine that time, to work the bucket that dug the hole that made the very body of water in which, twelve months later, he'd end up facedown, rocks in his pockets, as his brain cells died, one by one.

"Cubby Hollingsworth," Sal Perrone was saying. "The guy's an artist with an excavator. When he gets done with the cleanup here, you'll never know there was ever a tree here, or a house."

Was this supposed to be a good thing?

For several moments, nobody knew what to do. Then Al took charge. "Listen, everyone," he announced. *"Lo que importa es que todos están bien."*

The only thing that matters is that everyone's all right.

He took a moment to survey the wreckage. Ursula joined him.

"This family's had to adapt to some major events before. We'll get through this one."

"And let's not forget," Al said, reaching for Teresa's hand, "we've got a wedding to celebrate. There's a great meal waiting for you all, over at the tent, so what do you say we head over there and get some food?"

Al and Teresa had hired a company in Peterborough to cater the wedding dinner—platters of artisanal cheese, poached salmon and leg of lamb with fresh English peas, a salad of organic greens served up in a giant burl bowl, bread baked in a wood-fired oven, and a dark chocolate cake with fresh raspberries. Off to the side, for the vegan crowd, there was quinoa and kale salad, and some kind of nut loaf. In spite of the events that preceded the dinner, or maybe because of them, everyone seemed to have a big appetite.

Maybe the shared experience of calamity had bonded the group in unexpected ways. For whatever reason, the conversation was livelier than at most weddings Eleanor remembered. She finally managed to meet Teresa, who embraced her like a daughter, which she was now. The Mexican American contingent and the yoga contingent and the gender fluid and the programming tribe and the retired softball players could be observed in animated conversation. Most seemed to favor the catered meal over the healthy fare. Even one of the yoga group could be observed loading a second helping of lamb on his plate. Louise, for her part, mostly focused on the cake—some of which ended up in her mouth, some on her white dress—and on gathering up the retablos on everyone's table.

There were toasts, of course. Ursula spoke first, as the younger sister, followed by Teresa's brothers, then Elijah. Toby stood there beside him, but said nothing, and for a moment Eleanor registered the sadness of this.

Teresa's parents approached the microphone together. Her mother, Claudia, spoke in Spanish, but it wasn't difficult to get the drift of what she was saying. All a mother wants is for her children to be happy, and Teresa was. This filled her heart.

Cam waited until the Hernandez family had spoken before taking the microphone. Watching him make his way to the front of the room—the old, too-big sport jacket hanging on his frame like David Byrne's in that Talking Heads video of their youth—Eleanor was caught up short by a wave of unexpected tenderness.

He did not look well. She worried for him. And because of how they loved him, she worried for their children.

Now he stood at the microphone.

"I want to welcome you all to our farm," he said. (Then the words in Spanish, read from a card.)

"And though something surprising and . . . a little difficult . . . happened here this afternoon—speaking not of the marriage of my son and Teresa, of course, but about . . . you know . . . the tree—I want everyone to know that this remains a good day for our family. A great day."

He said some more things then, about Al, and about Teresa. "Our family is your family now," he said to her parents, without consulting his Spanish file cards. He had clearly practiced this part. *"Nuestra familia es tu familia."*

"And I want to acknowledge all the people who were part of bringing us where we are today," he said. One by one he named the children. Among the names that followed, though her absence at the wedding was notable, was Coco's.

"Most of all, I want to honor the woman who started all this with me," he said. He looked over in Eleanor's direction. "You were a wonderful mother to our children, Ellie." He paused. He looked tired.

"You are a wonderful mother."

Louise having reunited with her parents, Eleanor stood alongside Teresa and Al, who had not taken his arm from Teresa's shoulders the whole time. Toby joined them.

"I made you something," he said to Al, his voice soft and halting. "It's okay if you don't know what it is, Teresa. My brother can explain later."

He took two very small objects out of his pocket. At first Eleanor might have thought they were rocks, but they weren't. They were made from corks, with bits of yarn and pipe cleaners attached, and faces. A man and a woman.

"You can let them go in the brook sometime," he said. "Don't worry if you lose them, or it looks like they sink."

He paused and looked at them. His brother and his new wife, first. Then the cork people. "They'll always be out there someplace. The ocean, maybe."

There was dancing—a DJ, playing songs Eleanor did not know, mostly, though there were a few she did ("thrown in for our parents," Al explained)—Bruce Springsteen, the Rolling Stones, Van

Morrison, the Beatles. Also Selena. Freddy Fender. In honor of Toby, but also the recent news of Michael Jackson, he played "Billie Jean."

Louise stayed out on the dance floor for a good hour before Jake took her off to the house—the house that remained, the new one—to sleep.

When Ursula returned to the tent, she was carrying a box. She made her way to the table where her family was sitting and, dirty as it was, set the box on the tablecloth.

"Our time capsule," she said. "The way it worked out, we never had to dig it up after all."

Who would have guessed this? When the tree came down, and the roots pulled away from the earth, there it was: the time capsule the children had buried twenty-four years before.

If they thought they might find something profound inside—words that might suddenly illuminate their lives—they were disappointed. What they found, when they got the box pried open, was a package of Silly String, a Matchbox truck, a rock, a My Little Pony, a quarter with the date 1985, and a Snickers bar.

Then they noticed three worn-looking envelopes, each with a name on the front: Alison, Ursula, Toby. Al opened his first and read out loud the words he'd written almost a quarter century before, when he was eight years old.

"Dear Future Self," the note began. "I hope when you read this that you are happy, and I hope you turned into a good person. I hope you have your own computer. I think there will be a big future in programming. I bet your parents are going to be really sorry they didn't do what you told them and buy stock in Microsoft."

Ursula's next. "Dear Future Self. I hope by the time you read this, you aren't still this perfect person all the time. I hope you get to be real, finally."

"Der Foootur Slf," Toby had written. He'd been four years old, and still in possession of his fully functioning brain, when he wrote the note he now read out loud, grinning. "I hop u get gotes. I hop u r hapy."

"And I am!" he called out, hearing this. "And I did."

Eleanor danced. With Al, with Louise, with Teresa's father, José, and with Sal Perrone, who asked how long she was going to be in town.

She had thought about asking Cam to dance with her, as parents of the groom, but having seen the difficulty with which he'd made his way to the microphone earlier—Cam, the one of the Yellow Jackets who used to get around the bases faster than anyone—it seemed to Eleanor that he was in no small amount of pain. Dancing to some hip-hop song was the last thing he needed. And truthfully, she didn't have any desire for that, either, though when they played "Teach Your Children," she had to step out of the tent for a moment. That song always got to her.

. . . just look at them and sigh, and know they love you.

She looked out to the field—the peach tree they'd planted, the woods where the lady's slippers came up every year, the cornflowers. When she turned around, he was standing there. Cam.

"Most of what the kids like nowadays isn't our kind of music, I guess," he said. "I bet the young ones never heard of Crosby, Stills and Nash."

"I'm sorry about the house," she told him. "The tree."

"Nothing stays the same forever," he said. "If there's one thing life has taught me, it's that."

"You probably aren't up for a walk," she said. It was a question.

"The waterfall? I could handle that."

100.

you who are on the road

It was a stretch of road Eleanor must have traveled a thousand times over the years: first, alone, when she'd just bought the house, with her sketchbook and her pencils, setting off to draw, then pregnant that first time, and after, with Alison buckled into her Snugli and Sally following alongside, wagging.

When Ursula came along, they'd bought a stroller. Eleanor had studied the fancy model in a catalog and dreamed about getting it, the way some women dreamed about jewelry or cars.

All they could afford at the time was a very cheap one—the old umbrella style, which was difficult to push over a road as bumpy as this one, so bumpy in fact that often Cam just picked the whole thing up—stroller, baby, and all—and carried it the last stretch of road to the waterfall. She could see him now—his long, strong first baseman's arms holding the sides of the flimsy stroller, with Alison bundled into her bunny suit, strapped into the seat, her face serious, even then. Cam had lifted her over his head like an Olympian showing off his trophy to the crowd. *Just look what we made. A person.*

Once they were old enough, the children made the trip to the waterfall on their own steam—talking about that day's events as they made their way down the road, Toby skipping ahead, looking for turtles and efts, interesting rocks—the three of them singing the Seven Dwarfs' song from *Snow White. Heigh-ho, heigh-ho.*

When they got close to the place where the brook raced over the boulders—the water so loud in the weeks of first runoff that you had to yell to be heard—Eleanor made sure they held each other's hands.

"That's close enough," she'd call out. Toby, in particular, was always pushing the limits.

They'd stand together on the stone arch bridge—two hundred years old, built without mortar, the stones held in place by simple tension, one rock against another—and sometimes they threw pebbles in and sometimes a penny, making a wish.

"I wish nobody ever had to die," Alison said one time.

"I wish my dolls could talk to me." This was Ursula.

Toby wanted to fly. That, and talk to God, or Mr. T.

Over all those years of trips to the waterfall—even holding tightly to their hands as she always did—Eleanor had to fight the terror of seeing a child of hers standing there by the edge. The pictures that came to mind could drive you crazy, the pictures of what could happen.

You had to let your children venture out in the world. You couldn't always find the Barbie shoe. Children had to know pain, or how would they ever know what to do when they encountered it? Trouble would come, no matter what. The best you could do was to raise your children in such a way that when trouble found them—as it would—they'd be able to survive it.

Teach your children well.

Here was what Eleanor had learned, over the years since she'd wept over a chicken pox scab on her daughter's scalp and the bald spot it left there, believing that event qualified as a heartbreak:

The worst things, the ones that actually got you, were almost never the ones you spent your time worrying about. In all those years, nobody ever fell over the edge of the waterfall onto the rocks. That never happened, but plenty more did. So much else fell apart. So much floated away. So much had been broken.

Her son had incurred a brain injury in eight inches of water. Her best friend was murdered while filling up her gas tank. One daughter had stopped speaking to her—and that was the easy daughter, the one she could least imagine shutting her mother out of her life, the most considerate, the sweetest. At the time, Eleanor had not believed she could survive it when Al had spoken the words that day in the car—"We'll never forgive you. We'll hate you for the rest of our lives." Then Ursula: "You aren't welcome in my child's life."

I wish I had a river I could skate away on.

A person can survive a lot, it turned out. Those things change you. But you carry on. Toby had not become a violinist, or a geologist, or a swimmer of the English Channel, or a notorious diamond thief. He practiced yoga and took care of chickens and goats. Coco, the onetime queen of cartwheels, whose mother used to worry she'd tear a ligament on the uneven parallel bars, walked with a cane now, thanks to a collision on the highway between Timmy Pouliot's Harley and an eighteen-wheeler. The farm Eleanor had believed she would live on for the rest of her days was Cam's now. The house she'd loved, rubble.

Now here they were, just the two of them again. They had swum naked in this place once. They had conceived a baby here. Here was the place they'd launched their boats. Here was where Eleanor first met Timmy Pouliot, with a freshly caught trout in his cooler, and Darla. Here was where Eleanor had witnessed the sight of her husband locked in an embrace with their babysitter.

Cam walked very slowly now, almost as slowly as their children had when taking their first steps. Now he reached for her hand.

"I've got cancer," he told her. "It's not good."

The news hit her like a punch.

She turned her face to the racing water. Even now, in midsummer, it crashed over the rocks, but somewhere, a mile beyond this place, or three miles, or five—beyond the old people sitting in their cars listening to the radio, beyond the men with their fishing poles, conferring among themselves on whether the Red Sox had a chance in the playoffs, and the young couples kissing or smoking weed, and the mothers nursing babies; beyond the teenagers daring each other to jump off the rocks, and the ones, like Eleanor and Cam, just standing there taking it all in—all those human beings, figuring out how to live their lives the best they knew; count the ways—the brook would keep on running. Sometimes faster, sometimes slower, but the water never stopped moving. It flowed all the way to the dam in town, and beyond that to the river, which flowed to the ocean, which reached far as the horizon, and even farther than that.

Somewhere along this stretch of water, in among the rocks and weeds, so deep under you'd never see them, slept the cork people.

"I could take care of you," Eleanor said to the man who used to be her husband. "That might be a good idea."

They headed up the hill then. No house there anymore, but home.

Acknowledgments

Writing is a lonely occupation. When a writer completes a novel, or a draft of one, there is little she wants more than to hear the voice of someone she respects and trusts, offering up a response. This time, I was fortunate that a number of such readers and friends were willing to read my work—in several cases, in far rougher form than the one between these covers now. Large measures of gratitude go to Roland Merullo, Stephen Tolkin, Jane Miller, Helaine Banner, Peggy Cappy, Jordan Moffet, Kari Olivier, Peggy Cook, and my treasured lifelong reader and friend Graf Mouen.

The final revision on this novel was completed during the early months of the pandemic, where I had the great good fortune to be sequestered at my home on the shores of Lake Atitlán, Guatemala, with two writing students whom I'd invited to stay with me for what turned out to be six rich and extraordinarily productive months. Every evening, after a long day of work and a good dinner, we sat outdoors under the stars—looking out to a volcano and a lake—while I read out loud to them from this novel. These two young women offered invaluable suggestions—and (most precious of all) the gift of caring deeply about my characters. For this and so much more, my gratitude and love to XiRen Wang and Jenny Allsopp.

I want to thank Nat Stratton Clark and his mother, Jules Layman, for their generosity, guidance, and insight into the experience of gender transition, and that of being the parent of an adult child who makes this brave life decision. I wanted to include, in a novel about many aspects of family life and parenthood, the story of the transition of a child once perceived as a daughter to the person he knows himself to have been all along, a son, and to do so in a way that portrayed this situation not as a problem but rather, a liberation.

My thanks, also, to Nicole Tourtelot for her multiple readings of this book in its many stages; to Maria Massie, for her guidance and support; to Laurie Fox; and to Judi Farkas, for once again sharing her deeply insightful comments on the manuscript in ways that significantly transformed it. As always, I owe a debt to my longtime editor, Jennifer Brehl, who believed in me as a fiction writer at a time when I needed that faith and support most, and always inspires me to work harder, go deeper. I had the great pleasure of working with the terrific team at William Morrow—Nate Lanman, Stephanie Vallejo, Tavia Kowalchuk, and Eliza Rosenberry. I could not ask for better support or more thought and care given to my work.

For more than forty years, I have been the beneficiary of a precious gift in the form of readers who stand in line at my readings (or used to, in the days when writers still got to give readings, and readers got to attend them). I have learned so much from readers who tell me how the stories I write relate to their own, or who write to me to share their thoughts and feelings about their lives.

In addition to telling my own stories, my life's work has included helping other writers—and those still hesitant to call themselves writers—in the telling of theirs. To the hundreds of women and men—thousands, probably, by now (and I know your names)—who have trusted me with the truth of their experiences, I offer my profound thanks. It has been my honor to listen.

The readers and writers who are such an important part of my world have broadened and expanded my understanding of all the different routes by which a human being may get through her days and years, all the ways a person's heart can be broken or mended, the forms loss may take, as well as redemption.

In a life that has seen the loss of some treasured friends, the painful end of my young marriage, the deaths of my parents and a beloved partner, I have been fortunate to have acquired at least one great gift that may not have come my way without the passage of years. It's the ability to locate forgiveness—to offer it and humbly ask for it in return. For the lesson of what it means to forgive (to understand that there are seldom heroes or villains—just human beings capable of all the best and worst of human behavior) I thank every person who entrusted me with the truth of her or his or their experiences and was brave enough to recognize, in doing so, the part each of us plays in writing our family story. I offer this one as testament to what those who shared theirs with me taught me about love.